MAN AT THE SHARP END

MAN AT THE SHARP END

Mike Kilby

The Book Guild Ltd
Sussex, England

The Book Guild Limited
Temple House
25 High Street
Lewes, Sussex

First published 1991
© Mike Kilby 1991

Set in Baskerville

Typesetting by Unit Eleven Typeset
Burgess Hill

Printed in Great Britain by
Antony Rowe Ltd
Chippenham

British Library Cataloguing in Publication Data
Kilby, Mike
 Man at the sharp end
 I. Title
 823.914 [F]

ISBN 0 86332 556 4

To my wife and our three sons,
Guy, Marcus and Robert.

Thanks

The author wishes to acknowledge with
thanks the help received from
Lionel Stanbrook in his sharp appraisal
of the story.

Brief Authority

Bi-monthly meetings of the European Planning Committee helped to shape the future of the international vehicle business, and influenced the economic and social environment of towns, regions and even sizeable countries.

During a particularly long and controversial meeting which generated heated exchanges between European nationals and their US parent company colleagues, who were not particularly interested in the social and political implications of their actions, the Chairman called for a short break in proceedings, for passions to cool.

When the executives returned to the conference room some ten minutes later, written on the flip charts were the words:

Man, proud man,
Drest in a little brief authority,
Most ignorant of what he's most assurr'd. . . .

The words of The Bard from *Measure for Measure* seemed to be particularly appropriate.

1

TIME – Late Nineteen Seventies

In the early morning light, the electronic alarm began to beep urgently, but Mark Sanders was already wide awake, staring fixedly at a shadowed ceiling through slate-grey eyes, thoughts busy elsewhere.

Tall, lean, fifty years of age but still hard muscled, Mark Sanders lay very still, but under tension. Even in repose, he gave the impression of a powerfully coiled spring on a hair trigger. He was a tough man, work hardened by experience in the fiercely competitive international motor industry, and a tough day lay ahead. A lot of searching questions would have to be answered at that morning's meeting of United Motors' European Planning Committee, and the biggest question of all was would the giant multi-national corporation really pull out of vehicle manufacture in the UK?

Closer to home, there was another question, equally important. Mark was the only Englishman on the Planning Committee and, as such, had rather more than a detached and pragmatic business interest in the issues at stake. If the Corporation really did pull out of the UK, where precisely did that leave him?

He'd been awake for twenty minutes or more, lying in the half-light, going over the same ground again and again. He thrust out his left hand and hit the electronic alarm. The beeping stopped.

He had played a leading role in expanding British operations. It angered him to see the UK vehicle division in its current difficulties and sickened him beyond words to hear American and European colleagues write off Britain as an unreliable and uncompetitive source of manufacture. Wouldn't Americans on the Committee be similarly madder-than-hell to hear Englishmen writing off the US as a spent industrial force?

Dawn was coming up over the lovely North Buckinghamshire countryside, stirring Canada geese in the adjacent nature reserve into action. Mark raised himself by his elbows to get a better view of the feathered squadron which honked its way in V formation toward the eighteenth-century stone barn which he and Georgina had converted into a home.

Beside him in the bed, his wife reluctantly bestirred herself. Ten years younger than her husband, Georgina Sanders was tall, though not exceptionally so, and supple and slender rather than slim. She had jet black hair, and tiny laughter lines at the corners of her bright blue eyes and her mouth. She had never been a pretty woman but she was attractive. Men looked at her . . . and then looked again.

She opened her eyes in the growing light and shut them again, quickly. 'What time is it?' she groaned.

'Five' he replied quietly, still thinking through the potential problems in the day ahead.

'Uh?'

'Five o'clock. Go back to sleep. I'm getting up.'

'Why?'

'Busy day.'

'No, don't get up just yet,' she murmured, slipping a hand through his open pyjama jacket. She nuzzled his ear. 'Let's talk.'

'Sorry sweetheart. Must go.' Gently, but firmly, he removed her hand, now heading south from his navel. 'We can talk on Friday.'

'Oh, Mark . . . I wanted to now.' Suddenly she shot up in bed.

'Friday? But today's only Wednesday. Why can't we talk tonight or tomorrow?'

'No can do,' he called from the bathroom, turning on the shower. 'It's the bi-monthly meeting of the EPC.'

'Oh, God!' she moaned. 'Not again! What on earth do you lot manage to talk about for three days and nights that you haven't already discussed time and time again?'

Mark thrust his head out of the powerful jet stream. 'You'd be surprised. Beautiful bodies . . . Sex appeal . . . Exciting rides. . . .'

'Huh!' she said. 'Good job I know you mean cars.'

8

He re-entered the bedroom, rubbing his head violently with the thick Turkish towel wrapped around him.

'You do mean cars, don't you?' she demanded.

He grinned. 'You know me.' He bent to kiss her lightly on the lips.

She responded by clasping her hands behind his head pulling him towards her. 'That's the trouble,' she said. 'I do know you.'

He kissed her suddenly, quickly, hard and broke away. 'No time, love,' he said.

Georgina gritted her teeth and clearly and distinctly, uttered a very rude word.

Mark's grin widened. 'My feeling exactly.'

'Oh you . . .!' she said. 'That's our problem. I wish you would. More often!'

A pause. Then she said, 'This meeting . . .'

'Yep?'

'Something you said to Don Peters last night on the 'phone. Is UM really planning to pull out of this country? Is that what the meeting's all about?'

'It's on the agenda.' he said, knotting his tie.

'But would they? Could they do that?'

He laughed shortly. 'Afraid they could and they would, sweetheart, if they thought it made sense commercially.'

'But what about their employees? Over fifty thousand, aren't there? And what about us?' Georgina was now concerned.

'I don't know about us.' He zipped his trousers and shrugged into his jacket. 'UM's a huge multi-national. There are other places.'

'But the other fifty thousand families would be given the old heave-ho,' she said. 'And we could get the booby prize. We could go to Detroit.'

'It may never happen!' he insisted.

'Huh' she snorted. 'Detroit shouldn't happen to anyone. . . . But are you really saying that it might happen?' she insisted. 'Could UM be that callous?'

'International competition is callous, I'm afraid,' he sighed almost under his breath. 'The UK has elected to compete in Europe, and it's rough and tough with no holds barred. The UK either fights its way back to the top or it goes sliding down

9

the industrial league table until it's relegated to a lower division.'

'Football!' she exclaimed. 'Is that all it is? A bloody game? People's livelihoods are at stake. Their lives, even. Our lives, come to that.'

His voice was harsh. 'Do you think I don't know it?'

She was beginning to feel faintly sick. Was it all that inhuman and impersonal?

After a long pause she said, 'Why don't you get out of this corporate rat race, Mark, before we lose our self-respect?'

'The mortgage,' he said. 'The school fees, the insurances, the . . .'

'Oh come on!' She was angry. Then she stopped.

'Go on,' he said quietly.

No answer.

He spoke quietly. 'We couldn't opt out of the rat race even if we wanted to. We have no choice. We're committed. In Raleigh's words, "We are hostages to fortune." I am too far down the corporate track, Georgie, to think of opting out or turning back. In corporate management you are either going further up the ladder to New York Central Office, where it is dangerous to even think your own thoughts and positively lethal to express them, or you are going down and out.'

An uneasy silence lengthened between them.

Then in the burgeoning light she looked at him apprehensively. 'Which way are we going, Mark?'

Twenty miles away, in the adjacent county of Hertfordshire, the first rays of the rising sun warmed the rich golden stone of an eight-bedroomed manor house.

It was a big house, historic, imposing. It was also at least four centuries old, which was one reason why United Motors had acquired it.

Age suggested stability. It lent an air of authority. It enhanced the corporate image. Of itself, United Motors didn't have age, but it could buy what it lacked. Another motor mogul may have declared 'History is bunk!' but United Motors didn't believe it. Not if it enhanced the corporate image, it didn't. With its Tudor beams and a Regency ghost of doubtful authenticity, Wynfordingham Manor had been bought for the use of the American Managing Director of its UK Vehicle Division, and it had already paid for itself several times over with the picture publicity it regularly generated.

In the Manor's ground floor study fifty-one-year-old Don Peters drank his fourth cup of coffee, rubbed a rough, large-knuckled hand over his craggy, faintly freckled face, and again considered the papers before him.

Over the years, Don Peters had disciplined himself to need no more than five hours sleep in any night, and he had been up since half-past four working on the points he proposed to develop at that morning's meeting of the European Planning Committee. He had no doubt at all that they were points which would bring him into open conflict with his American colleagues and, in particular, with Clancy McGillicuddy, the Chairman of the Committee, who also happened to be UM's General Director of European Operations.

Nor was he under any illusion that the stance he was considering taking that day would be well received by UM's President, Nate Cocello, and the Corporation's top brass in New York. It wouldn't. They had long been of the opinion that UM should pull out of vehicle manufacturing operations in the UK and would brook no disagreement. Any personal decision he now took to swim against the corporate tide would damage his career, and not just in the short term during his temporary two-or-three year assignment in the United Kingdom, but permanently.

Don Peters was a rising star in the corporate firmament, with an impressive job performance track record to go with his hard-bitten appearance. He was being freely tipped to make it to the very top by colleagues who had worked closely with him in overseas operations, and by indiscreet members of the staff at New York Central office, who occasionally let slip the names of the front runners in the senior promotion stakes.

He had been awake since four, considering his options. He could go along with the corporate planning proposals and help to bring about the painful and difficult phasing-out operation as smoothly as possible; or he could fight on behalf of his division as he had fought throughout his career.

Either way he had a tough job to do. Either way he had to take local plant management, the trade unions, the Govern-

11

ment and the local authorities along with him.

In his previous overseas assignments he had never failed to come out on top. Now the Corporation wanted him to accept the hopelessness of a declining division and phase it out of European operations. If he carried out the task effectively without too much damage to the Corporation's international reputation, he could expect further promotion.

He would be sticking his neck out if he chose not to go along with the corporate planning proposals.

On the other hand if he could succeed in pulling the UK division out of the doldrums, his personal performance rating and standing in the Corporation would be unequalled anywhere in the world. He would be hailed as the man who had raised the dead.

He poured himself another cup of coffee and put a second cup on the tray. He was utterly convinced that he had accurately identified the reasons behind the division's poor performances over the last decade, and was absolutely certain in his own mind that he could pull the division round over the next year or so. It was the kind of challenge which appealed to his combative nature.

Rising from the table he carried the tray upstairs to his ex-model wife, Eleanor. She stirred at the sound of his footsteps on the stairs.

'That you, honey?' she called drowsily from under the sheets. 'What time is it?'

'Six thirty.'

He set the tray down on the bedside table. 'I'm just about to flee the chicken coop, sweetheart.'

'Jeez,' she moaned. 'Do you have to go this early?'

'Guess so. We got a tough one today.'

'Yeah . . . so you said last night.' Eleanor Peters raised herself in the bed and shook her mane of blonde hair. 'Jeez, I'm tired.' She was still, even in her mid-forties, the typical all-American girl, firm-fleshed and firm-breasted; dressed or stripped, a masterpiece of regular and expensive cosmetic engineering.

She still looked like the 'girl next door'; if you didn't look too closely. But she could sound, and act, like the girl next door lived in a house, not a home. 'Have you decided what you're gonna do?' she asked in a husky voice.

'Does it make any difference?' Don Peters asked gently.

'Sure as hell does!' she exclaimed, waking up to the realities of the alternatives. 'So?'

'I'm still thinking about it,' he said softly.

'Still thinking about it!' she cried in disbelief. 'Just what the hell is there to think about? You know what you've gotta do. Jeez, Don, is there any other way of looking at it?'

'Perhaps,' he said.

'And what the hell does that mean?'

He sat on the edge of the bed. 'Sure I know what the Corporation wants me to do. I've always known, and isn't that what I've always done?'

'Too damn right you have. There's no other way, honey,' she added flatly.

'But you could be wrong,' he said. 'This time, you could be wrong. I could pull the division round. I know it can be done. . . .'

'Aw come on, Don,' she said disbelievingly. 'Everybody, but everybody, says it can't.'

'Perhaps I could talk the Committee into giving me the time. If they gave me the chance. . . .'

'To prove them wrong, you mean? And what good would that do?' Her voice was hard. 'Too many people say it can't be done. It's a no-win situation, Don. You've just been handed a perfect escape route before you get dragged into that limey graveyard like the others before you. So get smart! Count yourself lucky to survive and jump on the corporate bandwagon while you've still got the chance.'

He smiled cynically at his wife's perception of the situation. She had an uncanny knack of smelling which way the wind was about to blow.

'What about the fifty thousand people who work for me?' he asked. 'What bandwagon do they jump on? The one heading for the soup kitchen?'

'Aw come on, Don. You're breaking my heart. Who cares what happens to those crazy bastards? Most of those guys have got a death wish anyway.'

'Some of them, perhaps . . . but not the majority,' he replied calmly.

'That's not what I hear from Darlene McGillicuddy,' she said unequivocally. 'And it's certainly not what Clancy thinks.'

13

He shrugged. 'I know. But if I don't fight for the people who work for me, who the hell will? I am supposed to be their leader.'

She stared at him in disbelief. 'This is me you're talking to, baby. This is Eleanor. Don't give me the conscience crap.'

'We all have one,' he said wearily.

She slipped out of bed. 'Don, honey, baby. . . .' She put her arms round him. Through her thin nightdress, her body was warm, gently firm, smooth. 'Let's get the pecking order straight, shall we? You have to fight for yourself and for me. You could go right to the top, and you know it. Others know it too. It stands out a mile. So don't blow it now, honey. Don't blow it to prove something you don't have to prove; or on account of any goddam conscience pangs.'

She slid her hands up to cradle his head and caress the back of his neck. Gently, she pulled his head down to her eager mouth.

'We can't afford conscience,' she said, huskily. 'We've gotta win. You and I are going to make it to the top of that goddam fourteenth floor, come hell or high water. Ain't that right, honey?'

She kissed him, wet open-mouthed, greedily.

'Come back to bed.' she said. 'Seems to me like your resolve needs some stiffening.'

He grinned suddenly; slid a hand down and round a firm buttock. 'Sorry,' he said. 'But I'm late already. Now . . . don't split your stitches. . . .' And he was away.

'You bastard!' she yelled, throwing a pillow at his vanishing back.

.   .   .

Up on Merseyside in one of the shudderingly depressing high-rise modern slums built by the Development Corporation in the new town of Kirkby, Fred Clasper was tucking into a breakfast of bubble and squeak. Opposite sat his platinum-blonde bedmate, Deirdre, polishing her nails.

In the prison-bleak outside corridor, the blue and white colours of Everton and the fiery red of Liverpool vied to take up the available wall space. Assorted graffiti picturesquely described the sexual proclivities of certain inmates of the

14

tower block, whose erotic feats defied belief.

Fred's mate, Albert Wheelwright, emerged from number 107 and shuffled his weary way along the filthy concrete corridor, eyes down for a full house.

Passing unit number 102, he thumped the bright red door with the side of his clenched fist without so much as a sidewards or upwards glance and followed it up with a resounding kick for good measure.

'Aye up there, Fred. . . . Time to get off the nest, wack. 'You'll do yourself an injury with all that exercise,' he yelled loud enough to be heard in the next street.

'Stick it up 'em today, wack,' he called over his shoulder. 'Nil carborundum. Don't let the bastards grind yer down . . . up the Reds. . . .'

'Up yours,' yelled back Fred Clasper from the smelly interior depths of unit 102, wiping his mouth on the back of his hand.

Albert swung a boot and an empty beer can was sent spinning against the mutilated Salvation Army poster alongside the vandalised lift. JESUS SAVES, proclaimed the message to the masses and underneath someone had scribbled, 'BUT KENNY DALGLEISH SCORES FROM THE REBOUND.'

Deirdre Clasper – for that was what the locals called her amongst other things – took her empty plate to the kitchen sink where it became part of an ever growing pile.

'Well, I only 'ope you know wot you're doin' . . . that's all I'm saying,' she said loftily, scrutinising the smelly heap.

'Course I know wot I'm bloody well doin,' Fred Clasper snarled from the table. 'My action sub-committee has got it all worked out like, step by step. You don't think we'd be stupid enough like to put it up to the full executive committee without a supportin' plan for strike action, do yer?'

Deirdre sniffed contemptuously over her beaker of tea. 'Bloody plans for strike action. That's all you and that bloody stupid shop stewards' committee ever think of. Don't you ever consider the possibilities of working for a livin' for a bloody change?' She sniffed contemptuously again, only more so.

'You know bugger all about it so why don't you shut up and do us all a favour?' Fred Clasper growled. 'You got a bloody mouth like the Mersey tunnel,' he added as an afterthought.

Deirdre Clasper shrugged her shoulders. 'I gotta mouth. I gotta mouth. I like that . . . and who's got the biggest mouth on Merseyside? Ask anyone at the plant and you'll get a unanimous vote on that question, that's for sure. . . . Fred bloody Clasper.'

'Yeah, yeah, yeah, yeah . . . so you keep on tellin' me. Put another bloody record on will yer?'

'No I bloody well won't,' she snapped defiantly. 'And I'll tell you something else too, Fred Clasper. You'll be making the biggest bloody mistake of your life if you take the lads out over this bloody rumour. They're in no mood for a strike I tell yer. They've had a belly-full of strikes. Well, I mean to say, it stands to reason. It's been strike, strike, strike.'

'You mean to say. . . . You!' Fred Clasper spluttered around the hot tea in his plastic beaker. 'Who the hell are you to tell me what the lads think? I'm the bloody convener, not you, . . .'

'And I work in the bloody canteen, you know,' Deirdre snorted. 'And that's where you hear what the lads really think. And I'm tellin' you something. They ain't got no stomach for this one.'

'Nor for those bloody meals you keep sloppin' up either,' he retorted.

'Oh funny' she said tartly. 'Trés drôle. So isn't it amazing how everybody, you included, keeps on coming back for more.'

'Yeah well. . . . You gotta eat something when you're working your guts out,' Fred Clasper declared. 'But, by Christ, I can tell you we're always bloody glad when we've had enough!'

Deirdre Clasper threw back her platinum blonde head and cackled. 'I like that! You workin' your guts out! That'll be the day, that will! You've never done a day's work since you've been at United Motors, and that must be twelve bloody years. We all know that! That's common enough knowledge!'

Fred Clasper rounded on his bed partner. 'I've worked my guts out for the lads ever since I was elected convener and they know it. What they've got today is largely due to me,' he roared.

'Yeah, you're right about that . . . that's what I hear 'em say . . . but it ain't what you think. They say you've got 'em all in the shit.'

16

Fred got up from the table. 'I've worked my balls off for the union and I defy anyone to say that I 'aven't,' he yelled.

Deirdre daubed a bright red lipstick over her open mouth, which did in fact resemble the Mersey tunnel.

'Come off it, Fred,' she retorted. 'You're a bloody press shop setter and you haven't set a bloody press in the twelve years you've been convener. Be honest now, have you? You spend every bloody day on that bloody soap box of yours mouthin' mouthin', mouthin'. You don't actually work for a living the way other men do, now be honest. . . ? They say you're a bloody professional agitator paid by United Motors to give those silly buggers in Personnel Department somethin' to do!'

Clasper grabbed his keys from the sideboard. He snarled. 'Well, all I know is that I'm workin' like hell for somethin' I believe in and that somethin' ain't bloody United Motors.'

'Then why the hell do we work there?' she asked.

He threw back his head in exasperation. 'To bring about the bloody change in society from the point where the action is . . . on the factory floor, you silly git. You've heard of the bloody Trojan horse, I suppose?' he added sarcastically.

' 'Course I 'ave, luvvy,' Deirdre said brightly. 'He won the three thirty at Doncaster last Saturday, didn't he?'

'Cor, bloody hell. . . !' Fred Clasper snorted. 'Come on, Antonia Fraser . . . we'll be late for work.'

'Late for what?' said Deirdre in disbelief. 'Work? You've got to be joking. Oh Fred,' she said. 'Fred, you know what? You do make me laugh! You really do. Late for work. I like that. That's rich, that is,' and she sniffed again.

2

The exterior of United Motors' Headquarters was bare brick and gaunt; a motley group of functional buildings which had first been used in the Thirties as an assembly plant for American manufactured trucks and cars. In the Second World War, the plant had been converted to assemble tanks and armoured fighting vehicles. Now it was the European nerve centre of one of the largest and most powerful multi-national corporations of the world.

Londoners who regularly drove past this grim group of buildings on their way to their City offices were blissfully unaware that behind that unprepossessing exterior corporate decisions were taken which would affect the economic and social destinies of cities, regions; even countries. Had the British people known what was intended for them as part of the United Motors, corporate plan, there would have been a riot. Even those local employees who worked within the Headquarters' buildings on a variety of service tasks had no hint of what went on inside the top security office block strictly restricted to the Corporation's overseas senior personnel.

Housed within this block was a totally windowless, electronically secure Conference Room, where the deliberations of the eighteen top executives who comprised the European Planning Committee shaped the destinies of nearly a quarter-of-a-million employees in Europe, including fifty thousand in Britain.

Long term planning decisions of the Committee, governing the investment of billions of dollars, effectively determined which countries would be the winners and which the losers in the decades ahead.

Such – at least in theory – was the influence of the European Planning Committee of United Motors, and of its members. But, of course, as is frequently the case with committees at which matters of great moment are supposedly decided, the real decisions were often made elsewhere, and in advance, by other even more powerful men.

By mid-afternoon on the first day of this particular conference, however, it had become patently obvious that things were not going to plan.

Presentation proposals from the divisional planning managers had given rise to more lively and controversial discussion than usual, and burly Irish-American Chairman, fifty-eight-year-old Clancy McGillicuddy didn't attempt to conceal his irritability.

'Goddammit!' he exclaimed. 'I thought we all agreed at the last meeting that we would progressively phase-out passenger car manufacture in the UK beginning with the new "Z" car.'

He glared around him. 'We also agreed to discontinue vehicle assembly operations in Austria, Switzerland, Portugal Denmark and Ireland, as additional capacity becomes available in Germany and Belgium. New plants are to come on stream in the new European locations to be determined by the special task force teams. That's what we agreed.' His voice was hard and harsh.

'This meeting is to discuss implementation and timing, not to question the basic strategy of the European plan. Unless that is . . . some of you are having very late second thoughts on the plan, in which case we had better discuss it. Though I'm damned if I know what Nate will say if I have to ring him tonight to tell him that. He'll hit the god-damned roof!'

The eighteen members of the European Planning Committee, comprising the managing directors and planning managers of the various divisions, were visibly ill at ease. Most kept their heads well down. They fully understood the implication of what McGillicuddy was saying. Nate Cocello, President and Chief Executive of UM had already let it be known that he considered this plan to be the right one for Europe. Second thoughts at this stage would put Chairman McGillicuddy and each member of the committee in the presidential dock, and very few executives survived that kind of ordeal with their reputations and careers untarnished.

Nate Cocello had climbed swiftly up the company ladder to Chief Engineer of the biggest vehicle division in the entire corporation, before becoming Vice President in charge of Overseas Operations, and finally, President and Chief Executive Officer. Throughout, his management style had stamped him as a force to be reckoned with.

He was more than just a brilliant engineer. He was sharply perceptive in locating and exposing management weaknesses, and had proved himself to be utterly ruthless in getting rid of poor performers at the operating plants and hacking out dead wood at staff headquarters. He was admired, respected, feared.

His personal staff included hatchet men who were regularly despatched to divisions around the world where budgets were not being met, or where plant or divisional track records were below expectations. The action they took was invariably bloody, bold and resolute.

Nate's pet hates were indecision, prevarication and Governments of any kind. He would rather make a wrong decision than none at all. His penchant for making on-the-spot judgements had been a decided asset as a line operating man, where he had earned the reputation as a man who always got things done.

Nate had never failed to beat his budget, an achievement which line managers were never allowed to forget. As President and Chief Executive Officer, however, at corporation headquarters, where he was concerned principally with future policies and long range business plans, his swashbuckling entrepreneurial style of management and arrogant disregard of the opinions of others, were distinct disadvantages in the view of a growing number of only slightly less powerful men in the company.

Nate Cocello would do well to watch his back.

. . .

The retired former President of United Motors, Ned Werner, was relaxing at home with his old and close friend, Ben Cartwright, who had become the President of the United States.

They were strolling together in the garden of Werner's Bloomfield Hills home on the outskirts of Detroit.

'I am flattered that you should wish to seek my opinion, Mr President; sorry, Ben, but Mr President comes out more

20

naturally somehow. . . . ' the silver-haired ex-motor man was saying. 'But for what it is worth, Nate is never happier than when he is dashing around solving day-to-day problems and putting out fires . . . at which I must confess he is brilliant . . . though I suspect that he would have fewer fires to put out if he paid just a little more attention to avoid creating them.'

He paused to admire his latest rose. 'What concerns me most of all, Mr President, is his unwillingness to come to terms with the new political, economic and social environment in which international business will have to operate around the world over the next decade.'

He shrugged. 'Sure, Nate knows the US business scene like the back of his hand, and if he is given the free rein he seeks from you, Mr President, and from overseas Governments he will continue to do a fine job for the Corporation; and I might add for the United States. But you and I know that he won't be given a free hand; particularly from overseas Governments; for all kinds of political reasons . . . economic, social and environmental. All the factors which Nate calls political bull-shit.'

He shook his head slowly. 'It is this personal disregard of the long-term political dimension which I fear will bring the Corporation into open conflict with overseas Governments which will rebound ultimately to the detriment of the United States.'

It was a rhetorical observation.

'Nate seems to think that he can run the world from Detroit; if only Governments would get off his back and let him get on with the job. But he can't do it. He must know that he won't be allowed to. So why does he keep baying at the moon?'

He sighed, took a rose between his fingers to admire it more closely.

'Just look at that, Ben; isn't it a beaut?'

The President nodded with a smile and they continued their stroll in the warm sunshine.

He sighed again.

'My personal view, for what it's worth, is that even if the Corporation's world operations would be better run from here in Detroit, I am not sure that it would be politically and socially right to attempt to do so. Which introduces another worry. Many of the younger high-fliers in the Corporation are

21

taking their cue from Nate. Every Government problem, every international question thrown up, is all a load of political bull-shit in their opinion. You know how it is, Ben. When father says "turn", we all turn.'

Ben Cartwright nodded slowly.

The President of the United States had listened to the ageing former President of United Motors with interest, and without interruption. He valued the motor man's judgement, which had been reliably accurate in the past, even when grinding the company axe. Now free from the discipline and bias of office his opinions were doubly welcome; even if he no longer carried the power and authority of the highest office in the huge multi-national.

'I am worried,' Ned Werner said, 'that Nate is already on a political collision course. If he can see it coming, but is too damned stubborn to admit it and amend the plan accordingly then heaven help the Corporation. But if he can't see it he shouldn't be in the driving seat. Either way, it seems to me the Corporation is in for a very rough ride.'

Ben Cartwright looked at him quizzically. 'Have you talked to Nate personally?'

'Hell yes. But you know Nate, Mr President. He thinks with his ears closed. Once he's made up his mind, it's like talking to the wall.'

The President was acutely aware of the political rumblings of discontent being heard in US Embassies and Consulates around the world concerning multi-national activities in general and the world car plan of United Motors in particular. Criticisms being voiced in Europe were especially forthright.

A report had been prepared by the European Commission which was to be discussed by Heads of Government at a summit meeting in Geneva the following month, this being the principal reason why he had sought a meeting with his old and close friend Ned Werner.

He needed to obtain a detached and objective industrial viewpoint, which he would then use to probe and question his own staff before seeking the collective views of industry and commerce and the personal views of leading industrialists; including Nate Cocello.

Three Prime Ministers had already been on their respective

'hot lines' to express growing concern at the sequence of events developing in their own countries and to examine the possibility of a common approach to the problems which would be debated at the forthcoming Heads of Government meeting. Questions were being asked in national Parliaments following the Commission's hard-hitting report, which was far from flattering to multi-nationals; particularly US Corporations.

Individual Governments were coming under intense pressure from Trade Unions, concerned about job security and the employment prospects of their members. In Brussels, Paris and London, union demonstrations had demanded Government action to control the activities of the multi-nationals.

Members of Parliament representing constituencies where multi-nationals were located were expressing concern about employment prospects in their region, arising from the world car plan of United Motors, with its plant closure possibilities. The President was aware that world plans like those of United Motors would have a significant influence on the economies of countries. It was understandable that Governments would wish to be involved, but, as a businessman hardened to the rewards and penalties of the marketplace, he was equally aware that Government intervention usually did more harm than good; as he himself had learned, the hard way.

As head of the most powerful country in the world, he knew that he would be expected to take the lead role at the forthcoming Geneva meeting, particularly as US multi-nationals had been singled out for special mention.

He held out his hand. 'I value your opinions, Ned. Let's keep in touch. This problem's not going away.'

.   .   .

In London, within the windowless electronically secure Conference room at United Motors' European headquarters, the uncomfortable silence lengthened as each member of the European Planning Committee absorbed the Chairman's warning.

Nate Cocello hitting the roof would not be a pretty sight!

23

The uneasy lull in proceedings was finally broken by Don Peters.

'The unions and the Government ain't gonna like it one little bit,' he drawled, in his matter-of-fact Indiana manner of speech. 'So I guess if we go ahead as planned we'd better fasten our seat belts for a very rough ride.'

'To hell with the unions,' bawled Chairman Clancy McGillicuddy. 'And I don't give a damn what the Government thinks. Those union bastards have screwed us long enough. Dammit, Don, they've had enough chances to make a go of things, but sure as God they always foul things up. Hell, we'll just go ahead without 'em in future. And as far as I'm concerned the Government can find out when it's too late for them to do anything about it.'

It was normal Company practice to go easy on a new incumbent and avoid giving him a rough ride until he was well and truly in the saddle. As Don Peters had only been in the UK hot seat for a relatively short few months, he could, under normal circumstances, reasonably expect to receive the support of his peers and superiors. As rumour also had it that he was destined for higher things nobody was particularly anxious to cross swords with him. Even his immediate boss Clancy McGillicuddy understood the wisdom of the Company maxim 'Be nice to your subordinate. You may need his support when he passes you on the way up'.

Quite apart from his first-class track record which justified respect, every member of the committee was aware that Don Peters was meticulously thorough in his groundwork. He would not have said what he had without giving the subject much thought. During his first six months in the UK much of his time had been spent preparing the ground for future action. He had visited the various manufacturing plants within the division, talking to plant managers, shop stewards, union officials, local mayors, the local press, Ministers and officials, not simply to introduce himself, but in an earnest endeavour to identify the causes of low productivity and union restrictive practices which had in recent years dragged the giant division down from among the top performers in Overseas Operations to near the bottom of the league.

Peters was already winning people over with his easy, but immensely persuasive style of management. He came across to people in industry and Government as a strong and sincere American, utterly dedicated to the task of lifting the UK division back to the top of the heap.

Moderate trade union leaders and shop stewards who had met him were reporting back to their members that Peters should be supported. The view they expressed was that their members' jobs were now in much better hands than those of his predecessor: an ascetic American finance man named Kauffman who kept such a low profile he was known by the unions as the 'bleedin' invisible man'!

Kauffman had always communicated through third parties and then only to announce further cuts, short time working, or more redundancies.

His stint as 'leader' of the British division had been a disaster. His absent management style had slowly but surely sapped the morale of both management and unions until a general feeling of hopelessness and despair pervaded the once great organisation.

Kauffman had no personal plans; only his orders from Detroit to execute a 'cut and hold' situation in the UK while the Corporation expanded the German, Belgian and French operations within the Common Market.

Unfortunately for Kauffman he couldn't keep his British division out of the red, as he executed his orders from Detroit. In consequence he was finally put out to grass back in America, pending early retirement.

Arising from the UK's belated entry into the Common Market in 1973, Don Peters had been brought in to get better utilisation of the ailing division's facilities, which were now operating at only fifty per cent of capacity, and with labour efficiency some forty per cent below its sister divisions in Germany and Belgium.

Peters had quickly identified what needed to be done to achieve the objectives; the most important first factor being to lift morale and replace despair by hope, with a plan of expansion. This was, in his opinion, a necessary first step in the process of persuading employees to raise productivity to the former levels achieved in the division's halcyon days, when it was top of the European league.

To raise productivity, the unions had to be persuaded to get rid of all the restrictive practices which had dragged the division down and nearly out. Peters knew that he had to break their now accustomed bad habits of stopping work, or disrupting production, at the drop of a hat, to air minor grievances, or to put pressure on management to resolve inter-union problems, which had been caused by the unions themselves. Constant disruption of the supply lines had driven the division's dealers to despair. Many had turned to other franchises simply to ensure continuity of supply.

Peters was slowly but surely gaining the confidence of local management, employees and unions, with the exception of a small hard core of militant shop stewards who refused, as they said, to 'be conned' by Peters. The dealers were also responding to him and were now less inclined to seek other franchises to protect their supply lines.

. . .

'Give me one good reason, Don,' said Chairman McGillicuddy, 'why we shouldn't phase-out the UK vehicle plants?'

He paused, waiting for a reply, but then continued. 'You agreed that the new "Z" car should be built elsewhere. In fact we all agreed. It was a unanimous decision of this committee. So why the second thoughts?'

Don Peters looked up at the Chairman and replied in his slow Indiana drawl.

'I agreed, that's true Clancy, and I still agree that we should build the "Z" car elsewhere.'

He showed absolutely no emotion in his voice or on his face.

'Our track record in the UK in recent years has been too goddam awful for the UK to be considered. We'd be thrown out anyway by the executive committee if we were crazy enough to propose that.'

'You're too damned right we would!' interjected McGillicuddy belligerently, nodding furiously to acknowledge the supporting nods coming from all around the table.

'But . . .' went on Peters. 'You Clancy, and the Corporation expect me to pull the division out of the red and into the black. How the hell am I gonna get better utilisation of existing facilities and drive the division into black numbers if the UK

26

plants are to be phased-out over the ten year business plan period?'

He tapped his pen lightly on the report before him.

'Maybe I'm wrong, but as I see it, the only way I can achieve the first objective set by the Corporation, is to raise labour efficiency, and to do that, I have to raise morale and give the guys and dolls some hope of better things in the future. But with the phase-out plan they ain't got no future. So how the hell do I sell that plan to management and the unions?'

He allowed his words to penetrate further before continuing.

'We can achieve the first objective, that's for sure; and I'm working like hell on it. But the second objective, Jeez, that's a no-win situation.'

There was a long pause as each member of the committee signified his recognition of the dilemma facing Don Peters, by keeping quiet. Chairman McGillicuddy sat impassively before nodding his head imperceptibly to register his understanding of Peters' difficulties.

'Look Don,' he said sympathetically, 'Nobody's denying you got a tough one, that's for sure.'

'You'd better believe it!' Peters interjected under his breath.

'Now if you guys can knock some sense into those fart-arsin' limey unions over the next year or so,' McGillicuddy went on, 'then maybe we can sell Nate the idea of retaining the UK plants in some form or other. But until they start coming through with the goods and keep coming through, over one hell of a long period, neither Nate nor anybody else on the Executive Committee is gonna give us the time o'day if we start pushin' the UK at 'em; and you know it. Right now, the UK is the kiss of death with Nate. He bursts a blood vessel every time he hears the name.'

Don Peters nodded to acknowledge the message being made by the Chairman as did most of the others around the long elliptical table.

'Yeah . . . you're right I guess,' he said. 'But give me time and we'll turn the plants round, that's for sure. There's nothing basically wrong that can't be put right. And most of the guys and dolls I've come across are just as good as you'll find in any of the plants in the States . . . or anywhere else I've worked for that matter.'

'Yeah, yeah, yeah,' McGillicuddy broke in impatiently, 'but they just won't damn well work. Isn't that right, Mark?'

McGillicuddy wheeled in his chair as he put the question to the lone Englishman in the eighteen-member committee.

Chairman McGillicuddy had addressed his question to Mark Sanders for more than one reason. He had been hard hitting in his criticism of the performance of UK vehicle plants, and the retrogressive attitude of the British trade unions, and, having done so, he was now seeking confirmation, from the only Englishman present in the room, that his criticism of Britain and the British was justified.

Mark instinctively sensed the trap. He knew from his own experiences that Don Peters was right in saying that UK plant people would respond given the right management leadership. He knew that Peters badly needed all the support he could get, from top corporate management, as well as from local plant management and the unions, and that without that support, the UK vehicle division wouldn't survive.

He also knew that McGillicuddy was equally right when he had said that it would be the kiss of death to propose that the UK vehicle plants be given another chance. Nate had been taken down that road too many times, and was now utterly sick of the name 'British'.

The eyes of everyone around the table were now firmly on the lone Englishman. If he supported Peters he would be judged to be a little Englander, not a Corporation man. It would simply confirm the reasons why corporate policy always favoured Americans for top jobs.

Peters was sitting opposite Mark but he kept his head down until Mark began to speak.

'My opinions are those of a components man, not a vehicle man,' Mark Sanders began.

'Yeah, yeah, yeah, we know,' interrupted McGillicuddy impatiently.

'But what d'ya think, Mark?'

'We would never sell Nate and the Executive Committee. . . .' Mark continued, only to be cut off by the Chairman.

'You're too damned right we wouldn't,' concurred McGillicuddy.

'We'd be pissin' into a gale force wind, and who'd be crazy enough to do that?' and he roared with laughter at his colourful description of a hopeless situation.

Don Peters looked up at the ceiling and winced. Others joined in the laughter which had eased the tension in the atmosphere. One or two managed a forced smile, which hid their distaste of crude language.

McGillicuddy's smile vanished quickly, however, when the Englishman added, 'But I take the view that we should support Don in what he wants to do.'

McGillicuddy exploded: 'Jeez! It's not a question of supporting or not supporting Don. It's a question of getting Nate's and the executive committee's approval. That's what it's all about. What's the sense in pushin' something that ain't got a snowball in hell's chance of gettin' acceptance?' Then he added, dramatically, looking round the room for support, 'Nate would have my guts for garters before I got halfway through the spiel.'

'I'm not suggesting that we should change the plan,' Mark continued calmly. 'We all agreed that the "Z" car is a new location project, and I still agree with that decision. But the phase-out of vehicle manufacture in the UK becomes critical in year six. Don has had less than a year to turn the UK division round, and we all know that if he can get the plants close to capacity volume over the next two years profits will start pouring through. The division's profit potential, above standard volume, is in fact much greater than the German and Belgian plants, because of lower British labour rates and employee benefits. So if Don achieves what he is setting out to do, Nate could be handing out laurels instead of brick-bats.

'Don's right when he says that he's got to have a plan which he can sell to management and the unions, if he is to win their support. So what's wrong with Don telling Nate, the Executive Committee, the unions, local management and the Government, that unless the necessary improvements are made, beginning this year, and continue to improve over the next two years to target objectives, the UK vehicle manufacturing plants will be phased-out over the following three? Nate would probably buy that.

'It provides the unions with the necessary incentives to improve efficiency, and lift their restrictive practices, and it gives Don the time he needs to turn the division round. It doesn't change the basic direction of the European plan, and if Don succeeds in years one to three nobody's going to object to amendments over the last five, if the UK division turns in the results.'

There was another long silence before Don Peters spoke.

'I'll buy that,' he affirmed to the Chairman. 'It's my neck on the block if we fail, but we won't. Hell I know the division's been in and out of the red now for more than five years,' he said, 'but it couldn't be any other way with plants operating at fifty per cent of capacity and with labour efficiency forty per cent below standard. We break even at fifty-eight per cent of capacity, which is damned low by general standards. If we can progressively lift production to standard volume of eighty per cent of capacity, we can make over three hundred million dollars operating profit. It can be done, and I'd like the chance to prove it.'

Clancy McGillicuddy was a realist, but his Irish ancestry also endeared him to a fighter. He remained silent for at least a minute, and nobody was foolish enough to interrupt his train of thought.

'If. . . .' he said reflectively, half to himself. 'If . . . if. . . .'

He was silent again. Then he looked hard at Don Peters.

'If we can raise production to standard volume. . . ? That's one hell of an "if" you've got there, Don!'

He added, 'In my book, permanently under-utilised assets aren't assets at all. They're liabilities to be disposed of. But if you can get better utilisation, I agree that things would be different.'

Again he fell silent.

'If . . . if . . . if.'

'OK,' he said eventually. 'I'll go along with it, if that's what you want to do, Don.' He looked around. 'Do we all agree?'

Heads nodded. 'Nothing to lose,' mumbled one.

'Wanna bet?' whispered his neighbour.

The Chairman, however, had his reasons for giving Peters his head. His subordinate's track record and the high personal esteem in which he was held at Presidential level made him too close a rival for comfort. McGillicuddy wanted that top job.

.   .   .

30

Clancy McGillicuddy was a man of action cast from the same mould as Nate Cocello. He was rude, crude and callously brutal toward any subordinate who had the temerity to disagree with him. He could, however, be charming and courteous when in the presence of the ladies.

On the public relations platform he would defend the interests of the multi-nationals and their ostensible targets which, of course, were quite different from their real objectives, with a polite frankness and sincerity which never failed to create a good impression of the integrity of the man and the Corporation. Behind the public relations facade in the highly charged corridors of power, he was a rough, tough and dirty in-fighter, who never flinched from putting the boot in, if he sensed that his own power base was threatened by an injudicious rival.

He would steal anyone's clothes, if he thought for one moment he could use them to his personal advantage; and often did.

A finance man by training, he had risen to the powerful position of General Director Europe not simply because he was a good bean counter, which he was, but because during his last three overseas assignments, he had been particularly fortunate to have been treasurer of divisions which had expanded under the creative leadership of enterprising managing directors.

Treasurers, as a breed of men in the Company, were only put at the top if the job requirement demanded the expertise of a butcher; in which case they could usually be relied upon to carry out top corporate instructions with effectiveness and relish. When the top requirement demanded the expertise of creative thinking managers, to expand the business, the top job was always given to engineers, sales or marketing men, or planners.

In his early days in the Corporation, McGillicuddy had hacked his way through several small plants in the USA which weren't performing as expected, leaving his personal trade mark as he went. If word travelled ahead to a plant that 'Gilly-the-Kid' was coming, it was in itself enough to send shock waves through plant management ranks.

In those days McGillicuddy never saw people as people, but as headcount numbers attached to dollar signs. The engineering

31

department, for example, didn't conjure up in his mind's eye research, development and design activities where the future products of the business were being developed. He only saw, say three hundred heads at an average cost of forty thousand dollars per head, plus ten thousand dollars for employee benefits. Say fifteen million dollars per year.

Cutting the engineering headcount by twenty per cent would save three million dollars per year. That was sufficient reason to use his cleaver.

Although he didn't realise it at the time, his big break came when he was sent overseas to an ailing division, alongside a new creative managing director, who was just as determined to expand the ailing division with a new product programme as McGillicuddy was eager and ready to hack it back with his butcher's cleaver.

The MD was even tougher and more determined than his treasurer, who eventually came to the conclusion that as he couldn't really fight the MD he'd better join him. It proved to be a very sensible decision, for thereafter he shared with the managing director the honour and distinction of achieving profitable expansion, which was the hallmark of the real manager in the eyes of top corporate management.

Two more similar assignments alongside dynamic managing directors and McGillicuddy's track record was established. He had proved to the brass that he could do a hatchet job effectively, but that he could also do the far more important and infinitely more difficult builder's job, with equal effectiveness.

At the age of fifty-eight, he was now General Director Europe, which made him one of the most powerful businessmen in the world, exercising control over more than two hundred thousand employees.

McGillicuddy was a man of action who went everywhere and did everything in a hurry, bustling energetically along at such a pace that his personal staff often had to trot to keep up with him. He liked that. A busier man there never could be, and yet he seemed busier than he was.

Big Clancy McGillicuddy had come a long way from his early 'Gilly-the Kid' days in the States, and was now the well-rounded international executive of great experience, high integrity and good repute.

His flamboyant and opulent lifestyle simply reflected what was expected from a man in his position.

And how he loved it!

.   .   .

The regional meeting of the Allied Union of Engineering Workers was in customary turmoil.

After extending fraternal greetings of solidarity, the brothers were, as usual, at each other's throats, not bothering for one moment about such semantic trivialities as keeping to the agenda.

Instead, the meeting followed its customary course, with one brother after another launching into an emotive tirade about industry and politics in general and nothing very much in particular.

At long last, after the lads had had their say, the grey-haired and distinguished-looking Chairman, Clem Bunker, who looked more like a prosperous banker than a Trade Union leader, raised his arms aloft and stared forever upward in statuesque tableau, until the noise eventually subsided.

'Ah, brothers,' he said softly in lilting cadence as he let his arms fall. 'You must all feel so very much better now that you've got that little lot off your chests. So shall we now address ourselves to the subject matter on the agenda, which is the reason for this special meeting being called at the specific request of the committee representing the shop stewards at the United Motors plants? Namely . . . to consider what steps we should take in response to reports circulating in the plants that United Motors is planning to phase-out vehicle manufacture in the UK.'

Bunker's calm and measured tones acted like a sedative. Most of the trade union members employed at the United Motors plants had come to like and respect him. He had spent twenty-five years working on the factory floor at the biggest UM plant in the country, progressing from shop steward to convener before taking up the full-time job of District Officer of the AUEW at the age of forty. He was promoted to Regional Officer at forty-five, where he quickly established himself as an up-and-coming national figure. Invitations followed to serve on several TUC national committees which brought him into close personal contact with Ministers and senior civil servants. His ability to think through a problem rationally, and debate the subject calmly, without rancour or undue bias, led to an invitation to serve on the influential Economic Planning Council, which advised the Cabinet. Members of this committee included other trade unionists, leading international bankers, industrialists and academics. One of the industrial members on the committee was Mark Sanders.

Bunker had no burning personal political ambition and had already declined an invitation from Labour Party Headquarters to stand for Parliament. He had reacted more favourably to overtures from the office of Prime Minister Hallershan who had recognised abilities which could be put to good use in one of the Nationalised industries.

Bunker had started work as an apprentice at United Motors at the same time as Mark Sanders. Their careers had run parallel, up to the age of thirty, before they went their separate ways: Sanders into management, Bunker to trade union affairs. Periodically their career paths crossed and they would find themselves jointly involved in local and national issues. Initially as a district official and a plant manager respectively, serving on the United Motors national negotiating committee, and more latterly as members of the Economic Planning Council.

Both men were frequently invited by the universities to present papers and debate topical industrial issues. They had a genuine respect for one another and enjoyed crossing swords in debate. In so many ways they were very similar characters, even to the point that they actually looked rather alike, and might be readily mistaken for brothers. Both were family men, Bunker with two unmarried daughters in their late teens, and Sanders with three sons, one of whom was still single.

Bunker's ability to debate problems calmly, without recourse to political cant and dogma, had made him as many enemies as friends within the trade union movement. Active trade unionists generally preferred to listen to men with fire in their bellies, who could rouse the lads to action. Only when fighting for election or re-election, or when addressing Annual Conference, would Bunker allow himself to mix it in traditional trade union style. That's what the lads wanted at

34

Conference, and that's what they always got. Lashings of histrionics with high-pitched crescendos and clenched fists. It wasn't very edifying, but it reminded members of their early days in the Movement, on top of a soap box. Conference wasn't so much a debate as a cross between a drama festival and a musical comedy. Bunker did what was expected of him on these occasions, but it gave him no pleasure to reduce his arguments to their lowest common denominator. He preferred to raise the level of debate to the highest common factor.

His enemies in the Movement were of the militant extreme left, who took the standard line that there was nothing to be gained from discussing issues rationally with Governments, nor from negotiating responsibly with employers within the law. The law was for others to obey, not for them. They were interested only in destroying the system.

They were well on the way to achieving that objective in the UK and saw Bunker only as one of the renegade bastards who, for too long, had helped the capitalist system to function. He had assisted in its perpetuation. He was assisting it now. In consequence, he was an enemy of the cause and a class traitor. Nothing less. It wasn't simply a question of distrust; they hated him.

'Right,' Clem Bunker said now, scanning the troubled faces before him. 'Who wants to kick off? Yes Fred,' he added nodding to Fred Clasper, the cadaverous convener who represented the Merseyside plants and who had immediately leapt to his feet after Bunker had metaphorically blown the kick-off whistle. 'But let's keep to the subject on the agenda, shall we?'

The tall, angular and hungry-looking convener cleared his throat.

'As far as we on Merseyside are concerned like, the lads 'ave 'eard this rumour which has allegedly come down from bloody mount Olympus, via the management and technical unions that the bloody Yanks are planning to close down all the UK plants and build new plants in Spain, Austria, Portugal, Turkey and from what we can gather, every other bloody country west of Tibet and east of Suez, except this bloody country. And the lads don't bloody well like it . . . they want to know what the bloody hell's going on!'

Clem Bunker nodded and held up a hand to temporarily restrain other speakers.

'OK brother Fred,' he began. 'But before we all work ourselves into a lather again, let's check out the rumour with the TASS member here. Brother George, can you throw any light on the subject?'

'It's right enough,' confirmed the thin well-dressed and bespectacled young man who represented the technical staff. 'We have been asked to do preliminary planning work on the new "Z" car, but the tip-off we are getting from the secretaries is that this is simply a blind to keep quiet the fact that a top corporate decision has already been made to build the "Z" car elsewhere; probably Spain. We are simply going through the motions of an exercise.'

'If the bastards do that we'll black the bloody vehicles!' somebody shouted above the din.

'If the bastards do that,' Clasper yelled, 'we'll dump the bloody foreign trash in the Mersey!'

The Chairman had to raise his voice to bring the meeting to order.

'I agree that losing the "Z" car would be a great blow,' he said. 'But that doesn't constitute phasing-out vehicle manufacture in the UK does it? And that is the subject of this meeting.'

'Ah, but it doesn't end there,' the thin young technician interjected. 'The secretaries are also saying that they have seen secret reports which are being circulated to the top brass, that the real intention is to pull out of the UK.'

There was immediate uproar at this disclosure with further cries of 'Stuff them!' 'Bloody Yanks' and 'All-out strike!' coming thick and fast from the body of the hall. The Merseyside convener, Fred Clasper, was back on his feet shouting expletives above the bedlam.

'Hang on a minute, brothers, just hang on a minute,' Bunker appealed from his prominent position on the platform. The noise gradually subsided. 'If Brother George is right –and I'm not saying he's not – then we have a lot of work to do, a lot of constructive work, to protect the jobs of our member's.

'You can say that again!' someone shouted from the back of the hall.

'I do say it again!' Bunker retorted. 'But I also have to tell you that I think it would be most unlikely that United Motors would have considered such a major decision without first raising the matter with Government. We are not talking about the jobs of a few hundred people – which would be bad enough, God knows – we are talking about the jobs of more than fifty thousand workers in the United Motors UK plants. When you add in their families, there could be a hundred and fifty thousand people directly affected by a decision like that.'

He shook his head firmly. 'Detroit wouldn't make such a decision. They couldn't. Not unilaterally. Not without prior discussions with the Government. And I can't believe that Whitehall wouldn't have leaked something out to the TUC if such a possibility were on the cards.'

Fred Clasper was on his feet again. 'I wouldn't trust the bastards in Whitehall any more than I trust the bloody Yanks in Detroit!' he shouted. 'They'd both sell us down the river if they got half a bloody chance! I wouldn't mind bettin' that there's a bloody conspiracy goin' on right now between Obergruppenführer Nate bloody Cocello and smilin' Jim Hallershan. Cocello's always poppin' over in his private bloody jet for cosy little fireside chats with the bloody Prime Minister. I'll bet the bastards are cookin' something up between them, and it won't be an angel's bloody delight!'

His harangue was getting through to some of the members who began to nod in accord.

'I say let's call their bluff like, with an all-out strike!' he yelled warming to the prospect. 'That'll flush the bastards out from their funk hole!'

For the next hour every brother was given an opportunity to have his say, Bunker made sure of that. When the subject on the agenda had been well and truly aired the majority accepted his proposition that 'the conveners at each plant bring the rumours to the attention of plant managers, stressing the depressing effect on employee morale, and seeking the assurance of top management that such rumours are without foundation.'

The second part of the proposition 'that the Regional Secretary be asked to take the matter up personally with the Chairman and Managing Director, Don Peters,' was also carried.

The notable dissenter to both propositions was Fred Clasper whose amendment calling for an 'all-out strike in protest' was defeated by a large majority. He left the meeting angrily, with the Merseyside shop stewards to begin their own meeting in the back room of a nearby pub.

Subsequently, Clem Bunker's meeting with Don Peters was arranged for the following Monday. Peters readily accepted the opportunity of meeting Bunker for the first time, to explain what he was attempting to do to revive the ailing giant subsidiary and, over the weekend, he rang Mark Sanders to get a second opinion on Bunker to that already given him by his Personnel Director.

'Be absolutely frank with him,' Mark Sanders advised. 'You'll need his support to achieve what you're setting out to do. He can be one hell of an ally where you'll need one most: in the inter-union boxing ring. That's my advice, for what it's worth.'

'That stacks up with what I've already heard, Mark.'

'When I ran the southern plant, Bunker was a great help to me,' Mark Sanders said. 'But the union commies hate his guts.'

'Yeah, those bastards hate the guts of anyone who's trying,' the American said sourly. 'Thanks for the tip, Mark.'

. . .

3

Clem Bunker was relaxing at home with his family on one of his rare evenings free from trade union duties. He was reclining with his feet up, sipping a large Scotch as he ploughed his way through a mass of reports and Government papers, which he had just received for the next meeting of the Economic Planning Council.

He sifted the wheat from the chaff with lightning rapidity, marshalling his own thoughts and going straight to the important issues, underlining sentences here and there and scribbling words in the margin. As usual his mind was racing ahead. He looked up, staring quizzically at the wall as his thoughts suddenly jumped track, triggered off by what he had just read.

Putting down the reports he stretched himself and eyed his elegant and still beautiful wife, Gwen, who was sitting opposite, reading a thriller.

'I thought we might ring Mark Sanders and ask him round for a drink tonight,' he said. 'That is, if he's in the country. I owe him a return match.'

Gwen Bunker looked up from her book. 'Why not?' she agreed. 'I haven't seen Mark for ages. But why do you call it a return match?'

Clem Bunker smiled. He crossed to the telephone, pausing to kiss her lightly on the cheek.

'There's something I'd like to talk to him about, rather urgently.'

'Oh dear, darling, must it always be work? Can't you ever relax without wanting to discuss things?' Gwen Bunker said. 'I'm sure the world wouldn't stop if you did. Invite Georgina along, too. That will clip your union wings a little.'

He lifted the phone and the younger of his pretty daughters who were playing chess stretched out on the hearth rug, called out, 'Ask his dishy son Andrew over as well, Daddy. I saw a photograph of him in a magazine the other week. Made me feel quite weak at the knees.'

'Once again sex rears its ugly head,' intoned her elder sister in a pseudo-American accent. 'Sister dear, don't you ever think of anything else?'

'What else is there to think of?' came the quick reply. 'It's a biological necessity. It improves the complexion by stimulating the phagocytes, so there.' She put out a tongue.

'Stimulating the what?' said Gwen Bunker.

'The phagocytes, Mother dear. I read it in a book.'

'At the sex shop,' said her older sister. 'Her local.'

'Really!' Gwen Bunker exclaimed in mock outrage. 'There are times when I truly despair of this generation.' She aimed a playful smack at the neatly rounded bottom of her youngest daughter, now kneeling to play the game, chin cupped in hands, elbows pivoting on the rug. 'We behaved differently, you know, when I was a girl.'

'Of course Mummy. You and Daddy held hands.'

'Safer that way,' said her sister. 'If you've got their hands under control. . . .'

'Did you hear what she said, Mummy? Isn't she naughty?'

Clem Bunker was speaking into the 'phone. 'Hullo Mark. Clem Bunker. I'm fine, and you? Will you be at the Whitehall meeting next week? . . . Yes . . . good. . . . I see from the notes that the PM intends to sit in on the East European trade discussions and I thought . . . yes . . . that's the idea. . . . About tonight, Mark, Gwen and I were wondering if you and Georgie would care to drive over for a drink? Oh I see . . . out to dinner . . . but . . . yes, could you? Yes, that would be fine. See you about seven fifteen then. Bye.'

His younger daughter signalled frantically.

'Oh and Mark, bring Andrew along if he's not doing anything. Might liven the old place up a bit. See you later then, cheerio.'

Bunker put the 'phone down. 'Mark and Georgina have a dinner engagement in London. They'll pop in for half an hour on the way up.'

'Oh good,' said Gwen. 'It will be nice to see them again.'

The younger daughter swept past her Father planting a

40

quick kiss on his cheek.

'Well played, Daddykins. Now for the warpaint. I'll need an hour for this one.'

'Will it make any difference?' called her sister after her as she bounded up the stairs.

Clem put an arm around his wife's waist.

'Mrs Bunker, are you sure these daughters are mine?'

'I have it on the very best authority that there is at least a fifty-fifty chance,' she teased. 'Now tell me what he said.'

. . .

'What are we doing fraternising with the enemy?' Andrew Sanders enquired. He sprawled across the back seat of his father's top-of-the-line company car, glancing through the latest *MEN ONLY*, as Mark drove swiftly down the M1 towards St Albans, his wife Georgina beside him.

'Do Chairman Mao Murray and Pope Clancy McGillicuddy approve?' he added, turning his head to one side to get a better view of the Girl-of-the-Month spreadeagled wide-legged across the centre page. 'Or is Brother Bunker about to sell his fraternal mates down the proverbial river?'

The Girl-of-the-Month was really something!

Andrew was twenty-two and in his final year at agricultural college, having decided at a very early age that under no circumstances would he follow his father into the motor industry; or any other industry, for that matter. He preferred to think that twentieth-century farming was not really an industry as such, but a healthy vocation for the discerning environmentalist, as opposed to the mechanistic existence to be found in a factory. The rat race was okay . . . for rats.

From early boyhood Andrew had been influenced in his choice of career by the fact that his father had spent little time at home in the evenings or weekends, always being too busy at the plant or, in later years, abroad on Corporation business. He was, however, sufficiently mature enough now to recognise that it was his father's willingness to work long and irregular hours which had taken him up the company ladder and provided the family with a lovely home in the country, and a public school education for himself and his two brothers at Millfield, Britain's most expensive school.

41

Andrew and his brothers respected their father's dedication which had taken him from the apprentice ranks to European Planning Manager, but he was also in their eyes a foolish workaholic who had got life's priorities all wrong. This was a view shared by so many sons and daughters of United Motors' executives. Some had left home when in their early teens, and were no longer on speaking terms with their fathers. Others had become drop-outs hooked on hard drugs. One had committed suicide. Many families had, in fact, paid a very high price in terms of pain and anguish, for a successful career.

When a family problem became public knowledge, sympathy was quietly expressed at the executive table, before colleagues moved on quickly to more important business problems. Nobody presumed to intrude in the personal life of a fellow executive; not even the Executive Personnel Director, who in any case was always far too busy to get involved in personal affairs.

A drop-out son or daughter, or even a suicide, was a delicate personal matter which did not concern the company, unless the executive's job performance was adversely affected by the stress and strain of it all. In that case he would be transferred to a less exacting job which would almost certainly affect his career prospects, his salary and bonus, probably for good. It was very rare for executives to bounce back from a sideways or downward move when you were above a certain level in the hierarchy of the Corporation.

.   .   .

'Is Bunker about to defect?' Andrew asked.

'You couldn't buy Bunker at any price,' his father told him in no uncertain terms. 'And surprising though it may seem to you and your college pals, I wouldn't even attempt to try. We are not all rogues in the motor industry, you know, contrary to what some of your more trendy pedagogues might have told you.'

'No perhaps not all of you,' Andrew conceded. 'That might be putting the ratio a little too high, I agree. So tell me, why are we deviating from the straight and narrow of the M1 to have a quick chat with the Bunkers?'

Georgina glanced quickly at Mark and put on a smile.

'Does there have to be an ulterior motive?' she asked.

Andrew murmured, 'No of course not.' Another wide-legged girl in *MEN ONLY* had engaged his attention.

He was a young man who could only think of one thing at a time.

The half hour spent with the Bunkers was friendly and easy. The wives, who hadn't seen each other for two years or more, chatted amiably about family affairs and their husbands' careers. Andrew and the two girls spent most of the time openly sizing each other up as they picked over record albums.

Clem Bunker quickly found an opportunity to take Mark to one side and came straight to the point, as they raised glasses.

'I'm seeing Don Peters on Monday,' he said. 'About these rumours circulating in the plants that United Motors is planning to pull out of vehicle manufacture in the UK.'

He was watching for any tell-tale signs in Mark's expression. The face of the industrial manager remained impassive.

'I know I can't expect to get a straight answer to a straight question from Peters,' the trade union leader went on, 'but I need to know more about the man, if the meeting is to be of any value to both of us. What sort of chap is he? I have met him, but literally only to shake hands on a formal introduction when he first arrived here.'

He took a gulp of his whisky.

'The reports we have been getting from the shop stewards and coveners have on the whole been very good,' he continued. 'Everyone seems to agree that he is a great improvement on Kauffman, but that's not saying anything. Any silly bugger would be an improvement on that bastard.'

Clem Bunker could feel his gall rising at the very thought of Kauffman and his massive personal contribution to the decline of the British vehicle division.

'How straight is Peters, Mark?' he asked. 'How far can I go with him?'

Mark smiled. 'All the way,' he replied. 'He's straight. One hell of a track record. I like him and I think you and he could hit it off.'

'How the hell can a union man hit it off with a hatchet-man?' asked Bunker in pained surprise. 'Closing plants is not exactly the ideal way of making friends and influencing people.'

Mark savoured his Scotch.

'I happen to believe that Peters is probably the division's best chance of survival right now,' he replied. 'Maybe its last chance,' he added.

'It's not in the man's nature to be a hatchet-man. He's a builder, not a destroyer. He's determined to turn the division round from the mess it has been in for the last ten years, and he'll do it if he's given the necessary support from the top and the bottom. He's planning long term, Clem. . . .'

'Long term!' Bunker exclaimed in surprise. 'Oh, come on now, Mark. From what I hear, short term is down and long term is out. Since when have Yankee Managing Directors of overseas subsidiaries ever planned further than the end of their own short term assignments? They're never in the job for more than two years. Their horizon is always this year's budget, and to hell with the future. That's someone else's problem after they've moved on to richer pickings and lusher pastures. You know it, and so does everyone else in United Motors!'

Mark smiled a little wryly. Bunker was too close to the truth to be contradicted. Nevertheless. . . .

'I can only repeat what I've just said,' he replied. 'Don Peters is no hatchet-man. His own future depends upon him pulling the division through. He's stuck his neck out on behalf of the division. If he fails, it's certain he'll be replaced by another character like Kauffman, and that really will be the end.'

Bunker had listened carefully, taking it all in. He shrugged his shoulders to signify he would like to be convinced.

'I don't trust the Yanks to represent British interests,' he said quietly. 'You only have to look at what American management has done to the British motor industry over the last ten years. Just compare the massive expansion achieved under British management in the late forties and fifties with what has happened under American management in the sixties and seventies.'

He ticked off points on his fingers.

'Profitable expansion under British management with not one bloody strike in twenty years. But what happened when the Yanks took over in sixty-four? Bloody mess from then on. Everybody in the division knows that the Yanks sent for more

Yanks, and they in turn sent for their mates, until a bloody great, highly paid Yankee caucus was established in all the top positions, totally insulated from local management and the workers. And what was the first thing they did? They bloody well ditched the output incentive scheme and imposed their own flat rate system, and then complained when productivity started to fall. Well it rose every bloody year before they took over, didn't it? And it fell every year afterwards. But do they accept the blame? The fault of bloody poor management? Do they hell! They blame it all on the unions!'

Bunker shook his head in disgust.

'And just look what they did to the dealer network. Their bloody marketing experts came over and wiped out every dealer who wasn't selling two hundred and fifty new vehicles a year. So what happened? All the hundreds of small dealers in the rural areas went over to the Japs and the Froggies and the Krauts, who were all looking for dealers in the UK at that time. Christ! The bloody Yanks handed them a complete and fully established dealer network on a plate, free and for nothing.'

He refilled Mark's glass, recharged his own.

'It's bloody tragic,' he said. 'Dammit, Mark, we had the biggest and most efficient motor industry in Europe up to the sixties. Second in the world only to the States itself. Bigger than France, Germany and Japan. Now look at us. Nearly bottom of the heap. And it's all happened since the Yanks took over.'

He took down a mouthful of Scotch.

'They kicked us out of their own country two hundred years ago so they could run their own affairs, didn't they? We don't blame them for that, do we? They were right to do so. So what's wrong when the boot's on the other foot? Would the American unions and the American public stand by and let Englishmen run American industry? Would they hell! Let's face it, Mark,' he ended sourly. 'American managers are put here to run the business in the interests of America. Not in the interest of Britain. Britain is expendable!'

.   .   .

Mark had listened to the union man without interruption.

45

There was no point in attempting to contradict him. He was too close to the truth for comfort. It was common knowledge that if a British manager failed to turn in the results expected of him he would be replaced by an American. And if an American failed he would also be replaced . . . by ANOTHER American. This was standard Corporation procedure by which Detroit built up total American control over foreign subsidiaries whenever local laws didn't prevent it. Detroit had all the freedom it wanted in Britain.

To replace a high-flying British executive with an American because his job had become too important to be left to the locals, the standard procedure was utterly cynical but very effective. He was either set new budget targets he couldn't possibly reach and replaced when, as expected, he failed to reach them, or else 'promoted' laterally into a management *cul-de-sac* where there could be no way out . . . except down.

Nobody in management was under any illusions. In this particular American multi-national the unwritten rule was that you could only go so far if you weren't an All-American boy.

As the only Englishman in one of the higher European echelons of the Corporation, a seeming exception to the rule, Mark was now under no illusions either. He knew that he would never become General Director Europe, or a Vice-President of the Corporation though, theoretically, both positions were within his reach. He now knew from bitter experience that the top jobs would always be reserved for members of the All-American 'club'.

Mark had almost made it as Regional Director Europe, some three years before. He had been asked by New York if he would take the top job if it were offered to him. In theory, it was the next logical promotion step in the onward and upward thrust of his career, for he was still under fifty and had been foolish enough to believe at that time that he really could be the exception to every unwritten corporate rule. The dis-illusion which had followed when promotion blew up in his face at the eleventh hour had left a permanent scar.

For as long as he lived, he would never forget that Friday when he had received a call from New York telling him to catch the Sunday morning flight from Heathrow for a meeting the following day with President Nate Cocello and the Executive Committee. Mark was to have given a presentation to Cocello and the Committee at the end of the following week, but this personal telephone call from Hank Berman, the executive in charge of Component Operations world-wide, had brought the date sharply forward and given Mark the news he had really wanted to hear.

It was Berman who had asked Mark some weeks before if he would take over as Regional Director Europe, if the job were offered to him. It was no secret that Berman and Frank Steiner, the Regional Director at that time, Mark's boss, simply didn't get on.

Mark flew to New York that Sunday a very happy man. He had made it to the top job in Europe in one of the biggest corporations in the world.

On arrival at The Plaza Hotel he had been informed at the desk that Frank Steiner wanted to see him immediately.

It was early Sunday evening as Mark rang his boss from his hotel room. Steiner had been in New York all that week and had presumably been involved in the discussions which had led to Mark being named as his successor.

'Hello Mark,' said the Regional Director with the reputation of being a man of few words. 'Come on round for a drink . . . and bring your presentation with you.'

Mark had expected to be greeted at the door of Steiner's suite with a handshake and congratulations, but it didn't happen that way.

His tough and uncompromising boss looked tired and surly and it was patently obvious from bloodshot eyes and odorous breath that he had consumed a great deal of alcohol during the day. But this was not unusual as Steiner was an alcoholic; as indeed were many of the top executives of the Corporation.

Frank Steiner could hold his liquor, however. He simply became more and more bloody-minded in direct proportion to the amount of alcohol he consumed. It was never really obvious to outsiders that he was ever the worse for wear, but those who were close to him, as Mark was, had learned to keep out of his way when he'd had too many. He was a hard and pitiless man who could be vindictively cruel when his tank was full.

'Come on in, Mark. Good trip? Have a drink? Was it Berman who sent for you?' Steiner asked, not giving a damn whether the trip had been good, bad or indifferent. He poured Mark a very large Scotch from one of the many bottles on the side table without bothering to wait for an answer. He knew Mark drank Scotch. All he was really interested in was a reply to his last question.

Mark took the Scotch, acutely aware of the undertone of hostility in Frank Steiner's voice and manner.

'Hank rang me last Friday, as I expect you know,' he said guardedly.

Steiner shook his head and topped up his own glass.

'Let's have a look at the presentation,' he said brusquely, motioning the Englishman to take a seat next to him at the circular table in front of the picture window.

The curtains were thrust back. The million and one lights of New York spangled and shimmered far, far below the penthouse apartment the Corporation maintained for its top men passing through.

Mark's mind was racing ahead as he took the presentation text from his briefcase and set a cartridge of slides on the table. He guessed what must have happened. The growling grinding animosity between Berman and Steiner must have erupted into all-out war with the latter now on his way down or out. Whether Steiner was actually aware of the changes taking place was a matter of conjecture. Mark himself was in a bit of a box for until Nate Cocello and the Executive Committee had confirmed Mark in the appointment which Hank Berman had said was his, Frank Steiner was still technically his immediate boss.

The only sensible thing to do, he concluded, was to act dumb and let Steiner ask all the questions. He slid through his presentation swiftly, leaving it to his boss to interrupt him.

But Frank Steiner said nothing. He allowed Mark to skip through the presentation at speed. But he missed nothing either. Drunk or sober, his brain was honed razor sharp. Nothing went past him.

'That's it,' said Mark looking up at the end of his rapid presentation. Steiner nodded and kept on nodding away for several seconds in contemplation.

'It's good,' he said finally. 'Damned good.'

48

Mark felt a sudden surge of compassion for his erstwhile boss who was now on his way down the corporate ladder after a lifetime in the Company.

Steiner rose from the table and half turned toward Mark. He had a curious smile on his harsh face which gradually hardened into a cruel leer. He picked up the text from the table.

'It's better than damned good ... it's excellent,' he exclaimed as he ripped selected pages from the text.

Mark was so totally taken aback by what Steiner was doing that he just stood there transfixed and speechless. The American tossed him the residue of the text he had just gutted and shook out a handful of slides.

'I'll use these in my introduction,' he said flatly. 'You can take it from there.'

Mark could see that Steiner had taken the key slides which gave the global picture and explained the objectives and strategy. The American had stolen the big scene and left the Englishman with the details.

Steiner raised his glass.

'To our presentation,' he said sarcastically. 'You can go now. I don't need you any more.'

Exploding in anger, Mark sprang at the American, seizing him by the throat with his left hand.

'You bastard ... you dirty unscrupulous bastard,' he yelled, winding up his right fist to strike the American.

'You are on your way out and you intend to take me down with you,' he shouted in a wild rage. 'You lousy underhanded bastard ... I'll kill you.'

Steiner's face turned puce as Mark twisted his tie in a vice-like grip but he still managed a supercilious smile.

'Go on. Hit me. Hit me,' he cried, coughing out the words. 'It will be the last thing you ever do in UM.'

Eyes blazing with uncontrolled anger, Mark raised his right fist to smash it into the American's vindictively cruel face. The supercilious smile broadened. He nodded encouragingly.

'Go on, hit me,' he repeated. 'Hit me.'

As if a light had been switched on to see things more clearly, Mark was suddenly aware that Steiner was setting him up.

He thrust the American into the deep armchair where he sprawled with a self-satisfied leer on his malicious face.

Mark stood over him and smashed his right fist into the palm of his left hand in frustration, sending the black onyx in his gold signet ring flying across the room.

'You shit, you devious bastard! I should knock the hell out of you, but I won't give you the satisfaction of bringing me down with you.'

He grabbed the text and slides and moved to grab the gutted edition in Steiner's clenched hand. The American jerked his hand back and away.

'Oh, no,' he said dismissively. 'These are mine, remember? For the introduction. I'm still your boss, you know,' he added knowingly. The malicious smile broadened still further,

With an armjerk gesture of disgust and contempt, Mark turned to the door, grabbing his briefcase *en route*.

'You unprincipled bastard,' he hissed, wrenching open the door. 'I hope you rot in hell.'

'Goodbye, Mark,' called out the American.

'And if I were you I wouldn't count my chickens on that promotion. No siree. Not if I were you.'

. . .

Nate Cocello was the last man to take his seat around the President's table on the fourteenth floor of the UM building. Hank Berman had taken Mark by the arm, guiding him to the chair with the name 'Hank Berman' embossed in gold on the backrest.

'Could be yours in a couple of years when I move on,' he said with a smile.

On entering the room, Berman had deliberately ignored Steiner who had taken an empty chair toward the end of the long table. Steiner's face was even harder and colder than usual, which was saying something.

'OK. Let's roll it!' called the President eagerly, settling back in his chair to enjoy the show.

Nate Cocello loved presentations for they gave him yet another opportunity to display his considerable knowledge of all aspects of corporate affairs in front of the Executive Committee. As President, he was the man who was expected to ask all the searching questions and to make the final pronouncements at the end of the session. The others would take their cue from him. They would only speak if he asked them for their views. If he didn't do so, only a very rash man would presume to speak voluntarily.

Hank Berman cleared his throat.

'Mark Sanders is going to take us through the Components Europe Ten Year Business Plan,' he said to the most powerful industrialist in the world.

Cocello nodded. He knew only too well that Sanders was in the driving seat. Nobody would attempt to put on a presentation to the President of United Motors without his prior approval and without him being properly briefed in advance. He had agreed with Berman that the Englishman should succeed Steiner who was being moved sideways to let Mark through. He looked over in Mark's direction.

'OK, Mark, let's get the wagon on the road,' he said cheerfully.

Knowing that Steiner had decided to give the introduction, explain the plan and grab the headlines of the proposals, Mark hesitated, but it wasn't necessary. Steiner was already on his feet and had gone to the podium.

'I'd like to introduce and explain the plan in broad outline, before handing over to Mark to take you through the details,' he began.

Berman looked at Steiner in astonishment; then at Mark before meeting the President's withering look. Nate Cocello had expected to hear Mark Sanders and only Mark Sanders. He hated surprises. They made him very uneasy.

Steiner pressed the button and Mark's first slide appeared on the large screen.

As he began speaking, Berman hissed agitatedly to Mark, 'What the hell's going on? This is your show, not his! What the hell's he doing up there?'

Mark was between the devil and the deep. Steiner was still his boss until all the acts of appointment had been completed. There was no way he could stop Steiner going to the podium.

'I think you should ask Steiner that question,' said Mark wearily.

'I can't stop him.'

But by that time, Berman was up on his feet, cutting off Steiner who was in full spate.

'Sorry about this, Nate. . . .' angrily he waved Steiner away from the podium, 'but Frank is not down to speak, and I don't know what the hell he's doing up there. This is Mark's show.'

'That's what I thought.' Cocello's reply was testy. 'I think we'd better adjourn.'

The atmosphere in the room was electric. Steiner stood transfixed at the podium, his face deathly grey. Berman hurried to the President's chair and whispered something in his ear.

Cocello rose slowly and cast a cold, withering look around him. Equally slowly, he walked towards the ante-room with Berman continuing to whisper apologies and explanations, words which would be of no real value or consolation.

Mark closed his eyes in mental anguish, knowing full well that his promotion had been shot to pieces, along with the last act of Steiner's career. The American stepped down from the podium and walked out through another exit, not bothering even to cast a glance in the Englishman's direction. He knew that he was finished anyway, and the fact that he had also ruined the Englishman's career was of no concern to him. Such people were incidental. 'A dime a dozen' was the expression he often used to describe non-American executives.

.   .   .

The organisational changes announced two days later shunted both Steiner and Berman into a management *cul-de-sac*. Steiner's successor as Regional Director Europe was not Mark Sanders, as originally planned, but the moon-faced elderly American, Patrick Muldoon, who had never put a foot wrong in a long and undistinguished career in United Motors because he had never ever put a foot forward without first testing the ground, and getting the approval of his superiors, earning for himself the reputation of the original fail-safe man, belt and braces with everything.

Pat Muldoon was a safe bet not to rock the boat. He could also be utterly relied upon to do whatever Detroit told him to do because of his complete faith in the Corporation and the infallibility of his superiors. Mark was asked to continue as head of planning and to also act as Muldoon's right hand man. He had no choice in the matter but to accept, short of leaving the Corporation. His salary was increased substantially to sweeten the bitter pill of disappointment and to ensure that the corporation retained his services. But his miserable return flight to London was in marked contrast to his eager outward flight a few days before.

From that moment on he would always be on his guard when working with Americans.

.   .   .

Clem Bunker was taking the glass from his hand.

'Let me get you another drink, Mark,' he was saying.

Mark snapped out of his reverie.

'What? . . . Oh . . . No thanks, Clem, we must be off.' He had been miles away, but had not missed Bunker's comments and question.

'I go along with much of what you say, Clem, but if you want my personal opinion, not just as a United Motors man, but as an old friend, give Don Peters all the help you can. He's going to need one hell of a lot of support if the division is to survive. I mean it.'

The trade union leader took his empty glass.

'That's what I needed to know,' he said calmly. 'Thanks for dropping in. It's been a great help.'

.   .   .

The dinner engagement at the French Embassy was a small but formal affair. The meal was excellent with a rare Romanée Conti to accompany the *Boeuf Wellington* which had been put on the menu for the Englishman's benefit.

But Mark was troubled by a remark that came with the brandy and cigars.

The Ambassador had reiterated that the French Government was very keen indeed to attract new European component investment to France under the United Motors' Ten year Business Plan, and had stressed that his Prime Minister had considered the matter to be of sufficient importance to have personally communicated his country's interest to Nate Cocello. That by itself was not unusual, since virtually every

European Government was keen to obtain the lion's share of new projects. Mark had been under great pressure from many quarters.

His general remarks took on a rather sharp edge and meaning, however, when he added, 'It must be very difficult for you, Mr Sanders, to form a detached judgement on European investment. You are an Englishman, after all. A Frenchman would certainly be expected to favour France; a German, Germany . . . naturally. It must be very difficult to take the coldly analytical view.'

Mark could not agree more.

'But, difficult or not,' the Frenchman went on, 'it is expected of you. Otherwise you will be open to criticism from every quarter. You must consider the situation objectively and, if you do, I am sure you will reach the conclusion that the right place for European investment is France.'

.   .   .

The Ambassador's remarks returned to him more than once on the drive back home to Buckinghamshire, only to be abruptly thrust to one side as the house came into view. The porch and sitting room lights were on. Andrew Sanders leant forward.

'Isn't that Grandad's car?'

It was parked in the driveway in front of the house.

Mark brought his car to a halt beside it.

'What's Dad doing here?' There was a note of anxiety in his voice.

'He didn't say he was coming, did he?'

'Not to me.' Georgina Sanders sounded every bit as anxious as her husband.

Tall and lean and in his late seventies, Mark's father was a man who had always carried his age very lightly indeed. But the last time she had seen him she had noticed a sudden sag to his shoulders and a tiredness that haunted the depths of his eyes.

He came to the door to greet them.

'Hullo, Georgina.'

He kissed her warmly and affectionately.

'Hullo Andrew . . . Mark. Hope you don't mind me

descending on you like this?'

'Of course not!'

'Fact is, I felt the need for a bit of family company, so I invited myself over for a couple of days, if that's all right.'

'You know it is,' Georgina said.

'Nothing wrong, is there Dad?' Mark couldn't disguise his concern.

'No, not really. Just a bit of over-tiredness, I suppose,' his father told him. And he smiled.

But there was something wrong, Mark thought. You'd have to be blind not to see it.

Later that night, sleeping uneasily, some small sound awakened him. He lay in the darkened room, listening, Georgina sleeping quietly beside him; but the sound, whatever it was, wasn't repeated. Nevertheless, he got out of bed and, on the landing, saw that a light was on in his father's room. Silently, he pushed the door open.

His father was sitting hunched up, bent forward in a chair by the bed, breathing heavily and with great difficulty.

'Dad! What is it? What's the trouble?'

Mark bent over his father, and the grey, haggard face of a suddenly old, old man stared up into his own.

'Got these pains in my chest. Mark. Just can't breathe.'

The gasping mouth tried to smile.

' 'Fraid Anno Domini has finally jumped me. Better than creeping up gradually. . . .'

He was admitted to hospital within the hour.

.   .   .

On his way to Heathrow the next day, Mark made a detour to see his father, remembering only at the very last moment to pick up a bottle of Scotch at a nearby off-licence. With the bottle deep in an inner pocket of his coat, safe from the forbidding eyes of authority, he approached his father's bed with mounting concern. The prostrate figure before him lay ashen-faced; seemingly lifeless. Then the old man's eyes flickered open.

He smiled tremulously and put out an old, grey hand. 'Mark' he whispered. 'How good to see you. Been thinking of you. Everybody's been here today, except you . . . but I knew you'd come. Are you off somewhere?'

'Yes, Dad. Paris. I'd rather not go. But I have to.'

'It's your job, Mark.'

Mark tried to smile.

'Anyway, it'll only be for a couple of days. I'll come and see you on my way home.'

'Don't be too long.'

Mark leaned over to kiss his father's cheek and the bottle in his coat pocket nudged the old man's arm.

'I know what that is,' was the immediate response. 'Just what the doctor ordered!'

Mark took the Scotch out of his pocket and held it up for his father's approval. The tassel round the neck of the bottle carried the distiller's trademark: a golden ball and the words 'AFORE YE GO. . . .'

Even now, the old man's keen sense of humour had not deserted him.

'How very appropriate,' he chuckled. 'No point in buying me Johnny Walker. . . .'

And then he started to cough. And gasp. And gasp again.

Nurses came with oxygen. Mark had to go. He called the hospital from Heathrow and was told that his father was fighting back. But when Mark arrived at the Hotel George Cinq in Paris there was a message waiting for him, to call Georgina.

'Mark,' she said tremulously. 'Mark darling. I'm so terribly sorry. Your father is dead.'

.   .   .

All the arrangements had been made for the round of meetings in Paris. There was a tight schedule to keep to; reports to write. Life had to go on. Business as usual. But alone in his room that first night, after all the hassle of the day was over, Mark poured himself a very large whisky and had his last drink with his father.

.   .   .

He flew back for the funeral, and the next day was back in

56

harness at UM's European headquarters in London.

And there, within minutes, Clancy McGillicuddy, the General Director of European Operations, was on the internal 'hot line'.

'What are we gonna do about Spain, Mark?' he asked.

'Do we have to do anything? After that last fiasco in Madrid, Nate's very firm instruction was to do nothing until further notice.'

'Sure, Mark. But the new Spanish Government is putting a lot of pressure on Nate to reconsider investment there. Suarez wants to mend bridges and open discussions. He's on a good will visit to the States right now, and has a meeting with Nate on Friday. I've got to fly out tomorrow for talks prior to the meeting. He wants our current thinking on Spain.'

'You've got my report,' Mark said. 'Nothing has changed except the members of the Spanish Government. Spain's domestic market is still heavily protected by a wall of highly discriminatory decrees despite the fact that Spain has now elected to join the same club. The Spaniards want the best of both worlds.'

'Don't we all?' McGillicuddy rejoined.

'Sure,' said Mark. 'But we don't usually get it.'

'Not unless we're ultra-smart. . . ?' McGillicuddy suggested.

'Or the other fellow,' Mark said, 'is incredibly stupid.'

'I couldn't agree more,' said McGillicuddy, 'but this really isn't our concern. Our sole responsibility is to the Corporation. Nothing else. We don't have to play the role of Solomon. Let the politicians do that.'

'I understood,' Mark said slowly, 'that our first reponsibility was for European operations.'

'Sure. Sure. The Corporation's European operations. So what are you saying?'

'Just that the only way Spain can win is if someone else loses. The only way we can meet Spain's local content and export-ratio requirements is to manufacture all the new components there, and progressively phase-out existing component plants elsewhere.'

Yeah,' McGillicuddy agreed heavily. 'It's all in your report.'

'Then shouldn't we sit down and discuss it before we

consider investment in Spain? To give Spain what it wants would call for a massive shift of manufacturing resources away from existing plants in Western Europe. Germany, France and Belgium would all be adversely affected. British operations would be decimated. We're talking about a total UM investment of over five BILLION dollars, Clancy, with annual product sales of roughly similar value. Spain would get most of it. Other countries would lose out.'

'Sure. Sure,' the American said wearily. 'You really do bleed for those British plants, don't you Mark?'

Mark's mouth twisted angrily. He could never defend even the smallest, the most minor of British interests without being accused of British bias.

'And wouldn't you be wearing your American hat, Clancy,' he said, 'if UM were talking about replacing most of Detroit production with imports from Mexico, or Cuba?'

There was a brief pause and then the American laughed down the line.

'Point well made, Mark. And taken,' he said. 'But why don't we leave the politics to New York Central office? Those guys feel left out if we don't give 'em something to chew at now and again. Mueller's always moaning about only having a rubber stamp operation these days, and he's pushing Nate to accept Spain's terms. Incidentally, Mark, there's a guy to watch,' he added. 'He's a tricky bastard. Hates decentralised operations now that he's in the centre himself.'

'I'll watch it.'

'OK, Mark. Then is there anything you want to add to your report or subtract?'

A last chance, Mark thought, to shift with the wind; if he wanted to.

'Nothing,' he said.

'OK,' said McGillicuddy. 'Then be ready to fly out to Spain for new discussions if necessary.'

'Sure. I'll keep the engine running.'

'Hey, Mark,' added the American. 'I was sorry to hear about your father.'

Mark was taken by surprise.

Clancy McGillicuddy normally talked of nothing but industry in general and United Motors in particular.

'Thanks, Clancy. Nice of you to say so.'

'We only get one,' the American said. 'The real one. And there isn't such a thing as a replacement. I truly am sorry.'

A pause.

Then swiftly, Clancy McGillicuddy added, 'I'll ring you from New York. Check?'

'Sure.' said the Englishman.

4

Mark's plane touched down at Madrid's Barajas Airport in the early evening. As he stepped from the plane he was hit by a wave of oven-like heat which bounced off a shimmering concrete apron. Even the Madrilenians winced. He was driven to the Hotel Villa Magna in the Paseo del Prado, a short walk from the famous museum. An hour or so later, showered, changed and briefly rested, he was welcoming an eminent Spanish lawyer as his guest at a working dinner.

The Corporation retained the best possible native-born legal advisers in every country in which it operated, and this working dinner was intended to provide answers to any last questions which Mark might have before he opened discussions with representatives of the Spanish Government the following day.

A considerable number of small, but important details were attended to, and probing questions asked and answered. Then the cigars and brandy arrived.

'There is absolutely no doubt at all, Señor Sanders, that the new Government is very keen to attract United Motors' investment to Spain,' the lawyer said.

He warmed his brandy, savoured its bouquet.

'The unfortunate episodes which led to the termination of the previous discussions you had with the Franco administration are things of the past.' He gestured expansively. 'We have a new democratically elected Government now. And the new administration is most anxious to reach an agreement with United Motors, which it sees as further evidence of its sincere desire to become a full participating member of the European Community.'

The orotund phrases rolled off the tongue, and the swarthy Spaniard lubricated his vocal chords with several generous sips from his balloon glass of Duc D'Alba before he continued.

60

'You will recall from your previous discussions with the last Government,' he said, 'that there are two Spanish laws which cover all motor industry investment in this country. The first law covers investment by a new company entering Spain for the first time, which stipulates that at least seventy-five per cent of the new company's finished product must be assembled from parts manufactured in Spain. In addition, the company must agree to export not less than two thirds of its total production and, furthermore, it must limit its penetration of the Spanish domestic market to no more than ten per cent of the previous year's vehicle registrations.'

Mark nodded. He was fully aware of the laws.

'Under the second decree, which applies to investment made by existing companies already established in Spain,' the lawyer went on, 'the terms and conditions are less onerous. A twenty-five per cent local content requirement. A twenty per cent export ratio, and no limit placed on sales penetration of the domestic market.'

The lawyer took a long pull at his cigar and eyed it thoughtfully.

'Both decrees are, of course, still operative under the new Government,' he said. 'And are not expected to be changed until Spain joins the Common Market.' He shrugged. 'Perhaps not even then. Things can be spun out a bit . . . you know?'

'Nevertheless . . .' and he spoke slowly and distinctly, 'some people in Government would like you to know in advance of your meeting tomorrow that the existing laws do not necessarily have to apply . . . rigidly. Not in every case. You understand me? They can be, shall we say, manipulated a little. But for this to happen, the nature of the investment by the company concerned must be of sufficient size and importance.'

'You always could bend them a bit,' said the Englishman.

'More now,' said the lawyer. 'That is the message. More now if the circumstances are right. Believe me.'

.   .   .

The meeting between Don Peters and Clem Bunker proved to be of considerable value to both men. Each found, to his

61

surprise, that he really did have much in common with the other, as Mark had forecast would be the case.

Representatives of the allegedly diametrically opposed forces of capital and labour, they nevertheless shared an unalterable conviction that it was absolutely essential to raise the efficiency, output and profitability of the United Motors' UK plants if the division were to survive.

Clem Bunker said at one stage, 'I want a bigger chunk of a bigger cake for my members! There's no future in trying to grab a bigger slice of a smaller cake.' Then he added, 'And I have enough nous to know that a bigger chunk of nothing is nothing.'

'We need each other,' Don Peters said. Then he asked, 'But what about the wild men?'

'The wreckers?' Clem Bunker made an abrupt, dismissive gesture. 'We've got to put them down. But, first, YOU'VE got to stand up to them. If management gets diarrhoea every time a wrecker so much as farts, what can the real grafters, the builders, in the Trade Unions do? I can tell you something about the British working man,' he said. 'By nature he's conservative. Not conservative with a big 'C' – though a hell of a lot of them are – but more importantly conservative with a small 'c'. He wants change, sure. There's got to be change. It's only through change that man came out of the trees. But he distrusts abrupt change. Over the centuries, and looking around him, he can see that abrupt change has brought the ordinary man and his wife and kids nothing but grief. So revolution is out. Evolution is in. He wants a better life for his kids than he's had, though if he's any man at all he expects them to have to work for it. And he acknowledges he's had an easier life than his father.

'If the wreckers get their way – and everybody knows this but them – the very first people up against a wall will be the wreckers themselves. After the revolution, agitators are expendable. The French Revolution guillotined Robespierre and welcomed Napoleon. The Russians had Trotsky hacked to death and welcomed Henry Ford.

'And can anyone really believe that Russia today is a Workers' Paradise? A 'Bureaucrats Paradise' yes. But a Workers'.... Come on...!

'We've got common interests,' said Don Peters.

62

'But of course. If we hadn't, would I really be talking to you?'

.　　.　　.

Fred Clasper, convener of the Merseyside's plant's shop stewards' Committee, was holding the floor, as usual, at the local branch meeting called to discuss the reports of the alleged impending closure of UK vehicle plants. He had made it brutally clear from the outset that no discussion was necessary. He favoured an all-out strike without equivocation.

One of the moderates had nervously reminded him of the resolution agreed at the regional branch meeting which Clem Bunker had chaired. This had resolved that conveners at each plant should bring the closure reports to the attention of plant managers and seek assurance that they were without any foundation before proposing further action.

'Don't you think we ought to do that first?' he asked. 'Before we talk of strike action? And don't you think we ought to wait to hear what Clem Bunker and Don Peters have got to say. . . ?'

'Christ, brother!' Clasper's tone was despairing. 'What can they say? What do you expect them to say? Like everything in the garden is bloody lovely? That's what they'll say as they sell you down the bloody river! Hasn't the penny dropped yet? They're in it together. They've got you by the goolies and they intend to keep you that way for as long as you let 'em.

'Plant managers?' He almost spat out the words. 'What the hell do plant managers know? They don't know what the hell's going on in Detroit, that's for sure. And that's where the decisions are made, brother. Not in the UK or here on Merseyside. That's where the real power is now, yer know.'

He warmed to his pet subject, and the words spilled out, thick and fast.

'With Obergruppenführer Nate bloody Cocello, the bloody stars and stripes All Action Man. With him and his bloody bunch of Harvard Business school whiz kids in Detroit, that's where. Peters and the bloody plant managers are just bloody puppets. Detroit pulls the strings and they all flip and flop about like bloody Bill and Ben the flowerpot men!'

That got the great guffaw that Clasper expected.

The Merseyside shop stewards loved knock-about soap-box oratory. It often provided more laughs than the stuff on the telly. Clasper knew he had the meeting with him right at this moment; but who could say for how long. He lunged for the kill.

'The only way we're going to protect our jobs, brother, is to tell 'em all to get stuffed!' he shouted. 'Strike action, that's the only way to bring the bastards to heel! That's the only weapon they fear, so let's stick it right up 'em. Where it hurts!'

There was an explosion of agreement.

'He's right, yer know,' cried a dull-looking, string bag of a man who was known to his mates on the shop floor as 'Mastermind'.

'We should stand up and fight, like, that's what we should do. It's the only way. It's what I've always said, yer know, what we suffer from in this union is a lack of apathy. That's the trouble, always has been. Lack of apathy. . . . Well, I mean ter say . . . stands to reason.'

'Just listen to bloody Mastermind,' one of the older shop stewards muttered to a neighbour.

'If brains were made of gunpowder he wouldn't have enough to blow his eyebrows off!'

'What's the point in doing anything at all?' a miserable-looking shop steward in the back row wanted to know. He answered to the name of 'Laughing Boy'.

'What can yer do? Yer can't do nothing. There's nothing yer can do. It's all sewn up. It's a complete waste of time. Yer can't do nothing.'

Clasper regarded him with contempt.

'Thank you very much for that positive contribution, Brother Perce. It's a bloody great help, wack. So why don't we just bloody well lie down and let 'em walk all over us? It would be much easier all round; particularly for United Bloody Motors. I like that, Perce. It shows real spirit. Bloody hell!'

A lean, small, elderly shop steward with thick horn-rimmed glasses and a shock of white hair was on his feet.

'Haven't we got to wait for the result of Clem Bunker's meeting with Peters before we talk of strike action?' he asked mildly.

'It's always bloody wait and see, isn't it?' a lilting Welsh

64

voice sang out from the back of the meeting.

'Too right, Brother Dai!' Clasper cried. 'You've hit it, boyo! Always bloody wait and bloody see!'

But the elderly shop steward persisted. Glasses off, jabbing the air with them for emphasis.

'But we've already been through this. We've agreed everything once. We should wait for Clem Bunker's report. That's what we decided at the regional meeting.'

Clasper dismissed the suggestion with a derogatory sweep of the hand.

'I keep tellin' yer!' he shouted. 'It's a complete waste of bloody time. We need action. Strike action, that's what. Bunker is a bloody Southerner anyway so he won't do anything but fart around the mulberry bush. He couldn't give a tuppenny damn about us on Merseyside. Everyone knows that. I'll tell yer this for nothing, wack. If it's a question of who's getting the chop, I'll lay you ten thousand pounds to a pinch of shit that it's us on the Mersey. Bunker'll see to that, you mark my words!'

'But why should he?' someone demanded.

'To protect all his bloody mates in the Midland plants, that's why,' Clasper declared warmly.

But the questioner persisted

'If the Midland plants are more efficient and more profitable than the Merseyside plants – as they say they are – what can Clem Bunker do? Isn't it obvious that if it comes to a choice the less efficient and unprofitable plants will be the ones to go to the wall?'

'Whose side are you on?' Clasper raved. 'We're talking about people here, wack. Not bloody profits. It's the whole rotten system that's wrong. That's why I say smash the bloody system.'

'He was furious, boiling over, his heart pumping. That was what it was all about. Capitalism had bought more than half of the workers. It was only a bloody moron who didn't know that. That's why the militant left had to fight every inch of the way for socialism. Well, he was a bloody fighter. Too right. His father had died like a pig in his own shit: a blackleg, a scab and a strike-breaker, in a riot outside the gates of a factory here on the Mersey in the mid-Thirties, even before he was born. But he himself was a fighter; just like his grandad had been.

Christ! Someone had to wipe out what his father had done, didn't they? Betrayed his own bloody class, that's what he had done, and got killed doing it. Serve him bloody well right! His Grandad had told him!

His Grandad had told him everything. He'd spat on the memory of his own son. It was his Grandad who'd brought him up. He wouldn't let his mother keep him.

'A bloody class enemy,' he'd called her. Said she'd been responsible for everything that had happened.

And there were still bloody class enemies now. All around. Nothing had changed. The bloody capitalists had bought the working class, like this shifty bastard in front of him. . . .

He lunged to destroy him.

'What you've just said,' he shouted, 'that's obscene! You know that? It's bloody obscene! We should be caring about people, not bloody buildings and machines. It's people who count. Perhaps not in your book, Brother, and certainly not in Herr Reichmarshall Cocello's book either. But in my book, Brother. They count in my book.'

He warmed to his task.

'You sound like a bloody clerical worker,' he sneered. 'And what the hell do they know? They take the bosses' view. So many little red numbers at the end of a line. But I tell you, Brothers, people count more with me than little red numbers. And they should count more with you. Because in Cocello's book it's you who are the little bloody numbers, Brothers. And that's all you are or ever will be, until you show that you've got some guts.'

His diatribe ended the argument.

His motion that a small action group sub-committee be formed to prepare plans for strike action in the event that no satisfactory answer was forthcoming from the Merseyside plant manager was carried by a majority.

·   ·   ·

66

5

Mark's flight from Madrid arrived at Heathrow some thirty minutes late. After a fast drive up the M4, well behind the rush hour traffic, and a relatively free passage down the Cromwell Road and Knightsbridge to Hyde Park Corner, he arrived at Marsham Street bang on time for the monthly meeting of the Economic Planning Council.

He bounded up the escalator rather than take the lift to Conference Room P3025 on the third floor and, slipping quietly into the chair reserved with his name, acknowledged with a reciprocal nod and a smile the silent greeting of the distinguished-looking Chairman, Lord Hampshire.

The meeting had just commenced with the Vice Chancellor of one of the universities expressing a view on British energy resources and the anticipated impact on the pound sterling and UK export prices.

Mark glanced around the room. The secretariat flanked the Chairman on both sides, representing the Department of the Environment, the Ministry of Industry, the Ministry of Energy and the Treasury. Members present included two famous international bankers, several well-known economists and academics, and four TUC members, amongst whom Mark acknowledged Clem Bunker, who nodded back with a smile. Four heads of major UK companies and three British managers of multi-national Corporations made up the rest of the company.

Mark removed the Government papers from his briefcase and settled into his chair, eyes firmly on the second speaker who had taken over where the Vice Chancellor had left off.

Long speeches were never made at the Council, Lord Hampshire saw to that, and axes were never ground by individuals or groups, except at their peril. Members were appointed by the Prime Minister to express a personal and detached viewpoint, on a wide range of issues, including

67

Government White and Green Papers; the former being Government proposals to be put before Parliament as intended legislation, and the latter as consultation documents for discussion, prior to the final preparation of a White Paper.

The Chairman's knowledge of a wide range of subjects had earned the respect of the Council, but his real strength was his ability to persuade members to freely speak their minds on controversial issues. In other places, the same people might well mouth banal platitudes or tired shibboleths, but never here; a fact which made meetings of the Council of immense value to Ministers and senior Civil Servants.

The debate on energy resources continued until noon at which time the double doors opened and Labour Prime Minister Charles Hallershan entered the room, accompanied by the Secretary of State for Trade and Industry, three junior Ministers and a posse of secretarial aides.

The Chairman rose to greet the first Minister of State with an outstretched hand.

'Good morning, Prime Minister,'

'Good morning, my lord,' the tall and donnish-looking statesman replied, taking the Chairman's hand with a warm and friendly smile.

'Please be seated everyone,' he added as he was led to the centre of a row of vacant chairs which had been reserved for his party, opposite the Chairman.

'May I say, sir, how nice it is to welcome you once again to our meeting,' Hampshire said. 'And also to welcome the Minister of Trade and Industry, who we are always pleased to see here. The next item on our Agenda, as you know, is East-West European trade, and I trust you will find the opinions freely expressed to be of interest and value.'

'Thank you, My Lord Chairman,' the Prime Minister's keen gaze ranged the room. 'I am quite sure that we shall. My colleagues and I particularly wanted to be present today to hear the Council's views. I hope we haven't been too much of a nuisance in disturbing your debate on energy resources.'

'Not at all, sir,' the Chairman told him. 'We had concluded our discussions. But before we move on, may I congratulate the Minister of Industry. Twins, I believe.'

The Minister smiled broadly.

'Thank you, my Lord Chairman. I am now what the PM has

described as a *pa de deux.*'

The laughter was general. As usual, the Chairman and Ministers had put the Council completely at ease, an essential prerequisite if members were to be persuaded to speak freely and in confidence, as among friends.

'Is there anything you wish to say, Prime Minister?' the Chairman asked. 'Before we open it up?'

'I am here to listen and learn,' Charles Hallershan replied modestly. 'But if there is anything to be said at the outset it is this. My very real concern with the economic and social implications of Britain's prolonged balance of trade deficit on manufactured products is only matched by the unease with which I view the present weakness of our defence capability.'

His voice was strong.

'In the past we have effectively defended ourselves against aggressors because we have had the capability rapidly to convert great industries and manufacturing plants from peacetime manufacture to weapons of war. Almost overnight in 1939 our factories at Cowley, Dagenham, Luton, Coventry and Birmingham switched from building cars to producing tanks and armoured fighting vehicles. In our shipyards, hundreds of warships and merchant vessels replaced passenger ships on the stocks. The same was true of our aircraft industry whose enormous expansion during the last war was made possible by the resilience and strength of other manufacturing sectors, including the components, sector. But gentlemen,' he moved his mouth wryly, 'what do we see today? We have been witnessing over the last decade or more the slow and inexorable erosion of our entire industrial base. It follows that our ability to defend ourselves against any would-be aggressor in the future has been immeasurably weakened by this debilitating process, for you cannot embark on an emergency programme to convert rapidly great industries to a wartime footing if you have no great industries left to convert!'

There was no movement around the long rectangular table. Charles Hallershan looked to the left and to the right over the top of his spectacles as he went on.

'We are all rightly concerned with the economic and social implications of our industrial decline. But it is my view that we should be equally concerned with the effect of this deterioration

69

on our defence capability. Whilst certain countries have been greatly expanding their own industries – including some, I might say, who have not been particularly friendly towards Britain in the past – we in this country have become large-scale importers of manufactured goods, instead of the producers and exporters we once were. The economic effects of this change are plain for all to see. We have fallen from the position of the Number One industrial nation in Europe, which we held in the fifties and early sixties, to joint eighth out of nine! And of course,' . . . his throwaway gesture indicated the inevitability of it all, 'our standing, our reputation and our influence in the world has deteriorated stage by stage and step by step with our industrial decline.'

He looked towards the TUC and industrial members who were sitting on his left, and leaned forward slightly to secure their personal attention.

'Now, gentlemen, there are many who say that none of this matters very much. Their point of view is that Britain's time of influence and importance in the world is long gone, some say rightly so, and that so far as my fears about our country's defence capability are concerned they are wholly illusory. The next war, so the argument goes, will begin and end in fifteen minutes. No time to convert industries from a peacetime to a wartime footing. No time to convert them to anything, in fact, except, possibly, radioactive dust. But I tell you, gentlemen, this is a dangerous delusion. If we are incapable of making a conventional response to aggression, we must either make a nuclear response to a conventional attack and ring up the curtain on the end of the world, or make no response at all and let the aggressor take whatever he wants.'

In the stillness within the room, he removed his glasses and rubbed at the lenses ineffectually with his tie, looking around all the while, a nervous gesture which kept attention focused on him.

'Gentlemen,' he said, 'I am sure no-one here would seek to deny that we ourselves have been largely responsible for our own industrial decline. We all share the blame for that misfortune. But I also have to tell you, from evidence in my possession, that we have also been helped on our way down by those who have ideological and strategic reasons for wanting to see Britain weak, powerless and afraid.'

70

Again he looked around him. . . .

'My Lord Chairman and members of this distinguished Council,' he said, 'please be assured that I in no way exaggerate the gravity of the situation. Would it surprise you to know, for example, that no fewer than forty agents of the Soviet bloc are currently engaged in industrial espionage in this country alone? We also have it on impeccable authority that no fewer than four thousand Soviet industrial spies are at work in Europe securing strategic defence information and, at the same time, sabotaging European industrial effort.

'Those agents naturally concentrate their activities in the high technology fields such as nuclear energy, electronics, computers and optics. Their contacts, more often than not, are unsuspecting management people going about their normal business of buying and selling products and services. Within this highly respectable cover, it is relatively easy for the agents to operate without drawing undue attention to their more devious intent. Their contacts provide the Soviet bloc with direct access to Strategic Defence information. Just recently, computer technology was sold to East Germany which told the Soviets all they wanted to know about a critical NATO defence system.'

He looked up to catch the Chairman's eye, but this was unnecessary. Lord Hampshire's attention was riveted on the first Minister of State.

'My reasons for wishing to attend your discussion today on the subject of East-West trade, My Lord Chairman,' Charles Hallershan concluded, 'was to communicate what I have just said, and to listen to the views of your Council, particularly those members actively involved in world trade.'

The Labour Prime Minister again removed his glasses and nodded briefly to the Chairman to signify he had said all he wanted to say.

Lord Hampshire sat up in his chair and glanced quickly around the table.

'Thank you Prime Minister. You have certainly made us very much more aware of the less obvious aspects of our country's poor industrial performance which we are all most anxious to correct. Now who will open the batting? What about you Mark? Got your pads on?'

To the Prime Minister, he said: 'Mark Sanders is the

71

European Planning Manager of United Motors, Components Operations, as you may remember from your previous attendances at our Council. He will, of course, be speaking as a private individual and not as a representative of United Motors.'

Charles Hallershan nodded.

'Of course.'

'Then sir, your first question. . . .'

The Prime Minister rubbed the palm of his right hand with his left thumb and went on rubbing, staring intently at his palm all the while, as if wishing to remove an offending spot.

'Thank you, My Lord Chairman. . . .' he began slowly.

Then he looked at Mark over the top of his glasses.

'Mr Sanders, for a long time you have been at what I believe is called the sharp end of industrial operations in both West and East Europe. That is to say, you have been concerned with selling, manufacturing and planning up front.'

Mark nodded.

'We now see Russian Moscovitchs and Zhigulis, Polis Ladas, Czechoslovakian Skodas, Bulgarian fork-lift trucks, etc., entering this country in progressively greater numbers every year,' Charles Hallershan said. 'But I am not aware that we are selling many British-made vehicles or components to East European countries. Why is that?'

'I suspect, sir,' Mark began, 'that you know the answer to your question.'

The Prime Minister nodded slightly and Mark cleared his throat.

'Well Prime Minister,' he said, 'provided he can persuade the British public to buy his product, any East European manufacturer is perfectly free to operate in the UK market under the same free trade terms and conditions as everyone else. He can establish his own dealerships with one hundred per cent financial and management control if he wishes to do so. He is free to appoint his own staff and even set up a local manufacturing subsidiary under his own total ownership and control if he so desires.'

'Quite so,' said the Prime Minister. 'And now tell me, Mr Sanders, what a British manufacturer must do to sell into East Europe?'

'There's a very simple answer to that, sir,' Mark told him. 'He can't . . . except with strings attached.' He gestured. 'Oh sure, they are keen to buy technology under a Licensing agreement, but even then they insist on 'buy-back' deals. Which means, of course, that you are selling them your expertise to enable them to manufacture your products, which you are then contracted to buy back from them as finished goods. Needless to say, this enables them to penetrate your domestic market while their own markets remain effectively protected from entry from the outside.'

'And to what extent is their so-called hard currency shortage a genuine impediment to free trade with the West, or is it simply a convenient excuse for imposing unilateral trade conditions?' asked the Prime Minister.

Mark shrugged. 'East European Governments claim, of course, that it is a shortage of hard currency which forces them to impose such conditions. But my own opinion, for what it is worth, sir, is that the Soviet Union considers it to be a very convenient mechanism by which it is able to exercise control, not only of the amount of East-West trade which is transacted in each Comecon country, but also of the precise nature of each and every item of that trade, to ensure that everything complies with the overall objectives of the strategic plan.'

Mark paused for a reaction.

'Go on, Mr Sanders,' the PM said.

'Well sir, if the rouble and other Comecon currencies were to be made freely convertible into Western currencies, a free secondary market would have to be established, subject of course the normal free trade laws of supply and demand which I would have thought is alien to their political beliefs. As things are, the existing procedures permit the Soviet Union to retain overall control of East-West trade, by which means it is able to dictate trade terms to the West, and effectively control Soviet bloc countries.'

The Prime Minister leaned forward.

'To sum up then Mr Sanders, would it be correct to say that East European countries are perfectly free to sell into our market and into the free markets of West Europe, but we are not given the same freedom to sell into theirs, unless we are willing to agree to specific terms and conditions which are always heavily weighted in their favour and ultimately

73

determined by Moscow?'

'Yes, sir,' Mark said. 'You could put it that way.'

'Is there any other way to put it?'

'I would have to think long and hard to find another way of putting it,' Mark agreed.

'And does United Motors think this is fair?' Charles Hallershan asked. 'And in the interest of Britain?'

'United Motors doesn't make the rules, Prime Minister . . . and I am, of course, speaking in a private capacity, and not as a representative of United Motors.'

'Quite so, Mr Sanders, and I value your personal observation. So do you personally think it is fair and in the interest of the United Kingdom?'

'No sir, I do not.'

The Prime Minister nodded gravely.

'Thank you, Mr Sanders, for being so frank and helpful.'

.   .   .

Three days later, the British Prime Minister was discussing East-West trade with the President of the United States in Washington, prior to the Heads of Government meeting in Geneva. Other subjects discussed at some length were multinational activities and the United Motors' world car plan with its anticipated effect upon Europe in general and the United Kingdom in particular.

Both men recognised that their respective countries faced similar problems as a result of similar political mistakes. Both countries had experienced prolonged and worsening balance of trade deficits, which had devalued their currencies and fuelled inflation. Both countries had pursued policies of increased financial and technical aid to poorer nations after the 1939-45 war, and both had given social objectives top priority in the past thirty years.

Both heads of state now viewed with growing concern the ever-increasing strength of hitherto hostile countries which were now beginning to dominate the world scene through the dedicated pursuit of industrial supremacy.

As President Ben Cartwright put it to Prime Minister Hallershan:

'You know, Charles, there is a strong body of opinion over

here which says that we've done it again. We won the military war to save Europe, and we've lost the industrial war. We sat on our laurels when the war was over and played Lady Bountiful, while Japan and Germany got down to the business of rebuilding their industries with dollars we gave them. We are now learning the painful lessons which your country learned when Britain was the major world power. We know now that everyone wants favours from the top man to improve their relatively poor positions in the league table. But what they want most of all is to pull you down. Abe knew what he was talking about when he said you can't make the poor rich by making the rich poor!'

The paradox was not lost on the Englishman.

'And when you are toppled from the number one position, you discover there is no shortage of volunteers to help you on your way down. Now sir, after that little baring of souls ceremony, can we agree on the steps we propose to take at the Geneva Conference on multi-national activities and East-West trade?'

6

The United Motors' World Planning Group was in session in Detroit, with Chairman Randy Mueller laying down the law.

'I don't give a damn what the European Planning Committee has to say about our proposals to grant technology and manufacturing 'know-how' licenses to produce vehicles and components in Russia and Poland. We call the shots here in this committee, and if the Limeys, Krauts and Froggies on the European Planning Committee don't like it, that's just too bad. I'm cheesed off with those European bastards telling us to watch our step. That's their goddam trouble. They are too shit scared to do anything!'

Randy Mueller was in his early forties, a comparatively young man to be appointed Chairman of the group which had been formed to advise the Board on world planning issues. The principal function of the group was to co-ordinate and consolidate the various plans submitted by the Regional General Directors on behalf of the divisions within their respective zones, and thus to provide an overview of what was going on worldwide in the vast Corporation.

This was the role of the group as determined by Nate Cocello and the Executive Committee, and as perceived and accepted by the General Directors. It was not Mueller's view of the Group's function. His personal sights were set on the World Planning Group ultimately assuming complete control of the planning functions currently exercised by the individual General Directors. For, by nature, Mueller was not a co-ordinator of other people's ideas and proposals.

He had jumped at the chance of becoming the Group's first Chairman, because it had brought him that much closer to the seat of power. He had made up his mind to beaver away on his inside track progressively to gather up more powers and duties until he had effectively wrested planning control from the Regional General Directors.

Mueller was an ex-Harvard Business School man, supremely confident in his ability to plan the world from Detroit. He was, in fact, the archetype American manager as seen from European eyes. Brash, loud-mouthed, aggressive and vulgar. Mueller had fought his way to the top with a display of all-out aggression which had paid off handsomely. He made up for his lack of experience and talent by bawling and bulldozing his way through. His rivals in the Corporation had the choice of either standing up and fighting him off, or getting out of his way. Most of them got out of his way.

His short assignment in Europe had provided him with a superficial knowledge of the European business and political environment which he had then used with devastating effect on his American colleagues, most of whom had never held line responsibilities outside the United States.

His presentations to Nate Cocello and to the top brass, always used words and titles such as 'Aggressive Sales Plan', 'Aggressive Marketing Proposals', 'Aggressive Action to be Taken', themes which were in keeping with the man's character.

Mueller knew that the giant Corporation carried all the necessary clout to power its way through with any planning proposal, irrespective of the long-term consequences on host Governments in countries where United Motors had a manufacturing presence. He just wound himself up, pointed himself in the direction he wanted to go, and simply blasted his way through every obstacle until he reached his objective.

If an obstacle happened to be a local Managing Director, or the Government of a country, so what? 'Let's get on with the war,' he would shout to his colleagues, 'and cut out all the Government bull-shit.' Virtually everyone in the organisation hated him, which made him eminently suitable material for promotion to top levels, where he would be in good company.

.   .   .

'Yeah I hear what ya say, Randy, but hang on a minute, will ya?' one of the more reflective Americans on the all-American committee interjected.

'The European Planning Committee is only reminding us that the objective is to prepare a plan which would permit us to sell vehicles and components in East Europe. I'm not sure they don't have a point.'

'Jeez, I know that,' exploded Mueller. 'Those guys ain't telling me anything I don't already know. But they haven't produced a plan, have they? Sure they've been fart-arsing around, but they haven't come up with the answer, have they? At least we gotta plan and we'll get approval, so stuff those guys.'

The reflective American came back.

'But they are saying that we haven't got a plan to SELL United Motors vehicles and components in East Europe.' He put a great deal of emphasis on the word SELL.

'They are saying that our plan is, in fact, selling the Ruskies and the Polaks our technology to help them to manufacture our vehicles and components for sale in both East and West Europe. They claim that our plan doesn't provide us with a sales penetration in East Europe, but permits them to penetrate our markets in West Europe with the 'buy-back' deal, which they say is great for the East Europeans, but a bloody lousy deal for West Europe.'

Mueller shouted back. 'They say . . . they say . . . they say! That limey bastard Sanders says it's a bad deal, and he can get stuffed! I'm not having any bloody limey tell me what to do!'

'Yeah I know, Randy,' persisted the other American calmly. 'But you gotta listen to the guy's point of view. He's spent a long time in Europe, and knows the scene pretty damned well. He's no novice at the game.'

'That's his goddam trouble,' yelled Mueller. 'He's spent far too long, marking time on the same goddam spot. We want action, not goddam opinions. He's not aggressive enough. Checks too many angles out. If you want to win the goddam war, you gotta take risks.'

'Yeah, I hear what you say,' came the reply. 'But he says that our last deal with the Bulgarians and the Slavs cost the European components' division twenty million dollars worth of body hardware and ignition products, just because we didn't check it out with the local guys. Don't forget, Randy, they had to fire a thousand people in England on account of that deal. I guess we'd be hopping mad, too, if the same thing happened to us. Maybe he's right. Maybe we will get our tits in the wringer with West European Governments, and the Commission, if we go ahead, I don't know . . . but as sure as hell I wouldn't ignore what he is saying. . . .'

'Aw shit! I don't give a damn what European Governments think, or the European Commission; and I care even less what Mister Smart Arse Sanders thinks!' shouted Mueller.

'Now for Pete's sake Josh, will you shut up and let us get on with the war. We gotta get this presentation licked into shape for Nate and the Executive Committee. And if Sanders and the European Planning Committee don't like it, well that's just too bad.'

· · ·

Before leaving Washington for the Geneva Conference, President Cartwright had a working lunch with Nate Cocello to discuss the probable effect of the United Motors' world car plan on East/West trade, and also to hear Cocello's views on the recommended guidelines for multi-national companies which the European Commission was putting forward for discussion.

Nate had listened uncomfortably to the President's exposition of the various problems that European Governments were already experiencing arising from global plans. He squirmed visibly when the President went on to cross-examine him on the benefits expected to be derived from the United Motors' plan to sell its technology to Russia, Poland and East Germany.

'Mr President,' he said. 'Please be assured that there is nothing, but nothing in our world car plan, or in our proposals concerning East Europe, which could be considered in any way detrimental to the interests of the United States. We believe that what we are doing, or proposing to do, will be to the advantage of this country, and the Corporation, and we hope that you will see it that way.'

The President shook his head.

'I'm not questioning your motives, Nate. I'm sure the Corporation's intentions are in the best interests of the United States. But European Governments are concerned that you are giving East European countries your technology and manufacturing expertise which will enable them to sell into West European markets with a 'buy-back' deal, while at the same time, East European markets are still effectively protected from penetration by the West.'

'But that's not strictly correct, Mr President,' Cocello replied. 'Our proposals include a plan to sell certain vehicle models from our West German subsidiary to East Germany, Russia and Poland, as part of a reciprocal deal. We believe that we are helping to develop East-West trade, which must surely be in everyone's political and commercial interest. I don't really understand what you mean when you say that West European Governments don't see it that way. That's not our reading of the situation.'

The President took a sip of water from the glass before him. 'Well, let me put it to you the way that it has been put to me, personally, by the Prime Ministers of both Britain and France. They make the point that the United Motors' proposals may be very good for East Germany, Russia, Poland and West Germany in that the deal develops trade between these countries. The principal losers are going to be France and Britain, who will have to pick up the import bill. As they see it, what's going to happen is this. . . .'

He ticked off the items on his fingers.

'United Motors sells vehicles and component technology to East Germany, Russia and Poland. Secondly, West Germany sells vehicles to East Europe and buys back components which Germany previously purchased from Britain and France. Adding up, isn't it? The only West European country that's going to benefit from the UM plan is West Germany, which just happens to be the only West European industrial country to be running a large trade surplus at a time when France and Britain are struggling to cope with ever growing trade deficits. Meantime, the Russians are laughing all the way to the bank.

'Sure, we in the US are not the losers in the deal,' the President said heavily. 'Nor the Corporation, naturally. But you can imagine what the Governments of Britain and France think of the deal. They are the losers in the Corporation's plan. I tell you Nate, I don't like the political implications at all.'

Nor did Nate Cocello. In particular he didn't like being carpeted by the President of the United States, no less, on something on which he had been inadequately briefed.

He had assumed that Cartwright had arranged this meeting to seek his views on East-West trade in general and to have his comments on the European Commission's guideline proposals for multi-nationals in particular. What he'd just been told by the President about the way West European Governments were expressing themselves was all news to him. Why the hell hadn't he been advised of their views? He'd have Mueller's guts for garters when he got back to Detroit!

His mouth was clamped in a hard line as he thought furiously.

'Europe's supposed to be a Common Market, but it's a damned Uncommon Market to me,' he began. 'I'm an engineer, Mr President, not a diplomat. Politics is not my line of business. I do what I believe to be in the best interests of this great country of ours and the Corporation I serve. That's quite enough for me to think about. But if you feel that we should take another look at our East European proposals,' he finished placatingly, 'of course we will do so.'

The President rose and led him by the arm to the window.

'I'd appreciate that, Nate,' he replied. 'For quite apart from the commercial angle there's a much bigger defence problem which I'd like the Defence Secretary to outline to you.'

He pressed a bell to summon an aide.

'You might not like getting involved in the European political scene, Nate,' he said, 'but I can assure you that when you've heard from the Defence Secretary about how it all impinges on NATOs defence capability you will agree with me that we really have no alternative. We have to respond to the objections our friends in Europe have raised. It's in our mutual long-term interests.'

The hard line of Nate Cocello's mouth was thinner than ever. He swore to himself that someone back in Detroit was going to pay for his embarrassment.

.   .   .

When Cocello arrived back at his Detroit office, sparks really began to fly. Mueller had received a message from Cocello's

81

bagman in Washington, to be in the President's office when he returned to Detroit, at six pm.

Mueller wasn't aware of the purpose of that meeting, but he had an unpleasant feeling, from the tone of the bagman's voice, that the top man wasn't too happy about something.

Just what it was, he soon found out.

'Jesus wept!' Cocello raged. 'Just what's wrong with you, Randy? Why the hell didn't you check out the political implications with Europe before taking us so far down that road? It sounds to me like we've been completely out-smarted by the Russians!'

He stalked up and down, scratching himself like an agitated ape.

'Why didn't you sound out McGillicuddy and Muldoon, to get the European viewpoint?' he demanded. 'Hell Randy, why didn't you just talk to Sanders? He knows the European political scene as well as anyone; Jeez, he damned well ought to! He spends enough time talking trade matters with the Commission and with European Governments. He could have steered you clear of the shit we're now in! Why didn't you talk to him? I don't like being made to look a fool in front of the President!'

He stalked about the room, scratching himself furiously as he went.

Mueller was well and truly in the doghouse, but in a curious way he was sensually excited by Cocello, as the big man stomped angrily from wall to wall, firing vituperative broadsides in all directions. Mueller loved a shouting match. It got the adrenalin going. He was going to give as good as he got. Answering aggression with aggression was the only way he knew. He also knew that Nate admired aggression in others; lots of aggression.

'Yeah, but hang on a minute, Nate,' he bawled. 'Just hang on a minute, will ya, and give me a chance to explain?'

Cocello stopped in his tracks, glaring furiously.

'Explain?' he shouted 'Explain? What the hell is there to explain? You dropped me in it with the President. And for why? Because you didn't think things through far enough!'

'But Nate, listen to me, will ya? Didn't we all agree to play this one confidentially, from Detroit? Didn't we? If we'd discussed it with McGillicuddy or Muldoon or Sanders we could never have kept it quiet. With respect, Nate, you've gotta admit that's right. And you'll recall that you agreed that we give the Russian Government an assurance that it would be handled that way.'

'Yeah, yeah, yeah,' Cocello interrupted. He had stopped stalking the room. His shoulders were beginning to sag. The fires of fury were being damped down.

'I hear ya, I hear ya,' he said. 'And we did agree just that. But we didn't think it through, did we? Or we wouldn't be in the mess we're in now. We've been outsmarted, Randy. The goddam Russians have done a wheat deal on us!'

His voice was incredulous as the truth struck home: they had been outsmarted commercially as well as politically.

'Who handled the negotiations?' he demanded.

'Kopensky and Walenska,' Mueller told him.

'Well put 'em where they can't do any more harm.'

'Yes, sir. You can bet on it. They're out. But I mean out.'

Mueller was all subservience now that the danger was over.

'I had a suspicion they were too damned soft, but they spoke Russian.'

'Yeah, you can say that again. They spoke the same goddam language. That's for sure.'

The President of United Motors picked up some papers from his desk, glanced at them, and looked up to demand sharply.

'Well, what the hell are you waiting for, Randy? Divine guidance? Unscramble the deal before it's too late. You hear me?'

'Yes, sir,' Mueller was on his way to the door. 'Yes, sir. It's done.'

'And Randy. . . .'

'Yes, sir?' Mueller paused, and swivelled on his heel to face the top man.

'Don't ever put me in that kind of situation again. Is that understood?'

Outwardly totally subservient, Mueller nevertheless held a little holiday in his heart. Nate was losing his edge. Age was beginning to tell. And time, he told himself, was on his side.

'Move over, Cocello!' he crowed silently.

Nate Cocello looked at him, thought he saw something he didn't quite recognise, and looked again.

'You'd better believe it,' he said forcefully.

. . .

Mueller carried out Cocello's instructions with care.

It was true that Kopensky and Walenska had actually negotiated the terms of the deal with the Russians, but their negotiating brief had been based on specific criteria which he himself had formulated, so it was important that they should not feel that they were being victimised at this stage for the failure of the Russian project.

Accordingly, they were both informed that they were urgently needed on a new project in Argentina where they were despatched on a manufactured no-win assignment. When this project ultimately failed, as it speedily did, Mueller could get rid of them in any way that he saw fit without any hint of blame for the Russian fiasco striking himself.

Or so he thought. But he was wrong.

In Detroit, on his Personal Appraisal File, under the heading PERSONAL QUALITIES, had long since been listed 'Aggressive. Dominant. Determined. Decisive. Dedicated. Ambitious'. But to these, other qualities were now added by Cocello at Mueller's next review.

He had identified what he had seen in Mueller's face that evening in his office, and he wrote: 'Ruthless in Pursuit of Ambition'. He added, 'Not afraid to get rid of poor performers'. And on even further reflection: 'Judgement not always reliable in political and commercial matters'.

It was this last sentence which would, like a ghost unseen, finally haunt Mueller.

. . .

Mueller was one of life's workaholics, a dedicated corporate executive whose appetite for work was as voracious as his ruthless ambition. At the age of forty-five, he was a comparatively young man to hold his senior position, and had every reason to believe that, given a reasonable run of luck, he would reach the top echelon of the Corporation by his early fifties.

In moments of delicious contemplation, he saw himself as the youngest ever President of United Motors, with a salary in excess of one million dollars a year plus bonus. But it wasn't just avarice which spurred him on, though it was one hell of an incentive. It was the thought of all that power which could be at his command. The influence and the sheer goddam economic and political muscle of the most powerful industrial corporation on earth! That was the consummation devoutly to be wished.

Power to control the lives of nearly nine hundred thousand employees spread around the world, and the rock-solid influence of the giant Corporation whose sales turnover was greater than the wealth of most nations. With that power under his control he could really plan world operations as he saw it.

The very thought of such a possibility dispelled all doubt that he was right to do what he was about to do. As far as he was concerned, there were no sacrosanct rules in love and war. Rivals were competitors, and competitors were there to be beaten and eliminated. In his book, the internal power struggle within the Corporation was every bit as important as the commercial struggle against UM's main competitors. It was a brutal battle where only the fittest and most brutal survived. You had to be aggressive and ruthless to win and nobody, not even Cocello himself, was more aggressive and ruthless than Randy Mueller.

He took up a phone.

'Get me Muldoon,' he snapped to his secretary.

'Yes, Mr Mueller. Is he in London right now?'

'How the hell do I know where he is right now?' Mueller shouted. 'Just find him!'

Minutes later, the connection was made.

Muldoon happened to be in his London office, and Mueller greeted him with uncharacteristic friendliness.

'Hi there, Pat, buddy boy!' he bawled. 'How's the gravy train? London still swingin'? Jeez, some people are born lucky! Yes sir, you've got it made over there! Say Pat, do me a favour, will ya? Put the 'phone down and ring me back on my private line right away. Rather important.'

The private line rang in Randy Mueller's office.

'Hey, Randy,' called Muldoon. 'We must be in real trouble for you to want me to ring you on your private line. What's the problem?'

'I'm the one with the problem,' replied Mueller. 'Nate has had a rough ride with President Cartwright over our proposal to licence and buy back vehicles and components from East Europe.'

'I'm not surprised,' Muldoon replied. 'Mark did warn everyone.'

'Yeah, yeah, yeah,' Mueller cut in testily. 'But all that political bullshit gives me a pain in the arse. We should be able to get on with the business of making and selling motor vehicles; instead of wallowing around in all this multi-government crap.'

'So what can I do for ya?' said Muldoon, wincing at the bad language which he abhorred.

Mueller exhaled a long drawn-out sigh.

'Waal . . . I guess I'm not too sure how to put it,' he said at length.

'Go ahead, Randy. I'm listening.'

'So,' Mueller said abruptly. 'Do you trust Sanders?'

Muldoon was taken aback by the directness of the question.

'What do you mean?'

He felt very uneasy.

'I guess I don't know how to answer you,' he said at last. 'He's been around here a long time. That's for sure.'

'But do you TRUST him?'

Muldoon sensed, rather than saw, very dangerous shoals ahead. He hedged.

'Well. . . .'

'How is it,' Mueller cut in, 'that within days of him sending in his report on our East European proposals we get the British and French Governments breathing down our necks primed to the back teeth with the very same points he has already outlined? Doesn't that suggest a leak to you?'

'No, I don't think so,' Muldoon said warily. 'You could say that he correctly anticipated their reactions.'

'Bull. The bastard's been selling us down the river. He's a smart-arse Englishman who's airing a grievance because you

86

got the job he was originally offered. If you ask me, he's getting his own back. He's trying to scuttle us.'

'Aw, come on Randy, he knows his job. That's all,' Pat Muldoon said uneasily. 'He'd be criticised if he hadn't anticipated their reactions, wouldn't he?'

'Waal ... Nate thinks we've been outsmarted by the Russkies because President Cartwright tells him so. And he says so because Prime Minister Hallershan and the French President have said so. And who primed them?. Three guesses. They wouldn't have a clue if Sanders weren't telling them what to say. How else would they know? Everything that's been going on, it's supposed to be confidential, isn't it? Confidential between Detroit and Moscow. So how come London and Paris got to know about it unless either you or Mister Mark Bloody Sanders leaked. . . ?'

'It wasn't me!' Muldoon said hastily.

'Then who's left?' Mueller demanded. 'I can tell you, nobody over here trusts the limey bastard!' He laid great emphasis on the word 'nobody'.

'You mean. . . .' Muldoon began uneasily.

'For Chrissake!' Mueller cut in. 'Come on Pat. I just got through with talking to Nate. He's madder than hell. We're all very concerned over here. You'd better get yourself in line, boy, or it could be o - u - t!'

'What do you want me to do?'

Faced with such a direct challenge, the reply was automatic and instantaneous.

'It's not what I want you to do,' Mueller said. 'It's what Nate wants you to do. He wants you to help ease Sanders out. We gotta do it gradually, you understand. Nothing obvious. Just take it slow and easy. We make life progressively more difficult and uncomfortable until he's had enough. Shouldn't be difficult between the two of us.

'Is that what Nate really wants?' Muldoon asked anxiously.

'Sure is!' Mueller told him. 'But don't ask him or me to put it in writing. You weren't going to ask us to put it in writing, were you?'

'Of course not!' Muldoon said hastily.,

'Right,' said Mueller. 'Now, you've got the message. And, incidentally, from here on in I'm going to send the confidential

stuff to you for your eyes only. You can decide what you want
to pass on to Sanders, but I'd be goddam careful if I were you.
Any more leaks about what we in Detroit are doing in East
Europe, and we'll know where Sanders got hold of the information, won't we?'

'But what about. . . .' Muldoon began uncertainly.

'Nice talking to you, Pat,' Mueller cut in. 'Say hello to
Eleanor for me, will ya?'

'Sure, Randy. Same to Darlene. And say, Randy. . . .'

'Yeah.'

'You could be wrong about him, you know. I don't really
like it.'

'Yeah, yeah, yeah. Sure, sure, sure. You're too nice, Pat,'
Mueller said. 'We'll throttle the bastard slowly. Have a nice
day. . . .'

.   .   .

The annual conference of the International Communist Party
had come to the end of its five day summer session in Moscow. Among the delegates from the UK was Fred Clasper
who, with the Scottish Regional Officer of the Transport
and General Workers' Union, were the Communist Party
approved spokesmen on the British Motor industry.

The international brotherhood had discussed and agreed a
ten point proposal, outlining guidelines for local action
groups, which had been submitted by the Italian Communist party.

The proposal re-affirmed that the basic objective of all
affiliated Communist parties, in each and every country, was
the destruction of the capitalist system.

To achieve this primary objective, guideline two called on
party members to oppose any measure which could be con-
strued as giving support to the capitalist system.

Guideline three re-affirmed that it was the duty of all members actively to disrupt and harass the workings of the
capitalist system, to ensure that it was unable to function
effectively.

Guideline four called on all members to seek election to
each and every position which provided an opportunity to
communicate the Communist viewpoint, and to influence

decisions in favour of the working classes.

Guideline five stated that it was essential that Communist party members stood for election on all local, regional and national committees, which represented the Trade Union movement.

Guideline six said that in those instances where the Communist party was not a major political force in a country, such as in the UK, members were encouraged to infiltrate the Socialist parties and work toward Communist objectives from internal positions of influence, if necessary by standing under a Socialist ticket.

Guideline seven proclaimed that in those countries where the Communist party was a major political force, such as in Italy and France, members were encouraged to fly the banner and to use every opportunity to get the eyes and ears of the media, to communicate the aims and objectives of Communism. Demonstrations, strikes, rallies were the most favoured means of getting attention, but other more violent measures were not ruled out, if such action could be supported under the basic criteria that the end justified the means.

In those instances where Communists and fellow-travellers had been hounded and jailed, for their actions and beliefs, the taking of hostages as a bargaining lever to obtain the release of loyal party members was supportable. Such hostages should be leaders of industry, and others who occupied positions of power in the capitalist system.

Guideline eight advanced the premise that the forces of law and order in capitalist countries were there to oppress the workers and to uphold the capitalist system. For this reason action should continually be taken to discredit the upholders of the law: the judges, magistrates, police and the armed forces.

Guideline nine called on all Communists actively to oppose all expenditures on defence.

The final guideline re-affirmed the long term objective of overthrowing the capitalist system by revolution.

A prerequisite of achieving this objective would be a total paralysis of the entire transport system, road, rail, air, sea, waterways, docks and shipping, to prevent the movement of goods and people. To achieve this objective it was essential that the various transport trade unions be firmly under the control of trusted Communists, at local, regional and national level.

One of the items on the five day agenda was the European Commission's report on multi-national corporations, which was due to be debated by heads of Government at the forthcoming Geneva conference. All members returned to their respective countries fully informed of the report, and armed with a twenty point action plan which they were instructed to put into effect to fight the international corporations, who were considered to be the instruments by which the capitalist system controlled the lives of the workers and usurped the power of the State.

It was moved by Italian party members and seconded by the Greeks that every possible step should be taken to disrupt production in the European plants operated by United Motors and Ford – the world's biggest multi-national employers of labour - in order to thwart world car plans.

As no United Motors, or Ford vehicle manufacturing plants were sited in either Italy or Greece, the Italians and Greeks were not likely to suffer too much from such disruption. More surprising, however, was the fact that the resolution was supported by the British, German and Belgian delegates, who could not be unaware that the take-home pay and job prospects of their members were going to be seriously affected. Insofar as the British delegates were concerned, the reason for their support lay in their passionate commitment to a totally integrated, nationally-owned public transport system, in which the State and the unions completely controlled the movement of people and goods.

At the end of a week's diet of red blooded Communism, Clasper flew back to London from Moscow with ideological batteries fully charged: ready, willing and able to continue the People's Struggle.

The other British delegate, upon his return, immediately contacted a senior lecturer at Ruskin College, Oxford, who also happened to be an economic adviser to the British Government. The Oxford don was particularly delighted to learn that all the detailed proposals to counter the world plans of the multi-nationals had been agreed unanimously.

He had every reason to be delighted, since it was he and his counterpart at Rome University, who had drafted the proposals in the first place.

.   .   .

Clem Bunker's meeting with the plant conveners was every bit as stormy as expected.

The meeting had been called to hear the results of the conveners' discussions with local plant managers and for Bunker himself to report the outcome of his discussions with Don Peters.

The conveners had given their reports, and Bunker was more than halfway through his. He had expressed the view that, in his opinion, Peters was not bluffing when he had said that he had been given just two years to change the ailing vehicle division from a loss into a profit. Peters had made the point again and again that, implicit in meeting the profit objective, it was essential that productivity – known in company parlance as 'direct labour efficiency' – be improved progressively, month by month, until it reached the standard rate expected by management. This rate, Peters had emphasised, was in fact no higher than the Corporation expected from its vehicle divisions in Germany and Belgium, manufacturing similar products with identical tools and equipment in plants with similar layouts.

Bunker quoted the comparative figures which Peters had given him. On Merseyside, direct labour efficiency was forty per cent below that of the German division. Absenteeism was ten per cent higher. Plant stoppages due to industrial disputes represented six per cent of the clocked working hours, compared with less than one per cent. Customer supply reliability was seventy per cent compared with ninety-seven per cent, etcetera, etcetera.

Bunker had also reported on the comparative figures per plant within the UK division, which showed the performance of the Merseyside plant to be significantly inferior to plants in the Midlands despite the fact that the Merseyside plant was the most modern of all in the group, having been built in the early sixties at the express wish of both Labour and Conservative Governments to bring employment and hoped-for prosperity to the area.

91

At the disclosure of these comparison figures, Clasper had hit the roof, claiming the figures were bunk and simply an excuse to close the Merseyside plant, which had always been made the scapegoat for poor management.

Without attempting to take sides, Bunker had asked Clasper to explain why eighty per cent of the stoppages at the Merseyside plant had been due to inter-union disputes, despite the fact that such stoppages were in breach of agreed national procedure. Clasper quickly dismissed Bunker's question as irrelevant. Company propaganda. He put the blame for the disputes firmly back in the lap of management.

'But how do you explain the fact that the company has changed plant managers several times in an effort to find the right answer?' asked Bunker. 'Most of them arrived at the plant with good, or even outstanding track records at other vehicle plants.'

Clasper refused to be corrected, and retaliated aggressively by blaming all the problems on the capitalist system, the multi-nationals and the Government. He was in full cry on his favourite subject when Bunker shut him up.

'Turn the bloody record off, for Pete's sake, Fred,' he snapped, displaying a rare show of temper. 'We've heard it all before. We're not interested in cant. We are here to discuss the company reponses to our fears about the plant closure rumours, and I am trying, for my part, to explain the company viewpoint as put to me by Peters, which was what this committee requested me to do. We have heard the conveners' reports of their meetings with the plant managers, including your own report, and I am attempting to give mine. Now if the committee doesn't want to hear it, so be it. I have other things to do with my time, but don't ask me to approach Peters in the future. If the committee wants to hear what I have to say, then shut up and hear me out.'

It had the desired effect, with Clasper remaining restlessly silent while Bunker outlined the Peters' plan, which included a productivity bonus scheme which would increase earnings by one per cent for each one per cent increase in direct labour efficiency.

The conveners listened without interruption. It was their jobs and their future at stake. But Clasper was having none of it. He contemptuously dismissed the productivity incentive proposal as a treadmill charter, and referred to the Peters' two year plan as a management con.

'If you believe that, you'll believe anything,' he scoffed. 'If we were stupid enough to give 'em the increased productivity, does anybody here think for one minute that they wouldn't find reasons for not payin' us the bonus? Course they would . . . it stands to reason . . . they're bloody management aren't they? We'd be puttin' our heads in a bloody noose, for Yankee-doodle-dandie Peters to jerk whenever he felt the inclination. We want work, and we want more money, without strings. . . . Stuff 'em.

He glared belligerently at his mates, defying them to disagree with him.

'Are you saying, Brother Fred, that you could raise productivity at your plant over the next two years, but that you won't?' Bunker asked quietly.

'I didn't say that,' Clasper retorted. 'But I suppose if you wanted to work yer arse off, yes. Yes, it could be done. But as far as I am concerned, we're not goin' back to no sweat shop days!'

His voice was rising.

'We've fought for union recognition. We've had to fight like hell to get control of the lines over many years, and we're not giving that up after all we've been through.'

'Yeah, Fred. But where has it got us?' asked one of the conveners.

'In the shit,' a representative of one of the Midland plants said sourly.

'It's got us union control!' Clasper shouted, incensed at the lack of spontaneous support from his Brothers.

'We are the masters now, and the bastard employers have to come to us, cap in hand!'

'Yeah, Fred. But as Brother Alf says, where has it got us?' asked another convener.

'In the shit,' the man from the Midlands factory repeated, derisively. 'That's where it's got us. For God's sake, why don't we stop kidding ourselves?'

He hadn't intended to address the meeting, but the others were now all looking at him and so he felt obliged to continue. In for a penny, in for a pound, he said to himself and he was on his feet.

'What's the point of refusing to face what we all know to be true?' he demanded. 'We all know that we have been restricting output as a bargaining lever, and I don't deny that I've done my share. But what have we ended up bargaining over? Our bleeding jobs!'

'Bloody Judas!' Clasper snarled. 'You bloody southerners would sell your union birthright for TWENTY pieces of silver. You wouldn't even hold out for thirty! Well, you can say and do what you like, but we're not having any of it up north!'

'Yeah, that must be the trouble. He's bloody frustrated. He's not getting any!' somebody sniggered in an aside which produced stifled laughter.

'I heard that!' Clasper snapped. 'Very funny, I must say!' He pulled a packet from a grimy pocket and thrust a cigarette into the corner of his mouth.

'Got a match?' he demanded of the Brother nearest to him.

'Yeah,' one of the Midland conveners told him. 'Your face and my arse!'

The stifled laughter now became uncontrollable, with Clasper finally seeing the funny side of things and joining in.

Bunker allowed the general merriment to run its course before intervening to take over the reins of the meeting again.

'OK Brothers,' he said at last. 'We all enjoyed that. Now it seems to me that we've got a few questions to ask ourselves before we can decide on the road to take. For a start, do we accept that the situation is really as serious as Peters and the plant managers say, or do we reject what they say out of hand? If we do accept that the situation is serious, do we go along with the company's proposals, or not? Are the company's targets realistic, for example? Can they be achieved within two years, to the satisfaction of the unions as well as the company?'

His gaze ranged across the men before him.

'Do we want to give the productivity scheme a trial run, or are we going to reject any form of incentive scheme which relates earnings to output? Finally, what alternative proposals might we put forward to safeguard the future of the UK plants and the jobs of our members?'

His questions seemed to meet with general approval, one of

94

the Midland plant conveners taking the view that the real issue was whether the company proposals were in the best interest of the workers, as well as Detroit.

The Merseyside conveners, prompted by Clasper, took a different view. They questioned whether the company's financial position was as serious as Peters and the plant managers claimed. They believed that they were being conned by the company into accepting the productivity deal and the two year targets under the threat of plant closures which would never happen. They favoured a total rejection of the company's explanation and its proposals, and moved that the unions should counter the threatened closures by all-out strike action.

A verbal free-for-all followed, at the end of which the majority took the view that they were over a barrel anyway and had no real alternative but to accept the posititon as described by the company. A resolution was moved and carried that 'the unions take part in joint discussions at each plant, to consider ways and means of making the necessary improvements, to achieve the target objectives over two years'.

Clasper continued with his objections to the end and finally left the meeting in disgust.

.   .   .

Don Peters was delighted when Bunker rang him that evening with the news. He was now in with a racing chance of achieving the target objectives.

When he put the plant managers and the divisional executives in the picture the next day, he ended the meeting by saying that without the support of Bunker and the unions, the company hadn't a hope in hell of surviving but with their support, they did at least have a racing chance. His letter, from the desk of the Managing Director which appeared on plant notice boards the following day, ended with an appeal for management and unions to pull together, to turn the plants around and to make the UK division the best outfit in Europe.

McGillicuddy was pleased to hear the news from Peters, but harboured doubts, which he kept to himself. Cocello and the Head of Overseas' Operations were equally pleased to hear the news from McGillicuddy, but were highly sceptical. They would believe it, only when it began to happen.

Mueller had no doubts at all that the British unions wouldn't play ball, and that within the two year respite period the division would be back to square one.

As Mueller put it himself to the World Planning Group.

'They've already gone too far down the wrong road . . . and it's a no-through way. Peters is crazy to kid himself that he can steer out of this one. He should have cut and run. At least he personally would have survived. That goddam limey grave-yard is already up to its arse with the carcases of managers who thought they had the answers to that god-forsaken division.'

7

At the Heads of State Conference in Geneva, the British Prime Minister was delivering a thoroughly uncharacteristic speech. Charles Hallershan was normally urbane, at times almost plummy. But he was not so now as he reviewed the adverse economic and social trends which had been developing in his country at an alarming rate in recent years.

'Can it be right' he asked, 'for a multi-national Corporation to be given total freedom to conclude a trade agreement with an East European country which results in a third country being obliged to pick up the import bill? I have numerous examples of such planning agreements which have operated to the detriment of Britain,' he said.

His gaze ranged the room slowly, to stop when it fixed on the President of the United States.

'Would not my friend President Cartwright feel as aggrieved as we do,' he said, 'if for example, the American motor industry were owned and controlled by British multi-national Corporations who planned to supply the large American market from, say cheap-labour plants in Mexico, or even Cuba, and to phase-out vehicle and component manufacture in the United States? I don't think it is necessary for me to wait for the answers to the questions I've posed' he concluded. 'We all know what the answers must surely be. But I have to tell you that these are typical examples of the kind of planning agreements which have been arranged between American multi-national Corporations and certain countries in both East and West Europe which have operated to Britain's detriment.'

He sat down to an uneasy and thoughtful silence.

In the speeches which followed, both the French and German Heads of State gently but diplomatically chided the British Prime Minister for placing the blame for Britain's problems at other country's doors. The British Prime Minister would have none of it, however, and leapt to his feet.

'I do not wish to attempt to defend the actions of my Government, or successive British Governments since the war which have manifestly failed to sustain the industrial, economic and political strength of our country and to satisfy the aspirations of our people', he declared bluntly. 'We must accept much of the blame for our industrial decline. But what I do say without equivocation,' he continued, with heavy emphasis, 'is that the present Government has learned from the lessons of the past twenty years and has no intention of making the same mistakes in the future.'

He turned to face the French and German Heads of State.

'You chide us, Monsieur le President . . . Herr Chancellor . . . for electing to tread the road we trod, the wrong road, as the industrial and economic record shows only too clearly. But other countries represented here in this room have also trodden the wrong road in the not too distant past.' His voice had an edge to it. 'We are not the only country in the world to have made mistakes.'

The room was very still.

'In the not too distant past, Britain played no small part in helping certain countries through their little local difficulties and in persuading others to tread the right road.' Hallershan continued quietly. 'But I do not wish to dwell on that unhappy period except to make the point that Britain would have been powerless to help anyone had we not possessed a strong industrial base. That base has been progressively eroded over the years to a dangerous level. But I am here to tell you, gentlemen, that we have no intention of allowing this decline to continue.'

His voice was strong.

'We intend to defend British interests in precisely the same way that other countries have defended theirs. We seek no favours, but we will have, we must have, we demand equal and fair treatment.'

Charles Hallershan sat down.

The French President shifted uncomfortably as others around him murmured politely. The German Chancellor gazed disdainfully at the ceiling. It was the President of the United States who eased the tension by tactfully introducing new suggestions. He was, nevertheless, privately delighted to hear the British Prime Minister making points which he, too, would have liked to have made but for diplomatic niceties.

He could not but reflect on how times had changed. The British had been renowned for their tact and diplomacy while Americans had been renowned for bluntness. Britain was now no longer top of the heap, and thus more free to speak her mind, while the United States had taken over the position of top dog, and was therefore obliged to be more diplomatic.

If Germany and Japan had defeated the United States and Britain would they have been as generous in victory as the Allies had been? Would there have been a Rommel Plan equivalent to the Marshall Plan? Or perhaps a Himmler Plan instead . . . ?

Germany and Japan were free and powerful nations today because the Allies had been generous in victory. Where would the United States and Britain be today if they had been defeated? He had often asked himself these questions.

Yes, Charles Hallershan's remarks should have made people think. He was right to put Britain first. As long as this didn't mean that American interests were put second. That couldn't be allowed, of course.

One had to know where to draw the line, President Cartwright thought.

8

Mark's wife, Georgina, was spending a few days with her mother in the Cotswolds while Mark was abroad on business. She had not been feeling too well of late, and needed cheering up. In fact, she had not been one hundred per cent fit ever since she had lost her fourth child during pregnancy. An operation had followed, and though she had been warned in advance that it would have its side-effects she had preferred to believe that she possessed enough resilience and determination to cope with all the anticipated problems and ride out the emotional storms ahead. This, in fact, she did do most successfully to a great degree. But periodically she suffered from a kind of depressive guilt complex which had a tendency to surface when she was alone. This was such a time, and so she had driven out to the Cotswolds for her mother's company.

Now she paused in turning the pages of *Country Life* and stared into space for a long moment, completely withdrawn from the world around her.

'Penny for them, Georgie,' her mother had said.

'What . . . ? Oh. . . .' Georgina put the magazine down.

'It's just that I'm getting rather worried about Mark, mother. He's sleeping so badly these days. Never more than two or three hours at a stretch, and always up before six. Often before four, in fact, when he has an early morning flight out of Heathrow. And he's so restless. I'm sure the job's getting through to him. The strain is beginning to tell. He's looking so old and grey these days.'

'But he is getting old, my dear,' her mother replied, casually rearranging the flowers on the deep windowsill of the long sun-splashed room.

'On the other hand, she added, eyeing her daughter sidelong, a bantering note entering her voice, 'are you sure that it's just the stress and strain of his job that's getting through to him, as you put it, and not the *dolce vita* of Paris,

Vienna, Rome, Athens, New York. . . .'

'Mother, he goes there to work.'

'No doubt. But all work and no play, as they say.'

'Mother, you really are incorrigible.'

'No . . .' her mother said slowly and smiled. 'Just remembering what all of those places were like; how exotic they were, when I visited them with your father when I was a young woman. I shudder to think what your father would have got up to if I hadn't been with him! All that spicy food and wine. . . . It doesn't exactly cool the blood, you know. It never cooled your father's.'

'Mother! Really!' said Georgina, grinning.

'If I can't tell you the truth at my age,' said her mother, 'what hope is there for me? If I'd given your father just half a chance he'd have been away gallivanting, I'm sure. Always had an eye for the girls you know, your father.'

'You make him out to have been a real Don Juan,' Georgina said. 'I'm sure he wasn't.'

'But of course he was, my dear . . . I'm glad to say,' her mother said. 'Kept me on my toes. You should never get too complacent, you know. Never take anything for granted, as the shoplifters' union says. Absolutely fatal. Are you sure you're making enough effort to hold Mark's interest?'

Georgina picked up the magazine again, but didn't open it.

'Oh, mother you do go on. Such a lot of advice in response to such a minor observation.'

Her mother moved to the other side of the room to pour a little water into a vase of gladioli.

'Other people, Georgie, are observant too. . . .'

'What does that mean?'

'That you must make the effort to be stimulating and interesting, my dear, even when you don't feel like it. You've got to try, my darling, or he'll seek what he needs elsewhere, that's for sure. Men are like that, you know. You can take it from me. And you did say that you and Mark are not getting together very often these days, didn't you? You don't want to give him an excuse to trade you in for a new model, now do you? Part exchange is all people seem to think of these days!'

Georgina sighed.

She tossed the magazine aside.

'I suppose you're right,' she said. *'Comme d'habitude....'*

She got up, stood by the window and looked out on the lovely Gloucestershire countryside.

'I know that I'm not exactly the most affectionate and stimulating of wives these days. It's not that I don't love Mark any more. I do. More than ever. It's simply that I'm not switched on to sex any more. Is that so bad? I just don't want Mark physically the way I used to ...'

She straightened a curtain.

'Of course,' she went on, 'I do try and tell myself that I want him in the old way. And from time to time I turn on all the old witchcraft to see if I still have that old black magic effect upon him. Surprisingly enough, it seems that I do. But when he switches on, I switch off. It's all very frustrating ... for both of us.

'It's all so much of a conscious effort,' she said, 'instead of the spontaneous combustion it used to be ... so we don't seem to bother very much about it. I don't really mind, and I don't think that Mark does. He always seems to be so tired, anyway, when he gets home. He just sticks his head into his papers, and then falls asleep. I simply wake him up to tell him it's time for bed.

'I suppose we don't really live together any more,' she sighed slowly. 'It's more like what politicians call peaceful co-existence. Sanders and Sanders, Mutual Friendly Society. Safe and dependable. The old firm.'

Her mother smiled wryly as she poured herself a drink.

'Won't you have one? she asked, holding her glass aloft.

'No thank you.'

'Might help you to relax a little to have the occasional drink,' Georgina's mother said.

Her daughter smiled and shook her head.

'You know I don't like the stuff ... and I've never needed it. Just being near Mark was enough to turn me on in the old days.'

Hot tears suddenly stung the back of her eyes.

'Are you happy, darling?' her mother asked gently.

'Yes, I am really ... oh, I don't know. Silly isn't it ... grown woman behaving like a young girl?'

She brushed quick fingers across her lashes.

'I love Mark, and I don't think I could bear to live without him, but we just go through the motions of affection. We don't laugh together and have fun the way we used to.'

She bent down to pick up the magazine again, only to toss it back on the table.

'There was a time when our relationship came first with Mark; before the children even, when they were small. Certainly before United Motors. But it's different now. It's United Motors first, and me last. I run a very poor third behind the boys. In fact,' she added as an afterthought, 'I'm not so sure that I don't come after the dogs now. He always greets them more affectionately than me when he arrives home. Pats them, strokes them, hugs them, tells them they're lovely . . . rolls on the carpet with them.'

'I thought you said that you didn't care for rolling on the carpet any more,' said her mother.

'Oh,' said Georgina, 'you know what I mean!'

Her mother slipped an affectionate arm round her shoulder. She knew that some of the sparkle, the zest and the humour had gone out of their lives when their eldest son, Adam, had left Millfield School at eighteen to live with a married woman. That he'd married her eventually had done nothing to diminish the shock.

Adam was the first of three handsome sons. Brilliant at sport, which pleased Mark in particular, and academically bright enough to be all set for Cambridge and a successful career. He'd just picked up his life and thrown it away. That was what Mark thought, and so did Georgina. But Adam, of course, saw things rather differently.

Nothing that either Georgina or Mark could say made any difference. Adam had made up his mind. Money didn't interest him; a career didn't interest him; what could have been a glittering future didn't interest him. He was determined, as he said simply, to put people before things. 'Unlike you, Dad,' he said without rancour, but it still turned the knife in Mark's heart. 'We never got to know and understand each other when it would have mattered. There was always something else; always United Motors. You never had the time. I don't want a life like that.'

For many months after Adam had gone his own way, Mark and Georgina lost all zest for life, making all kinds of excuses to avoid going to parties, particularly the United Motors' parties. Thus the rumour began to circulate among the American wives of overseas executives that Georgina had a drink problem.

The rumour was started by one of the wives who did have a drink problem. She had been jealous of Georgina's non-alcoholic air of calm self-assurance. The fact that Georgina was teetoal was incidental and didn't spoil the story.

'So no-one had seen her drinking. Wasn't that only because Mark had kept her out of the way? She was a secret drinker and a heavy one, the story went. It was getting embarrassing for Mark to take her anywhere. That's why they'd avoided the party circuit of late!'

The truth was that virtually all the wives of American overseas executives had a drink problem.

But lies have a way of making themselves into truths. Repeated often enough, even the most fantastic fable will become history. So, as the rumours gathered around Georgina thick and fast, someone in New York heard them once, heard them twice, and heard them again, and then believed they were true. And so on Mark's personal record the words finally appeared: 'Wife has drink problem.' And the trouble with history is that it cannot be rewritten. Only modified.

Thus from that moment on it was officially impossible for the personal records to contain no mention of Georgina's 'drink problem'. Simply year by year it was updated: 'Problem seems to be better,' 'No worse' or 'No longer a problem' . . . until the next annual entry.

Meanwhile as Mark and Georgina continued to keep a low profile during this troubled family period it was assumed by 'the girls' and their American husbands that Georgina's drink problem must be getting worse.

. . .

At company dinner and cocktail parties there was always a very strict observance of behaviour codes. The wives of the top men always expected to be seated in the correct descending order from the host, as befitted their husband's position in the Corporation, and woe betide the person who failed to get the pecking order right. If he or she didn't know who was senior to

104

whom then he or she should have made enquiries beforehand. There was simply no excuse for not knowing everyone's station.

Where individuals were of equal rank it was a particularly tricky business as one couldn't afford to offend the sensitivities of those who considered themselves to be of more elevated rank than in fact they were. In such situations, the clever host took a calculated gamble on who was likely to be going up in the near future, as opposed to the one going down. The grapevine could usually be relied on to provide guidance on the subject.

When gathering for pre-dinner drinks, the very top women always kept together and only deigned to let a woman from the lower ranks join them as a very special privilege. This screening procedure enabled the top women to run a critical eye over the wives of executives being considered for further promotion. It also gave the newcomers a whiff of the heady ambience at the top. The same procedure applied all the way down to the lowest executive level.

It would not be an exaggeration to say that the esteem and near reverence lauded on rank, position and the trappings of office by the American 'girls' in the overseas Corporation was more reminiscent of Edwardian England than modern day Europe.

As a European corporate executive, Mark was a step above the national executive. But as he was non-American, the wives were never quite sure where they stood in relation to Georgina, which made life difficult at parties, where the pecking order was all-important.

But, as the final arbiter, one thing was for sure. American executives were always paid a lot more than non-Americans, even when in hierarchical terms the non-American was the senior man. And since in their part of God's Own Country money was every bit as important, if not more important than position, they figured that this must mean that Americans came first.

Mark and Georgina mixed easily and naturally at company parties, chatting casually with anyone who wanted to chat to them irrespective of anything as specious as 'rank'. It wouldn't have entered their heads to consult the Corporation's organisational chart before deciding who they should talk to.

And who they should not.

Digging the dirt was the accepted occupation of many of the American wives, which Georgina and Mark found rather bad form, but often very funny. . . .

'Missed you at Charlene's party, Darlene,'

'Oh, was that a party she gave? Well, you could have fooled me. . . . Though I'll say this for her, she certainly knows how to select the right wine for the occasion. . . . Graves. . . .'

'Was that what it was? My husband said it tasted like death warmed up.'

'Say, did you see the fur her husband's secretary turned up in? Now that must have cost her something.'

'Yeah. . . . A few sleepless nights, I guess.'

'Jeeze, didn't he look bushed? Those late nights at the office really take it out of you . . . so he says.'

'Well, something is, that's for sure. He looks terrible. She was in fine form though I thought. Something's doing her a power of good. She really sparkled.'

'But I thought she was under the doctor?'

'She is, and it looks like she's responding to treatment.'

'Is that so? Well, would you believe it? Lucky old Charlene.'

'Hi, Charlene sweetheart, we were just saying what a swell party it is. Gosh, you look so much better. What's the secret? It can't be an apple a day, can it?'

'Wasn't it terrible about Hank Stephenson. Only forty-five. Everybody liked him who knew him . . . at least that's what all the secretaries said. Now I know what he meant when he always said 'thanks for having me'. Well, you never know when your number's up . . . that's what I keep tellin' my husband . . . but he takes no notice.'

'Gosh, I really like the dress you're nearly wearin' Mary Lou, I really do. . . . Saw another one just like it at Harrods. One of the floor walkers was wearin' it. Nice colour puce. It really suits you. No, I really mean it.'

Georgina was a puzzle to most of the Americans. They couldn't really fathom her out. But one thing was for sure, they recognised that she'd got class. She was attractive and possessed that unmistakable and effortless quality which is recognisable anywhere as style.

Georgina had almost fully recovered from the emotional shock of losing her fourth child and from the effects of the operation which followed.

Mark was fortunate. He could bury himself in his work and forget family problems during the day. Georgina was not so lucky. Her family was her life. She couldn't escape from family troubles, day or night.

Mark would continue to bring home masses of paper work which he would read avidly after dinner, scribbling little notes in margins before falling asleep in the chair. Sometimes he would take the reports to bed with him. Of late he never appeared to notice the beautiful woman beside him. The former seductress who had never failed to arouse him with a certain look, would now simply read a book or turn her back on him and go to sleep. She made no attempt to attract the attention of the man she still loved.

Her adoring husband and formerly insatiable lover now read his reports, and made little notes in the margin. He was now a Corporation man. Dedicated and fully programmed to operate and function at maximum efficiency. United Motors now held his rapt and undivided attention. She held his hat and coat.

. . .

Georgina turned from the window, her moist eyes glistening.

'I still love Mark, desperately ... I really do,' she said tremulously, trying hard to fight back the tears.

'Silly, isn't it ... I love Mark and I love Adam and Andrew and Christopher ... so why am I crying? It's really too stupid for words, isn't it?'

Her mother put a comforting arm around her shoulders.

'No more stupid than other family problems, my dear,' she replied affectionately. 'You are not at all unique you know. Most mothers go through the same experience at some time or other. Badge of our tribe, darling.'

She took her daughter's hands and patted them. 'You are not worried about Mark in any other way are you?' she asked, slipping away from her daughter to pour herself another drink.

'He's not ill, is he?'

'No, no ... nothing like that ... at least as far as I know.

107

He's just had his annual check up at the London Clinic. He says that he's been given a medical certificate of worthiness for another year's dedicated service, but that's only Mark's little joke. He always has to add the funnies. He can never say that he's going to the London Clinic for his annual check-up. He has to say that he's going for his twelve month's service. Still, I'm glad he's retained something of his sense of humour. He hasn't completely lost that. But he's begining to look so old and tired. He's beginning to worry me. Always falling asleep in the chair after dinner.'

'Well, there is nothing unusual about that,' interjected her mother. 'Your father did the same when he was forty, and he's still going strong at seventy. Perhaps not firing on all cylinders . . . but the old engine is still capable of useful working life . . . as I believe Mark would say. Though you wouldn't believe it to look at him.'

Georgina spluttered a laugh.

'Oh Mother, you are priceless. Poor Daddy, what he has to put up with!'

'What HE has to put up with? What I have to put up with!' She patted her daughter's knee. 'Now my dear, you were telling me about Mark, before I so rudely interrupted you.'

'Well, it's just that these days he's so tired and listless, which is so unlike him. The other day he arrived home from Madrid at four in the morning. I heard the car come up the drive and was surprised when he hadn't come to bed, so I went to the landing, and there he was sitting at the foot of the stairs with his head in his hands, fast asleep. He hadn't the strength to climb the stairs. He was utterly exhausted and looked so drawn and grey. He couldn't keep awake long enough to undress himself, yet, somehow, he had driven seventy miles from Heathrow. He could so easily have fallen asleep at the wheel.'

'What on earth was he doing coming home at four in the morning?' asked her mother. 'I thought there were no incoming flights between midnight and seven into London.'

'Oh, there was evidently another one of those dreadful strikes. He was due to take off from Madrid late afternoon, but there was an air traffic controllers' strike in France, and he was delayed five hours. Then when they eventually took off he was diverted to Stansted because of a baggage handlers' strike at Heathrow.

'By the time the airport bus had transported him back to Heathrow to pick up his car it was nearly two o'clock. He wouldn't listen to me when I said that he should have stayed overnight at one of the airport's hotels instead of driving home. But then, you know Mark. He was up again at six, and in the office on time as usual. He just wouldn't be late. Oh no, not Mark. Late for me perhaps, but not United Motors.' She sighed.

'He was off again the other day to Athens. Got up at four to catch a seven-thirty flight. Going on to Vienna and Budapest afterwards. I suppose I shall see him sometime late on Friday evening, exhausted as usual. He really does begin to worry me.'

'Did you say Athens?' her mother queried with a pained expression.

'Yes, why?'

'Didn't you hear the news this morning?'

'No, what news?' Georgina went cold. She hated flying and news of an air crash anywhere in the world always sent cold shudders right through her.

'Not an aircrash?' she asked tremulously.

'Oh my God, darling . . . I'm sure the news-reader said it was a flight from Athens to Vienna. Went down in the Alps.'

Georgina clutched at her throat.

'Oh, dear God. No, it can't be. There must be other flights. They would have phoned me!'

It was at that precise moment, making both of them jump, that the telephone rang.

They both stared at it. 'Oh God. . . .' Georgina said.

'Dear God. . . .'

Her mother picked up the receiver.

'Yes? Yes, just one moment.' Her voice shook. She held out the receiver.

'It's Mark's secretary. She wants to speak to you.'

Georgina shivered as she took the phone.

'I've been trying to reach you, but there was no reply from your home. I tried again a few minutes ago, and your daily said you were at your mother's.'

'Yes, Millie. I've been here since yesterday.' Even to herself, her voice sounded strange.

109

'Is anything wrong?'

'Mr Sanders has been trying to contact you. He rang me to tell you that he was having to fly on to Lisbon before going on to Vienna. Some trouble with the new revolutionary Government, I gather. He'll call you tonight. I'll ring him back to tell him to contact you at your mother's.'

Georgina's head swam.

'Millie . . . when did you last speak to him?'

'Oh, about an hour ago.'

'And he spoke to you from Lisbon, and not Athens?'

'No, he spoke to me from Vienna where he arrived last night. He tried to ring you at home from there. Tried several times and again this morning, that's why he rang me.'

Georgina heaved a great sigh.

'Oh, thank God!' she gasped.

'What did you say, Mrs Sanders?'

'No. Nothing, Millie. . . . Thank you very much for phoning me here. I can't tell you how relieved I am.'

'I don't understand, Mrs Sanders.'

Georgina sighed again heavily.

'My mother tells me that on the news this morning it said that a plane from Athens to Vienna had crashed in the Alps.'

'Oh, my God!' the secretary gasped.

'Mr Sanders would have been on that plane. It's the only daily flight from Athens to Vienna. Thank God he went to Lisbon.'

'Yes, Millie. Thank God . . . and Millie?'

'Yes, Mrs Sanders?'

'Could you get in touch with my husband and ask him to ring me here at my mother's just as soon as he is free to do so.'

'Of course Mrs Sanders. I'll phone straight away.'

.   .   .

9

Mark's meeting with Government officials in Vienna took place at ten in the morning, and by late evening he had secured general agreement to outline proposals which were to be the basis of further detailed discussions. These would be undertaken by a joint task force team comprising representatives of the vehicle and component divisions and Ministry officials. The next day he took possession of a company car and drove to Budapest for a meeting with the Hungarian Government, his secretary having made the necessary advanced appointments with specifically named people, thus ensuring the authorisation of the necessary entry visas.

The drive was not without incident. He had taken the E5 to Gyor and had been held up at the Austro-Hungarian border at Hagyeshalom for some four hours while guards drove the vehicle into an adjacent shed where it was jacked up and meticulously examined. The discovery of his special UK Government security pass, issued to members of the Economic Planning Council to gain access to high security Government buildings, didn't exactly help. The James Bonds of this world were issued with the same card: the near, but not quite, six of diamonds. Several phone calls were made to Government offices in Budapest, who in turn notified Moscow before he was finally allowed through.

He stopped briefly for a bowl of goulash at Komaron before taking the road to Tatabanya and Budapest, where he arrived at The Duna Hotel on the Danube in the late afternoon.

It was on leaving the roadside restaurant at Komaron that he became aware that the Polski Fiat which had pulled out after him, and which was still there as he entered Budapest, was the same car which he remembered being parked adjacent to the customs' office. He had slowed down for long periods to give the smaller car an opportunity to pass, but it steadfastly refused to do so, remaining just within sight for

111

most of the journey.

In addition to the hotel receptionist, who was expecting him as his secretary had booked the accommodation when making the necessary business appointments, no fewer than four Governments also expected him to arrive at The Duna Hotel: the Governments of Hungary, Russia, Britain and the United States.

The short, stockily-built middle-aged businessman reading a paper in the hotel lobby had taken a personal interest in Mark from the moment he had arrived. Mark had been aware of the undue attention he was getting but took no real notice. Homosexuals were always hanging around in all the top hotels, in both West and East Europe.

On taking the elevator to his room, the observer moved to the desk. After exchanging words with the receptionist, he entered a telephone booth and made a call. Later that evening in the cocktail bar he occupied a chair which permitted him to observe Mark without being observed.

When the Englishman left the bar to enter the dining-room the observer followed.

Mark browsed through the menu, and on looking up to casually take in the room's flora and fauna, noticed the man sitting in a corner position behind a large pot plant. Not wishing to give anyone a wrong impression of his sexual inclinations Mark quickly looked away.

On returning to his room an hour or so later, he was immediately aware that his belongings had been searched.

His briefcase was open, but nothing was missing, as subsequent examination showed. The intruder had also taken a new box of Bolivar cigars from a drawer, removed the outer wrapping and had deliberately placed a cigar carefully by the side of the box, precisely parallel to it. It was patently obvious that someone wanted Mark to know that he was being observed.

As this visiting card procedure was commonly practised by East European Government agents, Mark was not greatly disturbed: merely inquisitive to know why he was under surveillance.

He checked his clothes and briefcase for the second time. Nothing missing. Shrugging his shoulders, he lit the cigar, poured himself a large Scotch and settled down to prepare his approach to the next day's meeting with the Hungarian Government, which was to follow a short courtesy visit to the British Embassy for outline discussions with the Commercial Attaché.

.   .   .

Meetings with the Hungarian Government followed predictable East European lines. This was no exception. On the first day Mark was kept waiting for three hours while the obligatory phone calls were made to advise God knows how many Ministers and officials that he was on Government premises. As usual, no fewer than two negotiators were always present. Two began the discussions and they were joined periodically by further batches of two as the talks proceeded, until finally there were eight Hungarians around the table, four others having come and gone during the day's deliberations.

Mark had been invited by the Hungarian Government to pay a third visit to Budapest in a further endeavour to establish a joint venture trade agreement with United Motors, but as usual the East Europeans were inching their way toward securing a contract which would permit them to obtain United Motors' technology to manufacture components on a buy-back arrangement, while protecting their own domestic markets from import penetration.

Mark was steadfastly trying to lead them in a different direction. He wanted an opportunity to penetrate the growing East European markets, and was endeavouring to use the technology licence, which the Hungarians desperately needed, as a bargaining lever to achieve that sales objective. He tried to convince them that if they wanted their own manufactured vehicles to be equipped with the latest component technology to make them competitive internationally then they would have to give a little, and buy in certain Western components. To provide them with the hard currency they would need to do this, he was prepared to purchase raw materials from East Europe of the same value, this being the fundamental line he had taken at previous meetings. He saw no reason to significantly alter his strategic approach now.

Nor was he surprised that the Hungarians still found it difficult to accept his proposals. He had, after all, been here twice

113

before. What did surprise him was the fact that the British Embassy made no secret of the fact that it took the Hungarian line, rather than his . . . the British line.

The seesaw discussions continued for four days, with Mark resolutely countering the Hungarian proposals by advancing his own. He was well aware that East European Government negotiators were given very little room to manoeuvre by Moscow, and that even the smallest deviation from the strict and explicit instructions which the Russians would have sent to their satellite in advance of the meetings would have to be referred back to Moscow for clearance. In consequence negotiations were always prolonged.

The Hungarians made a great show of construing Mark's unwillingness to agree to their terms and conditions as evidence of unreasonable obstinacy, a sign that he wasn't really interested in forging bonds of friendship and trade with their country. British Embassy officials made no secret of the fact that they thought the same. Invited to the Embassy for pre-dinner drinks on the third day, Mark was buttonholed by an attaché who made it quite clear that it was hoped that the talks would be fruitful.

'We are most anxious to develop trade links with Hungary,' he said. 'All part of our effort to unfreeze the Cold War, don't you know.'

When Mark asked if that meant that United Motors was expected to be party to a one-sided agreement that virtually gave away its technology and West European markets, he was favoured with a polite smile in return, but nothing else. Mark returned to his hotel wondering whose bloody side the diplomats were really on. They were certainly damned keen to look after East European interests. Too damned keen, it sometimes seemed. But then, what the hell could you expect from Foreign Office officials who knew damn all about industry and commerce, and didn't want to know? Industry and commerce were certainly foreign to the Foreign Office.

On the penultimate day, after further exhaustive and exhausting efforts had failed to bridge the gap between the two sides, all the negotiators, except the group leader, were progressively called from the room. Mark stood up to stretch his legs, secure in the knowledge that no futher negotiations would take place since only one negotiator was now present.

He was therefore startled to hear the group leader say quietly, 'We want that technology and buy-back agreement, Mr Sanders. . . . So what do YOU want?'

For a moment, Mark couldn't believe his ears. But the emphasis had been unmistakable.

He poured himself another glass of water from the poor quality, cast-glass decanter: took a long, slow drink and then replied, 'I want only that which is best for my company.'

'Of course . . . of course. But what about your personal interests?' the elderly official asked ingenuously.

'Don't you have any personal ambitions, or targets . . . or appetites even?'

'I am sure that if I look after my company's interests, it will look after me,' Mark replied with an air of casual indifference.

The official shrugged broad, peasant shoulders.

'You really believe that?' he asked disbelievingly.

'Of course. Can you think of any reason why I shouldn't?'

The other man rose slowly; thoughtfully. He took a few paces forward and faced Mark.

'What I think. . . .' he said.

And then his face split into a broad beaming grin.

'What I think is that we've done enough talking for one day. Tonight we have special treat for you at best restaurant in all Hungary!'

He thrust an arm round Mark's shoulder and guided him to the door.

'The ghoulash is best you ever tasted. You will have to agree. It is real, authentic dish. Lots of peppers and spices. You like hot spicy dishes, Mr Sanders?' he asked mischievously.

Mark had to smile.

'The hotter the better.'

'Good. Then we must make sure you get it just the way you like it!'

The group leader helped Mark into his coat.

'We were, of course, hoping we celebrate joint agreement, all signed and sealed. But no matter. We still have tomorrow to convince you, before you leave us. So tonight we enjoy ourselves, and forget all about negotiations. What is the expression you use in England? "All work and no play makes Jacob a dull boy"?'

And he smiled his hard smile.

They were joined at the door by the other negotiators who had emerged from an adjacent room. Together they ambled down the dingy corridor and out into the courtyard, where a car engine responded immediately to the elderly official's raised hand.

As the car drew up before them, he addressed his colleagues as well as Mark when he said.

'Oh and by the way, Mr Sanders, it is our custom after lengthy late night discussions to invite negotiators and their ladies to this dinner. Ladies can see we truly work late every evening, instead of playing fool. I hope this arrangement you accept?'

All the negotiators beamed their collective agreement.

'Sounds a great idea to me,' said the Englishman. 'I'm only sorry that we still don't have something to celebrate.'

The old man dismissed the comment with a generous sweep of an arm.

'There is still time. There is always tomorrow.

A car will call for you at your hotel at seven thirty.'

'Fine.'

'Good. Then . . . until this evening, Mr Sanders . . . until this evening.'

. . .

When Mark returned to his hotel there was a message at the desk to ring Muldoon.

He took a shower and then made the call. Muldoon wanted to know how the talks were going, so that he could put McGillicuddy and, of course, Mueller in the picture, Mueller first. He wasn't too pleased to hear that little progress had been made.

'Sounds like you're wastin' your time, Mark . . . same as the last meetin' in Budapest.'

'I'm affraid so,' Mark replied. 'They still want the keys of the kingdom . . . and as far as I'm concerned, that's not on.'

'Yeah, I guess so, Mark,' said Muldoon. 'But don't lose sight of the fact that Central Office are expecting you to reach an

116

agreement of some kind.'

'That's easy,' said the Englishman. 'I just give them what they want, instead of what we want.'

'Yeah sure. I know the problem. Just try to clinch it, that's all.'

'That's right, Pat. We all know the East European problem. We just don't seem to be able to find the solution. . . .'

'I take it you propose to give a report on your discussions at next week's European Planning meeting?'

'Sure.'

'Good. You know that Nate is planning to attend?'

'Yes, I did hear.'

'Fine. I think you oughta up-date them on Spain, also.'

'Will do.'

'Why don't we get together on Monday, Mark, and you can fill me in before the Wednesday meeting?'

'Fine.'

'It will also give me a chance to introduce you to a new Detroit central office guy. Mueller wants him to work alongside you for a while to learn something of the European scene.'

'Who?'

'A guy named Klepner. Fred Klepner.'

'Don't know him. Who's he?'

'Ex-Harvard Business School. A guy on Mueller's staff.'

'Aren't they all. Hasn't he got anyone with line operating experience in Europe?'

'I guess we've all got to learn, Mark. Mueller wants him to learn from you.'

'What is he?' asked Mark. 'Mueller's bag man or his mole?'

'No. Nothing like that. He's just over here on a familiarisation assignment. Get some idea of the European environment. He'll also act as liaison with Detroit to keep Mueller informed of what we're doin'.'

'Ye Gods!' Mark exclaimed testily. 'Hasn't Mueller got any better ways of spending company money? What the hell would Detroit say if you or I wanted to have our liaison man sitting alongside Mueller to keep us informed in Europe of what he is doing in Detroit? You know the answer to that one.'

'Yeah, I guess so, but that's the way it is. That's what they

117

want to do, and we just have to go along with it.'

'Sure. They don't give us any option in the matter.'

'That's right.'

. . .

Mark was working on his report when the phone rang and the desk clerk announced that his host was waiting in the lobby.

Mark shut up shop and took the elevator to the ground floor. On stepping out, the first person who caught his eye in the spacious lobby was the middle-aged philanderer who always appeared to be around wherever Mark happened to be. It was getting to be too much of a coincidence. He concluded that the fellow had a specific job to do, and that was to keep an eye on yours truly, but why?

The elderly official who had led the negotiations, emerged from the mixed group milling around by the desk.

'Mr Sanders,' he called eagerly, walking briskly toward the Englishman with a broad smile.

'Or may I call you Mark since we have become so well-acquainted over last few days? Please to call me Bruno.'

'That's just fine, Bruno.'

'Good. Well now, allow me to introduce ladies. I am not going to bother about men ... you know them all too well.'

There were six ladies and five men. Three of the negotiators who had attended the discussions, obviously couldn't make it, or more likely, the expense account couldn't stand such a large party when there was nothing as yet to celebrate.

Mark was introduced to the wife of the elderly Bruno and then along a line of youngish and not unattractive women, until he came to the last, a devastatingly attractive redhead in her early twenties who looked every inch a top model girl; beautiful, poised and dressed to kill.

She greeted Mark with a 'Welcome to the Club' smile, her gorgeous green eyes holding his for a second or so.

In a husky voice she said in excellent English with the faintest of American accents, 'I'm Natalie. I'm afraid you have to put up with me this evening. I hope you don't mind too much.'

Bruno roared with laughter.

118

'Don't mind too much. . . . Of course he don't mind too much, do you, Mark? It's not every day man gets opportunity escort most beautiful girl in Hungary.'

Mark smiled at the devastatingly attractive Natalie.

'It certainly isn't,' he rejoined with a slight bow. 'I'm delighted. My lucky day.'

'Our lucky day,' boomed Bruno. 'It's our lucky day, for tonight we all going to enjoy ourselves and have little fun, after three days of very hard work, work, work. What was Bernard Shaw said?' he added, looking around for support. 'Work is curse of drinking classes. Is not it? Is not what he said? I think so.' He joined in the laughter. 'Curious socialist, that man Shaw, but what commentator!'

He ushered them toward the hotel entrance and the waiting cars.

'Did Shaw say that?' asked the beautiful Natalie as she sidled up to Mark on the back seat of the first car.

He was acutely conscious of the power pack perfume she was wearing. She turned quickly towards him throwing her long red hair over her shoulders.

'Is that right?'

Mark could feel her thigh pressed against his. His temples pulsed. She was completely available, that was the message. He exhaled sharply to clear suddenly blurred vision.

'No, I don't think so,' he said. 'Right church, wrong pew. He's got his Irishmen mixed up. It was Oscar Wilde I think.'

'Yes, I thought so. I read Shaw at University College, London, and I don't remember him saying that.'

'So you were at University College, were you?' Mark had himself under control again. 'That figures. You speak English beautifully. And do you remember Shaw's reply to the girl who approached him and said, 'Are you Shaw?'

'Of course,' she replied. 'I am certain!'

They laughed together and in the space of a few minutes had established a rapport. They could and would enjoy each other's company.

Her hand rested on his. It remained there for the rest of the journey as the convoy of cars drove at speed through the Hungarian countryside.

. . .

Before the cars arrived at their Country Club destination, Mark had mentally mapped out the course the evening was intended to take. He was too old a hand at the game not to be aware of the goodies in store, which would be all his to enjoy in return for favours.

The attractive Natalie was his for the taking; but he would have to pay a price. He would be compromised into accepting the Hungarian terms and conditions for a technology and know-how licence agreement, supported by a buy-back deal. He didn't agree with their proposals, but this was what some of the clowns in Detroit, like Mueller, wanted. That's what they expected him to negotiate and recommend. So, if that's what United Motors, corporate planning staff thought was a good deal for the company, why the hell should he attempt to negotiate far more difficult terms, or obtain a better deal for the company? He wouldn't earn any more medals for holding out for something better, which only he considered to be in the Corporation's best interests. And he would certainly lose stripes if he failed to secure an agreement of some kind, even if it were only an agreement of the kind regularly proposed by the Hungarians and the Russians.

He could announce to Bruno and the rest of the party over dinner that he had considered the pros and cons very carefully and had decided – in the best interests of East-West relations and to promote the greatest goodwill between United Motors and Hungary – that he would formally agree to their proposals in the morning, and recommend acceptance to his company. Thenceforward it would be a jolly, all-pals-together kind of evening after which, in the arms of a gorgeous Natalie, he would claim his reward.

As they arrived at the Club he had reached a decision.

.   .   .

Now that Mark had come to a rational conclusion, he was free to enjoy himself, and enjoy himself he would. As the apprentice boys used to say: 'If rape is inevitable, prepare yourself to enjoy it.'

The Tokay cocktails laced with heaven knows how many liqueurs got the party off to a lively start. The conversation was agreeably light and became increasingly more *risqué* as bottle after bottle of Hungary's finest wines washed down the spicey goulash and other exotic local delicacies. At the end of a superb meal spread over three most enjoyable hours, the party was mellow and at peace with the world, toasting one another with the fiery Slivovitz and singing each other's praises, between visits to the tiny dance floor.

The dimly-lit room pounded with noise as inebriated dancers cavorted to the wildly exciting music played at feverish speed by a demented gypsy quartet.

Toward the end of dinner Natalie concluded that it was time to begin the first act of her repertoire. Safely hidden by a table-cloth of heavy brocade which touched the floor, her opening number was more in the nature of an introductory piece. A kind of getting to know you overture. She rubbed her knee along Mark's thigh, the way a cat rubs itself against its master when it wants something. From the amount of thigh surface she was able to cover Mark concluded that it was a bloody miracle that she still remained seated.

Having whetted his appetite, to polite and smiling appreciation from Mark, she went into her next performance which was a rather complicated *entre chat* where she crossed her right leg over Mark's left and entwined them by interlocking their ankles. She then proceeded to scrape the calf of his leg with her instep. By alternately flexing and relaxing her leg muscles she was able to produce a very pleasurable pulsating sensation which earned Mark's approbation for originality and effect. She certainly knew her stuff. . . .

With the party getting higher and higher from the effects of more and more Slivovitz, and the demented quartet getting wilder and louder under the influence of a steady supply of free beer from grateful admirers, Natalie went into her finale; which could best be described as a kind of *pas seul erotica*, where the artiste does her own thing and really lets her hair down.

Her tantalising fingers, which had been tapping out little messages on his thigh, now began restlessly to explore the nether region, with the single-minded purpose of the devotee who knows what she wants and how to get it. Suddenly, Mark began to feel very hot and dizzy. The frenzied cacophany generated by the madhouse four which battered the ear in a continuous barrage, now came and went, crescendo, diminu-

121

endo, crescendo, in ever-increasing frequency cycles. One second, the raucous group was yelling like crazy, the next it was miming. Mark put a hand to his head to ease the ever increasing pressure pounding in his ears. He wanted to res train Natalie's fingers for fear of the consequences and to hide his embarrassment, but the sensations she was inducing were so exciting that he couldn't force himself to do so. To cover his confusion he took a large gulp of Slivovitz, which proved to be fatal. As the burning liquid hit the pit of his stomach, so her tantalising fingers strayed into the supersensitive zone. He gasped involuntarily. . . .

Bruno and his colleagues were still cavorting with wild abandon on the dance-floor. Natalie turned her head and nibbled Mark's ear.

'Enjoying my opening number, darling?' she whispered.

But abruptly, the elderly Bruno was returning to the table to fall into the chair opposite Mark.

'Oh, my! . . . that was fun,' he gasped. 'But I fear I am get-ting too old for it.'

'Aren't we all!' Mark said under his breath.

'Your health, Mr Sanders. Or, forgive me . . . Mark.'

Bruno raised his glass in salute.

'And your health also, Natalie. Are you enjoying yourself? Yes, you are, of course. Yes.'

'Fantastic evening,' replied Mark.

'Fantastic,' added Natalie, nodding to Bruno over her raised glass.

'Good, good, good. The drink is good, is it not?' he asked, cocking the glass in Mark's direction.

'Very good.'

'Yes it is. Drink is also a great easer of tensions, is it not?' he asked. 'A great easer of tensions . . . now let me see . . . what was it that your great master, Shakespeare, said about drink? We are very fond of Shakespeare in Hungary, you know. Are we not, Natalie? Frequent performances in Budapest. Mac-beth wasn't it? Now what was it he said?'

'You are getting close,' Mark replied. 'He said it provokes the desire and takes away the performance.'

'Yes, yes. That's it,' roared Bruno. 'Yes, that's it. Unfor-tunately.'

'We'll have to see, won't we. . . ?' Natalie whispered.

122

Bruno went on chuckling to himself for several seconds.

'Great man, Shakespeare. Great man. Such perception. Such perception,' he mused, lost in his own thoughts. 'Yes, yes.'

Mark excused himself and went to the men's room. Bruno leaned quizzically across the table.

'Well?' he asked Natalie.

'I'm earning my corn.'

'Does he like you? Yes?'

'What do you think?'

'Does he want you? Yes?'

'He gives me that impression.'

'Good. But you paid in full only if agreement is signed to our satisfaction.'

'That's understood.'

'Yes, that's good. He did seem to have gone quiet. Are you sure you interest him? Yes?'

'Quite sure.' She was about to say that he seemed to have liked the first course, but decided not to.

'Well, make him laugh, my dear. Dance a little. Make him happy. You know.'

She gave him a withering look.

'Don't tell me my business,' she said sharply. 'You stick to the office work and leave night shift operations to me.'

Bruno nodded.

'Keep him in bed in morning. We want him nicely tired and pliable,' he whispered.

'Natalie nodded.

'Get him to ring me at office and ask for meeting be put back after lunch. Hungarian tummy or something.'

'He won't want to get up, don't you worry. Except to come up for air,' she whispered.

Bruno smiled and patted her arm.

'Good girl, good girl. I knew you would be trump card, if we have to play it. Yes, I knew, I knew.'

.   .   .

Mark sluiced his face several times with cold water to clear his head and paused to consider what had happened. Then he considered what was now likely to happen.

123

It was eleven-thirty. He had drunk a lot, yes, but he was by no means drunk. He had enjoyed Natalie's 'opening number' and she had been enjoying herself too. That was obvious. He dried his face on the roller towel and tidied his hair with his hands. I bet she's good in bed, he reflected.

To his surprise, his body reacted to that thought with an immediate response. He had, of late, been under the impression that he was getting old. Now he realised that he had simply been out of practice.

He shook his head, straightened his tie, and returned to the table. Natalie was absent, in the ladies' room. He glanced around the dimly-lit club and there, sitting alone, but only a few feet away in a dark corner, was his limpet friend, the observer. Mark couldn't help but admire the man's dogged persistence. He must have driven like hell to have kept up with the fast moving convoy . . . unless he had already known where it was going.

Bruno and Mark talked obliquely about their negotiations during Natalie's absence. Mark danced with her on her return and then with each of the wives, before saying that he was ready for bed.

Bruno leapt to his feet.

'Of course. Bed. Mrs Bruno and I will see you to hotel for night-cap. The others can stay enjoy themselves. *Czárdás* are not for the old . . . I think so.'

They said their farewells to the rest of the party and made for the door. Bruno went ahead to summon one of the chauffeurs. In a wing mirror, as they drove away, Mark saw the observer hurrying down the steps to his car.

．　　．　　．

Mark was pleasantly squeezed between Natalie and Bruno's handsome wife, Nadia, on the back seat of the car. Bruno was in front. Arriving at the hotel the driver was told to wait in the forecourt.

'Just a quick nightcap and then Mrs Bruno and I go home. But then we much older. We need go to bed to sleep, do we not?' Bruno added, with a wink, as he ushered them through the lobby and into the lounge.

Natalie slipped a hand into Mark's jacket pocket and locked

fingers in his. He withdrew his hand as they sank into a settee.

Bruno ordered large brandies and raised his glass.

'Here's to successful partnership. Tomorrow we resolve outstanding problems and forge new fine links between Hungary and United Motors. To *Entente Cordiale*. Yes, to that.'

Mark raised his glass. 'To the successful resolution of our problems.'

Both men drained their glasses. The ladies sipped theirs.

Bruno rose to his feet.

'Come, my dear, we must go. That imposter, time, summons me to bed. To sleep, unfortunately.'

Mark rose with Mrs Bruno and helped to drape her coat over her shoulders. Natalie remained seated, sipping her brandy.

Bruno turned to Natalie.

'Good night, Natalie,' he said courteously with a slight bow. 'Happy nights to happy days. Ah, me.'

'Good night Bruno. Good night, Nadia' she replied with a smile.

The silence was deafening when Mark said, 'Oh . . . I didn't realise that you were staying in the hotel, Natalie!'

The beautiful redhead looked askance at Mark, whose face was expressionless. She turned to Bruno whose mouth had dropped open. He glanced quickly from Natalie to Mark and back again, seeking some explanation in their faces. Mark's told him nothing. Natalie raised her eyebrows in surprise. She turned to Mark, and with an imperceptible nod and an expression which unmistakably conveyed the message she wished to convey, waited expectantly for his reaction. He put out a hand.

'Let me help you with your coat, Natalie. You must be tired too,' he said with a faint smile.

Rising to her feet she tugged impatiently at the arms of her coat which she had thrown around her shoulders without help from Mark.

'Absolutely perfect evening, Bruno. Thanks for your company Natalie. I did enjoy it.'

Mark took her arm and led her toward the elderly official who stood with mouth agape.

'Perhaps I shall have the pleasure of your company again if we manage to conclude a successful arrangement with Hungary.'

'Not if . . . when,' interjected Bruno, regaining his senses and putting on a forced smile. 'Not if; not if, when.'

Natalie half turned to the Englishman.

'No doubt Bruno can put you in touch with me when the time comes,' she said with an air of complete indifference. 'That is, if you can make it,' she added with the slightest hint of contempt in her voice.

They walked slowly to the car, Mark taking Natalie's arm.

Restraining her gently to allow the elderly pair to move ahead he kissed her softly on the cheek.

'You really are fantastic,' he whispered. 'How do you think I feel right now.'

She looked intently into his eyes and gave the faintest of faint smiles. Her green eyes which had blazed with anger, softened appreciably.

As he helped her into the back seat next to Nadia he leaned forward and kissed her cheek again.

'Good night, Natalie, good night, Nadia. Good night, Bruno. See you in church.'

Natalie turned toward him, smiled and put out the tip of her tongue.

.   .   .

The last day's meeting went as expected by Mark, but not as planned by a more sober Bruno and his colleagues, who resolutely insisted on a licence and buy-back deal with Mark countering with a licence and export sales' agreement.

The discussions formally closed with both sides agreeing that no further action would be taken unless either side wished to put forward new proposals for further consideration.

Mark returned to his hotel and spent a quiet evening alone preparing his report and outlining the points he wished to discuss at the next meeting of the European Planning Committee. The observer was in the lobby when Mark came down to dinner.

At seven-thirty the next morning Mark was at the cashier's desk checking out, when he again spotted the limpet observer standing at the other end of the spacious lobby, ostensibly reading a newspaper. He thought for a moment or so and then walked toward his erstwhile shadow some thirty paces away. The lobby was deserted, apart from the two men, so his footsteps on the marble floor could be clearly heard. As Mark drew nearer, the observer turned his back and folded his paper. He turned to face Mark as the footsteps came closer. Mark smiled a broad smile and extended a hand. His shadow stiffened nervously. He was obviously taken by surprise.

'I thought I'd better come over to say goodbye,' Mark said, holding the broad smile. 'I'm leaving now. But then I suppose you know that. You seem to know all my movements this week.'

The stiffness went out of the stranger and he took Mark's outstretched hand with an equally broad smile.

'Driving back to Vienna now, Mr Sanders?' he asked in a guttural voice with an American accent.

'Yes. . . . That's the itinerary . . . as I'm sure you already know.

The observer smiled again.

'Did you have a successful business trip?' he asked.

'No, not really. But no doubt you will hear all about it . . . if you haven't heard already,' Mark replied.

The observer smiled again, but made no comment.

'Well, I think that's it. Cheerio then. It's "Home James, and don't spare the horses",' Mark said good-humouredly.

His shadow inclined his head in a tiny bow.

'Goodbye, Mr Sanders. *Bon Voyage.*'

Mark made the journey back to Vienna in about four hours, left the car at the airport for the office staff to collect, and was in London by late afternoon. He decided against going to the office. He hadn't seen Georgina for nearly three weeks and felt outrageously sexy. He drove, far too fast, from Heathrow and pulled into the drive, secretly praying that she was at home. He hadn't felt so potent for a long time. . . .

She wasn't there. He sat dejectedly at the foot of the stairs.

'Who the hell did the observer work for?' he asked himself out loud.

'The Hungarians, the Russians, the Americans or the British?'

10

Georgina arrived home from shopping at five-thirty, and was surprised to see Mark's car in the drive.

'Darling, how lovely to see you,' she called from over the top of her bulging shopping bag, planting a kiss on his cheek.

'I didn't expect you much before midnight. How have you been getting on? I read all about those awful floods in Athens and that dreadful air crash. Worried mother and me to death until your secretary rang. Why didn't you ring me? Thank God you changed your plans. Mother sends her love. Are you all right, darling? Really missed you.'

He took the parcels from her and dumped them on the kitchen table.

'We can talk about that later. Let me look at you. You look fabulous. Can't tell you how much I've missed you. More this time than most.'

He put his arms around her and kissed her long and passionately on the lips. His hands cupped her face and he kissed her again, running his fingers over her shoulder and down her back to caress her bottom.

She remained in his arms for what must have been a minute before drawing away.

'Humm . . . that was nice,' she said with an air of breathless surprise. 'Just like old times. You ARE pleased to see me . . . now let me see . . . where did I put that bag. . .? Ah there. . . .'

She walked toward the bag on the table and started to unpack the provisions.

'The dogs have gone for a walk over the fields with the Simpsons. Harriet's on heat . . . poor little thing, but she's looking beautiful. Now let's have a cup of tea and you can tell me all about your trip. I've so much to tell you too . . . while I think of it, Muldoon rang and said would you phone him as

128

soon as you get in. Not after midnight.'

He took her hand and led her toward the hall.

'You are coming with me, my girl,' he said decisively.

'Coming where, darling?' she asked quizzically.

'Where do you think?'

'Mark, really! At this time of day? The Simpsons will be back shortly with the dogs. Whatever would they say if they found us in bed? Anyway, I've just had my hair done and I don't want to spoil it.'

He swung an arm around her waist and pulled her tightly to his taut body.

'I don't give a damn what time of the day it is,' he whispered in her ear. 'And if the Simpsons come back while we are tossing around in bed, I'll. . . .'

'Mark, darling. What in the world has come over you? You're behaving like a randy young man. Shame on you. But we mustn't be too long.'

. . .

Later Mark spent a long time in a hot bath, meditating. He then called Muldoon who told him to be at The Inn on the Park that Sunday evening for a working dinner with Cocello and his entourage. The President was flying in that day for a series of meetings, including the European Planning Committee scheduled for the following Wednesday. An overnight room had been reserved for Mark at the hotel.

Over the weekend, Mark's daughter-in-law, Mandy, rang from London. She wanted Tigger (her pet name for Mark) to see the little Victorian terraced house they proposed to buy in Camden. Georgina liked it. Mark agreed to meet her at The Inn on the Park at four, prior to the meeting with Cocello. They would have tea together and then take a run out to Camden.

. . .

Mark was a little late arriving at The Inn on the Park having been held up by an accident on the M1.

Mueller and Muldoon were sitting in the open lounge on the first floor, which looked down on the ground floor lobby.

129

They couldn't help but notice the stunningly attractive young girl strolling up and down the foyer.

'I wonder how much she charges?' Mueller mused, eyeing her up and down lasciviously.

Muldoon was a devout Catholic and kept such carnal thoughts to himself.

'I wouldn't know,' he answered severely.

'Sure, Pat, sure. You don't do that sort of thing.'

Mark parked his car in the underground car park and entered the hotel carrying his overnight bag. He didn't immediately spot his daughter-in-law who had strolled to the far end of the lobby. Mueller and Muldoon saw Mark arrive and make for the desk and watched incredulously as the girl tripped eagerly up to him, calling out 'Tigger, darling'.

They watched in some amazement as the stunning girl threw her arms around Mark's neck and kissed him affectionately on both cheeks. He kissed her back. He then put his left arm around her waist as he filled in the registration form.

'Sorry I'm late, Mandy sweetheart. Accident on the M1. You look fabulous. Let me dump this case and then we'll have a look at this little love nest of yours.'

He turned to the receptionist.

'Will you arrange to have tea sent to my room, please. Straight away.'

'Yes, Mr Sanders. Of course, sir.'

'I know you will love it,' she said brightly. 'It's absolutely adorable.' They stolled to the lift, arms intertwined.

'How's that damned lucky son of mine?' he asked. 'Up in Scotland, I hear. Surveying property, so Georgie tells me. Hope that's the only thing he's surveying. You've got to watch these Sanders boys you know, Mandy. Can't take things for granted. Even a gorgeous creature like you.'

She pouted prettily.

'Stop teasing me, you brute,' she replied, digging him in the ribs with a clenched fist. The lift doors opened and they went in.

Mueller had watched all this with more than a lascivious interest. He slapped his thigh with delight as the lift door closed behind them.

'Well damn me, just look at that, will ya?' he cried, shaking his head in disbelief.

'So that's what Mister Sexy Sanders gets up to when he flees the chicken coop! Expensive sex kittens to ball around with, who call him Tigger, darling,' he exclaimed, mimicking the girl's English accent.

'Jeez, no wonder like you say, Pat, he's lookin' worn out. Hell, I'm not surprised. Who wouldn't be?'

He continued to shake his head in disbelief.

'What's his expense sheets like, Pat? Like, item one, for services rendered? One hundred dollars? How often does that little item appear? Once a week, matinées on Sunday?'

He threw back his head and laughed.

'Well, well, well. So now ya know!' He made a clicking noise with his tongue.

'Boy, oh boy, you gotta hand it to him. He certainly knows how to pick 'em. Jeez!'

Muldoon winced uncomfortably at his colleague's coarseness, which he considered to be quite unnecessary and in bad taste. Sign of the times however, he mused. He was glad that he was now close to retirement. He'd had enough. Business had become too crude, rough and dirty. He didn't like the new trends one little bit, and would be glad to turn his back on it all.

Mueller slapped Muldoon's thigh.

'Well buddy boy. That's somethin' else we add to his personal file. We've almost got enough to pull the rug out. Shall we tell Nate?'

'No,' snapped the elderly American. 'WE won't! YOU can . . . but not me.'

Mark did look tired and drawn at dinner and by the time the executive group finally adjourned for bed, well after midnight, he looked worn out. Nate saw fit to remark on it and had cast a knowing glance at Mueller. Muldoon looked at Mueller with pained disapproval.

It was Nate's customary manner to cross-examine overseas, senior executives before important meetings, to get a better feel for the subjects coming up for discussion and to enable his personal staff to prepare probing questions in advance which would be put to line managers.

Nate expected every top executive to have all the answers, but he also enjoyed tripping them up with unexpectedly detailed questions. He had grilled Mark over dinner on the components' situation in both West and East Europe, as seen from both Mark's position and from the position of West and East European Governments. He had asked numerous detailed questions about the situation in Spain, France, Greece, Turkey, Austria and Portugal and had mischievously provoked Mark when he had asked if he went along with the view currently being expressed in many international circles that the British were becoming ungovernable because of their militant trade unions.

By the end of the evening, the Englishman felt as if he had been filleted.

·   ·   ·

Nate Cocello's presence ensured a full attendance at the European Planning Committee meeting. As usual, Clancy McGillicuddy was in the chair. To the surprise of the German and French divisions, Don Peters won the day with the first item on the packed three day agenda; namely his proposals to regenerate the ailing UK vehicle division, Nate taking the view that the plans were unquestionably achievable, provided Peters was given full support by the unions and local management.

He then went on to emphasise the point that Don had his full support and the backing of corporate management. The sting was in the tail when he added that Don must be given sufficient time to make the necessary improvements and that one year was not enough. Everyone knew what Nate meant. This was the final make-or-break plan for the UK vehicle plants. It couldn't be any other way. As usual, Nate was firm but fair.

The second item on the agenda was Randy Mueller's world review of the vehicle market. He developed the theme that in the aftermath of the energy crisis of October 1973, which had seen vehicle sales plummet, the market had picked up again, and, although there had been an initial switch to smaller fuel-economy vehicles, all the marketing experts were reporting that the public was swinging back to bigger and more powerful cars once more.

The indications were that the public would continue to

move up-market in the future in much the same way as it had in the United States over the past seventy years.

He explained that small fuel-economy vehicles would be available to meet the anticipated growing demands of the developing countries, with the bigger and more powerful up-market models meeting the demands of the developed countries, which were predominantly the countries of North America and Western Europe.

He ended his presentation by saying that given freedom of choice in the world market place, he was certain that the public will continue to opt for the more powerful up-market models.

He ended with the words; 'United Motors is the number one vehicle producer in the world. Gentlemen, with the vehicle specification proposals I have out-lined to you today, we will continue to be that number one.'

Cocello and McGillicuddy had listened for some two hours without interruption. Getting the vehicle specifications right would determine the success or failure of the corporation over the next seven to ten years. Billions of dollars would be invested around the world based on their recommendations. The corporation's bottom line would be a black or red number depending on the outcome of their deliberations. The atmosphere in the room was heavy with the weighty responsibility they carried. They had to get it right.

McGillicuddy made certain that each and every executive responsible for the various vehicle operations in Europe had been given a chance to express a view, to ensure that the proposals were fully supported by the line managers. He didn't want anyone to say afterwards that they didn't go along with the proposals of the planners. The observations of the components divisions would be sought after the vehicle divisions had outlined their own proposals and debated all the marketing issues.

When he had satisfied himself that every vehicle man had had his say, he turned to Pat Muldoon.

'OK. Well, now let's have a component viewpoint on the vehicle proposals,' he said ingenuously.

'Pat, you guys have to design and make the components for the allied and non-alllied vehicle industry. What do you think of the vehicle proposals?'

133

Muldoon gulped hard. He wished he hadn't been asked.

'Well, I guess I shouldn't presume to express an opinion on the vehicle proposals,' he began obliquely, taking good care to be as non-committal as possible.

'That's the vehicle division's responsibility. We got enough to think about in components. But, as you've asked my opinion, I can only say it sounds OK to me.'

'Yeah. Thanks, Pat,' said the Chairman, none the wiser.

'How about you, Mark?' he asked, addressing the lone Englishman.

Mark knew instinctively that Mueller and the vehicle division executives would expect his support, or at least a non-committal reply such as Muldoon's. He would be *personna non grata* if he expressed an alternative view.

'I agree with Randy that given free consumer choice in an unconstrained European market, the buying public will progressively move up-market to larger, more powerful vehicles, along traditional market behaviour lines,' he began.

Mueller nodded vigorously.

'We think so,' he interjected, nodding in turn to everyone round the table. He had no doubts about the matter.

Mark paused a few seconds, then he added slowly.

'The multi-million dollar question, as I see it, from the point of view of components, is not what will happen in the vehicle market-place given a free and unconstrained market environment but what will happen if the market is not free and unconstrained?'

From the expression on everyone's face and the utter and complete silence and stillness within the room, it was clear that the Englishman's words had caused group paralysis.

The Chairman stared intently.

'What are you saying, Mark?'

'I'm saying, Clancy, that we know what we should do if we are given the necessary market freedom by Governments,' Mark told him. 'We should move along the lines outlined by Randy. But will we be ALLOWED by Governments to operate in a free and unconstrained market in the years ahead? That, in my opinion, is the first question we have to ask ourselves before we can move on to the question of future vehicle specifications.'

Mueller nearly burst a blood vessel.

134

'Goddammit, Mark!' he barked. 'How the hell can anyone guess what Governments are likely to do in the future? If we go down that road we haven't a hope in hell of comin' to a rational market conclusion based on the market knowledge we possess. How can we be expected to outguess Governments? We'd be crazy to try!'

He glared around him.

'Goddammit, the bastards don't know themselves where the hell they are goin' from one month to the next, let alone in the years ahead! Jeez, how often have we heard it said that a week is a long time in politics. It sure is to those bastards who operate on short-term political expediencies! But we have to plan long-term, not on the latest political opinion polls. I say let's keep the political bull-shit out of planning discussions and plan on the basis of the market we understand.'

He faced Mark across the table.

'For Chrissake, it's anybody's guess what's going to happen politically. How the hell can we forecast that?'

He looked at Nate for support. The President looked up at the ceiling.

'You may be right, Randy,' Mark agreed quietly. 'But if it was my money at stake, I wouldn't bet against Government intervention in the years ahead. All the evidence building up in the European Commission and in Government departments points to Government action – either collectively or unilaterally – to reduce oil consumption and lessen dependance upon OPEC countries. It seems fairly certain that the Commission will secure collective agreement to reduce European Community oil consumption by five per cent in volume terms over the next five years, and if the motor industry doesn't take the necessary voluntary steps to help hit that target, you can be sure that Governments will take the necessary interventionist steps to impose that discipline on us. They will increase taxes on oil and engine capacity to the point that the average consumer will have no alternative but to switch to fuel-economy cars even though, given freedom of choice, they would prefer to move up-market to bigger and more powerful vehicles. I'm afraid I can't be as confident as you seem to be that Governments will allow the market to move that way.'

He stopped, but Chairman McGillicuddy urged,

'Go on Mark.'

Mark looked down at his pen, tapped the table with it.

'I am not saying that the oil industry won't discover new reserves to change the energy outlook. Anything is possible. But what I do say is that it would be unwise to plan ahead on the assumption that the European market will be free and unconstrained without further considering the implications of a market hedged by Government intervention. If in the end we are going to have to adjust to Government action, whether we like it or not, then it seems to me that we ought to determine in advance what those constraints are likely to be and draw up an alternative plan of action which would enable us to operate successfully within those constraints.'

Mueller reacted with predictable aggression.

'Dammit, Mark, for years now Governments have farted around the energy issue. Hell, the Alaskan fields would have been on stream long before now, if it hadn't been for the delayin' tactics of so-called environmentalists and chicken-livered politicians. The only crises we have in the States are the ones caused by our own shit-scared Governments.' He paused for breath. 'I don't want to get side-tracked into forecasting political assumptions. You can't put numbers on assumptions.'

McGillicuddy sat forward, placing both hands on the long elliptical table.

'Well, let's discuss it,' he said. 'Mark is asking a basic question: will we be allowed to plan and operate along the lines proposed by Randy in an unconstrained market? Or will Governments intervene to influence the market and shape it the way Governments want it to go? One hell of a lot of business is at stake in getting the answer to that basic question right.'

'Sure Clancy, sure,' intervened the American in charge of marketing operations in the States.

'But every one of the US vehicle divisions, without exception, is planning on the basis of a free and unconstrained market. Our market analysis shows that eighty-two per cent of consumers will elect to buy a new vehicle of over two litre engine capacity. The US public has flirted with the small car and eighteen per cent like it and propose to stay with it; but eighty-two per cent don't want it. We have the small 'Z' car in the pipeline for those who do.'

The next person to speak was an ascetic elderly American responsible for corporate finance operations, who described how the profitability of both the corporation and its dealers would suffer if the market moved toward smaller fuel economy vehicles.

'The investment required to tool-up and manufacture a small vehicle is similar to that needed to produce a larger model, but the profit per car is about half.'

He simply wanted to make sure that everyone was aware of the financial implications.

'Fifteen per cent of ten thousand dollars is a hell of a lot better than fifteen per cent of five thousand,' he added. 'From a purely financial point of view we hope like hell that the market will continue to favour the traditionally large and more powerful vehicle, and I might make the point,' he went on, 'that this view is also shared by our dealers, by the oil industry and the steel industry.'

Several American executives responsible for different overseas operations activities went on to express similar views in support of the Mueller proposals.

'It's not easy,' said one, 'to fly in the face of US market trends over the past seventy years. The market has had its hiccups in plenty, and there have been some very bad years to sweat out, but it has always shown a remarkable resilience and an ability to bounce back. Over the years the US buying public has shown an overwhelming preference for bigger and more powerful cars. Are we to assume that over the next ten years the market will change the habits of a lifetime?'

'But the US market is not Europe,' Mark Sanders said firmly. 'I am not competent to judge what the American market will do, or what the American Government will do to influence its shape over the next ten years, neither would I presume to express an opinion on the subject . . . unless I am asked to do so. My observations relate only to my area of responsibility in Europe, which is a totally different market from the United States.'

Mueller shifted irritably in his chair, as did most of the Americans around the table.

'The United States is fortunate to be a major oil producer as well as a major vehicle manufacturer,' the Englishman added.

137

'But not one of the major West European industrial countries is an oil producer, with the exception of Britain, and that is a purely temporary phenomenon. Domestic oil prices in the States are half the prices paid by European consumers. Americans can afford to run big cars. But fuel economy is damned important to the car-buying public in Europe, as well as to Governments.'

He turned to address the Chairman.

'Can we really expect the five major vehicle producing countries of Europe, namely West Germany, France, Italy, Spain and the United Kingdom, to take the same view as the United States when it comes to a question of energy consumption and conservation? It's not just the possibility of a world shortage of oil which frightens European Governments to death, but also the economic effect of rapidly escalating oil prices on their domestic inflation levels, their trade balances and their currencies. Wouldn't everyone in this room be equally concerned if we were sitting in their position? Wouldn't we be considering, right now, the remedial action we should take?'

McGillicuddy glanced at Nate Cocello to see whether the top man wanted to enter the arena at that stage in the discussion. He didn't. But the imperceptible nod from the President was enough to tell him to continue to open up the debate.

'OK,' he said. 'Let's discuss the European implications of Government intervention.'

The talks continued throughout the afternoon and well into the evening, before they broke up for dinner. The next morning the debate continued. Just before lunch, McGillicuddy summed up, after having discussed the situation with Cocello following a short adjournment for coffee. As General Director responsible for all United Motors' operations in Europe, McGillicuddy instructed the vehicle and component divisions to prepare option plans for consideration, based on the assumption that the forecast volume growth of the European vehicle market through 1990 would not consume any more oil in volume terms than current levels. This meant in effect that Europe would continue to develop small fuel-economy vehicles.

Inevitably, Mark was given a rough ride by the vehicle divisions when it was his turn to outline his component proposals following his meetings in Greece, Austria, Portugal and Hungary. His recommendations that task force teams be now established to prepare detailed plans along the lines he had proposed were accepted for Austria and Portugal. But his failure to secure an agreement with the Hungarian Government led to Mueller being given the assignment to review the options, as he was the principal critic of Mark's tactics in that country.

Greece was put on the back burner for a subsequent meeting and Spain was now brought forward as top priority, arising from the initial discussions with the new Government and its declared intention to join the European Economic Community.

President Nate Cocello informed Sanders and Muldoon that he wanted to review the components' business plan for Europe at the next meeting. Mark had almost completed the plan, but he would be stretched even more than usual over the next few weeks to meet the new deadline date.

However, you didn't presume to explain to the President of United Motors that his deadline was tight. All his deadlines were tight. You just did what you were expected to do.

. . .

Mueller had brought his staff informer, 'the mole', Fred Klepner, to the EPC meeting. The newcomer had sat impassively at the back of the room, behind the committee members, listening intently to the discussions. He had been introduced briefly by Mueller at the start of the meeting as the man who would assist Mark Sanders in the preparation of his ten year Components' Business Plan. He would also be Randy Mueller's liaison between Detroit and Europe. The ex-Harvard Business School man who had never held a line operating responsibility outside the States was now considered to be ready to help the Europeans plan Europe.

Klepner had been well briefed by Mueller and fully understood the role he was expected to play in the rug-pulling act which was planned. He was to keep close to Sanders and Muldoon, learn the European ropes, keep Mueller well informed of everything that was going on, and forward advance copies of Mark's business plans and reports immediately they were available. His reward was the prospect of taking over Mark's European planning responsibilities when the world planning function was finally centralised in Detroit, which was Muellers dedicated objective.

Sanders had been introduced to Klepner by Mueller and Muldoon at The Inn on the Park meeting, and had taken an immediate dislike to the man.

Confident in the knowledge that he had the personal support of both Mueller and Muldoon, Klepner had adoped a truculent, all-knowing attitude from the start. He was aware that Mark was the fall guy, which put him one jump ahead of the Englishman on the inside track. He also couldn't resist his overwhelming desire to impress Mark with his Harvard qualifications to do the job.

Having been obliged to listen to Klepner pontificate on the problems of the European motor industry, in which he had never worked, but which he had read about in central office reports, Mark mentally switched off. When the braggart began to explain his solution to the Irish problem, pronouncing Eire 'Eeerie', Mark excused himself to get another drink.

. . .

Before leaving for Madrid, Muldoon had suggested to Mark that he should hand over his almost finished Business Plan to Klepner, who could at least start to prepare the fifty or so slides which would be needed to make the presentation to Nate Cocello at the next European Planning Committee meeting. Mark was not particularly keen to do so, as he had always taken the view that major presentations which determined the future of the business should be written and presented by the chief architect of the plan.

As the European Planning Manager who had personally written the two hundred page European Plan outlining its aims and the strategy by which its objectives were to be achieved, Mark considered it essential that the 'words and music' of the presentation should be his.

He was also mindful of the way that Steiner had stolen his clothes and ballsed-up his presentation to Nate in New York. He didn't want another fiasco like that and the only way to guard against it was to keep the presentation firmly under his personal control.

Muldoon was equally adamant, however, that Mark's very tight schedule in Spain wouldn't give him sufficient time to do the lot himself. At least, those were the reasons he gave. The truth, of course, was rather different. He insisted that Mark allow Klepner to do some of the preparatory leg work on the slide presentation.

'It will give Klepner a better insight and understanding of the European scene,' he said.

Reluctantly Mark agreed. He had no choice in the matter.

.   .   .

Don Peters was in his best 'get-up-and-go' mood. Nate Cocello had supported his plan to revitalise the UK vehicle plants, and Clem Bunker had been in touch to say that his proposals had general support. Morale was rising strongly, although on Merseyside support was mixed.

The American was firing on all cylinders with renewed energy and enthusiasm. He and his executive team were convinced they would succeed. For weeks on end they had worked well into the night to finalise the details of their proposals, but long hours meant nothing to Peters.

Long hours were part and parcel of the job, whether one was American or British; but there were important distinctions as perceived by the Europeans. Americans on overseas assignments only expected to be around for a year or so, often far less. They were therefore prepared to work long hours, particularly during the first few months, when they lived in hotels, awaiting the arrival of their families from the States. European managers were not on temporary assignment. They were obliged to work similar long hours pacing a succession of temporary American bosses; year after year, after year, after year.

And the distinctions didn't end there. American salaries were four to five times the salaries paid to British executives reporting to Peters, an enormous differential further widened by the operation of the company's annual executive bonus scheme. This was always expressed as a percentage of salary and, in a good year, could be as high as fifty per cent. Thus an

American executive doing similar work to his European counterpart could receive an income up to EIGHT times as great.

Not surpisingly many European executives felt they had legitimate cause for complaint.

Nor was this all they had to complain about. Americans working in Britain paid lower taxes and also received substantial additional benefits-in-kind covering a wide range of domestic expenses.

Notwithstanding these very real grievances, the local British management teams went into action, under Don Peters' direction, with morale and hopes high. It was their future at stake, also.

The response from the plants exceeded all expectations, with Plant Managers reporting substantial efficiency improvements. Both Peters and Bunker visited each plant in turn to get the message across, and a new spirit, or rather a re-awakening of the old fighting spirit of the forties and fifties began to spread through the division. People stopped looking for reasons why they shouldn't do something and, instead, started to look for reasons why they should.

Operators and line stockmen went out of their way to make sure that machines and assembly lines were never brought to a halt because of a shortage of parts. Maintenance men didn't wait for machines to break down before they repaired them, but made sure they didn't break down at all. In the machine shops, output and efficiency soared simply by ensuring that the machines were switched on at the correct time and kept running all the way through to the finishing bell, no minutes late, no minutes lost. The operators and setters weren't necessarily working any harder, but the machines certainly were. And it paid off.

Peters was looking for a twenty per cent efficiency improvement over the first year to meet his target objectives. In some departments they had passed that figure in a matter of weeks. 'We are on our way' was the heartening message from one plant manager, which seemed to sum up the general view from all plants, including Merseyside.

Plant managers issued daily progress reports at each plant and Peters passed on the consolidated divisional figures, adding further words of encouragement of his own. One of his first telephone calls was to Bunker.

'I'd just like you to know, Clem, how much I value the support you are giving me and the Plant managers. The response has been terrific, thanks in no small measure to you.'

'Nice of you to ring,' said the union man. 'From what I hear from the conveners, it sounds good so far.'

'Sure is. If we keep this up the UK will be back at the top of the heap again.'

'Will be a nice change.'

'You can say that again.'

'And Don Peters will be the blue-eyed boy again,' said the union man.

'Waal, I guess that will be a nice change too, Clem. At least that way I might escape the firing squad. But boy, I tell ya, I saw those guys load up,' he joked.

'Glad to be of help, Don. If the ship sinks we all go down with the captain, don't we?'

'We ain't goin' down, brother. No, siree. We're on our way. Bye now. I'll keep in touch.'

'Cheers,' Bunker said. 'Thanks for ringing.'

143

11

Cocello had agreed that Spain should be re-considered as an integral part of Europe now that it had applied to join the European Economic Community, and Mark was instructed to follow through his initial discussions with the new Government and evaluate its claim for new United Motors' investment.

Mark drove to Madrid over the following weekend, stopping off *en route* at Nantes to run his eye over a greenfield site recommended by DATAR, an industrial development arm of the French Government.

He had arranged a meeting with the Minister of Industry in Madrid for ten o'clock on the Monday morning, and drove away from his hotel on the banks of the Loire at five am on the Sunday planning to break the back of the further seven hundred miles to Madrid by late evening.

It was still dark as he nosed the powerful top-of-the-line model through the winding streets of the sleeping town and headed south toward the Bordeaux highway. On reaching the motorway intersection he opened up the powerful engine and sped along the deserted road with the speedometer needle hovering around one hundred miles an hour.

Easing himself into a more comfortable position, he lit up a cigar and settled down to the long drive ahead.

The motorway was deserted at that hour of the morning, so he pushed the engine up over the ton, glancing frequently in the rear-view mirror for any tell-tale police lights, and easing back at the approach roads to overhead bridges where they habitually lay in wait for the prey.

An orange-red sun appeared on the horizon to cast a thin pale blue haze over the countryside. Mark marvelled at the loveliness of the dawn. How did Shakespeare describe such a dawn? he asked himself. 'Night's candles are burnt out and jocund day stands tiptoe on the misty mountain tops'. The

Bard was exactly right as usual. He smiled. Life was beautiful.

The sun rose quickly and where only the occasional vehicle had been visible on the road ahead, he now met cars in twos and threes and then in a steady stream. He switched on the radio and caught the tail-end of a BBC discussion on the farming industry. He thought of Andrew, and wondered how the son of a non-farm-owning father would make his way. Would he make any money in farming, or was money relatively unimportant? Had he, himself, got his values all wrong? He didn't know.

He saw rather more of Andrew, now that he was only a few miles away at agricultural college, compared with the previous ten years spent at Millfield school, where he had lost touch with all three sons, particularly his eldest son, Adam, without even knowing it. Was it all worth it, he asked himself? The well-paid treadmill to buy the expensive education and finance the sky-high mortgage on the home in the country? He supposed so, he reflected, acknowledging with a wave of his left hand the frantically-waving arms of laughing children on the rear seat of the school outing bus he was just overtaking.

The sun rose higher in the sky as he approached the outskirts of La Rochelle, making good time so far.

He recalled the day he and Georgie had taken their eldest son Adam to the famous Somerset school to have the rule run over him by the equally famous and eccentric headmaster.

An hour's chat with the boy in the headmaster's study, interspersed with an odd assortment of questions, followed by half an hour in the nets, where the eccentric pedagogue had spun leg breaks and googlies off a full length to bring the eager boy forward on the front foot to middle the ball most of the time; unlike the wayward boy in the poem, 'who never swerved nor lost his grip, but snicked the ruddy lot to slip'.

Then on to the athletics' track in shorts and spikes to run the half mile with the captain of athletics, who paced the panting boy all the way, urging him on, on, on to the line where the head and the athletics' master snapped their watches before going into a confidential huddle, while Adam lay writhing on the sward heaving his heart up from his superhuman efforts.

He recalled the agony of uncertainty for ten year-old Adam, for Georgie, for himself, as they awaited the verdict, and the undisguised joy on the boy's face when he heard the headmaster tell his parents that he would have him. Fantastic. Great. Terrific. Super. Marvellous. Mark could see the boy's beaming face now. Joy unconfined. He had made it. He had won. He was there. The effort was worth it. It was a blissfully happy family trio who wandered the school grounds, arms linked, laughing joyously at heaven knows what. Adam had made it to one of the finest schools in Europe. In a strange way, Mark and Georgina had felt they had made it too.

That was an achievement, wasn't it? Mark asked himself, dropping through the gears to slow down in response to the flashing warning lights ahead. Yes, of course it was. It did mean something didn't it? It meant something to Adam and to Georgie and himself. They were all doing their best to achieve something, weren't they?

He recalled how at that time he had just been made Plant Manager of the United Motors' south of England factory. He hadn't really been able to afford to send his sons to an expensive school, but Georgie and he had agreed that they would rather spend any additional income on the education of their three sons than on themselves. Fortunately the headmaster was fully aware of the problems facing parents with more than one child and had agreed to take the others at the appropriate time, allowing Mark to spread the fees over twenty years through an insurance scheme. He was now halfway through paying off the debt.

He smiled as he recalled what he had said to his sons, many years later, when they had asked him when the last payment would be made on their education. 'When you lower me in my box,' he had replied.

Why, oh why did Adam opt out some eight years later when he was eighteen? But clearly, he was very happy now and lived a very contented life, so why should recollection be so painful? Maybe it was Adam who had got it right. Maybe it was Georgie and himself who had got it all wrong. He didn't know. It was all very confusing.

Would he and Georgie have been happier opting out of the rat race? Settling for the simple life? Home at four-thirty to five. Sport to play and watch. Hobbies to enjoy. Books to read.

Music. The theatre. More frequent walks in the countryside with the dogs. More time with the children when they were at a formative age. Gardening, fishing, thinking, writing, loving. He didn't know.

He looked up at the sign coming up fast. Approaching Bordeaux. It was just before nine. Time for coffee and a croissant.

He made Biarritz by lunchtime and after a short break for a quick snack was off again heading towards Hendaye and the Spanish border. There were no problems with the customs' formalities at Irun and he drove on as fast as the mountainous conditions would allow in the oppressive heat of the afternoon. The heat was bouncing off the white concrete roads to create a dazzling haze which made driving very tiring.

By the late afternoon he was approaching Burgos and beginning to feel the strain of some twelve hours of almost continuous driving at high speed. His head began to ache and he felt sick. It was beginning to be doubtful whether he would reach Madrid that evening, but he would have to do so if he was to make the meeting with the Government at ten the next morning.

He wound back the sunshine roof to its full extent, the incoming rush of hot air raising the noise level inside the car several decibels.

He felt so hot and uncomfortable and his head was really beginning to pound. He would have to stop for a drink at the next roadside café. Sweat was running down his cheeks. Taking out a handkerchief, he mopped his face and forehead. Hell, it was hot! He shook his head to clear his vision. As if in a trance he drove on.

What the hell was he doing, belting down a bloody hot road in Spain on a Sunday afternoon to get to a meeting on Monday morning, when he could be sitting at home in the garden with Georgie and the dogs, reading the Sunday papers and sipping a nice long cool drink in the more agreeable English sunshine? Eighty degrees was a darned sight more comfortable than a hundred. You grilled at that hellish temperature. God it was hot! Was it all worth it? Did United Motors think any the more of you? Did they hell! Did anyone give a damn where he was or what he was doing this Sunday afternoon, as long as he made it to the goddam meeting on Monday morning, and reported back to Muldoon and McGillicuddy the same evening. No, of course not!

Muldoon would be on his yacht in the Hamble savouring the delights of the Hampshire Solent, and indulging the not-inconsiderable pleasures of being a United Motors' American executive on overseas assignment. McGillicuddy would probably be stretched out in the garden of his beautiful Hertfordshire country home sleeping off the effects of one too many gin and tonics.

Then what the hell was he, himself, doing here in this bloody uncomfortable heat, racing like a bat out of hell to his next assignment? Was it masochism, or sheer bloody stupidity? He wasn't going to be promoted any further, that was for sure. That bastard Steiner had seen to that in New York. So what the hell was he doing rushing around like a blue-arsed fly in the dedicated interest of the great Corporation? He must be mad! Out of his cotton pickin' mind, as some of his American colleagues would say.

Hell it was hot! When was that roadside café coming up? His head was fit to burst. Near and yet so far. Virtually there in the top seat as Regional Manager of Europe . . . until that bastard Steiner had stuck his knife in. The scheming, dirty, shifty, unprincipled bastard!

He found himself saying the words out loud.

But Steiner wasn't the only underhanded bastard at high levels in United Motors. He didn't trust loud-mouthed Mueller any further than he could throw him. He was only interested in one thing, and he'd sell his grandmother to be one step closer to it. He and Steiner were birds of a feather. They made a great pair of unscrupulous bastards!

'God my head aches,' he moaned. 'I feel terrible. Better stop soon. Must get a drink. Mouth as dry as old boots. Where the hell is that café?'

I'll never forgive that bastard Steiner for what he did to me in New York. Never, never, never! He buggered up my future, after thirty years' service, and he didn't give a damn. I was a bloody expendable limey, one of the two a penny boys, to be used as required by VIP visiting Americans, and cast aside like an old clout after they had got what they wanted.

He mopped the streams of perspiration which poured down his face. He felt sick and tired,. So sick and tired. Where the hell was that café? He was feeling really rotten. Mouth like an emery cloth. Steiner was very good at destroying people. Had a gift. Destroyed me. Sure, I still went on after he knifed me in the back that day in New York, but I was effectively finished as a rising executive from that day. From then on I've just been going through the motions of the highly trained corporation executive responding to situations and events as programmed without any real feeling for the Corporation, or respect for most of the top people who run the organisation. My beliefs in the Corporation and the integrity of the men at the top were shattered by Steiner. Oh sure, the pieces have been stuck together and I'm operating as new, but the flaws can't be hidden, can they?

I'm a patched-up executive, OK for operational use but not suitable for pristine display in the front office.

Better get another handkerchief from the case. This one's wet through. Ah, a nice stretch of straight road ahead. Can really open it up now. Must be a café soon. Get there quicker. Hell, I feel tired . . . can hardly keep my eyes open . . . better stop soon . . . I'm bushed.

The noise was deafening, as if the engine had suddenly blown up. His head shot back against the headrest as the powerful car tore off the road at over a hundred miles an hour into scrubland.

'What the hell . . . !' he yelled in petrified terror as his panic-stricken eyes flashed crises messsages to his startled brain. Brown, green objects zoomed up and flashed by at lightning speed, the loose earth lashing the wheel arches in an ear-splitting cacophony as the coupé raced out of control across the scrub.

Mark knew instinctively that he was a dead man. At that speed on rough ground he would die in less than a second. He clung frantically to the wheel in the ridiculous notion that it would give him some degree of control over the runaway vehicle which swerved, slewed, bounced, weaved and leapt into the air as he held on for his life. He daren't brake. On that loose surface he would have rolled over a hundred times at that speed. The car hit the ground again and tore off into the scrubby bush, careering first to the left, and then to the right as the wheels smashed over the rocky ground.

The next moment a rising mound appeared from nowhere and the screeching vehicle leapt some ten feet in the air.

'Georgieeeee,' he yelled in mortal anguish, believing her name to be the last sound he would utter on earth before he was projected into the vast unknown to meet his Maker.

His head hit the edge of the sunshine roof, but somehow he still managed to hold onto the wheel at full arms' length, before crashing back into the driving seat. Oh, dear God, he pleaded as the vehicle crashed to earth again and tore off in another direction.

'Bloody hell!' he yelled as the uncontrollable coupé flashed

149

between two trees at breakneck speed. Would it never slow down? Dear God, why wasn't he dead already?

The vehicle continued to swerve and bounce beyond control until the build-up of soft earth under the wheel arches gradually slowed it down to a speed which enabled him to regain control. He guided the car toward less rocky scrub. Why couldn't he use his left hand to change gear? Because he needed it to hold on to the bloody wheel, that's why, he told himself.

The heaving machine came to a stop. He was now facing the direction from whence he had come. The reddish-brown dust had still not settled from the point where he had left the highway, nearly a mile away, the crazy course he had travelled being clearly visible in the spiral dust cloud which hung above the searing ruts gouged out of the soft earth. It was deathly quiet. Far away, a heavy truck ambled on its way to its destination, passing the point on the highway where Mark had left the road. The driver must have seen the skid marks and the cloud of dust; but even if he did, he didn't care.

Mark closed his eyes and prayed out loud.

'Our Father, who art in heaven, hallowed be Thy name . . . Dear God, thank you for saving my life. . . .'

His body was soaking wet with fear and he felt dreadfully sick, but was too weak to move. For several minutes he just sat there, paralysed by the frightful experience. Then he began to choke with nausea, but couldn't vomit, his heart pounding with great aching thuds which hurt his ear drums. His body continued to heave uncontrollably as he gulped air into an asbestos mouth. He hadn't the strength to re-open closed eyelids, or to raise a finger.

For some five minutes or so he just sat there, head resting on the padded wheel, breathing heavily and muttering thanks to God.

Raising his head slowly to survey the scene again he became more acutely aware of the stabbing pains in his head where it had struck the roof. He pulled the rear view mirror into position. He could have just stepped out of a shower; but there were no gaping wounds and only a trickle of blood.

'How lucky can you get?' he whispered.

Gradually taking stock of himself and the interior of the vehicle, he became more aware that the numb pins-and-needles feeling in his left leg and left arm hadn't gone away. It was only cramp, he was sure of that. He had been sitting at the wheel for the best part of thirteen hours. It was only when he continued to experience difficulty in moving these limbs after rubbing them for some time with his right hand that he began to ask himself if he had suffered a mild stroke.

After some ten minutes or so he was able to slide out of the driving seat to inspect the damage to the car. The vehicle was covered in reddish-brown dirt with pieces of yellow and brown bracken sticking out from under the wheel arches. Embedded between the front fender and the grill was a sizeable bush. Incredibly, there appeared to be no body distortion and to his surprise he was able to open and shut both doors of the coupé. Even the tyres were unpunctured.

He was now able to move his arms and legs with a little more freedom and proceeded to rub himself vigorously while stamping on the ground. He glanced at his watch. It was nearly six o'clock. He was suddenly no longer tired. On the contrary, he had never felt more wide awake in his life, although he did feel weak. He could make it to Madrid provided the car was driveable. Prising the packed soil from the wheel arches and kicking the tyres to check the pressure, he returned to the driving seat. The ignition light was still on. Turning the key, the powerful engine roared into action.

Very, very slowly and with great care he drove back to the road, re-tracing his tracks and marvelling at his outrageous luck in avoiding the hundreds of sizeable rocks and gullies which would have smashed his car to smithereens.

On re-entering the highway he was surprised to find the car behaving as normal. The tyres made a lot of noise until the last of the muck had fallen from the wheel arches, but after a mile or so this had cleared and the car sounded as good as ever.

Little by little, he opened up the engine until he was racing toward Madrid as fast as road conditions would allow. He pulled into the underground car park at the hotel Miguel Angel at eight forty-five that evening.

Taking the lift to the lobby, he felt some concern that he was dragging his left leg a bit. After signing the register he ordered a light meal to be served in his room; took a shower; rang Georgina to tell her that he had arrived safely in Madrid and

151

turned in for an early night.

The next morning he felt fine, though the heaviness in his left leg still disturbed him.

. . .

His meetings with the Government went without hitch, Ministry officials now making it quite clear that they were most anxious to avoid the mistakes made by the previous administration. How easy it was, he thought, for Governments to put the blame on their predecessors, even easier than in industry. By the third day, Mark was able to construct the guide lines of a plan based on the Government's latest laws, rules and regulations.

When Mark put it to the Minister that to meet Spain's local content and export ratio requirements it would be necessary to phase-out certain component operations in the rest of Europe, particularly in Britain and France, the Minister simply shrugged his shoulders.

'How do I explain such a plan to the British and French Governments?' Mark asked facetiously. He knew what the answer would be. The Minister shrugged and smiled enigmatically.

'I am sure that United Motors will think of something,' he said.

Mark's arrival in Madrid had been deliberately leaked to the press by the Government, the Spanish newspapers carrying statements in the business sections to the effect that a senior European executive of United Motors was in the capital to discuss the possibility of manufacturing components in Spain.

Mark had been advised by McGillicuddy and the lawyers in Detroit to keep a low profile, and to avoid unnecessary rumours circulating in the world's press. Some hope.

Keeping a low profile was becoming more essential of late, not so much in the interests of avoiding top level embarrassment or commercial security, but simply to secure the personal safety of the negotiators. Terrorist groups in several European countries had kidnapped, injured and killed local and international executives, particularly those who represented the major multi-nationals. Although Italy was top of the league in the terrorist stakes, Spain was running a close second

152

following the death of Franco and the fall of the authoritarian Government.

Mark Sanders received his first threat when the hotel porter at the Miguel Angel handed him an envelope with his room key and his copy of the London *Financial Times*. At first glance Mark had taken it to be one of the usual letters of introduction he often received from local suppliers who wished it to be known that they were very interested in offering their services to United Motors in the event of the company establishing manufacturing operations in their country.

Mark sat in his room reading *The Financial Times* and sipping a Scotch before opening the envelope. On plain white paper were typed the words: 'WE DON'T WANT UNITED MOTORS IN ESPAÑA. GET OUT SEÑOR SANDERS.' It was signed ETA.

Mark sat staring at the words. He had received threatening and abusive letters in the past from obvious cranks, but this was different. This was signed by a terrorist group which had already killed or injured many industrial and political leaders. It had the look of authenticity, stark, simple and chilling.

He was not sure what to do. If he brought the note to the attention of United Motors, via Muldoon, it was more than likely that the top brass would think that he was over-reacting to a kind of threat which was becoming commonplace. If they thought for one moment that he was getting scared they would take immediate steps to bring him back to London, and replace him with someone of sterner stuff. Being scared of threats was not the hallmark of a top corporation man.

He could expect a similar reaction from the Corporation if he brought the note to the attention of the local police.

He thought very carefully of what he should do, and decided to do nothing unless he received follow-up threats from the same source.

At dinner that evening, he found himself repeatedly thinking about the note. It gave him an uncomfortable feeling which shamed him. As he raised his wine glass to his lips he noticed that his hand was shaking.

.   .   .

On the Friday of that week Mark was leaving the offices of the company's lawyers in Avenue Capitan Haya around six-thirty in the evening, when a Jeep screeched to a halt and three men in rough khaki battledress leapt from the vehicle, and ran toward him brandishing automatics at the ready.

The Englishman stopped dead in his tracks, expecting the worst, and to his great relief, they raced past him to take up security positions outside the Palais de Congressos, a few yards away, where the President of the European Commission, Mr Roy Jenkins, was due to arrive.

Mark's heart was thumping like crazy.

He resumed his leisurely stroll down the avenue to his hotel with a superficial air of casual indifference, but he was perspiring copiously. But then, it was damned hot, he told himself. He had also better take that stupid smile off his face. People might get the wrong impression.

. . .

That weekend Mark decided to take a break from the work routine. He was feeling rather jaded and nervy. A complete change from Government officials, lawyers and the never-ending phone calls from London, New York and Detroit would re-charge his batteries, which were going rather flat. So Saturday was spent at the Prado among the paintings of El Greco and Goya. In the evening he went to the bull-ring, but for the first time in living memory the banderilleros and picadors went on strike to reduce the wide pay differentials between themselves and the matadors.

The corrida began as usual with the parade, after the paying customers had been relieved of their pesetas, before the President autocratically announced over the loud speaker system that the corrida was now cancelled due to the non-appearance of the banderilleros and picadors. Upon this announcement all hell broke loose. Cushions rained down on the hapless officials and matadors from all quarters. Whistles and cat-calls rent the air. Spain was being afflicted by the British disease.

The following day he took the car from the hotel garage and drove at a leisurely pace out of the city along the road to Valencia. Some forty miles or so beyond the outskirts of the capital he took the right fork to Chinchon, which he had been recommended to visit by the lawyers.

The afternoon was very hot with temperatures hovering around the hundred mark as he meandered at not much more than walking pace up the winding and dusty road toward the historic village. The characteristic smell of Spain, which is so noticeable to the visitor, was particularly strong as it wafted in through the lowered windows and open sunshine roof.

Red-brown furrows criss-crossed the patchwork-quilt fields, which rose in the foreground and then fell away to reveal hazy mountains rising majestically in the distance overlooking the valley. Up ahead, on one of the many bends in the spiral road, Mark could see a reluctant donkey carrying a huge load of vegetables on its back, with a peasant perched high on top under a large sombrero. The temperamental creature proceeded on its laborious way in fits and starts. Mark drove slowly past glancing sideways at the peasant to nod a friendly greeting, but the Spaniard was fast asleep.

The old village suddenly came into view, perched between mountain ledges like a crows' nest at the top of a tree. Mark drove through the ancient porchway which led to the square, except that the square, in this instance, was round in the shape of a bullring. The overall appearance was infinitely more pleasing to the eye than anything which could be conceivably contrived by a whole army of architects striving to reproduce the same visual effect.

The plaza was obviously used as a bullring, for in front of the buildings massive wooden pillars had been erected at regular intervals with wide recesses cut away to take the heavy wood blocks piled nearby. These would be slotted into position to form the barriers between performers and spectators on the days of the corrida. Hemingway would have loved the place. Vintage Spain.

Mark was sitting outside one of the small, grubby cafés, drinking thick black coffee and sipping a glass of the local sweet liqueur which claimed to be a digestive aid, when the reluctant donkey, which he had passed on the mountain road, ambled through the archway into the plaza without any guidance from its master, who was still fast asleep under his huge sombrero.

The donkey crossed the village square and stopped outside the general store. To awaken his recumbent master he jerked his head up and down sharply which rocked the load of vegetables piled high on his back shaking the peasant from his siesta. He awoke with a start and slid down from his mobile hammock. The unintelligible rumbling of a greeting with which he acknowledged the presence of the portly Sancho Panza of a store keeper who had emerged from the depths of the shop, must have been along the lines of *'Buenos dias, señor, como est a usted,'* but it sounded to Mark more like one long rumbling burp. He sat watching the two men argue in low monotones over the quality and price of the produce. Buying and selling components in the modern international market place, he thought, was really only a derivative of the ancient transaction being argued out over the back of the donkey between a willing seller and a not so willing buyer.

After languishing over coffee to absorb the charm of the village, Mark strolled past the dusty shops stopping to buy a piece of the hard black smoked ham, which he had come to like as an *hors d'oeuvre*, and a bottle of the local wine. He then meandered through the archway to mount the tiny cobbled street which led to the battlements of the old castle.

The view from the top, overlooking the valley which fell away into the far distance, was breathtakingly beautiful. Mark sat on the stone parapet enjoying the magnificent view, whilst savouring the hard smoked ham which went down well with the vino. It was utterly peaceful and quiet, save for the occasional bird cry. This was the way to relax and unwind, he mused.

He had been there for some five minutes or so when another lone stroller came up the cobbled street and paused a few feet away to also enjoy the view. Mark looked up and nodded toward the casually dressed young man in his late twenties who looked in his direction.

'*Buenos dias,*' Mark said, out of courtesy.

'*Buenos dias, Señor Sanders,*' replied the young man with a smile. 'It's very beautiful, señor, is it not?'

Mark stiffened.

'How do you know my name?' he asked. Who are you?'

'Who am I, señor? Someone who brings you good advice,' the young man replied. 'We have not been formally introduced. But you could say that we know one another. I believe you received my associations' little letter of introduction. It was delivered to your hotel. The Miguel Angel I think.'

Mark's pulse rate quickened. He slipped down from the parapet which now seemed uncomfortably dangerous.

'Yes, I received a letter,' he replied. 'But I receive lots of letters.'

The young man scraped the stony ground with his right foot in much the same manner as a fighting bull getting ready to charge.

'I don't think you would mistake this letter, señor,' he said coldly. 'At least, I should perhaps say that you would be most unwise to do so. But you are an intelligent businessman, so I think you will come to an intelligent decision. You will bring our message to the attention of your masters in Detroit, will you not?'

'If you say so' Mark replied calmly.

'We do say so! the Spaniard snapped. 'We are rather disappointed that, as yet, you don't seem to have taken our letter seriously. It is, I assure you, a very serious request.' He added menacingly, 'We are not in the habit of giving advice more than once.'

Mark maintained his outward air of composure, but he wasn't kidding himself. His heart was thumping.

'But what reasons do you have for wanting me to communicate your message to my company?' he asked cautiously. 'Your Government has invited United Motors to build new manufacturing plants in Spain. If we decide to do so, isn't that in Spain's interest?'

'You underestimate our intelligence, Señor Sanders, and that is not a sensible thing to do,' the Spaniard replied. 'You would not wish me to remind you that any investment made by United Motors in Spain will be made in the interest of United Motors and the United States, and not in the interest of Spain and the Spanish people.'

But why should investment not be in the interest of both countries?' the Englishman asked. 'I see no reason for any conflict of interests, if the plan is a good one.'

The younger man moved closer to Mark.

'Let me make our position quite clear to you, señor,' he said venomously. 'We are not interested in the situation as you see it. We see things rather differently. You either listen to what we have to say, and take action on what we are instructing you to do, or we will take appropriate alternative steps, which would be less agreeable to you personally.'

He glanced in the direction of the cobbled street below where two men were leaning against a bench seat looking up in their direction.

'It would be quite easy for my friends and I to take you to our colleagues right now, señor. But we have nothing against you personally, as yet. Let's keep it that way. Carry out our instructions, *por favor*.'

The young Spaniard stepped back a few paces and stood there grinning from ear to ear, before turning away to join his colleagues on the street below. He paused, turned and called out in a loud voice:

'Please convey our letter of introduction to your company, Señor Sanders. It is as you say, in our mutual interest.'

.   .   .

Mark waited several minutes before returning to his car which he had parked in the square. It had been broken into. The lock barrel on the driver's side hung from the door handle. His jacket, which contained his wallet and his Government security card, had been removed. He found the jacket and the wallet five minutes later at the side of the road some two miles outside the village. The only items missing were a few thousand pesetas and his Government security card. At least they had the courtesy not to throw away the more personal items in his wallet, he mused.

Back at the hotel, Mark reflected that it was pointless to phone Whitehall on a Sunday to report the stolen security card. He would do so the next day.

He sat quietly in the lounge for most of the evening contemplating the action he should now take. He had previously taken the view that he would advise Muldoon if he received a second follow-up letter. What reasons were there for not doing so now?

He put a call through to his Buckinghamshire home and told Georgina that he hoped to be back in England within a few days.

'You would love the charming old village I visited today, Georgie. About forty miles out of Madrid, high in the mountains. Chinchon. Vintage Spain. Oozes character and history.

Most interesting place.'

'Lucky old you. Some people have all the fun. Why don't you take me with you to some of these more interesting places? Would I queer your pitch with the local señoritas?'

'Can never cope with more than one at a time, darling,' he joked.

'I'm not sure you can even cope with one these days,' she said. 'I'm becoming the forgotten woman. Dangerous, you know, Mark. Guess what forgotten woman are apt to get up to?' She laughed. 'You know what they say, darling. In every nice girl there is a wanton woman trying to escape.'

'Is that what they say?'

'So they tell me.'

'I'd like to meet that wanton woman some time.'

'How about next week?'

'Can't wait.'

.   .   .

Mark continued his discussions with Government officials and by Tuesday evening had obtained sufficient information to review the situation with Muldoon and McGillicuddy in London.

He proposed to disclose the letter and the threat at that meeting.

He phoned Whitehall on the Monday to report that his Government security card had been stolen, which didn't go down at all well. He was asked to kindly give a full explanation of the loss by 'popping-in' to Marsham Street when he was next in London. He flew to Heathrow early Wednesday morning and explained the loss of his card to the security people, who clearly thought it was all rather tiresome. He was issued with a replacement card accompanied by an admonition to try and be a little more careful in future.

'We don't exactly hand these things out to all and sundry, you know,' said the pinstriped official. 'Supposed to be rather very, very hush hush. Can't have any old Tom, Dick and Harry flashing them around. That wouldn't do now, would it?'

His meeting with Muldoon and McGillicuddy in the afternoon went reasonably well, with the latter taking the view that the terms and conditions demanded by the Spanish Govern-

159

ment provided the Corporation's specialists and lawyers with
sufficient information to discuss the subject in more detail.

McGillicuddy made light of the letter and threat.

'Dime a dozen,' he said indifferently. 'Get 'em all the
time.'

12

Mark picked up another car at the London plant and drove up the M1 to his home in north Buckinghamshire. Turning off the motorway at the service station he entered a different world. Driving very slowly over the narrow bridges spanning the fast flowing streams which stemmed from the River Ouse, he noticed that a massive flock of coots had flown in while he had been away. There must have been two or three thousand on the river banks and the water.

Pulling the car off the narrow country lane, Mark pressed the button which activated the power-operated windows. It was early evening and very still. Soft white clouds remained motionless against an azure blue sky. Between the many breaks in the cloud the rays of a thin evening sun shafted down at an acute angle to spotlight the pastoral scene.

Away to the west a flock of Canada geese was heading home to descend on one of the larger lakes in the distance. In the foreground another smaller flock was taking off from the little lake on the south side. Squawking madly in what appeared to be a family squabble over the direction they should take, they suddenly closed ranks, as if by order, and formed a perfect vee behind their leader. They then wheeled in unison into a shaft of light which held them for a second or so before they soared over the car and away.

Standing in shallow water amongst the tall reeds on the banks of the river, Mark counted eight herons, all motionless, their necks inclined upwards at precisely the same angle, as if in silent prayer.

On the river banks to the east, mallard and teal were pecking away at their undercarriages and, in the meadow flanking the lane, two hares were squaring up.

High overhead, barely visible or audible, a jumbo jet began its gentle descent to Heathrow. Mark looked up at the tiny speck in the stratosphere and imagined he could hear the air hostess requesting passengers to fasten their seat belts. He looked again at the beautifully unspoiled Buckinghamshire countryside. It was great to be home again.

He drove leisurely up the country lane and ascended the hill, before bearing left along the escarpment. Away in the distance, tucked between a fold in the surrounding hills, was home.

Mark always experienced the same feelings of contentment when entering the home straight. Today he felt particularly pleased to be back. Gently nosing the car down the hill into the village, he turned off the road into the gravelled drive which led to the eighteenth-century stone barn.

Hearing the wheels of the car on the gravel the two young golden retriever bitches, Honey and the pick of the litter, Harriet, bounded through the hall to get a better view of the intruder from the dining-room window. Standing on their hind legs with front paws resting on the deep window sills, they saw Mark getting out of his car and went berserk. Racing back into the hall with tails wagging furiously, they almost knocked Georgina over. She had also heard a car come up the drive, and was heading through the hall to the porch.

She opened the heavy oak doors and the dogs swept past her bounding across the drive to their master who was opening up the car boot to remove his luggage. Mark turned, just as the dogs took off together in a huge leap which struck him in the chest, knocking him backwards into the boot where he sat, legs dangling, with both arms wrapped around the excited dogs. Looking up, he saw Georgina standing at the open door with a welcoming smile.

'Hello, darling,' he called waving with his right hand while trying to keep the dogs at bay with his left.

'Welcome home, sweetheart!' She flung her arms around him.

'Such a long time!' she gasped in his ear as they hugged each other tightly, the dogs retiring a respectful distance to sit and watch the homecoming with tails swishing excitedly over the gravel.

'I've missed you so much, this time,' she told him breathlessly. 'Can't think why. Really forgotten what you look like. Let's have a look at you. Hum, not bad, considering your age and everything I suppose. . . .'

'It's great to be home, darling. I've missed you too,' he whispered in her ear. 'Don't know why I feel this way. Must be Spring!'

.   .   .

During Mark's absence in Spain, 'the mole' Fred Klepner had spent countless hours going over the Ten Year Business plan which was to be the subject of the presentation Mark was to give to Nate Cocello at the next Planning Committee meeting.

Klepner had studied the plan with a sense of shock.

He had arrived in Europe knowing nothing about the European motor industry or the Continent's political and economic environment, except from what he had read on the subject at Harvard Business School and in Detroit Central Office reports. He had been under the erroneous impression that Europe was just one big common market, similar in size to the United States, operating under free trade concepts, and with common laws, rules and regulations. He had therefore assumed that the preparation of a European plan would be broadly similar to the planning practices normally followed in the United States.

In consequence, he had read the two hundred page European Plan with open-mouthed incredulity. It was a totally different planning world from the United States. The plan was also prepared in a different way from those drafted by the US divisions, as it had to be to give proper consideration to the problems and needs of a totally different planning environment.

For the first time since leaving the Harvard Business School of Management Klepner now began to have a glimmer of understanding of the many important practical differences between Europe and the United States.

The first section of the plan developed all the major assumptions upon which it was based. These assumptions detailed the principal factors under separate headings, such as Political, Economic, Technical, Commercial, Environmental, Energy and so on. These headings were then broken down to test the assumptions by critical analysis, country by country identifying the common European factors and the variables.

163

In developing the short list of manufacturing locations he proposed to establish to produce the new products which would incorporate all the latest technologies, he had detailed the comparative costs of manufacture per country and identified the economic and commercial advantages and disadvantages of selling components into specific European countries from single and dual manufacturing sources. It was patently obvious to Klepner, now that he had read the plan, that the European trade environment was not as he had been led to believe.

He spent the entire first week reading the plan over and over again.

Two days before Mark returned to England, Klepner spent a whole day with Muldoon going over the plan. The upshot of this meeting was that Muldoon phoned Mueller and Klepner was on the next plane to Detroit with photostat copies of Mark's plan, for Mueller's eyes only.

. . .

Mark arrived at his office expecting to have a few clear days ahead to finalise the European Business Plan and prepare his presentation to Cocello. But it didn't happen that way.

He received an internal phone call from Muldoon, who told him that McGillicuddy wanted him to go on to Dublin immediately.

The Irish Prime Minister had evidently made a personal approach to his compatriot, the Chairman of United Motors, Tom O'Reilly, pleading for more American investment to help the 'auld counthrie'. The Irish never allowed their expatriates to forget the debt they owed the Emerald Isle.

United Motors had already built a component plant in Dublin a few years before, at the specific request of the Chairman, but it had never operated profitably. It had been plagued by excessive absenteeism, restrictive practices, inter-union demarcation lines and poor product quality.

Mark's quarterly reports which highlighted the plant problems were not well received by the Chairman – according to his personal staff.

'You don't win any medals by questioning the Chairman's

judgement, Mark' said his personal assistant, advising him to 'tone it down a bit' in future Dublin plant reports.

Notwithstanding the plant's poor track record, Tom O'Reilly considered it to be his bounden duty to respond to the call for help from his compatriot, the Irish Prime Minister, and so he phoned McGillicuddy, who readily agreed, and Mark was instructed to contact the PM's office.

There were, in fact, many Irish Americans in United Motors at high management levels, all of whom had a nostalgic affection for the 'auld counthrie', and indeed for anything Irish; but that was because most of them had never actually been there. The majority preferred to believe the picturesque stories passed down by parents and grandparents, which were, of course, accepted as the gospel truth.

The Chairman, for example, was one of no fewer than five Irish Americans to have held the top job in UM.

Tom O'Reilly was an ascetic former Treasurer of the Corporation who had been never known to smile even when the company's blue chip shares soared to dizzy peaks on Wall Street. It was, however, reported by his personal staff that he did manage a smirk when he had been told the story of how his arch rival and competitor had been conned by his countrymen on a flag-flying visit to the 'auld counthrie'. He had agreed to make a financial contribution of $50,000 from the family trust to help finance a social club to be named after him. The local paper made a front page headline of 'Henry's magnificent $500,000 gift'. The motor magnate was furious and rang the Editor to say so, whereupon the latter apologised profusely adding that he would make a front page correction in the next day's edition.

Henry surrendered. Some two years later, on completion of the social club, the magnate was asked if he would like something suitable inscribed over the portal.

'Yeah,' replied the motor man irritably, 'you can say "I came amongst you and you took me in".'

Tom O'Reilly liked that story. It actually made him smirk . . . so it was said.

The UM Chairman was cast from a similar mould but with coarser ingredients. O'Reilly was impossible to please and suspicious of everybody and everything. He trusted nobody, not even fellow Catholics on the Board. But if it could be said that he did have a weakness for something, it was for Ireland and the Irish.

. . .

Mark could ill-afford to be away from his office with the presentation to Cocello looming large on the horizon, but the next day he was on his way to Dublin.

The taxi crossed the Liffey and made its way down O'Connell Street to Government House. The talkative driver hadn't stopped chatting from the moment Mark had entered the cab. He was better than a music-hall turn. There was no question of doubt but that the Irish had been blessed with the gift of the Blarney. Most of them could express themselves with a lilting eloquence which left the English spellbound. Who was it who said that the Irish took the English language and threw the words up in the air just to see how they all sparkled as they came tumbling down?

. . .

Mark's meeting with the Irish Minister of Industry and his loquacious officials was pure theatre. The problems experienced by United Motors at its Dublin plant, which the Englishman advised were the major factors which would influence future investment decisions in Ireland, simply melted away into insignificance under their mellifluous tongues.

They had excuses, or as they preferred to describe them, fair and reasonable explanations, for all the problems which had beset the Dublin plant. The exceptionally high absenteeism on Mondays and Fridays, which necessitated employing thirty per cent more workers than was economically justified, was not so much caused by the demon drink; but because . . . etcetera, etcetera. . . .

The reason why timekeeping was particularly bad on Tuesdays, Wednesdays and Thursdays, when employees did turn up for work, was because the buses were so unreliable. The local transport authority simply couldn't get spare parts from the British to keep the buses on the roads. If only the British would pull their socks up things would be different.

166

The reason why absenteeism was non-existent on Thursdays was not just because it happened to be pay day. Ah ha, no; it wasn't quite as simple as all that, don't you know, although of course it was an incentive day, and the Irish loved incentives.

Regarding the strikes, disputes and restrictive practices which had plagued the Dublin plant, these were all unfortunate legacies of the British system which had been foisted upon the Irish since before the First World War. The Irish Government was resolutely determined to rid itself of the British system which had done so much harm to the economy.

When Mark reminded them that the plant was relatively new and that with the exception of the American Managing Director and Treasurer, was manned throughout by Irish men and women, they countered with, 'Ah yes, but it's the Trade unions, you see.'

And when he pointed out that these were Irish, not British Trade unions they were talking about, it was sadly admitted that the English disease had poisoned the minds of many impressionable Irish trade unionists and that it would of course take time entirely to eradicate malign English influences from the land of Saints and Scholars.

To be sure, unemployment was a mortal sin to shame all good Christians and the Government was appealing to international companies to help solve the problem.

Meantime, it would greatly help if United Motors could see its way clear to build another factory in Ireland, particularly if it could be built in the South West, where the Prime Minister was having to face re-election in a year's time. Very generous financial assistance would be given by the Government, in the form of a grant of up to thirty per cent of capital and remission of all taxation on export sales for ten years.

The fact that in the whole of South West Ireland there was not sufficient labour to man a new United Motors plant was not seen by the Minister as any kind of problem; simply as a little local difficulty.

.   .   .

Later that morning he was flown to the South West and shown a beautiful industrial site with excellent access to the adjacent port facilities. Unfortunately it had just been earmarked for housing. There was, however, another very similar site in the area, which was really better than the site they had already seen. The trouble was that nobody could quite remember where it was exactly, but everybody knew it was around there somewhere, that's for sure. So they all went off to lunch with the mayor, while a messenger was sent to the Registrar of Births, Marriages and Deaths to get the necessary information.

Mark had often said to his American colleagues in Detroit and New York that the sales' promotion literature put out by the Irish Development Authority to attract internationally mobile inward investment was superior to anything produced by any other European country. Unfortunately the practical problems of operating a large plant in Ireland were totally unrelated to the glowing words in the glossy literature, and to the enchanting phrases which slid so eloquently off the honeyed tongues of Ministers and officials.

In reality, the unhappy experiences of United Motors at its Dublin plant had effectively ensured that no major future expansion would be undertaken in that enigmatic country for many years. Cocello would effectively see to that, whatever Chairman Tom O'Reilly might think.

When the Minister had ended the meeting with the words, 'Now, Mr Sanders, what can we do to persuade you to put more investment in Ireland?' the Englishman had replied, 'The best advocate you could have, Minister, to influence more investment in your country, is a local plant manager who consistently turns in good results, year after year.

'Such a man, with a good track record can fight for his plant and his people on the very strong grounds that investment in his region has been proven to be successful.

'Our Dublin plant has consistently failed to produce the expected results, and it is this unfortunate experience which will weigh heavily against any further investment in Eire; in much the same way as it has weighed heavily against the UK. The most eloquent advocates in United Motors, Minister, are those with beautiful bottom lines,' said the Englishman.

.   .   .

The executive jet took off from Cork airport and landed at Dublin in the late afternoon. Mark was driven to the Gresham Hotel by the head of the development authority. On the way he stopped the car in the city centre to point out dozens of parking meters, all capped with hooded covers.

'Now I'd like to show you sometin' which I'm sure you would appreciate,' he said pleasantly, wagging a finger at the objects ahead.

'Now you see all dose little parking meters dere, snoozing under dose little black sleeping caps? Well a few weeks ago the city fathers installed dose nasty little tings at a cost, believe it or not, sir, of some turty tree tousand pounds, and the day afterwards dey declared the whole area a no waiting zone.'

He threw back his head and roared with laughter.

'Now isn't dat Irish, Mr Sanders?' he exclaimed enjoying the joke on himself, which was one of the more agreeable characteristics the Irish had in common with the English.

Mark then told him of the occasion when he had been driving down O'Connell Street some twenty or so years before, when he had inadvertently misunderstood the hand signals of the policeman on traffic duty, and had moved off before he had been cleared to do so.

The policeman had ordered him to stop by his foot.

'You are English, are you not, Sor?' he had asked with haughty disdain. 'Sure, I taut so,' he added. 'Now sor, is dis your first time in Dublin? Ah it is. For sure dat explains it all!'

Then pulling himself up to a great height, he went on.

'Now sor, I'm goin' to be tellin' yer sometin'. If you'se happen to be comin' here to Dublin at some time or other in the future – which praise the Lord you will be, for tis God's own city – and you happen to be driving down O'Connell Street and you see me standin' here like dis, with me arms up; then whether I'm here or not, you stop.'

He had stood there with left arm aloft and right arm horizontal and remained in that statuesque position for some thirty seconds.

'Now, is dat understood, sor? Fine, then be off with you and may God give you a good day.'

. . .

The other Ireland raised its ugly head at Dublin airport. Mark's name had been called over the loudspeaker system.

He answered the phone to be told by an anonymous member of the IRA that he shouldn't attempt to return to Ireland if United Motors decided against further investment in that country.

Once again the sharp contrast was drawn between the charming and friendly people one came across in everyday life and the murdering hate of the evil terrorist minority who eagerly blew innocent men, women and children to Kingdom come.

13

While Mark was in Dublin the head of the French Development Authority DATAR paid a courtesy visit to Detroit to make the point to Nate Cocello, and Chairman, Tom O'Reilly that France was keen to attract very much more United Motors investment.

The fact that France had already received the lion's share of new European component investment over the previous five years was beside the point. That was past. France wanted the lion's share of all future European investment too, and was most concerned to hear that the Corporation was also considering investment in Spain, Portugal, Austria, Ireland and the UK.

It was put to the two top men and to the Vice President in charge of Overseas' Operations that the interests of France could only be adequately served by Frenchmen, and not by Americans or Englishmen. The fact that Sanders, an Englishman, had produced the plan which had changed French plants from ailing and unprofitable operations in the sixties, into expanding and profitable divisions in the seventies was discreetly overlooked.

Mark had actually transferred certain expanding and profitable product lines and manufacturing facilities from the UK to France to consolidate a new range of components at French locations. All hell would have been let loose by the French plants and the French Government if the boot had been on the other foot and anyone had attempted to transfer products and facilities from France to the UK.

The top men had listened courteously to their visitor's observations and requests without reaction. Under his breath, the Vice President was telling him to get stuffed. The French Government would object to Jesus Christ being head of European Operations, on the grounds that He wasn't a Frenchman.

In his capacity as world-wide planning coordinator, Mueller had been invited by Nate Cocello to attend the meeting as an observer. He had listened to DATAR's views with great interest, and from a totally different viewpoint to that of the Vice President. Mueller wanted to bring world planning under his personal direction and control from Detroit. He could understand – so he said to the top brass after the Frenchman had departed – why the French took exception to an Englishman holding such a key position in Europe. He could also understand why they objected to London being the European headquarters of United Motors.

Chairman Tom O'Reilly took a similar view but for different reasons. He had been against the choice of London as the location for European Headquarters when he had been Treasurer. As an active supporter of the 'Irish cause' he hated Britain and the British.

'I guess those European Government bastards would object wherever we located European headquarters,' said Cocello. 'The French hate London, but they would also object to Bonn, Rome, Brussels . . . you name it. It would still be wrong until you mentioned Paris. Then it would be right.'

'The same goes, I guess, for other Governments,' said the Chairman. 'There is no single acceptable location, as they see it, unless it is in their own country. The French hate London and the British, but then, who doesn't?' he added maliciously.

'Waal,' rejoined Cocello. 'If the Europeans fight like hell over new investment and where European headquarters should be, maybe we should consider running everything from here in Detroit, the way it used to be. We could do it, of course.'

'Sure could,' added Mueller eagerly, and received a look of cold disapproval from the Vice President in charge of Overseas' Operations for his unwarranted opinion.

'Well, why don't we chew on it a bit?' asked the ageing Chairman.

'Maybe we should,' replied the President and Chief Executive Officer.

'Randy, would you put down something for discussion by the Executive Committee?'

'Yes sir, Will do.'

. . .

Mark Sanders spent the next few days in his office, working late into the night to finalise the ten year European Business Plan and to summarise the massive document into a sixty minute presentation illustrated by thirty slides.

Fred Klepner had been in and out of both Mark's and Pat Muldoon's offices, which were only a few yards apart, like an eager beaver. He would grab a completed section of the overall plan from Mark's private secretary just as soon as she had typed it, and dash off to his own office down the corridor to study it carefully many times over, before taking it along to Muldoon to keep him in the picture.

Klepner played the usual corporate cat and mouse game of making at least one or two word changes on each and every page so that his own secretary could re-type each page under her initials and the initials 'FK'. This practice achieved twin objectives. It gave the European plan anonymity by not identifying the author of the plan, while his own copy under his own initials and those of his secretary would tell Mueller and his Detroit colleagues that he had a hand in its formulation, which is what Mueller and Muldoon wanted people to think.

As presentation day grew closer with Mark racing against time to complete the plan and finalise the slide illustrations, so Klepner read and re-read it until he had almost learnt it off by heart. So complete was his total immersion in the subject that he actually began to believe that he had assisted Sanders in the plan's preparation. His delusions were those of a messenger boy who assumes that because he takes the Chief Architect's drawings to the print room, he has played a leading role in the design of the building.

A few days before the European Planning Committee was due to meet, Mueller decided to go for the jugular.

His suggestion that United Motors should progressively wind up its European, South American and Asian regional headquarters and plan, direct and control world operations from its home base in Detroit, had been well-received by most of the top brass who liked the big bold approach of running

173

the world the way it used to be . . . from Detroit.

They were under no illusions that they could do a better job from Detroit, but they had become increasingly concerned that they were getting out of touch with what was happening around the world, and that the tail was beginning to wag the dog.

The European zone, for example, was growing twice as fast as the United States' zone, and now employed a quarter of a million people.

This situation went against the grain, as the top brass always needed to be on top of every situation and on top of every executive if they were to do their jobs to their own sastisfaction; not necessarily in the best interests of the Corporation, that is to say, but in their own best interests. Mueller's proposals appeared to be more in tune with their own thoughts at that particular time. For this reason he was given the green light to prepare more detailed proposals for further consideration.

Confident in the knowledge that he now had the general support of most of the top brass to his world control plan, Mueller considered that he was now in a much stronger position to start pulling the rug out from under the Regional Area Managers. And, as the biggest zone by far was Europe, he would begin there.

His plan to appoint Klepner to succeed Sanders as European Planning Manager, based on Detroit rather than London, was working out to perfection. Klepner had been doing everything that was expected of him acting as Mueller's eyes and ears in Europe.

It was now necessary to give Klepner visibility in front of Cocello and the top brass.

Muldoon was no problem. He wouldn't mind taking early retirement. He was over sixty and a relatively wealthy man, with a wife who was financially independent. He would welcome the chance of retiring to his yachts.

McGillicuddy wouldn't relish the idea of giving up the General Director's job as European overlord, but he was also sixty and could be kicked upstairs for a year or so before taking early retirement. He certainly wouldn't be short of a dollar or two.

Sanders was a bit of a problem. He was in his early fifties

174

and couldn't be retired early, except on a very much reduced company pension. But . . . so what? He could count himself lucky to have got where he had got in an all-American company. He could be offered an MD job in one of the UK divisions which he would obviously turn down; but so what! From now on the locals would do what they were told to do by Detroit, and if they didn't like it they could take the option of either getting out of their own free will, or being booted out. He'd had enough of all that European political crap about overseas subsidiaries also having to represent the interests of the local host country where United Motors had a manufacturing presence. Bullshit. Their one and only interest was to serve the interest of the Corporation in the US of A and anyone in a top position overseas who didn't understand that number one lesson would soon have his nose put out of joint. From here on in, Randy Mueller was going to start calling the shots.

He reckoned that his chances of making the Presidency before he was sixty were now better than ever. He should make a Vice Presidency within five, the Presidency within ten. President Randy Mueller, the all-American boy who had made it from right here in his little ole home town of Detroit.

He rose from his enormous desk and lit a big cigar – it couldn't have been a Havana – and strutted around his vast office like a peacock, admiring his reflection in the long mirror. Randy loved himself and everything he stood for. It was surely great to be an American going up in the greatest company in the world and in the greatest country in the world. God bless America, and piss on the rest.

He walked to the phone, pausing on the way to take another admiring look at himself in the mirror.

'Miss Kopensky,' he barked.

'Yes, Mr Mueller, sir.'

'Get me Muldoon.'

'Yes sir, right away, sir.'

'And Miss Kopensky.'

'Yes, sir.'

'Have a nice day, Miss Kopensky.'

'Thank you, sir; have a nice day yourself, sir.'

'I will, Miss Kopensky, I will.'

. . .

'Mr Muldoon on the line, sir.'

'Hi ya, Pat buddy boy. Happy Thanksgiving.'

'You're a bit early, Randy. You puttin' the clock forward?'

'You could put it that way. A long way forward.'

'I don't get it.'

'No buster, but you will, you will.'

'Quit stallin' around Randy, will ya. What is it?'

'We got ourselves a new ball park,' said the man from Detroit. 'Nate and the Executive Committee have agreed in principle to phase-out all regional activities and bring the whole god-damned shootin' match right back here to Detroit, where I always said it should be.'

'You gotta be kiddin'.'

'Nope. I'm deadly serious. I produced some option plans and they took to it like a duck takes to water.'

'What, Nate and the Executive Committee?'

'Yep. Well . . . with a few exceptions.'

'You serious?'

'Course I'm serious.'

'You amaze me. That's a major organisational change. Fundamental policies.'

'Too damned right it is. And yours truly is in the drivin' seat. So hang on for the ride, Pat. It's all systems go.'

'And where do I fit in under the new organisation?' Muldoon asked. 'Do I get early retirement on full pension?'

'Sure do. Yes, siree. Just what you wanted. Now you can quit the heat of the kitchen and swan around on those yachts of yours you got stashed around the world.'

'Yeah, guess you're right. It's gotta be better than work.'

'At your age. You better believe it.'

'What about McGillicuddy?'

'He'll be all right. He'll be kicked upstairs for a year or so before taking early retirement.'

'And Sanders? What about him? He's only in his early fifties.'

'Yeah, well. We ain't gonna have no limey runnin' Europe from Detroit, that's for sure. It's got to be an American. You and I are gonna recommend Klepner. He's been doin' what he's been told to do, and feedin' me back all the inside information I need. I can trust him. He's the kind of guy I'm lookin' for to head up regional planning. Someone who will carry out Detroit instructions. I don't want Mister smart arse Sanders on my Detroit team.'

'Well, what's gonna happen to him?'

'Don't know for sure yet, but there won't be any European corporate jobs left after we centralise everything in Detroit. He can be offered a divisional job in one of the UK divisions I suppose.'

'Come off it, Randy. He won't go back to divisional work after ten years at corporate level. He couldn't possibly accept such a demotion.'

'Well, he ain't comin' here to Detroit, that's for sure. And I can tell you, buddy boy, that he's *persona non grata* with the US vehicle divisions after his comments about the future European trend toward smaller fuel economy vehicles at the EPC meeting.'

'Well that's the way things are goin' over here, and that's the way he sees it goin' in the future, under the Government constraints he outlined at that meetin'.'

'Well all I'm tellin' you, Pat, is that he's made a lot of enemies. Those guys don't like being questioned by Europeans. We run this business . . . not Europeans.'

.   .   .

Muldoon stared into space, his face expressionless.

'Hey Patrick. You still there?'

'Yeah, Randy,' Muldoon sighed forlornly. 'I'm here.'

'I want you to get Sanders out of the country just before next week's EPC meeting and keep him out until after the meetin's over. I want you to give the European components presentation to Klepner.'

'What's that?'

'No, correction. I want you to introduce the plan and then hand over the presentation to Klepner. You can introduce him as the guy you and I appointed some months back to work with Sanders on the preparation of the Business Plan. That way we can see that he gets the credit. It will also make it easier when you and I recommend him to take over from Sanders when we pull it back to Detroit. If Klepner's gonna get his job he may as well do the spiel. We can go easy on him with the questions, but I want Nate to be impressed. Get it?'

'Yeah . . . I guess so, Randy . . . if you say so. But I gotta tell you that I don't like it. It stinks.'

'Yeah, yeah. But before you can make an omelette you gotta break a few eggs, ain't that so?'

'But the Business Plan is his baby, Randy. He's put that whole damn thing together, almost single-handed. And it's not gonna be easy to get him outta the country. . . . He'll fight like hell to present it. I just don't like it.'

'Aw come on, Pat. You're making me cry. OK, so you lose some and you win some. Sanders loses. We can't all be winners. Anyway, don't you worry none. You'll be all right. Just do what I say, will ya? There's no point in you tryin' to swim against the tide now, is there? At your age, you'd drown!'

Muldoon winced visibly at the younger man's cruel analogy. But he was right. There was no point in swimming against the tide. At his age he really would drown and nobody in the Corporation would give a damn.

'Are you sure, Randy, that Nate and the executive committee agree with your proposals?'

'Of course I'm sure. What the hell do you think I've been talkin' about the last few minutes? Hey and listen, Pat, I don't want to see or hear any reference to that part of the plan which shows that we can save up to a billion dollars a year by supplying components from the European plants to fit US manufactured vehicles. That's not on. The US components divisions would hit the goddamned roof if that proposal was ever given the light of day. Is that understood?'

'Well, I hear what you're sayin' Randy, but I don't necessarily agree with ya. Mark was asked by McGillicuddy for some ideas by which European plants could reduce corporate operating costs on a world wide basis. Mark's right. European component manufacturing costs are lower than in the States, and we could save the Corporation around a billion dollars a year by purchasin' components from our European plants. So what's wrong with puttin' it up for discussion?'

'Because the US components divisions ain't gonna like it, that's why! We'd have a full scale fight on our hands with those guys if we went ahead with that proposal!'

'Yeah, but hang on a minute, Randy. Isn't that exactly what you are proposing to do in reverse? You and the Corporation have been telling us to purchase from our new subsidiaries in Taiwan, Korea, Singapore and even from Japan, for God's sake. Mark has told you guys many times that European Governments and European plant people ain't gonna like that one little bit, particularly when their own Far East markets are heavily protected. So what's different about Mark's plan to sell components from our European plants into the United States, if we can save the Corporation a billion dollars a year by doin' so?'

'Whose side are you on, Pat?'

'The Corporation's, Randy. Whose side are you on?'

'The Corporation's and Uncle Sam's. Aren't you?'

'My responsibilities are European, so are Mark's. If the Corporation wants to turn our suggestions down, so be it. But we represent the interests of our European plants, as well as the overall interests of the Corporation. How else do we explain to Plant Managers and to Governments that it's right for the Corporation to purchase products from non-European sources, but it's wrong to supply European components to the United States because the US divisions wouldn't like it?'

'Since when has the interest of the United States come second, Pat?'

'Since when have we had a Corporation plan which is not truly multi-national, Randy?'

'Since the year dot,' said the younger American with finality.

Muldoon was beginning to get an uncomfortable feeling that he was pushing his opinions too far, something he had never done in his life. He sensed the danger and eased back.

'Guess you're right, Randy,' he said submissively.

'Sure I'm right, Pat. You know that. Look, I'm simply tellin' ya to drop it out of the presentation, that's all. The executive committee won't go along with something which doesn't have the support of the US divisions. You know that. So why don't you do as I say and drop it? We will amend the plan from this end when we pull it all together. Just don't include it in the

179

presentation, that's all. Sanders has already got the US vehicle divisions lined up against him. No point you adding the component divisions as well. Be smart. Do as I say.'

'Yeah. I suppose you are right, Randy. It's a no-win situation.

'Attaboy. Now you're talkin'.'

'But I don't like it, Randy. It's dirty.'

'Yeah sure. But you'll do it?'

'What choice is there?'

'None, I guess, if you're still interested in your own future.'

'How do I get him out of the country? As I say, he'll fight like hell to give the presentation.'

'Don't worry. We'll cook somethin' up from this end. We got Government bastards crawlin' all over us out here with their beggin' bowls at the ready. How does he fancy Iran or Turkey? They are the two latest to join the beggin' bowl line. They'd love to see him down there. Lambs' eyes and bulls' bollocks for dinner. He'd just love that. I'll be in touch shortly to tell you what we've cooked up. Must go Pat. Nice talkin' to ya. Have a nice day.'

Muldoon lowered the phone slowly, shaking his head sadly. My God, what was the Corporation coming to when unscrupulous people like Mueller were influencing its future and the destinies of countless loyal, hardworking and respected executives on overseas operations?

What in the world would the company be like in a few years' time if such people were in the driving seat?

Well the answer to that question, he supposed, was that there wouldn't be an overseas Corporation to worry about.

What would be the world reaction when the full implications of the new World Car Plan under the new centralised organisation became more obvious?

What would be the reaction of local managers, of Governments, of the employees and the unions?

He shuddered at the thought of all the potential conflict situations ahead.

He was glad he was getting out.

14

Mark could hardly believe his ears when, two days before the EPC meeting, Muldoon told him that Nate wanted him to fly out to Istanbul right away.

It was true that a major problem had just cropped up which demanded immediate attention. The Corporation's major vehicle assembler in Turkey was in serious difficulties, due to the fact that the new Government had slapped an embargo on the importation of components to conserve its diminishing currency reserves. United Motors had received two urgent requests for assistance; one from the local Managing Director, who needed help to resolve his serious plant problems, and the other from the Turkish Prime Minister requesting UM investment support to reduce the country's massive trade imbalance. All this was fact. The fiction was that Nate had instructed Mueller to arrange to get Sanders down there quickly, when he had done no such thing.

Muldoon spun the line that the deteriorating situation in Turkey was clearly more important right now than the EPC meeting. Events there were taking much the same course as they had in Portugal, and as Mark had resolved that problem in double quick time, he was considered the best man to deal with this new problem situation.

All very flattering, but. . . .

The Englishman sensed that the big personal build-up was a blind to hide Muldoon's real reason for wanting him out of the country. He knew full well that the only circumstances in which a regional planning manager would not be expected personally to present his Ten Year Business Plan to the President of the Corporation was if he was already earmarked for promotion and it was desired to give visibility to his successor, or if he was on his way out. Mark knew that he would never be promoted after the Steiner incident so he concluded he must indeed be on his way out, or being moved sideways. Sensing the

181

game which was being played, he decided to throw several balls in the air for Muldoon to catch, if he could.

So he said that he would take the next available flight to Turkey immediately after the EPC meeting.

No, that was no good. Istanbul was expecting him. Meetings had been set up. Nate wanted him there straight away; like today; tomorrow at the latest.

'Well, give me a few minutes,' Mark said, 'and I'll ring the Prime Minister's office in Istanbul, to see if they'll agree to a short postponement.'

'No, you can't do that,' Muldoon replied hurriedly. 'It was Nate himself who had the meetings fixed up, and he wouldn't want them changed.'

'But nothing can be more important than the Business Plan,' Mark insisted. 'Nothing, but nothing, is ever allowed to take precedence over that meeting. Dammit, it's the future of the European components business I'll be talking about.'

'Yes, I know that, Mark,' the American countered. 'But Nate has specifically said that you are the man he wants to fly out to Turkey. I'll have to give the presentation on your behalf. After all, I am the Regional Manager.'

'But you never give the planning presentations. That's my bailiwick,' countered the Englishman, with growing resentment in his voice and manner.

'Yes, I know that, Mark, but. . . .'

The American couldn't continue the charade any longer.

Lowering his head, he said, 'I'm sorry, Mark, but that's the way they want it, and that's the way it's got to be. Klepner can check out the slides for me. They are all done, aren't they, and the text?'

Mark nodded his head.

'Yes, sure. Everything's finished.'

He only realised the finality of the phrase a second or so later. Muldoon didn't know quite what to say.

'I know you have worked your arse off to produce the plan, Mark, and it's a great one. No doubt about that. But if Detroit has its reasons, it has its reasons. It's as simple as that. I'll hold the fort and fill you in when you get back.'

Mark turned towards the door. It was pointless to argue further. Muldoon was simply carrying out instructions.

'Fill me in ... that's just about it, Pat, nice choice of words.'

He opened the door and turned toward the American.

'Who are you going to hand the presentation over to, after you have given the introduction?' he asked quietly.

They both said the name together – 'Klepner.'

.　.　.

Mark was sick at heart as he drove home that evening. He had a blinding headache and simply wasn't thinking of what he was doing as he swung the car off the slip road to enter the motorway. His thoughts were fiercely occupied elsewhere. Without even glancing in the mirror, he crossed the inner and middle lanes into the fast lane and, in fewer than ten seconds the speedometer needle was registering one hundred and fifteen miles an hour, but Mark was oblivious of the fact.

.　.　.

Suddenly conscious that he was flashing past vehicles which appeared to be dawdling, he glanced at the speedometer. He was doing one hundred and twenty! He jerked his foot off the accelerator and glanced in the mirror, heaving a sigh of relief that nobody was on his tail. Slowing to seventy, he made his way home.

He very rarely spoke about business matters to Georgina and decided on reflection against recounting the day's events except to say that he was leaving for Istanbul in the morning, and would be away for three or four days.

.　.　.

The Tri-star jet was two hours late on take-off from Heathrow, and then had to abort on the runway at lift-off point due to a sudden failure of one of the engines.

The pilot slammed the powerful jets into reverse thrust, bringing the giant plane to a halt just before he ran out of runway. In a very matter-of-fact voice he apologised for the shut down, due to engine failure, adding laconically that he had left ten thousand pounds worth of tyres on the runway.

'British Airways will not be at all pleased with me.' he remarked casually.

'There goes another Brownie point.'

. . .

By the time the plane approached Istanbul in the late afternoon, Mark had put away several large measures of single malt Scotch.

Mechanically he had taken each drink offered without thinking, for the simple reason that he had spent the entire journey staring out of the cabin window into the infinity of space.

His meeting was not until the next morning, so he could switch off for a few hours. He needed to do just that, for he was tired, morose and bitter and, for the first time in his life, feeling very insecure.

Gazing out into the blue, he asked himself if this assignment was his swan song. Must be, he concluded. Nate would never have taken him off the presentation if he wasn't being moved sideways or demoted. But why? To make way for Klepner, Mueller's pet poodle? It had happened before, to make way for Muldoon. Why shouldn't it happen again? If you couldn't trust the bastards then, why should you trust them now?

He closed his eyes. What made Nate and the executive committee think that guys like Klepner and Mueller knew more about the European components' business than the Europeans? What the hell would the US component divisions say if the executive committee was stupid enough to appoint Europeans to manage components operations in the United States? No prizes for guessing the answer to that question.

The blonde hostess leaned across him to re-charge his glass for the umpteenth time. His favourite Scotch, Glenlivet. Good old George and James Smith. Now there were two characters you could trust! So easy to relax and forget your troubles when you had a glass of their malt in your hand. . . .

He jerked forward with a start to find the hostess fingering with his seat-belt clasp.

'Just arriving at Istanbul sir. Please fasten your seat belt.'

. . .

Fred Clasper, the militant Merseyside convener, was a desperately worried man. Things weren't going at all well within the UK vehicle Division. Even his own notorious plant, which had consistently gone downhill for ten years under his active leadership, had been steadily increasing efficiency and output for several weeks without interruption. Morale on the shop floor was higher than it had been for a long year and an unhealthy atmosphere of optimism and hope pervaded the plant. Union members were openly expressing the view that there was a real chance that the ailing division would now pull out of its dive with the Peters' Plan, which had been fully supported by Bunker and a two-thirds majority at the plant.

To Clasper's disgust, the majority had voted against his recommended call for strike action and he now sensed all too painfully that he was beginning to lose control of his members. Management was once again managing, something which he had never allowed to happen during his ten years as convener. Arising from Clem Bunker's endorsement of the plan, new methods had been introduced which were greatly increasing earnings through higher productivity. Restrictive practices, which Clasper had fought so hard to introduce, were being discarded at a rate of knots in the quest to increase efficiency, output and earnings.

As a lifelong Communist, Clasper knew that it was absolutely essential to wrest control of the workers away from the plant management. He had exercised effective control of the labour force for ten years at the giant plant and had been able to bring the workers out on strike at the drop of a hat. It was he, Clasper, who dictated to management the size of the labour force they would require to produce a given number of products, regardless of any figure which management might arrive at by employing accurately measured work standards. If in effect, Clasper said that three men must be employed to do two men's work, then that was it.

On those occasions when he had felt the need to demonstrate his power to management, he would create an instant departmental dispute which always had the immediate effect of lowering that day's efficiency to below fifty per cent. Since the plant manager was never able to make up a day's loss of output which pulled down his monthly overall efficiency figures on which he was judged, it was never difficult for

Clasper to prove his point.

As he had always succeeded in getting his own way, the workers had been inclined to go along with him, even when their instincts told them that he was wrong. They really had no choice in the matter for he had always been able to threaten any dissenters, or strays, with the loss of their union cards. Successive personnel managers had always caved in to his demands as they knew full well that Clasper would win a stand-up fight.

Yet an uneasy feeling had been steadily growing among the ten thousand workers employed at the plant that the benefits which Clasper's militancy had achieved were illusory. Increased earnings, grabbed as a result of strike action rather than earned by increased productivity and profitability had always been subsequently eaten away by inflation. The Corporation was also no longer expanding its British operations, in marked contrast to the frequent expansion of its plants in Germany, Belgium and France.

Every long service worker employed at the plant and within the division knew that union restrictive practices had lowered productivity to below the levels achieved on the continent. These more loyal long service employees had an intuitive feeling that the division would ultimately go out of business in the UK if it continued to operate in the way it had behaved over the previous ten years. Even the notoriously militant workers at the Merseyside plant were now beginning to recognise that distinct possibility.

It was generally recognised that Clasper was not the man to dismantle restrictive practices, nor to co-operate with management to make the necessary improvements in labour relations if they were to keep their jobs in future. The majority now believed that Bunker's more realistic approach made more sense. Clasper was beginning to be seen by his own members for what he really was: a born agitator and trouble-maker who was great to have around when plant managements behaved like bastards because he was one too and would give as good as he got in a stand-up fight. But he certainly wasn't the man to have in the driving seat on the union side when both management and workers were striving for the sheer survival of the company, and needed to work together if they were to pull through.

It was being said quite openly on the factory floor that the only place Clasper would lead them to was the end of the dole queue.

The Communist convener could both feel and see that he was losing control. Fewer workers bothered to listen to him when he called meetings to protest against the Peters' Plan. He was also being subjected to cat-calls and ridicule. At one such meeting a heckler had got a great round of cheers from the assembled throng when he had told Clasper to get off his bloody soap-box and do a day's work for a bloody change.

To his disgust he found that the workers would no longer respond to his call for mass meetings during working hours. They now told him, in no uncertain terms, that if he had something important to communicate, he could do it in the plant car park during the lunch break, or after working hours. They were not disposed to lose both output and earnings by downing tools.

In desperation Clasper called a private meeting of the hard core left-wing stewards under his convenership, who could always be relied upon to fight against management and the capitalist system.

. . .

The British people had just elected a Conservative Government, headed by Britain's first ever woman Prime Minister, who had already earned the reputation of being 'the best man for the job' in the Conservative Party.

Within days of taking office, she had invited Don Peters to explain the problems which had bedevilled the British vehicle plants during the sixties and seventies and to outline his company's plan for the future.

Living up to her reputation, Peters found that she had done her homework thoroughly. She was tough and uncompromising.

She noted, she said with a pained expression, that output from the UK Vehicle Division of United Motors had been falling steadily over the previous ten years. At the same time, UM imports had been steadily rising, including very substantial imports from UM Vehicle Divisions on the Continent which had greatly expanded their total output and exports over the same period.

'United Motors used to make a very healthy contribution to Britain's export drive. Now you are the biggest single contributor to our balance of payments deficit,' she said acidly.

'Trends of this nature don't simply happen, do they?' she asked with feigned innocence.

'It has to be planned that way, does it not?'

She wanted to know what the UK Vehicle Division was doing to correct its appalling track record of recent years, particularly when compared with its Continental plants. She then ticked off several points she wished to make.

Don Peters had been pleasantly surprised to find the Prime Minister's forthright manner lived up to her advance publicity. The United Kingdom had a serious balance of payments problem in manufactured goods, which was only partly disguised by the revenue beginning to flood in from North Sea oil, which had a limited life. The problem had been seriously aggravated by the poor performances of UK vehicle producers – his own company foremost among them – and the Prime Minister naturally wanted to know what he was doing to correct the adverse trend. It was a straightforward and most pertinent question. He would have posed the same question if he had been sitting in her position.

For nearly half an hour, the American explained the plan which the Corporation had recently approved. He then answered the many penetrating questions put to him. In answer to one such question, he replied that he was pleased to say that he was now being given full support by the unions which drew the sharp retort. . . .

'NOT BEFORE TIME!'

Before she dismissed him she said unequivocally that it was the Government's intention to rebuild Britain's weakened manufacturing base and reduce the ever-growing importation of manufactured products.

'If industry doesn't help me to achieve the objectives of the Government, we will have to take appropriate alternative steps,' she had said with a steely smile.

'But I hope that won't be necessary. Thank you so much, Mr Peters for the chat. Most helpful. I will invite you to dinner when you correct your trade imbalance.'

Mark booked into The Istanbul Hilton in the mid-evening and, after a shower, returned to the lobby where he purchased a thriller before retiring to the comfort of an easy chair in the lounge.

He continued to drink quietly for another hour before going in to dinner. Afterwards he adjourned to the cocktail bar for a nightcap.

He was now feeling pleasantly intoxicated from the effects of a steady supply of alcohol, which had lifted his flagging spirits. He was now more at peace with the world of United Motors. Sipping a large Armagnac and enjoying the heady aroma of a Havana cigar, he had come to terms with the fact that life could, and would go on. Whatever lay ahead, maybe it was for the best.

All is for the best in this best of all possible worlds, he mused, blowing a great cloud of smoke into the air above him. That's what Voltaire's Pangloss had said, wasn't it? And just look at the problems which had faced poor Candide.

Maybe it was time for a change, anyway. Thirty years was a long time to stay with one company. Should have got out after the Steiner incident. Fool not to have done so. Early fifties is leaving it a bit late. Over fifty policy comes into effect. Fate perhaps. Do I believe in Fate? Really don't know.

'There is a tide in the affairs of man, which taken at the flood, leads on to . . .' heaven knows what and where.

A voluptuous blonde hooker in a long white gown entered the spacious bar. The front was slashed all the way down to her navel to reveal rounded breasts, which rose and fell temptingly like a couple of ripe peaches.

Just inside the entrance, she turned to survey the *clientèle*, making sure as she did so that all the men got a tantalising glimpse of a very long and elegant leg exposed through a side slit.

The bar was fairly full, with groups of local worthies and their wives and a clutch of broody businessmen. From the attention which focused on her, it was obvious that the blonde would make a sale in no time at all. Eyes turned as she walked slowly across the room, brushing by this man and that. To his surprise, she stopped when she reached Mark's chair and took the vacant seat beside him, nodding casually in his direction and flashing a devastating smile as she carefully arranged herself on display. She crossed her slender legs very slowly so that the panel of her dress fell away to reveal long, shapely limbs plus a glimpse of white satin briefs.

Mark smiled the appreciative smile of a man who was just looking, not buying.

Must be too expensive for the locals, he mused. Perhaps the fiddle sheet didn't run to outside entertainment more than once a month. Soaring inflation, perhaps. Up sixty per cent this year in Turkey, he'd read in *The Financial Times*. No . . . wait a minute. Devaluation of the Turkish lira. Down forty per cent. That's it! She's after the export business. She gives a much better exchange rate and gets forty per cent more lira for every pound, deutschmark or dollar she takes. Not bad, eh, when you're giving your all for your country?

She smiled again, which Mark again returned, even though he was not in the running. Just an interested bystander, studying the form in the paddock and placing bets on who would be the jockey who would saddle her up. Chap at the far end of the bar in a grey pin-stripe clearly fancied his chances. Been ogling her up and down ever since she'd entered the room. Down boy, down! She's too expensive for you, even after allowing for devaluation.

Where on earth were the Germans? They could afford her. God only knows how many lira there were to the deutschmark these days. Must be bloody millions.

He watched her fumble for an intentionally long time in her handbag for the means of lighting the Turkish cigarette she held aloft in her left hand, only a foot or so away from Mark's head.

He was an ungallant swine for deliberately not coming to her aid, but in truth he really wanted to see which of the likely lads, would dash forward. Surprisingly, there were no punters.

At long last she looked up imploringly from the depths of her tiny handbag, which prompted Mark to produce his lighter.

'Thank you,' she said, blowing a thin wisp of smoke in the air.

'I thought you'd never respond. Are you waiting for some-one?'

Her voice was cultured and unmistakably English.

'No, not really,' he replied. 'Just enjoying the parade in the paddock,' he added casually.

'So you ARE English,' she said. 'I thought so. Always give yourselves away, you chaps.'

'Is that so?' he asked. 'Do tell me, and what gives a destitute Englishman away in a foreign land? Decadence?'

'Style,' she replied, throwing her long fair hair over her shoulders and flashing him the toothpaste smile again.

'Style?'

'Style.'

He raised his eyebrows in surprise and softly sang the words of the song.

'So you've got, or you haven't got . . . style.'

She finished the next line, 'If you've got it, it stands out . . . a mile.'

They laughed together.

'Sanders. Mark Sanders,' he said, introducing himself.

'Will you have a drink?'

'Love one. White lady,' she replied. 'Destitute Englishman,' she scoffed dismissively. 'My eye. With those shoes? British and Harrods to the last. Name's Virginia, believe it or not. But my friends call me Ginny. More appropriate.'

'So that's what gave me away. My shoes. Well, bless my soul,' he said, with an air of exaggerated surprise.

'They haven't got holes in have they?' he asked in mock horror, glancing at the sole.

'I wondered why you sat next to me, when you obviously had the field to play. Why pick on me?'

'I've told you. Style.' she replied, with her winning smile.

'And yes, I do like the company of my compatriots. Miss home quite a lot. Daddy fell from grace, poor dear. Lost everything, so I came out here. Well, a girl's got to live, hasn't she?'

She added brightly, 'Much easier to be a fallen woman when you're miles from home. Must keep up the family tradition you know. Daddy always did say to do what you do best, and I am very good at it . . . so they say.'

'Are you now. . . ?' he replied.

'Excellent references.'

She took the cocktail which the waiter had just brought.

'Cheers,' she said, raising her glass to him.

'Happy nights to happy days.'

'Bottoms up,' Mark said, raising his glass in return.

'Of course. Bottoms up. Now that's an English expression I haven't heard in a long time. Must use it in the future. Very English and most apt.'

Mark glanced round the room.

'Look, sweetheart, mustn't keep you away from the punters. By the looks of 'em, they are all champing at the bit to place their bets. And you are the hot favourite, bonny lass. No doubt about that. The others haven't a look in. Not in your class.'

'Aren't you a gambling man?' she asked provocatively.

'No, not me. Not any more. With my luck, Ginny, I'd lose if I backed the only filly in a one horse race,' Mark told her, suddenly conscious of the fact that his speech was beginning to slur.

'You couldn't lose with me,' she said. 'I'd give you a very good run for your money.'

'I bet you would. But it's not your performance I'm worried about, sweetheart. It's mine.'

'Never lost a rider yet'

'Always a first time,' he said. 'Bit out of practice,'

They laughed together at the sexy banter.

'I like you,' she said. 'I like men who make me laugh. Especially in bed. I give encores, you know, when I'm happy.'

'At no extra charge?'

'No extra charge.'

'Bully for you,' said Mark approvingly. 'Always satisfy the customer if you are looking for repeat business. Reminds me of a piece of graffiti outside Saint Martin-in the-Fields. The poster said: "All ye who have sinned, enter here" and a bright girl had written underneath: "All ye who have not sinned, ring Maida Vale 123456".'

'Must remember that,' she laughed. 'Free advertising.'

'Smart girl. You'll go far.'

'How far do you want me to go?'

'I'm not sure I'm physically in good enough shape to take the excitement of the ride,' he said, raising his glass to her.

'Maybe you ought to find yourself a younger jockey.'

'Nonsense. You look in good shape to me, and anyway, I prefer more mature riders. They pace the race so much better.'

'Ah, the filly who prefers the leisurely canter to the short-lived gallop,' he said appreciatively. 'How eminently considerate. So what odds do you lay me finishing the course on the bookie's favourite?'

'Fifty,' she said promptly.

'Fifty to win is a lot of money to lay out on an untried filly.'

'Not this one, I promise you.'

'Dollars, or pounds?' he asked.

'Pounds of course. What do you take me for?' she asked in mock surprise.

'My dear Ginny, that's not in question. We've already established what you are. We are simply negotiating the price. . . ! As I think George Bernard Shaw once said.'

'You beast. Hardly the way to win friends and influence people,' she replied, pouting prettily.

'You can soon go off someone, you know.'

'Sorry. My mistake. Mosht ungallant.'

He blinked and shook his head to bring the room back into focus. His speech really was slurred now.

'So let's have a shtirrup cup before that happens.'

He signalled the waiter.

'Great idea.' she said. 'Bottoms up!'

.   .   .

A few minutes later, feeling decidedly the worse for wear after the last Armagnac had been downed, Mark moved unsteadily into the lift with his voluptuous mate.

As they entered his room, she reversed against the door, closing it with her bottom. Draping her arms over his shoulders, she cradled his head in the palms of her hands, pulling him toward her to close a hungry, wet open mouth on his.

Restlessly exploring with an eager tongue, she eased his

jacket from his shoulders. It fell noiselessly to the thick carpeted floor. He tugged at the zip on the back of her dress while she unbuttoned his shirt and removed his tie.

She let the dress fall, pushing him away gently to slip out of tiny white satin briefs. She was naked as she drew him towards her.

Her hands slid under his shirt, unbuckling, unzipping, thrusting on downwards. She kissed him again on the lips before mouth followed the path her hands were taking.

'Do you like me?' she whispered.

'Ask a silly question,' he gasped. 'Fantastic!'

And then, suddenly, without warning, a bomb-burst of excruciating pain exploded inside his skull and sent him reeling.

Head clasped in hands, he sprawled on the bed, gasping for air, as the room swayed crazily from side to side. It was sheer hell.

Frightened by what had happened, the girl bent nervously over him.

'Are you all right?' she asked tremulously, taking care not to touch him.

He struggled breathlessly to find the words.

'Yes . . . be all right . . . terrible pain . . . give me a few minutes . . . be OK.'

She looked at the crumpled figure who was fighting for breath on the pillow, perspiration pouring down his anguished face.

'Shall I get you a drink?' she asked.

He nodded.

'Scotch . . . on table.'

'Cigarette?' she asked.

'No.'

She poured two glasses and gave him one. In the semi-darkness Mark could see her movements. She had a most beautiful body which looked opalescent in the half light. He took a gulp at the Scotch and gave a wry smile at the injustices of this world which caused him to be smitten with another one of those blinding attacks just when he was about to make it. Well, they always said it was the only way to go and he believed it.

He was perspiring heavily as he sipped his drink, gazing

wistfully at the voluptuous creature who stood naked before him in the half light with a look of scared concern on her young face.

'Shall I get a doctor?' she asked, at length.

'No. I'll be OK.'

'Are you sure?'

'Sure. Feeling a lot better already. Thanks.'

He moved himself into a reclining position, head against the padded headrest. The room started to sway again and the pains in his head intensified.

'Told you I was too old a jockey,' he joked. 'Fell at the first fence.'

He was about to say 'game to the last' but thought again.

She smiled at his efforts to be funny.

'I was looking forward to the ride. Frustrated filly. Entered then scratched. What a palaver.'

'Have to be a stewards' enquiry,' he said painfully.

'Lot of money went on the favourite.'

'Under starter's orders, so I'm afraid no stake money refunded.'

'Of course,' he said. 'Jockey to blame.'

She walked to the bathroom and returned with a towel to mop his sweating face.

'That feels good. Thanks,' he said.

She sat on the bed, mopping his brow. He closed his eyes. Not a bad looking devil, she thought. More than just a few grey hairs here and there. Plenty of lines on his face, which she hadn't really noticed before, but which were particularly noticeable now. No matter. They gave him character and sex appeal. About fifty, she thought. Why was it that she always found herself attracted to older men? More interesting, she supposed. She liked a man with a sense of humour. Had a good figure. Quite looked forward to his love-making. Pity.

She continued to pat his face with the towel. Wonder who he is? she thought. International business man, that's for sure. Written all over him. Married. No doubt. They all were. Wife who loves him, but who has gone off sex. How often had they said that. No ring on his hand, but that was nothing to go by. Very few married men wore rings these days. Can't blame them. Better chance to play the field.

He was breathing less heavily now. Perhaps he was asleep. She dabbed his forehead.

'Are you asleep?' she whispered.

'No,' he whispered back.

He wanted to say: 'With a girl like you in the room?' but was too exhausted to make the effort.

She kissed him lightly on the lips and rose from the bed to get dressed. Taking his jacket from the floor she opened his wallet and took out two twenties and a ten before returning the wallet to the inside pocket. Putting the money in her bag she checked her face in the mirror and walked back to the bed.

'Are you asleep now?' she whispered.

'Yes,' he whispered back, with the faintest of faint smiles.

'I've taken the stake money,' she said. He nodded imperceptibly.

'Sorry you . . . but it wasn't my fault, was it?' she said.

He gave a slow shake of his head.

She pulled the bed cover over him.

' 'Bye darling. Feel better soon. Look me up again when you are next in town, won't you? We must complete the course.'

.   .   .

Mark woke to the strangely sad and beautiful cry of the Muezzin, whose plaintive voice drifted across the ancient city to greet another dawn.

The pains in his head had subsided, but he felt dizzy and sick, which he concluded was not surprising, considering the amount of alcohol he had drunk the day before.

He attempted to go to the bathroom, but found that his left leg wouldn't respond. It felt heavy and lifeless, in much the same way as it had felt that day in Spain when he had gone off the road. He rolled on to his side and rubbed the leg vigorously with his right hand. After a few minutes he heaved himself out of bed, but his leg let him down and he fell backwards. From a sitting position he rubbed and thumped the leg until it responded sufficiently for him to drag himself to the bathroom.

196

It was five o'clock. Hauling himself back to bed he lay awake for some time, before falling asleep. When he awoke again it was seven. To his great relief he found that the pains in his head had almost gone and that he could now move his left leg, albeit with some difficulty.

After a while he was able to stand. He then walked slowly and gingerly towards the bathroom, keeping as much weight as possible on his right leg.

A hot bath, followed by a cold shower worked wonders for his circulation, and he was now able to move more freely, though still with a pronounced limp.

He shaved, got dressed and took the elevator to the breakfast-room. He felt in reasonable shape, as he entered the local MDs office.

15

Nate Cocello, President of United Motors, had flown into London from Detroit with a posse of Vice Presidents to attend the bi-monthly meeting of the European Planning committee.

Chauffeurs had met them at their Inn on the Park hotel, at seven o'clock sharp; and at five minutes to eight they had taken their seats around the long elliptical table at European headquarters to ensure the meeting began on time, at precisely eight o'clock.

Randy Mueller was darting from one Vice President to another like an agitated blue-bottle. He was first on with his presentation, and had been there since six-thirty to make sure there were no slip-ups with his slide presentation.

He began by saying how glad he was to be in Europe again, which gave him an opportunity to outline some of the developments taking place in other regions of the world, and to describe the next phase in the development of the world car.

He highlighted the different approaches being made by the regions, putting sufficient emphasis on the distinctions and duplications to enable the assembled company to draw their own conclusions: namely, that the international business was getting too big for the regions to handle, and that the variations would lead to unnecessary proliferation if they weren't effectively controlled and directed by Detroit.

European General Director Clancy McGillicuddy coughed and spluttered at the innuendo and the local European Managing Directors weren't exactly overjoyed. They cast furtive glances at one another. Nate Cocello allowed a knowing smile to cross his face at what he knew would be the natural reactions of line managers. He had been one himself.

Mueller strode through the presentation aggressively. Was there any other way? Throwing up slides to make a point here, and stepping aside from the podium to develop a theme there, he exuded great confidence in the future of the great corporation.

He ended his presentation of forty-five minutes precisely, with the words, 'We have been the number one in the United States for many years, now we aim to be the number one in Europe, in South America, the Middle East. . . .'

'And all stations west of downtown Detroit,' whispered Don Peters under his breath.

The President and Chief Executive Officer looked around the table.

Spotting Muldoon, he asked, 'Any comments, Pat, from a components' viewpoint?'

'Not at this stage,' Muldoon replied nervously.

'How about you, Mark. . . .' began the top man, his eyes searching the long table for the Englishman.

'Say, where is Mark?' he asked, not being able to spot him. 'He's here, isn't he?'

There was an uncomfortable and meaningful silence. Other executives had already asked themselves the same question. The main item on the agenda was the Components' Business Plan. It was really Mark's show. Where the hell was he?

'Ah. . . . He couldn't make it,' Muldoon replied breathlessly. 'Fred Klepner here is standing in. That's right, Randy, isn't it?' he asked, calling across the table to get the question off his back.

'Yeah, Nate,' Mueller interjected confidently. 'We got problems in Turkey. Mark was out there at the time, so we asked him to help us sort it out. He's taking a few days' vacation out there, right now, so Pat and I thought it would be a good idea to let Fred Klepner stand in. He's been helping Mark put together the Business Plan and the presentation. That's right Pat, isn't it?' he asked, getting the tricky subject off his shoulders.

'Yeah. That's right, Randy,' the nervous American replied, almost choking on the words.

The top man was both amazed and damned angry that Mark wasn't there. Dammit, the Components Plan was the main subject on the agenda. He himself had specifically told Mark and Muldoon that he proposed to attend the meeting.

What was more important than that? And surely, nobody in his right mind would take a few days' vacation and miss out on the opportunity of selling his own plans and proposals to the President of the Corporation?

He shrugged his shoulders, his face expressing his thoughts. Every executive around the table could see that he was visibly annoyed by the Englishman's absence. They were under no illusions. If the Englishman hadn't blotted his copybook before, he certainly had now.

'OK. Let's move on,' said the President after a long and pregnant pause.

'Ye Gods!' he muttered, loud enough for all to hear. 'Can you beat it!'

.　.　.

The components presentation came on after lunch.

Muldoon nervously introduced the plan, saying that as Fred Klepner had been over on special assignment from Detroit to help Mark in the final preparation of the Plan and the presentation, he would hand over to Fred and let him take the committee through the proposals.

Klepner's big moment had arrived and the ex-Harvard Business School man strode confidently to the podium.

He had worked long hours to acquire a complete understanding of the Plan and to learn Mark's presentation word for word. He proceeded to explain the Plan, starting with a brief review of the world components market which positioned Europe to the rest of the world and led straight into the Plan.

The political and economic background and outlook was described, country by country, together with the principal assumptions on which the Plan was based. This led into a technical and commercial appraisal of European competition and the anticipated market changes over the next ten years.

Existing low profit products were to be corrected with a cost reduction and profit improvement plan, or phased out where such improvements were not economically feasible. New products were to be introduced with new plants to be located from a short list of low cost countries: namely Spain, Austria,

France, Portugal and the United Kingdom.

A manpower resources' plan summarised the personnel requirements by skill category and headcount, together with the required training programme.

The financial plan showed the investment impact on sales, profit and return on investment per year over the next ten years, while the financing plan described how the investment was to be financed: namely, from borrowings in the early years until the plan became self-financing from funds accrued from current operations, in year four.

The forty-five minute presentation concluded with a summary of the overall effect of the Plan on total European operations.

It appeared to roll forward and unfold under its own natural momentum, to reach its clearly defined objectives. It came across to Cocello and the committee in such a way that the presenter couldn't help but benefit from being associated with it.

Klepner stepped down fron the podium and waited for questions and observations.

'Fine plan you have there, Pat,' said the President approvingly. 'I like it.'

Turning toward Klepner he nodded his approval.

'Excellent presentation, Fred. Obviously a lot of thought has gone into the plan. It's good. Fine job.'

Klepner kept a straight face, but was overjoyed at the top man's response.

'Thank you, sir.'

Randy Mueller put the first question but, before doing so, added his congratulations to those of the President.

'Good show, Fred. You've done a fine job over here,' he said, omnisciently, with the air of a superior conferring praise on a subordinate.

'Would you care to explain to the committee why you are considering the UK in your short list of countries to be considered for the new investment proposals. I thought we'd all agreed at previous meetings that, with minor exceptions, all the major new plants would be located on the continent?'

The question was simply a put-up job, Mueller having previously primed both Klepner and Muldoon. The question was designed to give Klepner the opportunity to express a contrary view to Sanders, which, in effect, was that there should be no further new investment in the United Kingdom.

'We've included the UK on the short list, at this stage,' said Klepner, 'because Mark says that when the task force teams come to prepare the comparative cost studies in detail they will find that the economics of manufacturing certain new products will almost certainly favour production in the UK. Mark takes the view that if the UK is not to be considered for other than economic reasons, then that's a matter for the committee and the Corporation to decide. But he wants all the facts to be presented to the committee before a corporate decision is made not to invest in the UK.'

'What do you, personally, think about that approach, Fred?' Mueller asked.

'Well, I guess I agree with the committee's original view that we should not put any major new investment in the UK,' Klepner replied, knowing full well that this line would be supported by Mueller and most of the Americans around the table.

Mueller turned to Muldoon.

'What do you think, Pat?' he asked.

'Muldoon coughed nervously

'I tend to agree with Fred,' he replied.

Mueller then turned to the American Managing Director in charge of the British Components' Division, who was due for another assignment after nearly two years in the UK. He too knew the score.

'What do you think, Hal?' asked Mueller.

'Waal, based on the UK track record in recent years, I guess I gotta go along with Pat and Fred,' he replied, shaking his head slowly.

Cocello had listened without interruption. He addressed Muldoon.

'Let me get this straight, Pat,' he said, shaking his head in disbelief. 'You gotta European plan which includes certain major new investment proposals in the UK subject to detailed economic justification by the special task force teams. But you and Fred and Hal don't go along with UK investment. Is that right? Is that what you're sayin'?'

Muldoon shuffled his papers nervously.

'Waal, I guess I am and I ain't,' he replied.

'What the hell does that mean?' asked Cocello irritably.

Muldoon looked to Mueller for support.

'Waal, I guess I'm all in favour of the European plan,' he stuttered. 'I agree with you Nate . . . I think it's a good one, a damned good one. But I also agree with Randy here, and with Fred and Hal, that I'm not so sure about the UK side of the plan.'

'The President grunted and turned his attention to McGillicuddy.

'Sounds to me, Clancy, that you European guys ain't quite made up your minds about the UK,' he said.

Turning to Don Peters, he added, 'How about you, Don? They tell me that your proposals tomorrow will show the UK coming good . . . is that right?'

Don Peters smiled and nodded his head.

'That's right, Nate,' he replied confidently. 'You'll hear our proposals tomorrow but we are now beginning to see real signs of a big improvement at our UK vehicle plants. All the indications are that we are now forging ahead. We think that the UK is bullish in the years ahead and we are backing our judgement with further investment proposals.'

Several Americans around the long table, including Mueller and the head of the British Components division, were shaking their heads slowly. Peters saw their reactions and knew instinctively that he was going to have one hell of a fight on his hands the next day to convince the committee of his vehicle division proposals.

.   .   .

Fred Clasper's disruptive plan had been well prepared. In addition to the work of a small but dedicated group of left wing militants who held shop stewardships at the Merseyside plant, he had received expert academic advice from two university lecturers who were sympathetic to the Communist international cause. One was a lecturer at Oxford, the other at Liverpool University.

Like all such schemes prepared by left-wing militants, this plan was aimed at putting the company in a 'Catch 22' situation. Namely, whatever action the company took, it would be blamed for the ensuing conflict. To this end, one of the younger Communist shop stewards in the plot had agreed to be the fall guy. It was not a particularly difficult decision for him to come to, since he was going to emigrate to Australia anyway.

Company rules stated that, before a person could be dismissed for misconduct, two previous warning notes had to be formally given to the offender, placing on record the gravity of the offence. Dismissal following automatically if a third serious offence was committed.

The young Communist shop steward had no difficulty in obtaining the first two warning notes. He had switched-off the assembly track one Friday afternoon, half an hour before finishing time, ostensibly on the grounds that the overhead conveyor was unsafe and a danger to line operators working below. The foreman had naturally hit the roof over the loss of thirty minutes' production, which would pull down his departmental output and efficiency target and had roundly reprimanded the shop steward for taking such unauthorised action without first bringing the alleged safety hazard to his attention, in line with normal company standard practice.

There was, of course, no such safety problem, as the safety inspector subsequently confirmed, and the steward was given the first of the warning notes, as planned.

He obtained the second by pretending to trip over an unseen obstacle, which inadvertently threw him against the foreman, knocking him to the ground and depositing his daily schedule papers all over the floor. Both men had leapt to their feet and had been restrained from using violence by the mates of the shop steward, who just happened to be on hand.

One of the two witnesses, who also just happened to be the convener, Fred Clasper, claimed that a second warning note was unjustified as the foreman had been knocked down unintentionally. Nevertheless, as planned, a second warning note was issued.

After both incidents, Clasper had made it known, throughout the plant, that the young shop steward was being victimised and harassed by the foreman while on legitimate union business. It was alleged by Clasper that the foreman had his knife in the young kid who was only doing his job. 'The foreman is out to get him' was the expression making the departmental rounds.

Clasper and the conspirators timed the third offence to coincide with the visit to the UK of the President and Chief Executive Officer of United Motors, Nate Cocello, as this would provide maximum publicity to the planned strike. An attempt would then be made to drag Cocello into the dispute by Clasper making a public appeal to the President to reinstate the sacked shop steward over the heads of plant and divisional management. Either way, Clasper would win. The strike would once again demonstrate the power of the unions and would also restore Clasper's own flagging personal influence and power over the workers.

.   .   .

While Don Peters was on his feet on the second day of the meeting of the European Planning Committee, explaining his plan to rejuvenate the ailing British vehicle division, Fred Clasper was also on his feet setting in motion his scheme to put the final nail in its coffin.

Don Peters knew when he went to the podium that the odds were stacked heavily against him gaining the support of Nate Cocello and the committee.

The American's performance at the podium was masterly. He began by saying that with the UK vehicle division's track record over recent years, he couldn't really expect to receive any support to the plan he was about to describe. He then went on to identify each and every major problem which affected cost and profit performance, quantifying each problem area and finally consolidating the total cost penalty at no less than four hundred million dollars. He then described his proposals to reduce that cost penalty and turn the division from an operating loss into a satisfactory profit and return on investment. Finally, he threw up slides showing the improvements which had already been achieved over the last three months.

What came across to Nate and the committee, most of all, was Peters the leader. He had been given a tough assignment and he was in there fighting like hell on behalf of the British vehicle division. He gave credit to local management and to the unions, singling out the name of Clem Bunker for most of the industrial relations improvements coming through.

He ended his hour-long presentation with the words, 'We are on our way toward making the division one of the best goddamned outfits in overseas operations, and I just want to be given the chance to prove that the plan which I have outlined to you today is the right one for the British operation, for Europe and for the Corporation.'

Even Americans round the table, who didn't give him a snowball in hell's chance of getting approval to his plan, had to admit that he was still in there, fighting like a demon for a lost cause.

He handled the many questions in masterly fashion, particularly the probing questions from Cocello. He was in the hot seat for more than three hours. He had gone to the podium at eight o'clock. By noon he had obtained Nate's approval and had won the day.

.   .   .

The Merseyside convener was aware that President Nate Cocello was coming to the UK for talks with British and European management. The grapevine always flashed advance notice of such events, though it was never hard to guess when a VIP visit was imminent because of the frenzied housekeeping activity at each plant which always preceded it.

Clasper saw Cocello's arrival at Heathrow on television. When asked by an interviewer if he was pleased with the performance of the British plants, the President had replied that although past performance had been bad by traditional British standards, he was now happy to say that in recent months a marked improvement had taken place. This enabled him to look forward with confidence to continued improvements which would put the British plants back at the top of the performance league, where they used to be, and where they belonged.

Clasper had other ideas, however. On the day that Don Peters was on his feet at the EPC meeting, fighting for the survival of the British Vehicle Division and the jobs of the fifty thousand people it employed, Fred Clasper was setting in motion the third and final stage of his scheme to sabotage any possible chance of the company's recovery.

206

It had been arranged by the conspirators that the young shop steward, who had already collected two warning notes as planned, would take out a set of spark plugs in his lunch box at the mid-day break. One of the conspirators would ring the foreman to tip him off that the shop steward could be caught red-handed stealing company property if they searched him at the gate. The foreman would naturally advise the security men on the gate, and Personnel Department, which would result in the steward being apprehended and instantly dismissed. He would plead that the plugs had been planted by someone who bore a grudge against him, and the story would be quickly put round the plant that it was the foreman himself who had fixed it, to settle an old score.

Credibility would be given to the shop steward's story by having his lunch box placed in an unauthorised position on the assembly track from which the foreman would have to remove it, and be seen doing so.

Everything went according to plan and at noon the steward was stopped at the gate. The spark plugs were found in the lunch box as arranged and he was immediately dismissed in accordance with company practice. In itself, the offence justified instant dismissal under company rules. The two previous warnings received by the steward made it inevitable.

Clasper was present in the Personnel Manager's office when the offence was read and the dismissal notice formally handed out. That afternoon the convener communicated his version of the story to the shop steward's committee and within an hour every department was buzzing with the news. It was well known that the foreman and the shop steward in question were always in dispute, and it appeared to the majority that the foreman had, in fact, set him up to get rid of him and to settle an old account.

Production was severely disrupted in all departments during the afternoon as the shop stewards spread the message. At four o'clock they fed back the feelings of the workers to the convener, and at five minutes past four, Clasper took the giant plant out on strike, advising the Personnel and Plant Managers that they wouldn't return until the sacked shop steward had been re-instated.

The majority had no wish to stop work, particularly after the great strides which had been made in recent months, but they weren't going to be sat on either. To them it sounded like a straight forward case of victimisation by the foreman.

.   .   .

The message that the big Merseyside plant was out on strike was conveyed to Don Peters at the EPC meeting. One of the secretaries entered the conference room with a message to ring the Plant Manager urgently.

'The plant has stopped work,' she added.

The pain on the American's face was clear for all to see as he rose from his chair and left the meeting to make the call. On his return, he immediately communicated the bad news to his boss, Clancy McGillicuddy, and to Nate Cocello, by handing them a copy of the statement put out by the Plant Manager. Nate closed his eyes and shook his head in disbelief. Clancy McGillicuddy was furious. What in God's name had happened to the British?

Peters nodded his agreement.

'Yeah,' he sighed. 'Yeah, Nate. I know. I know.'

The President shook his head.

'I'm not blaming you, Don. You've worked your arse off to solve this problem. But they ain't gonna let anyone help 'em. Those Merseyside bastards are hellbent on destroyin' themselves and every poor management sod unlucky enough to be involved with the plant. It's a bloody graveyard of top talent.'

'Yeah. Yeah, Nate,' Peters sighed again. 'I'm afraid it looks that way. But the plan is a good one, and it would work, if only they'd give it a chance.'

All the infectious enthusiasm had gone out of his voice and manner.

'Sure. But they won't,' the top man replied. 'So we'll have to change direction. I'll tell Mueller to get a team down here from Detroit to get things started. The locals ain't gonna like it, but they've ballsed-up their chances. From here on in, we go back to the original plan to phase-out vehicle manufacture in the UK and import instead. Passenger cars from Germany, Belgium and the proposed Spanish plant, and commercial vehicles from our new joint venture operation in Japan. We just can't take any more risks by manufacturing in the UK. It's

208

too damned unreliable. Don't you agree, Clancy?'

'Wish I could disagree with you, Nate, but I can't,' replied the European General Director.

.   .   .

After dinner that evening, Cocello instructed Randy Mueller to set up a task force team from Detroit to come up with a phase-out plan for vehicle manufacture, and a phase-in plan for supplying the UK market from imports,

'It's gotta be the right thing to do,' agreed Mueller readily.

'Today's events only confirmed what we already knew.' Cocelleo nodded sadly.

As an afterthought, Mueller added, 'What about the Components' Plan? Do we go ahead with the UK side of that? Or do we phase that out, too?' He hurried on. 'Guess we should be consistent, shouldn't we? We can hardly tell the Finance and Executive Committee that the British are unreliable at the vehicle plants, but as solid as the Rock of Gibraltar when it comes to components.'

'No, we can't,' Cocello agreed. 'Though for some totally inexplicable reason that seems to be the truth. But you're right, Randy. The Components' Plan would lose all credibility if we included the UK. Better tell Muldoon to make the necessary changes.'

Mueller immediately saw his opportunity.

'Why don't I get the Detroit task force team to co-ordinate both the vehicle and components' phase-out plans in the UK?' he asked. 'Sure as hell the locals ain't gonna like doing it themselves. We'd be fightin' a never-ending rearguard battle with those guys. Sanders also ain't gonna like it, that's for sure. He'll be fightin' for his European Plan as submitted; including the UK element.'

'Yeah. Perhaps you're right Randy,' said the top man. 'Maybe you should take both plans on board and control them from Detroit. At least that means that we can do it our way. Sanders can't be all that interested in the Plan if he takes a few days vacation rather than give the presentation. Jeez, that amazes me, as well as riles me.' he added, shaking his head in disbelief.

'What makes a guy like that behave that way? I just don't understand it.'

Mueller never turned a hair, or felt a twinge of remorse. As far as he was concerned, he had just knocked another competitor out of the promotion stakes.

'It's gotta be right, chief,' he replied enthusiastically. 'I don't think we can really plan overseas' operations effectively, until we get full planning control from Detroit. The European operation is too damned big a slice of the corporate business to be left to the locals. Today's events only confirm what we've been sayin'.'

The President and Chief Executive officer gazed into his Scotch. He was still uneasy about Mueller. He remembered what he had put on his personal qualities' file: 'Judgement not always reliable in the political and commercial area'.

He looked long and hard at the younger executive as if trying to sum him up.

'OK, Randy,' he said after a long pause. 'Go ahead. The Committee agreed in principle to your initial proposals. Not unanimously, mark you, but the majority. Put up a detailed proposal for consideration when we get back, and we'll see if they buy the specifics.'

16

That same evening Mark Sanders was dining alone in Istanbul after a satisfactory series of meetings with the local Managing Director and the Turkish Minister of Economic Affairs.

He had declined an invitation to dinner, as the stabbing pains in his head had been getting steadily worse throughout the day. They were now blindingly bad.

He placed his unfinished cigar in the ash tray and rose from the table, leaving his brandy untouched. He had decided to go to bed early.

After lying in a hot bath for an unusually long time, he stretched out on the bed, eyes closed, hoping that the pains would go away. But he couldn't get the thought out of his head that in London, that very day, Muldoon and Klepner had given HIS Ten Year Plan to Cocello.

The more he thought of the two carpet-baggers standing up at the podium, the more intense the pains in his head became. He put a hand to his forehead to ease the pressure.

Nate couldn't possibly have believed that the Turkish problem was more important than the European Plan. Not in a million years. In which case the reason was blindingly obvious. Muldoon had more than hinted at what was happening. Detroit was paving the way for Mueller to take over and run the whole bloody show from America. That's what he had always wanted to do, and Klepner was his advance guard. His mole. His trained pet poodle who had been sent to Europe to reconnoitre the scene and steal Mark's clothes. He would then take over the European Components' planning activity when everything was centralised in Detroit.

He thumped his pillow with his fist. The bastards are at it again, he said to himself, vividly recalling the Steiner incident in New York. Only this time it's curtains. He was finished. This had got to be the end of the road. He stared at the ceiling.

How would he and Georgina change their lifestyle after all

those years as a corporate executive? How would they live? What would happen when the monthly cheque was no longer paid into the bank? What about the mortgage and the school fees? They go on for ever. Well, until sixty-five, and that's a hell of a long way away. What would they do in the interim? They'd have to move to a smaller house, that's for sure.

My God, how would he tell Georgina? It would break her heart to leave the lovely old stone barn in Buckinghamshire. How could he keep Andrew at Agricultural college? Well they would, somehow or other. They'd done it for Adam and Christopher and they'd do it for him. But how would he break the news to Georgina that he'd let her down after all these years?

He fell asleep, but the pains in his head were still there when he awoke in the morning.

. . .

Clem Bunker was in a rare-rage. He had completely lost his temper when he had heard the news that Clasper had taken the giant Merseyside plant out on strike. Bunker had received the message from a convener at one of the Midlands plants, who was also hopping mad. And so, he said, were all the shop stewards at his plant, who were expressing the view that, once again, the Merseysiders were taking the law into their own hands, breaking national agreements and overturning official union policy.

The Midlands' shop stewards knew it was only a question of time before the strike affected supplies to their own plants and those in the South, jeopardising the recovery plan which had been producing such vast improvements in performance. Morale had been at its highest for years, up to the moment that the news had reached them that Merseyside was out.

'Clasper's behind this!' Bunker was furious. 'He was dead against the plan and now he's doing his damnedest to wreck it.'

'That's what everyone round here is saying as well,' the convener agreed. 'It's his Commie mate who got the chop. And nobody believes Clasper's version of the story. It's all too bloody coincidental.'

'Is that really the majority view at your plant?'

'Well, it's not often the majority express themselves without

212

some prompting from the shop stewards,' the convener replied, 'but in this instance the reaction was instantaneous. We heard the news over the radio at lunch break and I tell you, Clem, my lads are really up in arms. Nobody believes this cock and bull story about the sacking incident. They all know that Clasper's behind it. Who the hell does he think he's kiddin'? He's certainly not kiddin' my blokes.'

'Is that what the majority are really saying at your plant?' asked Bunker.

'Loud and clear,' replied the convener. 'They are sick to the eyeballs with Clasper and his bloody political conscience strikes. A hell of a roar went up in the canteen at lunch break when one of the shop stewards said that Clasper would go on fighting on behalf of the workers until every bloody one of them had lost their jobs. That's what my lads think about Mister bloody Clasper. The question is, Clem, what are you going to do about it?'

'I'm going to contact all the plant conveners, when I put this phone down, and call an emergency meeting,' Bunker told him. 'In the meantime, get the shop stewards at your plant to take an accurate reading of the majority viewpoint without influencing the men either way. Initially, I want the gut feel of the members. We can take final readings and decide on an official union line when we know all the facts. I'm going to ask the other plant conveners to do the same.'

'OK, Clem,' the convener said quickly. 'Will do.'

That evening, Bunker phoned Peters at The Inn on the Park to tell him that he had called an emergency meeting of plant conveners to help resolve the Merseyside problem. He was dismayed by the American's response.

There was more than a hint of weary resignation in his reply. All the old fighting spirit and enthusiasm had gone.

'Yeah. OK Clem. Thanks for ringing. and thanks for all the effort that you have put in personally. Just sorry it has turned out this way.'

He sounded like a beaten man.

News of the strike made headlines in all the British newspapers. It was also given in-depth coverage on television and radio that evening, with *News at Ten* running it as the lead story in the first half of the programme and coming back to it again in the second.

Clasper was interviewed outside the giant Merseyside plant and predictably blamed management for deliberately provoking the strike.

'Are you really saying that the company is to blame for the strike?' the man with the microphone asked, thrusting it under Clasper's chin.

'Well you don't think my lads would be out here just for the bloody exercise, do you?' Clasper demanded sarcastically. 'Course they're to blame. Stands to reason. And my lads are staying out until Management reinstates the innocent victim.'

'And is that the only thing which would influence you to call off this strike, which is obviously doing great harm to the company and the country?' the interviewer asked.

'Nothing more and nothing less,' replied Clasper. 'I'm already havin' to ask the lads to exercise great restraint over this particular issue. They want me to insist that the company sacks the foreman before they go back, but I've told 'em I won't be a party to victimisation either way.'

'Thank you, Mr Clasper,' said the interviewer. 'Now back to the studio.'

And there the newsreader told the British people that efforts had been made to obtain an interview with the local Plant Manager, who had declined to comment. The President of United Motors – who was in London at that moment – had also declined to comment on a local issue which, he had said, was a matter for local management.

The inference viewers gained was that management was to blame in one way or another.

. . .

When he returned to the States, Mueller lost no time in carrying out Cocello's instructions to direct the phase-out of UK vehicle operations from Detroit, and to prepare detail plans to centralise European and world planning activities.

His first step was to request that all copies of the European Vehicle and Components' Plan be withdrawn from circulation.

Having thus effectively stopped the Plans dead in their tracks, he then proceeded, in the name of the President, to dry

214

up the outward flow of all planning information from Detroit, so that, from that moment on, only he and members of the world planning group would be aware of what was going on, worldwide, at the planning stage.

Mueller thus gained immediate planning control of world wide operations, even before he had formally received top management approval to proceed.

The President had given Mueller an inch, but he had already taken a mile. This tactic was not unusual in the Corporation. Mueller had simply used his privileged position to advise the General Directors that he was operating on the instructions of the President. He would use that authority to his own personal advantage.

17

Mark Sanders returned from Istanbul feeling exhausted, depressed and ill. The blinding headaches he had been experiencing in recent weeks were taking their toll, and he looked grey and drawn when he arrived home.

Lately, Georgina had been worried by the general deterioration in his appearance. But now she was visibly shocked by the drained and haggard-looking face which kissed her.

She wanted to say, 'You look awful, darling,' but decided against it.

'What kind of a trip have you had?' she asked instead.

'Oh, not too bad,' he replied wearily.

She took his suitcase and placed it at the bottom of the stairs.

'Come into the kitchen, and we will have a cup of tea. I've so much news to tell you. All sorts of things seem to have happened while you have been away this time.'

Mark smiled thinly and kissed her affectionately on the cheek.

'Tell me about it,' he replied. 'I could do with a good laugh.'

'Why darling? What's the matter? Trouble at t'mill?'

Mark slipped an arm around her slim waist as they walked from the hall into the kitchen.

'Perhaps it's old Montezuma's revenge,' he replied. 'Must be getting too old for this globe-trotting lark, or else my misspent youth is catching up on me. I'm rapidly coming to the conclusion that this is a young man's game.'

'Nonsense, Mark. You're still a young man ... well, youngish.' she said, trying to tease him out of his apparent lethargy and depression.

'Let's have that cup of tea and you'll feel better.'

'Ah, fill the cup, what boots it to repeat, how time is slipping underneath our feet,' he quoted with a sigh.

'Oh darling. What a sad sack we are today. Is that how you feel? Shall I accompany you on the violin? Now let me tell you all the news.'

She poured the tea.

'Christopher has been promoted after only one year. The Chairman of the company told him he was most impressed with the contribution he's made to the business, and that he could go right to the top if he keeps it up. I knew you'd be delighted to hear that.'

She sipped her tea.

'Next . . . I've found a super husband for Harriet. Champion of the breed at Crufts last year. Lives in the next village, believe it or not. Absolutely magnificent dog.'

'Lucky Harriet,' said Mark.

'What else? Ah yes; a Secretary at the Ministry of Industry wants you to ring him. Seems they want you to address the European Commission on European industrial development. In Dublin, I think she said. Something about the factors which influence multi-nat location decisions. Anyway, you'll know what it means when you see it. I've written it all down. Oh and yes . . . a chap from Conservative Central Office rang up to say they'd like to know if you would be prepared to stand for the European Parliament. He sounded somewhat to the right of Genghis Khan. I said I didn't think so, as you were rather busy, but I'd pass the message on. Hope I did the right thing. I said you never knew where you were from one week to the next. He said that would do nicely. Just like the American Express advertisement. Perfect credentials apparently, for European parliamentarians.

'Now what next? The Chicheley-Smythes have bought an absolutely super villa in Sardinia and say we could rent it if we'd like to. I've seen the photographs. Gorgeous location overlooking a quiet bay. It sleeps ten with a permanent staff of three. Only a thousand pounds a week, yacht included. I'd love that for two or three weeks, wouldn't you?'

'We wouldn't want to stint ourselves,' Mark said facetiously, 'four or five, I should think. . . .'

'And we could take the family,' she said. 'We haven't had a family holiday for years. I'd like that. But we can talk about that later. And I've decided to take up riding again. Don't ask me why. Just got the urge, that's all.'

217

She gave him a beautiful smile, which lit her lovely face.
'Well, how's that for starters?' she asked.
He had heard that expression before.
'Is there more?'
'Now let me see. Ah, yes . . . Andrew's coming home for the weekend so I thought it would be nice to have a drinks party. I've invited the Bunkers, if that's all right. I like Clem and Gwen and the girls would be nicer company for Andrew.'
'Fine,' agreed Mark without much enthusiasm. 'If Clem can make it, that is. I heard about this latest Merseyside strike in Istanbul. Could finish off the UK vehicle division,' he said forlornly, 'and Don Peters,' he added, shaking his head. 'Some of the stupid bastards won't be satisfied until we no longer make a single vehicle in the UK. Then I suppose they'll say it's all management's fault, and people will believe them. And who the hell IS management?' he demanded, his voice rising. 'People like me, who've worked their guts out to expand the business while the militant bastards have been working their guts out to destroy it.'
Georgina was nodding agreement. She patted his wrist.
'I'm quite sure you're right, dear. But we weren't talking about the motor industry and the never-ending management-union saga. We were talking about Andrew coming home for the weekend and having the Bunkers round for drinks. And I do wish you wouldn't swear like that when you talk about business. You never used to swear, you know. At least, you didn't when you were with me. But you do now, darling, and I do wish you wouldn't. You are becoming so hard and bitter and it's not really like you.'
Mark sighed.
'I'm sorry. It's just. . . .'
'It's just that there really is trouble at t'mill,' she said quietly. 'That's it, isn't it? You weren't going to tell me. You were just going to worry about it alone. You let me go rabitting on. . . .'
He hugged her; kissed her cheek.
'I'm not sure yet that there really is something to worry about.'
'But you think there is.'
He nodded.
'I have a horrible feeling that UM is about to reorganise

218

world-wide planning operations and, if that happens, it's curtains for the European organisation and for me.'

'Curtains?' she said. 'What exactly would that mean?'

'Early retirement.'

'Mark, you're not serious!'

'I think it could be on the cards. They could transfer me to Detroit, or somewhere. I don't know, but I don't like the signs.'

'Oh, Mark,' she said. 'They wouldn't do that to you. They just couldn't. Not after all you've done for the Corporation. They couldn't be that unfair and ruthless.'

His expression was wry.

'My dear, they'll do whatever they feel is necessary to do. Sentiment, loyalty, service and track record, none of these things will come into it.'

Georgina took him in her arms and kissed him on the lips.

'It's all so ridiculous that we're not going to even think about it any more,' she said firmly, hiding her fears.

'Now come into the garden,' she added, smiling. 'I want to show you the clematis. It's a mass of colour.'

.   .   .

Lying in bed that evening, they talked a lot about their life together. They recalled their first days. The county ball. The Paul Jones and the emotional somersaults when the music stopped and they came face to face for the very first time. The wedding. The birth of their first son, Adam, and then Christopher and Andrew. The children growing up with all the laughter and tears. Schooldays and the void they both felt when the boys went off to boarding school, followed by the joy unconfined when they came home at the end of term. Mark's promotions and progress up the company ladder. New and changing homes. Friends lost and friends gained. Family achievements and disappointments.

Notwithstanding current problems which they discussed lightly, it had all been wonderful.

They fell asleep in the early hours of the morning, holding hands.

.   .   .

The next day Mark arrived back at UM's European headquarters in London and received an early call from Muldoon. He went down the airless corridor to his Boss's office, said hello to the secretary, and walked into the large oak-panelled room which was as big as the lobby of many a sizeable hotel.

Muldoon rose immediately from his enormous black leather chair to greet him, coming from behind the vast desk with hand outstretched.

'Hello Mark. Have a good trip?' He took the Englishman by the arm and ushered him toward the easy chairs arranged around a long rectangular coffee table.

Instinctively, Mark felt uneasy. Why the hand on the arm and the over-friendly approach? Muldoon never emerged from behind his desk to greet colleagues. Only visitors and VIPs got that special reception.

Muldoon poured the coffee.

'How did the Planning meeting go?' Mark asked him. 'What was Nate's reaction? Did he and the Committee go along with my proposals?' he added.

'It went fine,' Muldoon said. He seemed somewhat uneasy.

'Klepner did a good job.'

'How did he handle the questions?' Mark asked. 'He doesn't have the inside knowledge to deal with questions.'

'Oh, OK really. I handled some and so did Mueller. But Klepner did OK. He didn't let the side down.'

Mark nodded.

'What was Mueller doing answering questions. He was there to ASK them. He doesn't know the inside track any more than Klepner.'

'Maybe not, but he soon will,' Muldoon replied quietly.

'And what does that mean?'

Muldoon seemed to be taking a long time over his coffee. He evaded Mark's eyes.

'He's goin' to head-up world planning operations from Detroit.'

'He's already co-ordinating the regional plans to provide a world picture. So what's changed?'

Deep down he knew.

'He's not going to just co-ordinate and consolidate any longer,' Muldoon said, with increasing nervousness. 'He's gonna

220

plan, direct and control worldwide planning operations from Detroit, including the regional planning functions.'

Mark's expression was one of faked incredulity. His gut feelings had been right.

'You've got to be joking!' he scoffed. 'I know that's what Mueller's always wanted, but Nate and the Executive Committee would never fall for that bloody empire-building game! The regions are far too big and complex to be handled from Detroit and even if they were foolish enough to believe that they could do it more effectively – which they can't – they would be crazy to try.'

'I know, Mark, I know,' Muldoon said. 'But that's what they're gonna do.'

'It will boomerang,' the Englishman said heatedly.

'Overseas Governments and local nationals just won't stand for it, particularly when they get to know what's going on. That's one corporate plan that can't win, not in the long term.'

'I know, Mark. But they think they can run everything from Detroit and that's the way the organisation is going to be restructured. They are working on it right now. We will know the details in a few weeks' time. Couple of months at the latest.'

Mark said quietly:

'And how does that affect the European organisation?'

'The organisation will be wound up. I'm taking early retirement.'

'And me?'

Muldoon shrugged.

'Not certain yet. But my guess is early retirement too, unless you're prepared to go back to divisional work. Local MD perhaps?'

The Englishman snorted.

'You know I can't go back. Who the hell can? In any case, you know as well as I do that the MDs are always American.'

'Well, there won't be any European job functions, that's for sure,' Muldoon said. 'There'll be a direct link between Detroit and the line managers in each country, with Detroit calling the shots.'

'Don't they realise they're playing with political dynamite?'

Mark demanded. 'Mueller won't give a damn about the effect of a corporate plan on Europe and on individual countries. If he wants to import vehicles or components from Taiwan or Singapore or Hong Kong into Europe, he'll go ahead and do it, regardless of the economic consequences for the European countries concerned. The only thing you can be sure of is that US interest will always come first.

'Oh, and there's one more thing you can be sure of,' he added sourly. 'They won't plan to supply the US market from imports. You can bet your bottom dollar on that! Jesus wept!' he continued, hackles rising. 'Mueller will have the power to make or break whole areas of Europe. He's the last guy in the world who should be given such power. The bloody man's power drunk already.' He was angry and bitter.

'I know,' Muldoon agreed sadly.

'Then what are you and Clancy doing about it?'

'Look, Mark,' Muldoon said forlornly 'What's the point? The wheels have already been set in motion. We're not gonna change anyone's mind. You know that.'

His tone was abject.

'Sorry you're takin' it so bad,' he added miserably.

'How else should I take it?' Mark demanded. 'It's my life which is about to go down the plughole. I'm not an American on a brief overseas assignment. I've spent my entire working life in the European components' business. I've grown up in it. It's in my blood. I've built plants and managed them. Designed products and marketed and sold them. When I was an apprentice there were two component plants in Europe, and now there are seventeen, and I've had a hand in establishing the last twelve. What the hell do you expect me to say? Oh, is that what they are proposing to do? Well bully for Mueller and the Corporation? I'll go and collect my hat and coat!'

'I know how you feel, Mark,' Muldoon said sadly.

'Do you, Pat? Do you? You're sixty-one and have been looking forward to retirement. I'm fifty and have a long way to go. I don't think you can see things the way I see them.

'Well, perhaps not,' Muldoon agreed. 'But I can understand how you feel.'

The Englishman nodded and poured himself more coffee.

'So what's going to happen to the European Plan?' he asked.

'Mueller will drive it from Detroit, with one or two amendments agreed at the EPC meeting,' Muldoon told him.

'What amendments?'

'No further plant investment in the UK.'

'I suppose Mueller saw to that,' Mark said sarcastically. 'He really hates our guts! God help the British plants under the new regime!'

Muldoon shook his head.

'No, it wasn't that. It was the strike at Merseyside. That was the last straw as far as Nate was concerned. Up until that news hit the Committee, Don had won the day with his UK Vehicle Division proposals. But as soon as Nate heard about the latest strike, that was it. End of story. He instructed Mueller to phase-out vehicle manufacture in the UK.'

Mark nodded.

'How did Don take it? He was beginning to win through.'

'He's very upset. Naturally. It's the first time in his career he hasn't come out on top. Mueller is taking over the plan, and Don is being transferred back to the States. Public relations job or something similar. Just think of it, a man of his talent and ability stooging around the media.'

'So when's he going back to the States?' Mark said.

'It won't be announced for a week or so, but he's already been told. He'll fly out inside the month.'

'And what do you and I do now? Mark enquired. 'Start emptying the files?'

Muldoon made a face.

'Afraid so. Klepner will take over the files and ship them back to the States. He'll be Mueller's European components' Planning Manager in Detroit.'

'Klepner?' Mark uttered in mock astonishment. 'The man knows nothing about Europe. He's a novice. A bloody charlatan!'

'I know it sounds crazy, Mark,' Muldoon said. 'But there it is. We have no choice in the matter. I was instructed to tell you, and I have. New York and Detroit will come up with an attractive separation package, you can be sure of that. They've already told me you'll get the maximum terms permitted under British law. The Corporation wants to do the right thing by you.'

223

The two men rose from the table together.

'Sure. We have no choice in the matter,' said the Englishman.

'There has to be losers as well as winners,' said the American. 'I guess we're both losers, Mark.'

. . .

The Englishman returned to his own palatial office and sat with his head in hands. Another of his blinding headaches had developed and he felt a tight sensation in his chest, which made breathing very painful and difficult. His secretary entered the room.

'Can I get you a coffee, Mr Sanders? You don't look at all well. Shall I get the doctor?'

He looked up and smiled.

'No thank you Millie. I'm all right. Just a headache. Be OK in a minute. Would love a cup of coffee though.'

'Are you sure I shouldn't get a doctor?' she asked.

'No thank you. I'll be OK. It's only a headache.'

Millie had her reasons for being concerned. The petticoat Mafia at the top of the organisation always knew what was going on, often before the top executives themselves. Millie and the secretaries of Pat Muldoon and Clancy McGillicuddy were all close friends. They had got together over the weekend to discuss the implications of the confidential letter the two Americans had received from Randy Mueller on behalf of Nate Cocello. Major changes were afoot which affected their respective bosses.

By the time Mark reached home that evening, the pains in his head were excruciating. He decided against telling Georgina about his meeting with Muldoon.

He would wait for the right moment. This wasn't it.

18

Mark had a very full fortnight ahead, for which he was grateful. It gave him little time to think of his own problems.

First, there was a meeting in Whitehall of the Economic Planning Council, followed by the conference at Trinity College Dublin, at which he had been invited to speak on the subject of European investment. He had accepted the invitation gladly, knowing full well that it would be his last opportunity to speak in public as a European executive of United Motors. He hoped to make it a fitting swan-song.

· · ·

At the Economic Planning Council he had expected to see Clem Bunker, but he was absent, holding his own meeting with the vehicle plant conveners in an attempt to determine the truth about the sacking incident and to resolve the dispute. What he didn't know, couldn't know, was that nothing he could now do would make any difference. There had been trouble on Merseyside just once too often, and muddle-headed militants who believed that revolution was spawned in deprivation and poverty would be able to hold a little holiday in their hearts, secure in the knowledge that several more thousand British workers had been gulled into inflicting poverty and deprivation upon themselves.

· · ·

Opening the meeting of the Economic Planning Council, the Chairman, Lord Hampshire, surprised members by announcing that the Prime Minister intended to sit in on the transport debate, which was the subject of a White Paper about to be discussed on the floor of the House. As this was the first item on the agenda, the Prime Minister made her appearance at ten thirty-three, immediately after the Chairman had made his announcement.

After the usual preliminaries and courtesies from the Chair, the Minister of Transport outlined the Government's proposals before the Chairman threw the subject open for discussion. But, before doing so, he asked the Prime Minister if she wished to say a few words.

The 'Iron Lady' as she was called, smiled the steely smile which was so familiar on the television screen and in the press.

'I am here to listen and learn, my Lord Chairman,' she said in her clear and authoritative voice.

'But I am particularly interested to know if the United Kingdom incurs a significant transportation cost penalty on its exports to Europe which puts this country at a commercial and economic disadvantage to the rest of the Community. I am also keen to know,' she continued, 'if any such cost penalties operate to our disadvantage when European investment decisions are made, in particular those international mobile investment decisions which are made by the multi-nationals. I understand that Mr Sanders has accepted an invitation to address the European Commission on the subject in Dublin, and I look forward to hearing his observations.'

Lord Hampshire had folded a piece of paper which was being passed around the table. It arrived in front of Mark with his name on it. He unfolded the paper.

'Don't put your pads on, just yet,' it said. 'Want you to come in lower down the batting order.' It was signed 'H'.

The Chairman of the National Docks' Authority opened the batting by reviewing plans to meet the ever-growing volume of docks' traffic, particularly the substantial growth in roll-on, roll-off between Britain and the continent.

The Chief Highways Planner followed, outlining the Government's intentions to provide further motorway links between industrial centres and the ports. He also described the various channel tunnel options currently being studied by the Ministry. The rail, airways and waterways chiefs then outlined their plans, before the Chairman threw the subject open to the Council members.

Several members then questioned the planning assumptions of the Chief Planning Officers, making pertinent observations based on their own particular knowledge and experience. Mark Sanders was called by the Chairman after an hour's discussion.

'Now let's have a multi-national view point,' he said cheerfully. 'Particularly on the points raised by the Prime Minister. Mark would you like to face the next ball?'

Mark smiled and nodded.

'Before we begin, Mr Sanders,' the Prime Minister said, warmly, 'will you tell me which hat you will be wearing today? Your European hat, or the British one?' she smiled a thin smile.

The Chairman smiled. Mark smiled. Everyone smiled.

'Whichever one you wish me to wear, Prime Minister,' he replied.

'Can we see you in both?' she rejoined. 'Then we can judge which one we prefer.'

'I'm afraid I don't look particularly good in either,' Mark said, 'but, putting on my British hat first: yes, Prime Minister, the United Kingdom is at a considerable disadvantage when multi-nationals consider investment locations in Europe. The transport cost penalty, to which you referred, varies of course with the nature of the product being manufactured, and ranges from two per cent to twenty per cent in the motor industry.'

'So why is it called a penalty?' the Prime Minister asked. 'That's right, isn't it? Transport cost penalty?' she added with a pained expression.

'Yes, Prime Minister.'

'But why? Surely the expression suggests that we are being penalised into paying more than our EEC partners. How can this be? We ship exports to Europe and it costs X pounds. Our partners in the EEC ship their exports to us, and again it costs the same X pounds. So where does the penalty come in?'

'It comes in,' said Mark, 'when you consider exports as a proportion of total output. A European plant will probably sell around four fifths of its total output on the European mainland, principally within the so-called Golden Triangle countries of West Germany, France, Belgium and Holland at the centre of the market. The remaining one fifth of output will be exported to the long-distance peripheral markets of

227

the United Kingdom and Italy, etcetera, so when you export from a UK manufacturing base you ship four fifths of the output over relatively longer distances, hence the UK transport cost penalty.'

The Prime Minister was nodding agreement long before Mark had finished.

'Yes, I see. But doesn't that mean that most of the European investment will always tend to go to the centrally placed Golden Triangle countries who occupy this privileged position rather than to the United Kingdom and other peripheral countries who are in less favoured areas?'

'Yes, it does mean just that,' Mark said.

'But such a situation simply strengthens the strong, and weakens the weak, doesn't it?' the Prime Minister said, eyebrows raised.

'How does a large industrial country, such as the UK rebuild and expand its industrial base, and correct a worsening balance of trade in manufactured products, if investment location decisions by the multi-nationals go against it on such grounds?'

'I am afraid, Prime Minister, the answer is that we have to be more efficient than our European competitors.' Mark answered in a matter of fact voice.

'Transport costs do impose a penalty. We've got to live with it. And beat it. We've got to absorb these costs by being super-efficient.'

Again the Prime Minister was nodding her agreement.

'But,' Mark continued, 'transport costs are only one of the factors which have placed British industry at a disadvantage in recent years.'

'And what are the others, Mr Sanders?'

'If you'll forgive me saying so, Prime Minister,' Mark replied cautiously, 'successive British Governments and the trade unions haven't exactly helped.'

The steely smile was glimpsed briefly.

'I think that's something you are really going to have to explain, Mr Sanders,' she said quizzically in a pained expression.

'If you will allow me to say so, Prime Minister,' he continued, 'Britain has consistently lost out because. . . .'

He had been speaking for some five minutes or more with force and conviction, carried away by the things which concerned him greatly. Now, suddenly, he had an uneasy feeling that he had allowed himself to go a little 'over the top'. At these meetings viewpoints were expressed in a suitably detached manner.

'I'm afraid I've gone on a bit, My Lord Chairman,' he said apologetically. 'I think I've said enough. Probably too much.'

'Not at all,' put in the Prime Minister, reassuringly. 'It's only when you let your hair down that others can see the real person hiding under the hat. I personally have found your candour very refreshing. It's such a change to hear someone say what he really believes. . . .' and a warm smile blazed. 'Almost never happens in politics.'

The laughter was general.

'Now Mr Sanders,' she continued, 'can we ask you to wear your European hat? Spain and Austria are peripheral countries aren't they? So why is it that your company, and certain other major multi-nationals, plan to invest heavily in those countries?'

She cocked her head to one side after she had posed the question.

'Spain erects huge barriers which make it difficult, if not impossible, for vehicle and component imports to enter that country,' Mark said. 'So if my company wishes to supply the domestic market of this large and expanding population, it has no alternative but to manufacture from within the country itself. Spanish rules and regulations then determine what percentage of total output will be exported and what the local component content will be.

'Similarly, the Austrian Government has made it clear that unless multi-nationals manufacture vehicles or components within the country to correct its trade deficit, then it will be obliged to take appropriate steps to close its domestic markets to their products.'

The Prime Minister clasped her hands together.

'How very interesting. And pray do tell me which countries will have to accept the exports of motor vehicles or components from Spain, say, as a result of anything which might be agreed between United Motors and the Spanish Government?'

As Mark began to reply, she said the first name with him, nodding her head the while.

'Great Britain . . . of course, of course. And is that free and fair European trade, Mr Sanders?' She asked with more than a hint of sarcasm in her voice.

'My company doesn't make Government rules and regulations, Prime Minister,' he replied. 'We comply with them or we are excluded from these markets.'

'Quite so. But would you accept that such discriminatory rules and regulations operate to this country's clear disadvantage?'

'Of course,' Mark agreed. 'Without question.'

The first lady nodded and went on nodding for several seconds in quiet contemplation before putting two further questions to him concerning European regional incentives, Government grants and subsidies and their cost distorting influence on investment location decisions.

Mark answered in the traditional matter-of-fact manner, parading all the relevant factors and letting the facts speak for themselves.

The Prime Minister departed a short time later with the Ministers of Transport and Energy escorted by Lord Hampshire. In all, she had spent ninety minutes at the meeting.

During the lunch break, the Chairman took Mark to one side.

'Before she left, the PM told me how pleased she was that you were so frank. And she's delighted that you have accepted the invitation to address the European Commission on the subject in Dublin. She's looking for ways and means of redressing Britain's excessive contribution to the European budget which, as you know, is the highest in the community. She believes that with your practical experience at the sharp end in Europe you will be able to provide much needed ammunition to support her appeal which is to be submitted to the Commission and the Council of Ministers.

.   .   .

The next day, Mark told Millie, his secretary, that the Corporation's plans for reorganisation would involve the elimination of regional management. She had been expecting the news, because of her privileged position in the 'Petticoat Mafia' but it none-the-less visibly upset her.

She had what was generally regarded by other top secretaries as the most interesting job in European component operations, and took a great personal interest in her work. As a long-service employee she knew from first-hand experience the contribution Mark had made to the expansion of the Corporation over the years.

'It isn't fair!' she exclaimed angrily.

'Fair or not,' Mark said, trying to speak lightly, 'it's what's going to happen. The parting of the ways, I'm afraid, after all these years. But don't worry. It has already been agreed that you'll be offered another position within the Corporation at the same salary.'

The classically attractive forty-year-old secretary smiled uncertainly. Her eyes brimmed.

'I'm not really concerned about myself. It's so heartless and unfair after all you've done.'

'That, as the Americans say,' Mark told her wryly, 'is how the cookie crumbles. I suppose I'm going to miss the old firm after all these years. And I'm going to miss you too,' he added with a smile. 'We've worked together for a very long time.'

She blinked and touched the corners of her eyes.

'Certainly have.'

'I've really enjoyed working with you, Millie. Thank you,' Mark said with sincerity.

'And I've enjoyed working with you too. I really have,' she blurted, and hurried from the room into her own adjacent office. And there, privately, she cried.

. . .

It was a demoralised Don Peters who drove away from The London Hilton and the all-American farewell party that had been laid on for him by Clancy McGillicuddy.

In response to the many toasts from his American colleagues he had made a light-hearted speech at dinner, which belied his deep disappointment at being sent back to

231

the States on a Public Relations assignment.

Sure, the newly created position with its impressive job title sounded important, but that was only to impress the media and the public. It impressed no-one at corporate management level. Don Peters had failed in his UK assignment and had effectively blown his chances of being moved further up the corporate ladder to a Vice Presidency and, maybe, to the Presidency itself.

He turned the car into Park Lane and drove quickly and skilfully through the maze of traffic converging on Marble Arch to emerge in the correct lane for the Edgeware Road.

By his side, the magnificent cosmetically-engineered Eleanor graphically expressed what she thought of the farewell party through blazing eyes which darted alarmingly under false eyelashes. She wasn't demoralised. She was absolutely livid.

'Don't you ever put me through that situation again,' she snarled through clenched teeth, tugging irritably at the sleeve of her mink jacket.

'I've never been so uncomfortable in all my life. It was utter humiliation.'

'Aw, come on now honey . . . it wasn't that bad,' he replied dismally, pulling over to allow a wailing police car through the heavy late night traffic.

'Huh,' she scoffed dismissively. 'Who's kiddin' who? It was sheer bloody hell listening to all those fatuous nincompoops saying what a great guy you are. Bullshit! Sure you're a great guy in their eyes . . . you've done 'em all a favour by writing yourself off the promotion list. Jeez, they couldn't conceal how pleased they were. It made me want to throw up!'

He screwed up his eyes with pain. She was right of course, he knew that, but her words hurt just the same. For the first time in his career he had failed to produce the goods and that hurt his pride. He was also finished as a rising executive. He had been shunted into a side-line and was now out of the mainstream traffic for good. He knew that.

Trance-like he drove down the Edgware Road, responding to the multitudinous traffic lights with mechanical movements, while the agitated Eleanor continued to lash his unreceptive ear with a never-ending stream of abuse.

He reflected on the options which had been open to him,

one of which had led to his downfall. Eleanor was right when she had said at the very beginning that he should have gone along with the corporate planning proposals to phase-out the UK Vehicle Division as a manufacturing operation. He would have survived if he had accepted the plan in the first place and done what the Corporation had wanted him to do instead of putting forward his own counter proposals. But that was easier said than done. How could he have accepted such a proposal without letting down the fifty thousand people who worked for him? He was their leader. If he didn't fight on their behalf, who the hell would?

He switched on the headlights as the car entered the M1 at Brent Cross. Eleanor's waspish voice ranted on and on.

'You should have seen the smug self satisfaction on the faces of those bitches as they lined up to kiss me,' she rasped.

' "So sorry, darling",' she mimicked. ' "We're really goin' to miss you both, we really are. . . . " The lousy hypocritical bastards! I could have spit in their eyes!'

She swung her head in his direction.

'Well for God's sake say something,' she yelled. 'Even if it's only "Goodbye". Don't you have any feelings for what I'm goin' through?'

'Waal, I don't exactly feel too good myself,' he replied morosely.

'Then, why did you do it?' she cried bitterly. 'I said you were crazy not to go along with the Corporation's proposals, didn't I? But you wouldn't listen to me. Oh no! Not you, you had to be the good guy. You had to do a Custer. Well, look where it's got you. And do you think for one minute they care a damn about you? You've got to be joking. And what about me? Do I go back to modelling for a living?'

'What choice did I have?' Don Peters asked with a shrug. 'I couldn't have lived with myself if I hadn't put up a fight on behalf of the men.'

'Waal, how are you gonna live with the Corporation execs from here on in?' she asked caustically. 'And how am I gonna live with those two-faced blue-rinsed bitches back home? We're both losers, Don, and everybody knows it. How do we stomach that without choking?'

He winced visibly.

'I'm sorry honey . . . I know I've let you down . . . but we'll

233

get by.'

'Get by. . . ! Get by!' she yelled. 'I don't wanna get by, Don, I wanna get on. You and I have always been winners. I wanted you to make it to that goddamned fourteenth floor just as much as you did! You could have made it too, if you hadn't been so stupid.'

'How do you think I feel?' he asked. 'But I had to make the effort, on behalf of the Division. It would have worked too, if I'd been supported.'

'But you weren't supported and it didn't work . . . so what have you achieved?' she asked sarcastically.

'The Corporation isn't interested in effort . . . it's only interested in results. You know that. So where do we go from here?'

'You tell me,' he said flatly, with the air of a tired and unhappy man who has had enough.

And she did. Over and over again.

.   .   .

It is said that nothing so concentrates a man's mind as the knowledge that he is to be hanged in the morning. It was Sunday and Mark was working on the address he was to give at Trinity College, Dublin. To his pleasant surprise he discovered that he was now able to think with an objective clarity which stemmed from the knowledge that he was now free for the first time in his life to speak his mind without fear or favour.

He had touched on some of the reasons why the United Kingdom had been outsmarted and disadvantaged when he had spoken before the Prime Minister at the meeting of the Economic Planning Council. Now he would debate the subject in depth before a cosmopolitan audience of European and international politicians, bureaucrats, academic advisers and international managers.

.   .   .

Having dined 'not wisely, but too well' on one of Georgina's extra-special Sunday lunches, they were relaxing in the garden of their Buckinghamshire home when Mark broke the news.

234

In a very low-key, matter-of-fact way he described the meeting in Muldoon's office and explained Detroit's decision to eliminate regional management. Throughout, Georgina remained calm and expressionless.

'Does that mean we shall see a great deal more of each other than we have in the past?' she asked.

'I should think so,' he said. 'Much more.'

She smiled.

'I think I would like that.'

Mark returned her smile.

'But what about our standard of living?' he said. 'That will have to change if I don't land a job with much the same salary, and jobs like that don't exactly grow on trees, you know, particularly when you're over fifty.'

'Nonsense, my dear,' Georgina told him. 'You'll be snapped up in no time.'

'But what if I'm not? We're still faced with the mortgage and school fees. They won't go away.'

'In that event, we'll just have to lower our standard of living, won't we?' she said. 'It doesn't particularly bother me. I don't crave all those materialistic things we used to crave when we were young. Not any more. Oh, I don't deny that it was all great fun striving to get to the top,' she went on, 'but we've done it, haven't we? We've made the effort together. And if we didn't get to the very top, well, it was near enough, wasn't it? And what do we have to prove? That we're both getting older? That you still want to compete in a young man's race, even though it might kill you?'

She gripped his hand.

'We've had a lot, and we've got a lot,' she said. 'We've lived good and bad times together and, no doubt, we'll share more. I'm not afraid of the future and, knowing you as I do, nor should you be. You'll win through. You'll show them all!'

She stood up and kissed him lightly on the lips.

'Now if you'd like me to tell you what I really think of United Motors after all these years, I'll do so.' she said. And her voice took on a keener edge.

'But I don't really like swearing, and I'm sure you've already sworn quite enough for both of us. So, for the moment, we'll just leave it at that shall we?'

She linked an arm through his.

'Now let's take a walk over the fields with Honey and Harriet. The countryside is looking beautiful right now.'

19

The drinks party was evaporating slowly as guests said their goodbyes. Clem Bunker was talking to Mark in the garden.

'Lovely home, Mark,' said the union man. 'Will you be able to keep it?'

Mark stopped in his tracks.

'So you've heard already,' he said. 'Bush telegraph still as reliable as ever.'

'Never fails,' Clem replied, adding, 'Don Peters told me.'

He shook his head sadly.

'I really am sorry, Mark. Do you know who is replacing Peters?'

'Not a clue. Hasn't been announced yet.'

'Another American, I suppose?' said the union man.

'Bound to be.'

.   .   .

They sat at a circular wrought iron table shaded by a willow.

'Do you really think the Division could go out as a result of this latest strike? Or is it just another 'Cry Wolf' situation?' asked Bunker after a long pause.

'The Division's been going out for the last fifteen years; slowly but surely.' said the ex-management man.

'This is the last straw.'

The union man winced.

'To be honest, Clem, it started to go out twenty years ago when we failed to join the Common Market at the outset. All the new industrial investment was switched to the continent. The UK was effectively a back number from that moment. The new plants on the continent then did a better productivity job, and that was that. The more the UK Vehicle Division restricted output, the more sure it headed for the final chop.'

Clem Bunker was shaking his head, sadly.

'You know, Clem,' Mark continued, 'if we ARE going to fight our way back to the top again we are going to have to do it by our own collective efforts. Nobody else is going to help us. The Americans? Ha. . . . That's a laugh. . . . The Russians? Now there's an alternative for you. The Workers' Paradise that still can't feed its own people.'

Mark raised his glass in salute.

'We've been fighting each other like spoilt kids instead of fighting the real enemy, our international competitors. That's our stupidity,' he said sadly as if unburdening himself of a great guilt.

'People like you and me,' Clem replied with a smile, raising his glass.

Mark nodded and smiled back.

'Yes, I suppose so, Clem. People like you and me. At least we are builders, not bloody wreckers,' he added in mitigation.

'Bully for us. Let's drink to that,' Clem said.

'To the builders of this world.'

.   .   .

Andrew and Vicky appeared on the terrace.

'Don't tell me that you two are talking shop,' Andrew said. 'Don't you ever switch off?'

'Andrew, my dear boy, your father and I are talking matters of great pith and moment,' replied Clem.

'Ask your mother and Gwen to join us in the garden, will you Andrew?' Mark said. 'And bring another bottle with you. This stuff is very more-ish. Clem and I are getting addicted.'

'Daddy tells me that you were apprentices together at United Motors,' Vicky said.

She half-turned as her mother and Georgina joined them.

'Amazing isn't it, Mummy? They even look alike, don't you think?'

'Yes, I suppose they do. . . . ' Gwen Bunker looked from one

238

man to the other, cocking her head to one side as she appraised the merchandise.

'Do tell us about your apprentice days, Daddy,' said Vicky. 'What was it like? Did you fight over the same girl friends?'

'No' said her Mother. 'They kept the fighting till later when they sat on the management-union joint negotiation committee. I used to hear all about it. Mark said this and I said that.'

'Nostalgia ain't what it used to be,' interjected Andrew, quoting the latest college graffiti.

Clem grinned.

'Do you remember, Mark when you had to strip naked and tie that sack around your waist?' he asked.

'Do I remember! How could I ever forget!' said Mark, holding a hand over his eyes.

'Whatever happened?' asked Vicky.

Punctuated by interjections from Mark, Clem told the story of how Mark had fallen into a barrel of high viscosity oil while standing on the lid to get at another barrel with his hand pump. He had been stripped naked in the oil store, where the incident had occurred during their very first month as apprentices, and his clothes triumphantly borne aloft to the plating shop to be washed in one of the hot water tanks.

When the news hit the factory floor, young girls were sent off to the stores with requisitions to get a good look at the loin-cloth apprentice. One young girl who had stood giggling at the hapless Mark for more than ten minutes was told that she could go back to her department as she'd waited long enough. When she objected that she shouldn't be sent back empty handed, she was shown what had been written on her requisition. 'Please supply: ONE LONG WEIGHT'.

'But how did you come to go your separate ways?' Vicky asked as the laughter subsided.

'What influenced you both?'

'Well,' said Clem. 'I know what influenced me. It was a man named Arthur Billstock. A toolmaker. I was put to work with him on the same bench and he not only taught me tool-making, he also taught me about the trade union movement and the kind of society he wanted to see.'

'Ah, the local militant,' said Andrew.

'No, not at all,' Clem replied.

'In fact he was really a very quiet and rather reserved man, who preferred to keep in the background rather than hog the limelight. We talked a lot during those months on the same bench together, and it was his influence which set me on the trade union path. If it hadn't been for Arthur Billstock, I would probably have taken the same road as Mark. That was the road we apprentices were expected to take. Must have been crazy not to do so. Might have ended up with a house like this,' he added with a laugh.

'He's always been a bit funny in the head,' joked Gwen.

'How about you, Mark? What influenced you?' she added.

'Well,' said Mark, topping up their glasses. 'I suppose I should have followed Clem into the trade union movement. We apprentices were never short of advice on what was wrong with society and the system. But I found it all too negative and depressing. Success was supposed to be reserved for those with silver spoons in their mouths. I well remember the words of an old foreman who said to me, 'Son, even if you have the talent and ability to take you to the top, there is still no guarantee that you will ever get there, or even half way. But as sure as God made little apples, you certainly won't get there if you don't make the effort.' That clinched it for me. I suppose that simple precept from that old foreman stood me in good stead for thirty odd years, until now.'

'Why until now, Dad?' enquired Andrew, unaware of his father's predicament.

'I suppose I should have said up to now,' Mark replied disarmingly.

'Perhaps it will help me over the next thirty,' he added as an afterthought.

'But you are both very similar men, from similar backgrounds and with the same basic objectives in society,' Vicky said, with the air of a very puzzled young lady.

'Don't you still want the same things?'

'Oh, but we do,' her father told her. 'We both want to improve things; to build a better world. I thought that I could make my contribution by joining the Trade Union movement, and improve things from there.'

'And I thought I could make mine by designing and making better products, and selling them to the world,' said Mark.

'Now how about something to eat? I'm starving.'

. . .

A few days later the national press carried the headlines that the UM plants in the Midlands had now been made idle as a consequence of the Merseyside strike. The flow of supplies into the Midlands from the Merseyside works had dried up completely and with no apparent end to the stoppage in sight, lay-offs took immediate effect. Feelings were running high at all plants, but for different reasons.

The news that Don Peters was being replaced had been received with great disappointment and alarm throughout the Midlands by management, unions and employees alike. Disappointment that they were losing the best American MD they had ever had, after less than one year, and alarm in the knowledge that his demotion almost certainly meant the end of the recovery and expansion plans, and possibly the end of vehicle manufacture in the UK. Such was the state of concern at the Midlands plants that conveners and local members of Parliamant were demanding intervention at Government level.

Some of the thirty thousand workers employed at the Midlands plants, incensed by the idleness forced on them by the Merseysiders and alarmed at the bleak prospect ahead, stormed through the streets to Clem Bunker's regional office demanding action to get the Merseyside plants back to work. Bunker was jostled, heckled, spat upon and sworn at as he tried to keep some semblance of order to explain the action he had already taken. After two very noisy and unruly hours, with the local police trying to keep law and order, the angry mob reluctantly dispersed.

On Merseyside, the plant had split into two factions over the strike; those who supported Clasper in his demand that the strike be continued until the sacked shop steward had been reinstated, and those who took the view that Clasper was playing power politics with their jobs at stake. The latter demanded that the strike be called off to avoid even worse news. This view represented the thoughts of an ever-growing majority whose intuitive feeling was that the Merseyside plant was heading for total and irreversible closure with the loss of

241

ten thousand jobs. Clasper was becoming more isolated, with his dwindling support coming from a small core of left-wingers who considered the fight to be a question of principle, namely union solidarity against management.

Bunker's early efforts to bring about a settlement had been angrily brushed aside by Clasper, who told the regional officer in no uncertain terms that his help was not needed. The Merseyside members would resolve the dispute in their own way without his help.

Bunker knew instinctively that Clasper could not, and would not, resolve the dispute himself and that the effects of the stoppage would very soon be felt far beyond the confines of United Motors as one supply industry after another experienced a precipitous drop in demand.

He also knew that if Clasper was to be toppled from his influential position as plant convener – which was essential to the long term recovery of the plant – he would have to be seen to be toppled by his own members, acting in their own interests. He therefore resolved to keep out of the way and let Clasper hang himself.

The Midlands' plants had been putting great pressure on the Merseysiders to call off the strike, as a result of which a mass meeting at Pier Head, Liverpool, had been demanded to vote on the question of a return to work. Although this had initially been rejected out of hand by Clasper, he had been left in no doubt that his members would hold their own mass meeting without him if he chose not to call it.

At the same time, hundreds of workers in the Midlands' plants who had heard about the Pier Head meeting on the grapevine now decided to drive up to Liverpool to influence the return to work vote.

Confident that Clasper would be brought down by his own members without any interference from him, Bunker concluded that his best course of action would be to emulate Brer Rabbit on this occasion, and 'lie low and say nuffin'.'

.   .   .

Mark's address to an international audience at Trinity College, Dublin, came as a shock to European Commissioners, Government Ministers and their academic

242

advisers. He had been invited to speak on the factors which influenced investment location decisions as seen from the viewpoint of a European Industrial Planning Manager. He was the fourth of twelve speakers over the three day conference, the others being Ministers, Commissioners, Economists and Academics, and had been introduced by the Chairman as 'The Man at the Sharp End'.

He had based his paper strictly on his own practical experiences, working within the labyrinth of conflicting laws, rules and regulations imposed by individual Governments within the EEC, EFTA and East Europe. He sought to show how the laws imposed by certain countries to attract internationally mobile inward investment could only operate to the detriment of other states. He exposed the many devious ways in which Governments bent the rules of free trade in their favour, while flying the free trade banner.

He described how the Japanese used a laser beam strategy within a poorly drafted law to penetrate the European market while protecting their own domestic market behind a dynastic organisational structure which only permitted import access when the dynasty deemed it politically expedient to do so.

He itemised the steps by which East European Governments gained access to the free markets of West Europe, while denying the same freedom of access to West European manufacturers, and revealed how reciprocal trade deals negotiated with the multi-nationals resulted in unsuspecting third party EEC Governments being saddled with the import bill.

He then went on to describe the very considerable commercial and economic disadvantages experienced by peripheral industrial countries compared with the enormous advantages enjoyed by the privileged centrally placed Golden Triangle countries and called to question the entire concept of a European budget which incredibly penalised the poorer peripheral countries instead of applying the penalty the other way round.

He concluded his forty-five minute address by commenting on the political factors which influenced investment location decisions and emphasised that future multi-national planners would do well to have a much more sensitive appreciation of the social and political implications of their actions. Government intervention would inevitably follow if Governments had reason to believe that their interests were not being fairly served.

He sat down, knowing in his heart of hearts that for as long as Randy Mueller had a major part to play in UM's corporate planning, his basic criteria would be: 'Is it good for the Corporation? Is it good for the United States? And, above all, is it good for Randy Mueller?'

Delegate after delegate during the three day conference subsequently referred to his address to confess that the real world of the International Planning Manager was a totally different world from that perceived by politicians and their academic advisers.

One distinguished-looking delegate, who Mark recognised as the Chairman of the British Conservative party, introduced himself to say that people with his experience should put themselves forward to serve in the European Parliament.

'I am going to put your name on the list we are drawing up,' he said grandiloquently.

'I feel sure that one of the industrial constituences would be interested in a chap with your industrial background.'

20

Shortly after his return to England, Mark received an invitation to address an all-party Committee of Members of Parliament.

He was invited to develop his Dublin address with particular reference to the economic and commercial disadvantages of peripheral industrial countries, such as the United Kingdom, within the EEC. He was also specifically asked to speak not as an executive of United Motors, but as an Englishman.

As he had been invited to dine with Members afterwards, his secretary had booked him into The Howard Hotel, a few hundred yards from Parliament Square on the Victoria Embankment, overlooking the Tower of London to the east and the Houses of Parliament to the west. As Mark strolled from the hotel and crossed the road to the riverside walk, he had a strange feeling that the evening ahead would re-shape his future.

Outwardly he was calm and composed as he walked in the warm evening sunshine towards the House, but like the swans gliding serenely across the water, he too was paddling like hell underneath.

Big Ben struck the quarter hour and he checked his watch. Ahead of him, the tail-end stragglers of the daily rush hour traffic scurried across Westminster Bridge. The House of Parliament loomed up and his heart began to thump. He recalled the first time he had seen the impressive building as a schoolboy on a day's outing to see the sights of London.

He could picture the scene as if it were yesterday. The history master had gathered up his flock and had paused outside the source of power in the Commonwealth and Empire to eulogize on the great men of the past who had entered the hallowed portals. Mark was one of twelve young boys and girls clustered around him to lap up his words of wisdom.

'Through these portals passed such illustrious men as Pitt, Walpole, Disraeli and Gladstone, to carve their names on the glorious history of England,' he had said to his young and captive audience.

At the mention of the name Disraeli, Mark had been transported into a world of his own.

His grandfather had been a master baker and, in one of the many family stories Mark had heard at his grandfather's knee, he had been told of how his great-grandfather had served Benjamin Disraeli with a standing daily order of twelve French loaves, burnt and rasped. It was the burning and rasping bit which had fascinated Mark. His grandfather had explained that the only true way to bake bread was to burn it black and then rasp off the burnt extremities with a coarse file. Mark had adored his grandparents and would listen spellbound to their stories for hours on end.

The history master had interrupted his reverie with a smart clip round the ear.

'Stop daydreaming, Sanders, will you boy? Give us, pray, the benefit of your undivided attention. Now sir,' he had continued acidly, gripping Mark by the ear, 'tell me, if I may be so bold as to ask, precisely what I have been talking about.'

'Disraeli, sir. Twelve French loaves, burnt and rasped, sir.' blurted the surprised boy, and the other children giggled hysterically.

'You stupid boy,' cried the master. 'What in the world are you talking about? If it's not cricket and Frank Woolley it's something else. Now it's twelve French loaves, burnt and rasped, whatever that means. I despair of you, boy. One thing for certain, Sanders, you won't be coming here to the Mother of Parliaments to give us all the benefit of your profound wisdom. It'll be some factory workbench for you boy, where, if you continue to dream your stupid little daydreams, you'll end up chopping your fingers off. Is that understood?'

'Yes, sir.'

Mark had been twelve at the time and beset by emotional turmoil. His parents had recently parted. Now he recalled how, on the second night after his mother had left home, he had climbed out of bed in the late evening and slipped unnoticed from the house to run over a mile to Bournemouth Central Railway Station to catch a train to nearby Christchurch, where his mother had gone to live with her sister.

It was a cold night in late autumn and the rain had lashed down unremittingly. By the time he had reached the shelter of the station he was soaked to the skin. He had paid three pence at the booking office for his ticket and, after waiting ten minutes or so on the cold and draughty platform for the next London-bound train, he had arrived at Christchurch some ten minutes later to run through torrential rain toward the group of cottages which flanked the open park in the town centre.

He was not certain which cottage his aunt rented during the winter. In the spring and summer she lived in a cottage on the banks of the river Stour just below Tuckton bridge. Mark had spent many idyllic summer days sailing and fishing with his brothers and his aunt on the beautiful river, but had never been to her winter cottage.

The rain continued to beat down upon him as he ran across the dark and sodden park just before midnight. With the exception of one cottage, where a light still shone in the window, all the others were in total darkness. Mark ran to the one and only cottage with the light and was as surprised as his aunt when she opened the door.

She gave a great gasp of anguished amazement at the sight of the drowned rat of a boy standing before her, the rain pouring off his sodden hair to run in rivulets down his pale face.

'Oh my God, Mark sweetheart,' she cried, pulling the soaked boy to her bosum.

'Grace,' she called out to his mother, 'it's Mark.'

His beautiful and adored mother quickly appeared from the sitting-room and hugged him nearly to death on the doorstep. But despite his repeated and heartfelt pleas to his mother to come home, she steadfastly refused to do so, and she never did. The divorce was made absolute two years later.

.   .   .

Mark stood for a few moments at the corner of Parliament Street and Bridge Street. It was nearly forty years since the history master had bawled him out on the pavement over there, in front of the House of Commons.

'One thing is certain Sanders . . .' he had said, 'you won't be coming here. . . .'

Mark crossed Parliament Square and even the statue of Churchill appeared to be growling at the sorry state of affairs in the land where a pettifogging ex-apprentice was invited to address Right Honourable Members of both Houses.

He climbed the steps leading to the central lobby and was stopped by a burly policeman who asked the nature of his business.

'Name's Sanders. I am addressing an all-party committee,' Mark replied, feeling rather important as he uttered the words.

'Bully for you, sir,' replied the policeman with a smile.

'Go ahead sir.'

Mark passed through a security screen to make his way to the impressive central lobby where the Chairman of the Committee was already waiting to receive him. It was six twenty-seven.

After the usual pleasantries he took Mark along one of the labyrinth of corridors flanked with busts of the famous, and stopped before a heavy oak-panelled door attended by a liveried usher. After exchanging a few words, the usher opened the door and Mark was escorted into a debating chamber shaped in the form of a horseshoe, with a raised dais at the open end upon which were two heavy oak chairs, one for the Chairman and the other for the speaker.

The room had seating capacity for about eighty and Mark saw that it was about half full. Before being taken to the platform, he was introduced to those members of the Committee who happened to be milling around the entrance. He recognised familiar names and faces from all parties, and also noticed that everybody carried copies of his Dublin paper.

He was then escorted to the dais, where the Chairman launched into a brief introduction.

'Your Dublin paper whetted our appetite, Mr Sanders,' he said in conclusion.

'We now look forward to the main course this evening.'

Mark rose from his chair fully aware that politicians believed themselves to be the best informed people in the world, which made them a very sceptical audience for any speaker. They sprawled across the padded benches before him with the somewhat jaded air of men who expected to hear nothing new. He began jocularly by saying that he rose to address them with some apprehension, reminded of a piece of graffiti he had seen on a Whitehall notice board which had read, 'I used to be indecisive . . . but now I'm not so sure', which brought a few chuckles from the floor.

'I propose to describe the very considerable commercial and economic disadvantages incurred by the United Kingdom by comparison with other European countries when investment locations' decisions are taken by multi-nationals,' Mark continued.

'And also to offer some suggestions as to how the UK handicap could be reduced and its disadvantages turned to its advantage.'

A few eyebrows were raised at such unequivocal presumptions.

'You have also invited me to wear a British hat,' Mark continued.

'It will be a pleasant change to do so.'

He began by giving several examples of how Governments in both West and East Europe had obtained major United Motors' investment projects by highly discriminatory and blatantly unfair means, which had operated to the detriment of the UK.

He was suddenly thrown off balance by the hurried departure of a Minister. He was aware that Members had to come and go at irregular intervals at the behest of their lords and masters when the House was in session, but he feared the worst. He faltered, cleared his throat, drank liberally from the glass before him, and continued.

His morale was uplifted a few minutes later when the same Minister returned with a gaggle of additional members evidently called from the floor of the House. Mark warmed to the task and continued with renewed confidence.

'There are many instances where UK investment and product costs have been up to twenty per cent below other European countries, but the investment has still been located on the continent because of unfair political pressures and highly discriminatory practices,' he added to gasps of pained surprise.

249

'The Treaty of Rome rules on competitive costs and prices have been blatantly disregarded by certain countries and the multi-nationals,' he added.

'Just consider, for example, the adverse economic effect on Britain of Ford's highly discriminatory investment plan agreed with the Spanish Government. . . .'

For the best part of an hour he exposed what was really going on in the international motor industry. His audience was very quiet. Hardly a muscle moved.

'Corporate plans of the Fords, UMs and Chryslers of this world influence and shape our destiny. They determine whether Britain is to be a winner or loser country. Sadly for Britain they have already made the decision that Britain is to be a loser country,' he said dramatically.

Pained expressions crossed the faces of the now alarmed politicians.

'For example,' he went on, 'The corporate plan of United Motors is to phase-out vehicle and component manufacture in the UK and import its requirements from new plants on the continent, from East Europe, the Far East – including Japan – and from the United States itself, with the loss of fifty thousand UK jobs, one hundred and fifty thousand if one includes jobs lost in the UK supplier chain.' he added.

There was a gasp at this disclosure. Constituency problems now loomed large.

'By the late eighties the global plans of the major US multi-nationals will have created a massive UK trade deficit of around seven billion pounds which will go on increasing with the growth of the number of vehicles in use. These companies have been Britain's top exporters in the past. Seven years from now they will be Britain's top importers. What will be the effect on the pound sterling and on Britain's economic standing in the world as the trade gap widens? What will be the effect on employment?' he asked ominously.

'And yet, this frightening scenario I outline to you this evening is precisely what will happen arising from the global plans of these major American-owned multi-nationals.'

Mark's voice had trailed away to a whisper. His words had produced group paralysis. Not a muscle moved.

Mark was now speaking out with a vengeance. For the first time in his life he was free from corporate restraints, to say what he really thought. He had no qualms in doing so. If those with inside knowledge of the facts didn't speak up for Britain, who the hell would? That was his justification.

His eyes ranged the room.

'The Prime Minister has clearly stated her intention to bring about the industrial regeneration of Britain to correct the decline of the last few years,' he said vigorously. 'She has appealed to industrial leaders to help her redress the trade imbalance.'

'What price the American contribution toward that objective?' he asked in a hushed tone.

'How can the Prime Minister achieve her national targets when US corporate plans move in a diametrically opposite direction to compound Britain's trade problems. What would the American Government say if the roles were reversed?' he added to nods from all quarters.

Mark paused again to take a very long drink.

'Fortunately Britain can win if we learn from past mistakes, and I would now like to conclude by outlining certain strategic proposals for your consideration, which would put Britain firmly on the upward path to meet the Prime Minister's long-term objectives.'

Mark then described a ten point plan and summarised its resultant effect. The UK vehicle and component industry sectors alone would progressively benefit to the value of eight billion pounds sterling by year five. This would correct the Motor industry trade imbalance without the need to export one additional unit. Unemployment in the sector would be reduced by two hundred thousand, and existing manufacturing capacity, previously made idle by imports, would once more be fully utilised, thus improving operating profit and return on investment.

Mark ended his address by saying, 'The European and international trade war is really between those Governments who fix the rules of the game to suit themselves, and those who play the game according to Treaty of Rome rules. Britain has been a loser country in a manifestly unfair trade environment. It has allowed itself to be outsmarted by governments who are not afraid to bend the rules in their favour, aided and abetted by American multi-nationals whose allegiance is to the United States, naturally. Britain is expendable.'

He looked around him.
'Why not think and act as Great Britain Incorporated?'
he asked.

. . .

Unbeknown to Mark, one of the titled politicians present also
happened to be an international banker and financial advisor
to several US corporations. He phoned New York immediately after the Westminster meeting. A voice at the other end
said wearily in a faintly Irish accent.

'Ah well. I suppose we will have to take appropriate action
will we not. . . . Thanks for putting me in the picture,
Patrick.'

The magnate placed the phone back on the receiver . . .
slowly.

'Thorns left to fester . . .' he mused.

'Maybe we should contact the special outside Agency.'

He thought very, very carefully for a minute or more and
then picked up his private phone and dialled a number.

. . .

Two days later, Mark received a phone call from 10, Downing
Street, asking for permission to publish the Dublin paper, and
his submission to the House Select Committee, as an appen-
dix to the Government's proposed White Paper shortly to go
before the House. He readily gave his approval.

At Question Time in the House, the Prime Minister agreed
that a paper submitted by a European Planning Manager, now
being studied by the Government and the European Commission appeared to offer real solutions to Britain's excessive
contribution to the European budget.

Mark received several letters and phone calls from Members of Parliament, all but one in support of his two papers
and proposals. The Member who wrote to express his disagreement invited Mark to the House to discuss his reasons
for taking the opposite viewpoint. He received Mark in the
central lobby and took him to the Members' tea room for a
chat over a pot of tea.

He was a young lawyer of about thirty in his first year in

Parliament, who had sufficiently impressed someone in Government to have been given the job of Junior Minister at the Trade office. He came straight to the point in a rather superior manner, saying that he was a European federalist and that, in his opinion, it didn't matter a tuppeny damn whether industrial investments took place in Germany, France or the UK. He went on to say that it was irrelevant whether Britain had an industrial base at all if it could be shown that it would be more sensible, from a European point of view, for Britain to become a service nation importing its manufactured product requirements.

Mark listened aghast at the naive and dangerous idealism of the young, starry-eyed politician, who was light years away from knowing what really went on at the sharp end of European and international trade.

'If you believe that, sir,' said Mark with as much politeness as he could muster, 'you will naturally not share the concern I have expressed in my papers. We are obviously poles apart. Do you wish to discuss the subject further, or would we both be wasting our time?'

'Wasting our time, I think.' said the young Minister, forcing a laugh.

'But as I have invited you here, let's discuss the subject a little further at least.'

Mark asked him how he could reconcile his views with what was clearly Britain's basic needs; the need to maintain a strong manufacturing base as a defence capability; the need to correct a massive and worsening trade deficit on manufactured products; and the need to provide talented school-leavers with creative career opportunities in the manufacturing sector as designers, physicists, chemists and engineers as opposed to the more mundane jobs in the service sector as warehouse-men and handlers of other countries' goods.

The young politician shrugged his shoulders.

'Irrelevancies,' he said dismissively.

'Top talent will always be in demand where the jobs are, and if the jobs are on the continent, so be it. National trade deficits will become meaningless under a European monetary system with a common currency. And as for defence,' he went on, 'Britain would be defended by arms manufactured in Germany or France just as well as by arms manufactured in

253

Britain, if this were necessary for good economic reasons.'

Mark raised an eyebrow.

'Your belief that Germany or France would unfailingly defend Britain and British interests against an aggressor is not one that I share. Does the Minister of Defence share your views?'

'No, he does not!' snapped the Junior Minister of Trade.

'Thank God for that,' Mark declaimed.

'Your views are too simplistic for me,' said the young politician loftily.

'As you say, we are poles apart. Let's leave it at that.'

He rose to leave and Mark followed.

'Before you entered Parliament, what did you do?' Mark asked.

The young man's head went up.

'I was ... I am ... a barrister.'

'But you are a Junior Minister of Trade. You're not attached to the Attorney General's office,' said Mark with an air of feigned surprise.

The Junior Minister pulled himself up to his full height of five foot three, and in a plummy voice rich with haughty disdain said, 'What difference does that make?'

'Well, you wouldn't expect an industrial manager to be made Attorney General, would you?' Mark asked.

The young politician tugged at an ear lobe and eyed him narrowly.

'By that remark, I take it you mean that I know little or nothing about industrial or trade matters?'

Mark looked him straight in the eye.

'I think it would be a great presumption on your part if you thought you did,' he replied firmly, putting the young man down.

The self-important politician smiled coldly.

'You have a nice way of expressing yourself which, I suppose, reflects your industrial background.'

The word 'industrial' came out like a swearword.

'Good day to you, sir,' the Junior Minister said formally.

'Thank you for responding to my invitation.'

They shook hands, but it was clearly on the unspoken understanding that they could still come out fighting. They went their separate ways: the young politician to the floor of the House to promote new industrial and commercial legislation which would, no doubt, exercise his legal mind, and the industrial manager to the central lobby, and the way out.

.   .   .

Mark drove home along the M1 reflecting that the French and Germans in particular would be pleased to erect monuments to the idealistic young English politician who had said all the things that Britain's trade competitors wanted to hear. The Germans had got their priorities right. Unlike Britain, they put national industrial supremacy first and foremost. European interests were secondary to national objectives, except where European political unity carried more clout in the international political scene.

The British had been taken to the cleaners because foolish politicians in post-war Britain had elected to produce sociologists instead of engineers, and the predictable end result was that Britain had been short on wealth creators and long on spenders. The creative and talented nation that gave birth to the Industrial Revolution and produced more inventions and patents per head of population than any other country in the world, had turned its back on industry and commerce.

Mark felt bitter and sad. Sad that his country had fallen from the top of the European industrial league, to joint eighth out of nine, and bitter toward the foolish leaders who had been largely responsible for its decline. The supercilious young Minister of Trade was a typical product of the British post-war school of Parliamentarians whose motto should have been 'words not deeds'.

In the eyes of such politicians, industrial managers were not seen as the creators of the nation's wealth, and the providers of job opportunities for the people, but as despoilers of the environment; obsolete men, peddling obsolete views, who didn't really fit in with the new social scheme of things. They were yesterday's men. In their eyes, Mark Sanders was such a man.

21

When Mark arrived home there were two letters, postmarked Detroit, waiting for him. One was a personal letter from the President of United Motors, Nate Cocello, thanking him for his services to the Corporation. The other was from the Vice President in charge of Overseas' Operations, thanking him for his personal contribution to the expansion of European Component Operations.

Mark read the letters twice. He presumed they had been written for him to use as references for his next employer, but he tore them up angrily.

The next day Muldoon told him that he was returning to the States at the end of the month to take his enforced early retirement, after a short holiday on the Hamble. Mark's compensation and pension terms would be spelt out to him by New York within the next two weeks, after they had checked out the maximum terms permissible under British law.

'It has already been agreed that the company will be as generous as British law allows,' Muldoon said reassuringly.

'The company wish you to know, Mark, from Nate Cocello down, that your work over the years is sincerely appreciated. I know that the organisational change has come as a shock to you, as it has for me, but we want to part company after all these years, on the best and friendliest of terms. I am assured that you will be well looked after,' he reiterated.

'In the meantime you are free to do whatever you wish to do over the next few weeks. If we can be of any assistance to you in finding another job, please don't hesitate to shout. No doubt you will wish to say 'Goodbye' to all your many friends and colleagues in industry and Government, so please feel free to do so in whatever way you feel appropriate.'

Mark nodded.

'Yes, sure. Thanks.' he replied indifferently. The big, soft and pliable American smiled nervously.

'Oh, incidentally Mark, I understand they want to use your office and mine for a couple of visiting Americans on assignment over here for a couple of months. Hope you haven't any objection. You can use the Treasurer's office until you leave, if that's OK by you? He's on vacation.'

Mark nodded.

'Do I have any choice in the matter?'

'Sure you do,' the American replied. But he didn't sound certain.

'If you'd rather not move, OK. I'll tell 'em to make other arrangements in the interim.'

Mark shook his head.

'No. I'll use the Treasurer's office. As you say, I won't be around much over the next few weeks anyway.'

'OK, Mark. I'll tell 'em to go ahead.'

. . .

Mark never saw Pat Muldoon again. The American cruised the Solent for a few days while Mark was tying up the loose ends, and returned to the States without paying another visit to his office.

He slipped into the obscurity of retirement, after more than thirty years in the Corporation, in much the same way as he had operated during his entire working life: unobtrusively.

He was particularly anxious to return to the States before Mark left the company, as he simply couldn't face the prospect of having to spell out to the Englishman the compensation terms and pension proposals which New York had worked out.

Just one glance had told Muldoon that they were very far from being as generous as he had encouraged Mark to believe. They certainly bore no relationship to the eminently satisfactory compensation and pension which he himself would receive. It would have been very painful for Muldoon to have to pass on the bad news, so he decided to leave for the States and let the Detroit executive personnel Director handle Mark's affairs.

True to form, Muldoon simply did as he was told to do irrespective of the rights or wrongs of the decision. To the end of his career, he had complete faith in the Corporation and in

257

the infallibility of his superiors.

The following Sunday Pat Muldoon stood in what had formerly been his local church at Gross Pointe, Michigan, and sang to the heavens, 'If I can help somebody, as I go along, then my living will not be in vain. . . .' without paying the slightest attention to the meaning of the words.

He had always been a very religious man, which had helped him a lot in the Corporation. He looked around the congregation and saw many old and familiar friends and colleagues. They smiled as they caught his eye. He smiled back. The word had already got around that Pat Muldoon had decided to take retirement in his old familiar surroundings, after a lifetime's dedicated service to the great American Corporation. People liked that. Pat Muldoon had come home.

.   .   .

The Director of Personnel responsible for the personal affairs of overseas executives rang Mark from Detroit to say that compensation terms had now been worked out, and that he would be visiting England the following week to discuss the subject with him.

'Pat sends his best wishes, Mark, and says he's sorry that he won't be there to say 'Goodbye' and wish you luck. See you next week.'

'Yes, sure. Next week then,' said the Englishman.

.   .   .

The union meeting at the Pier Head in Liverpool was in uproar. Fred Clasper had shouted himself hoarse in his frenzied efforts to persuade the vociferous gathering of several thousand employees from the strike-bound Merseyside vehicle plant to continue the strike until management climbed down and re-instated the sacked shop steward. He was being heckled, jeered and booed by the vast majority, which included several hundred workers who had driven up from the Midlands' plants to influence the vote.

Clasper's small hard core of left-wing supporters, which included a phalanx of students from Liverpool University, had formed a noisy group immediately in front of the improvised platform, which consisted of a large wooden CKD crate with the Vehicle Divisions' name stencilled in large black letters on each surface. Clasper stood alone on the box, clasping a hand microphone to his ranting mouth.

The vituperative messages which poured forth in a veritable torrent of abuse were repeatedly drowned by the dissenting majority who kept up an incessant chant: 'Return to work. Return to work. Return to work.'

Clasper screamed back at the chanting mob that they were management lackeys who had been conned by Peters, and sold down the river by Bunker.

He yelled for union solidarity to support the strike and to bring management to their knees, but to no avail. His members had had enough. He knew that he was now powerless to influence the way they would vote. He had underestimated the new mood of his members who had become sick and tired of the never-ending series of disputes, which they knew in their consciences had been driving the Division ever closer to bankruptcy. Clasper was stranded. He had missed the ebb tide. Faced with the stark reality of a choice between jobs or no jobs, the majority had elected to work. It wasn't a straight management versus union dispute; it was job preservation. The unions didn't pay their weekly wages; the company did.

They would support the union if they thought it to be in their interest to do so. They would not back the union in a political fight with the company, or allow themselves to be used by Clasper in a power struggle between the convener and management. If it was a question of company survival, or union survival, the company would always win.

'Piss off, Clasper, you've had your day!' yelled a burly figure at the back of the crowd, who was cheered to the echo for his advice.

'Go home, you bum, go home, you bum, go home, you bum, go home,' sang another to the tune of *Auld Lang Syne*. Within seconds, the sing-song chant had been taken up by the vast majority.

'Go home, you bum, go home, you bum, go home, you bum, go home; go home, you bum, go home you bum, go home you bum, go home.'

Clasper looked out at the sea of open mouths which

259

chorused against him. The chants were now accompanied by signs as one member after another thrust a right arm in the air to stab a pointing finger at the man on the platform.

'Go home, you bum, go home you bum, go home you bum, go home; go home you bum, go home you bum, go home you bum, go home.'

Clasper yelled back at the chanting mob.

'You bloody stupid gits! You bloody sheep! You arse lickin' lackeys! You servile scum! You bloody shits. . . .'

He was shouting at the top of his voice into the microphone but save for a few at the front of the crowd, nobody could hear a word because someone had cut the amplifier cable.

A new chant was now taken up.

'Clasper out. Clasper out. Clasper out. . . . ' followed by 'Return to work. Return to work. Return to work.'

Clasper threw the useless microphone to the ground and thrust a rolled up newspaper aloft, which he brandished furiously in his left hand. Thumping the paper with his other hand he continued to yell at the chanting mob, but couldn't be heard above the din. In disgust he threw the paper into the crowd. Almost by return, he was hit by a missile which looked like a rotting cabbage. Other miscellaneous missiles rained in on him as he clambered down from the improvised platform with the help of his small band of left-wing brothers.

'Dump the bastard in the Mersey!' yelled a high pitched voice which rose above the chanting mob. Within seconds a new cry was taken up.

'Dump the bastard in the Mersey! Dump the bastard in the Mersey! Dump the bastard in the Mersey. . . . '

Hands grasped the now frightened convener as his mates fought to keep the pressing mob at bay. Overwhelmed by the sheer size and strength of the surging crowd, Clasper's supporters suddenly got the message and broke rank, dispersing into the milling throng.

Police helmets could be seen bobbing above the crowd as a small corps of police officers attempted to force their way through to rescue Clasper from the hands of the mob. Before they could reach him, however, he was borne aloft like a javelin and carried to the quayside a few yards away where he was dumped unceremoniously into the murky waters to a great cheer from those who were close enough to witness the event.

260

Then as if by magic the crowd melted away to let the struggling policemen through. Clasper was soon hauled out of the water by the forces of law and order, something he had never bargained for in a lifetime's fight against them.

Within two minutes the mob had completely dispersed, with the exception of the odd copper or two and a few stragglers who were loth to leave the scene of all the fun. One of them picked up the rolled newspaper which Clasper had flung into the crowd.

'I wouldn't have thought *The Times* was Clasper's favourite paper, exactly,' he muttered to his mate.

'Must have a good racing correspondent,' came the reply.

'The bastard likes the nags.'

'That figures wack. Bloody nagger by nature, etcetera.'

His attention was drawn to a red circle which had been drawn in the Business Section with the name JUDAS scrawled in large block capitals.

He read out loud, 'Mr Clem Bunker, regional officer of the Amalgamated Union of Engineering Workers, has been invited to serve on the social affair's directorate of the European Commission. The appointment has been approved by the Prime Minister.'

He cuffed his mate's ear with the paper.

'Well, stone me, wack,' he chuckled. 'The bastard's even against that.'

'He's against every bloody thing,' replied his mate.

'Never 'appy unless he's miserable.'

.   .   .

Back at cell number 102 in Kirkby New Town, Fred Clasper made a momentous decision to emigrate to Australia.

'Well it's fairly obvious that you can't go back to the plant, innit?' agreed his platinum blonde flatmate Deirdre.

'Well I mean to say . . . it stands to reason like . . . don't it?' she added.

'You couldn't do that now, could yer? No of course not . . . but I ain't leavin' Liverpool to chase bloody wallabies. I like it 'ere. Well, it's 'ome like, where all yer friends are, innit?' She put her nose in the air and sniffed.

261

'Give over, will yer,' pleaded the disconsolate convener, slapping jam on his butty.

'Don't you ever leave off?'

'No well . . . I shouldn't 'ave said that I suppose cos you ain't got no friends any more, 'ave yer? Not now you 'aven't . . . even if you 'ad some before they dumped you in the Mersey, which I suppose you did 'ave . . . at some time or other like. . . .'

'Aw for gawd's sake give that bloody tongue of yours a rest will yer?' Clasper sighed. 'I'm tryin' to think . . . believe it or not.'

'Well, don't try too hard, luvvie, or you'll burst a blood vessel,' she called above the noise of the open tap as she filled the kettle for more tea. She sniffed again.

Fred Clasper was a malcontent by nature, one of the curious breed who are never happy unless they are miserable. But discontent was one thing. Helpless misery was another. Now, briefly, possibly for the very first time in his life, he felt helplesss and miserable at one and the same time.

The death of his beloved grandfather had brought him misery but, at the same time, it had also given him strength. It was as if, gasping out his last breath, that battered, bitter and vindictive old man had somehow injected him with some small portion of his own bitter resolve. That was both why and how he had fought all his working life for what his grandfather had believed in – worker control of the means of production and distribution, and the establishment of a Communist society where means were related to needs.

Now after twelve years as convener at the huge Merseyside plant where he had effectively established shop-floor control after a long and bitter struggle, he had been thrown out by his own union members.

He shook his head sadly at the cruel injustices of this world.

'Bloody management-brainwashed gits,' he muttered.

'What's that, Fred luvvie?' she called from the stove.

'Stupid bastards,' he mumbled on.

'Come again, Fred?'

'I said stupid bastards!'

'Well I like that . . . that's rich that is after all I do for you. I really appreciate that, Fred . . . I really do. I cook for yer and I keep house for yer and all that . . . and that's the thanks I get, well thank you, mate.' She sniffed several times.

Deirdre was plainly upset and would have droned on indefinitely if Fred hadn't shut her up.

'Aw for gawd's sake shut that bloody trap of yours, will yer? I wasn't talkin' to you. I was thinkin' out loud.'

'Oh well, that's different, she agreed, after having her faith restored in human nature. 'But you might apologise.'

'Apologise! Apologise! What the bloody hell is there to apologise for? I didn't call you a stupid bastard, did I?' he yelled in exasperation.

'I was talkin' about those bloody stupid gits at the plant, wasn't I?'

'Well, yeah, but they don't exactly consider you to be the greatest thing since sliced bread, now do they?' she opined.

'I don't care what they bloody well think. Bloody management lackeys . . . that's what they are . . . scum of the earth. . . .'

'Well, let's have another cuppa tea, luvvie, and forget all about it . . . it's not worth it. You ain't gonna change the world no matter what you do.' She sniffed again.

He took the steaming beaker from his flatmate.

'Well, are yer comin' or ain't yer?' he asked after a long and noisy sip at the cup that cheers.

'Coming where?' she asked.

'Bloody Australia, of course. Where the hell do you think?'

'Oh, Australia. . . . Do you really want me to come?'

'Course I do or I wouldn't have bloody well asked yer, would I?'

'Why Australia?' she asked, breathing on her recently painted nails.

'Cause that's where the bloody new action is gonna be,' he replied testily.

'How do you know that?' she asked with an air of surprise.

'Cause I bloody well know. I'm in the movement, ain't I?'

'Well yes I know . . . but Aussie land is on the other side of the world ain't it?'

'So what! Bloody United Motors is not the only one to have a bloody world-wide corporate plan.'

'Australia. . . .' she toyed with the name.

'Well . . . be a change I suppose . . . and we do get along very well, don't we, Fred?' She sniffed and went on sniffing.

. . .

The Pier Head incident proved to be the turning point which led to a new period of industrial peace within the giant Vehicle Division, unfortunately too late to avoid the massive investment switch to the Continent which was already under way with the newly approved corporate plan.

Wholesale changes took place within the management and trade union organisations, with the good going out with the bad.

The convener who replaced Clasper, for example, at the Merseyside plant, was elected because he had stressed to the union membership that the best way he could serve their interest was to help make sure that the Merseyside plant became the most efficient plant in Europe.

'We know from past experience where the other route takes us,' he said to loud applause.

'Downhill to the Labout Exchange at the bottom. From here on in we are going to be winners, not losers. For years we have been a low productivity low-wage plant and we have ended up losing our jobs and all the new investment opportunities. From here on we aim to be a high-productivity high-wage plant. That's the best way I know to protect the jobs of our members.'

Sadly for Britain, sadly for industrial peace on Merseyside, the change-of-heart had come too late. Plants closed, men were sacked, industrial decay and unemployment spread like a leprous blight across the whole of the region and insidiously crept down into the Midlands. Fred Clasper may have moved on to a new fighting ground but he, and men like him, left behind their destructive trade-mark on Britain for more than a decade.

. . .

Mark couldn't believe his eyes and ears when the American Director of Overseas' Executive Personnel spelt out the compensation terms under the early retirement deal.

He was to be given two weeks' salary for each year of service. This would give him eighteen months' salary as compensation for loss of office, and his pension was not to begin until the eighteen month period had elapsed.

Mark's face hardened into an expression of bitter hatred. He had been deeply hurt twice before by the Corporation, but this last kick in the stomach on final departure was the last straw. He flung the contract at the feet of the American.

'You call these terms generous?' he demanded angrily.

'I call it a bloody insult!'

The American was visibly shaken by the Englishman's angry response.

'Sorry you feel that way about it, Mark. You can keep the company car,' he added quickly.

'You sure the Corporation can afford it?' Mark asked sarcastically.

'What did Muldoon say?' he added sharply.

'Waal,' said the American, 'there was nothing much he could say, was there? Rules is rules, after all.'

'That's right, isn't it?' Mark scoffed.

'He wouldn't say much would he! He's all right Jack! He's got two thirds of a bloody great American salary four times greater than mine for doing similar work. That gives him a pension nearly ten times greater than the one I've got. I'm not surprised he didn't say much. Who the hell would want to rock the boat on a deal like that! Do YOU think that's fair?' he shouted angrily.

'But you're not an American, Mark. You're an Englishman. . . .'

'So. . . .'

'So bullshit!' Mark exploded.

'I've been an Overseas' Corporation Executive for the last ten years and I've always been told that the reason the Corporation couldn't pay me the salary it paid to Americans doing similar work was because my salary had to be related to British salary scales.'

'Yeah, that's right. That's Corporation rules.'

'So why am I not being compensated for loss of office

according to British scales?'

'What's that?'

Mark said clearly, 'Accepted British practice is at least one month's salary for each year of service. And pension rights begin immediately, not at the end of any bloody eighteen month period. And that's for run-of-the-mill managers. For executives there is virtually no limit.'

The American shook his head worriedly.

'I'm sorry, Mark, but Corporation rules are rules. The Corporation can't make an exception in your case.'

Mark smashed a fist on the desk in a defiant gesture.

'You've been making a bloody exception in my case ever since I've been on the corporate payroll' he yelled.

'Some bloody rules! One for Americans. Another for the rest of us.'

Mark moved angrily toward the door. He had had enough.

'I'll take it up with higher authority, if that's what you want,' said the American nervously.

'I could bring your views to the attention of the Vice President in charge of Overseas Operations' he added placatingly.

Mark threw back his head and laughed sarcastically.

'You'd never keep Jupe awake long enough to listen to the arguments. Ye gods, even when he is awake all he ever says is let's sleep on it. . . .'

The American smiled at the accurate description of the Vice President whose reputation for always falling asleep at meetings had earned him the nickname of Mogadon Man.

'But I will speak to Jupe if you would like me to do so,' he replied.

'Can't do any harm. But I don't think it would do any good.'

Mark jerked the door open and turned to face the American eyes hardened with anger.

'Yes, maybe that's not a bad suggestion,' he said slowly and deliberately.

'Speak to Jupe by all means on my behalf. Tell him to stuff it up his arse.'

.   .   .

On returning to his office the following Monday, Mark was surprised to find that it was now occupied by visiting American auditors.

'Couldn't you wait for the body to be removed?' he said quietly.

The two Americans leapt to their feet.

'Sorry, Mr Sanders.'

It was the older man, who had been occupying Mark's large black leather chair, who spoke.

'We weren't expecting you back. We were told you were using the Treasurer's office. Do you want us to leave?'

'No,' Mark said with a sigh.

'No, don't bother. I knew you were coming. Sooner than I thought.'

'Your secretary organised the transfer of files and your personal things,' the other American said.

Mark nodded.

'Fine' he said, reflecting on the finality of the situation.

'Then I'll leave you to it.'

And he walked out of his office for the very last time.

.   .   .

The Treasurer's room was all dark teak furniture and the walls were hung with portraits of the top men in the Corporation, unlike the walls of Mark's office which were covered with coloured aerial photographs of the many European component plants which had come within his planning responsibility.

Flanking the portrait of the Chairman, Tom O'Reilly, were those of the President and Chief Executive officer, Nate Cocello, the Head of Overseas' Operations, Mogadon Man, the General Director, Europe, Clancy McGillicuddy, and Pat Muldoon as Regional Manager of European Component Operations. Mark was one level below Muldoon, so his portrait didn't make it among the VIPs.

'Thanks, Pat,' he said sardonically, nodding at Muldoon's picture.

'Hope I can do the same for you some day.'

He sat on the top of the large expanse of teak desk and stared coldly at the men who had made it to the top of one of the biggest corporations in the world, employing nearly one million people. A bitter smile crossed his face as his eyes ranged over the top men in the giant corporation.

He picked up the correspondence and miscellaneous papers in the in-tray and quickly scanned the contents. OECD reports, technical journals, but no reports of future European Planning Committee meetings in Geneva, or Paris, Lisbon, Rome or Madrid, and no minutes of previous Planning meetings with resolutions which called for immediate action. Nor were there file copies of his reports to the top brass on the European Business Plan, or copies of the vehicle divisions' plan for the private and confidential attention of Mark Sanders. He was already struck off the circulation list and would soon be off the payroll.

He looked around the room. None of the four phones would ring if he remained at the desk all day. The white, hot line certainly wouldn't. He was a redundant executive and nobody rang a redundant executive, except to say 'Goodbye'.

He opened the door which led to the secretary's annex. Her chair was empty and would remain empty until he left the company. The electric typewriter was covered by its hood and would remain covered while he was still there.

There was just no point in remaining on the premises when you knew you had to go, as Muldoon had said. It was too painful.

'Use the remaining few weeks to say your goodbyes and to find another job,' he had said.

Mark smiled the bitter smile of a disillusioned corporate executive and walked out of the office, closing the door slowly and carefully behind him.

.   .   .

Two days later, Mark arrived back at his temporary office to check the in-tray and tie up any loose ends. To his annoyance he found that the Treasurer's office was now completely empty except for the four telephones set down in a row on the bare boards of the floor. Even the carpet had been removed. He shook his head sadly. Couldn't they have waited just another couple of weeks until he had officially retired at the end of the month? Nothing surprised him any more.

He closed the door behind him and walked slowly down the corridor until he reached the top of the marble staircase, passing his own office and Pat Muldoon's without wishing to take a last look.

For one brief moment he paused to reflect on the finality of this his last visit which closed a thirty year chapter of his life; then with a wry smile he descended the impressive stairway. He was glad he was getting out. Glad, glad, glad. For the first time in years he felt what it was like to be a truly free man.

Mark crossed the imposing entrance hall and went out for the last time.

.   .   .

At home that evening, Georgina asked Mark if he had any future plans he wished to discuss with her.

'What will you do, darling?' she asked affectionately.

'No, sweetheart. It's not what will I do. It's what will WE do?' he replied, rising from his chair to kiss her lightly on the forehead on his way to the Scotch decanter.

'Yes, of course, darling. That's what I meant to say.

'What will WE do?'

'Well, I thought we might take a holiday in Canada,' Mark said.

'Vancouver Island and the Rockies. We don't have to rush. We've got all the time in the world.'

'That would be marvellous. Just the two of us with nothing else to think about but each other for a few weeks. Can't think of anything nicer. But what about after that?'

'We'll talk about that later,' Mark said, sipping his Scotch thoughtfully.

'Maybe I'll write a book and then take up that offer to have a go for the European Parliament.'